He would kiss her now . . .

It was why she had brought him here, to get that kiss he was about to give her before they had been interrupted.

Niels lowered his head until his mouth covered hers. His lips lightly brushed over hers. But when Edith raised her hands to slide them up his arms, his tongue traced the crease between her lips.

Edith instinctively opened to him on a little sigh and he caught her lower lip between his, and drew on it teasingly. Then he tilted his head as his tongue swept to fill her mouth and the sweet tempo suddenly changed.

She clutched his shoulders tightly as his mouth ravished hers. It was as if the passion they had shared by the loch had been merely restrained when they'd been interrupted, and now he had unleashed it.

By Lynsay Sands

LYNSAY SANDS

Surrender to the Highlander

AVONBOOKS
An Imprint of HarperCollinsPublishers

Excerpt from *Twice Bitten* copyright © 2018 by Lynsay Sands.

SURRENDER TO THE HIGHLANDER. Copyright © 2018 by Lynsay Sands. All rights reserved. Printed in the United States of America. No part of this book may be used or reproduced in any manner whatsoever without written permission except in the case of brief quotations embodied in critical articles and reviews. For information, address HarperCollins Publishers, 195 Broadway, New York, NY 10007.

First Avon Books mass market printing: February 2018
First Avon Books hardcover printing: January 2018

Print Edition ISBN: 978-0-06-246898-7
Digital Edition ISBN: 978-0-06-246888-8

Cover illustration by Victor Gadino

Avon, Avon & logo, and Avon Books & logo are registered trademarks of HarperCollins Publishers in the United States of America and other countries.
HarperCollins is a registered trademark of HarperCollins Publishers in the United States of America and other countries.

FIRST EDITION

18 19 20 21 22   QGM   10 9 8 7 6 5 4 3 2 1

Surrender to the Highlander

Prologue

Niels STARED AT HIS BROTHER-IN-LAW BLANKLY for one moment and then exploded, "Are ye daft? We're no' going anywhere near Drummond. We're traveling to McKay in the north. Drummond is south."

"Aye," Geordie agreed next to him, scowling at their sister's husband for good measure. "We only stopped here to drop off Rory and see our sister."

"I ken," Greer growled, his eyes shifting from the four Buchanan brothers sitting at his table to the upper landing, as if expecting his wife to appear at any moment.

Niels followed his glance, but there was nothing to see. The landing was empty. He looked back to his brother-in-law in time to see his mouth firming with determination as he turned his attention back to them.

"I ken it would add to yer journey, and I'd no' ask, but Saidh is really worried about her friend Edith Drummond. In the last letter she had from her four weeks ago, Edith was feeling poorly, and she's no' heard from her since. Saidh's had no' response to her last three messages and is concerned."

"Then send a damned messenger," Niels snapped impatiently. "Good Lord, man. Drummond is almost as far south as Buchanan and then it's another day's ride east. We'd ha'e to ride all the way back there, and then return here just to continue on with our original journey."

"It would add at least a week to our travels," Geordie put in, scowling.

"More," Alick commented with a grimace. "We have to ride slow with the cart." Shaking his head, he said, "Niels is right. Ye'd do better to send a messenger."

"Did you no' hear me just say that Edith has no' responded to the last three messages we sent?" Greer growled with frustration. "Me last messenger could no' even get inside Drummond bailey. He was made to leave the message at the gate. He returned with no news at all. Saidh is bound and determined to ride to Drummond herself and see that Edith is all right."

"So?" Niels asked with bewilderment. "Saidh has traveled before and will again. What—?"

"She is *with child*," Greer roared as if they had forgotten that little fact.

"Aye, with child, no' dead," Niels said with disgust. "Good Lord, she has five more months before the babe is due. Surely ye're no' trying to wrap her in swaddling and keep her from doing anything jest because she—Good Christ!" he ended with dismay as Saidh appeared at the top of the landing and started down the stairs. His dear—usually lithe—sister looked like she'd swallowed a calf . . . or two. Good God, her belly was so swollen and rounded out she could be carrying three calves in there, he thought with dismay. She looked so ungainly he feared she would overbalance and roll down the stairs like a ball.

Apparently, he was not the only one with that concern, for Greer MacDonnell was even now leaping to his feet to rush to his wife's side. They all watched in silent amazement as he hurried up the stairs, scooped her up into his arms and carried her down the rest of the way.

"I told ye to ha'e yer maid fetch me when ye were ready to come below," Greer was saying with exasperation as he approached the table.

"I am with child, no' cripple, husband," Saidh grumbled with irritation. "I am perfectly capable o' walking without help."

"Mayhap, but I can no' bear to watch it," Greer growled, setting her in the chair next to his with a care not presently notable in his voice. "Every time ye start down I fear ye'll just tip forward and roll down like a—" Greer's words died on an apologetic grimace as he noted Saidh's stiff expression. "I jest worry," he ended lamely and then offered a conciliatory smile and said, "I'll let Cook ken ye're below and ready to break yer fast."

"Thank ye, husband," Saidh murmured, smiling when he bent to press a kiss to her forehead before moving off. She watched him cross the great hall for the kitchens, her face soft with affection and appreciation, both of which were definitely absent when she turned back to her brothers. Her gaze slid over their gaping expressions and then she gave a little huff of disgust and snapped, "Well? Are ye no' pleased to see me?"

Niels raised his eyebrows at the grumpy question and let his eyes drift to settle on her overlarge stomach. "Aye. We are all just surprised that there is so much to see."

"Ye look ready to burst," Alick said with awe. "I thought ye were only four months along?"

"I am," she muttered unhappily, one hand rising to rub across her protruding belly. "I think I may be carrying two bairns."

"I'm thinking six," Geordie said, and promptly received a hard kick from their sister for his trouble.

Niels bit back a laugh and turned to Rory, eyebrows raised. "Should she be this big a'ready?"

Rory snapped his mouth closed and stood to move to Saidh's side. Placing a hand at her elbow, he tried to urge her to her feet. "We should retire above for a few moments."

"Above stairs?" Saidh asked with a scowl and then shook her head and jerked her arm free of his hold. "Nay. I jest got below. Besides, I'm hungry and—"

"And I need to examine ye," Rory countered firmly. "Ye can eat after."

"Or," she suggested just as firmly, "Ye could examine me *after* I've eaten."

"Or, I could examine ye right here in front o' everyone," he said in a tone of good cheer that didn't soften the threat.

Saidh's eyes narrowed, and her hand moved to the *sgian-dubh* at her waist. "Try it and I'll skewer ye where ye stand."

"*Saidh*," Rory complained with exasperation, and then heaving out a breath, tried reason. "Ye're much larger than ye should be at this stage in the game, lass.

It can be dangerous. I need to listen to yer heartbeat and see that it's no' under strain. I also wish to—"

"I'm fine," she said grimly, and when he opened his mouth to argue further, added, "But I'll make a deal with ye."

"What's that?" Rory asked, and Niels couldn't help noticing his brother was suddenly wary. He would have been himself. One never knew what would come out of their sister's mouth.

"Promise to accompany me to check on Edith and I'll let ye examine me," Saidh said firmly.

Rory scowled. "Saidh, ye can no' seriously be thinking to ride a horse in yer shape. Ye—"

"Fine. Then I do no' need examining," Saidh waved away his diatribe and turned to face the table.

Niels lowered his head to hide his amusement as Rory cursed, but then his brother heaved out a breath. "Fine. If ye let me examine ye, I'll see what I can do fer yer friend Edith," he said shortly. "Now . . . will ye please let me examine ye and be sure all is well?"

Saidh relaxed and even smiled faintly, but then she grimaced and said, "Aye. But give me a minute to rest at least. 'Twas a tiring bit of business getting below."

That last part was admitted almost shamefully, which told them that it was true. Saidh disliked showing weakness.

"I shall carry ye up," Rory offered gently.

She blinked at the very suggestion and began to laugh, but it died quickly as Saidh looked Rory over. Eyes widening slightly, she took in their previously lithe brother and said, "Ye've put on weight and yer arms have muscle."

"Aye." Niels grinned at her comment. "He's been

working out in the practice yard with the rest o' us ever since we got home after escorting Dougall and Murine to Carmichael."

"Why?" she asked with surprise.

Rory grimaced and answered, "Our brothers have been working hard at convincing me that while kenning how to heal others' injuries was good, it may be prudent to learn how to defend meself as well so that I could remain healthy enough to do so." He smiled crookedly and added, "After all the trouble both ye and Dougall and yer mates ran into recently, it did seem they may be right."

"Aye," Saidh said solemnly. "They are."

Rory nodded, and then raised an eyebrow. "Shall I carry ye up?"

Heaving a sigh, she shook her head and stood up. "I'll walk. Ye can hold me arm though to be sure I do no' overbalance and tumble backward down the stairs."

Rory merely nodded and took her arm to lead her away.

Niels watched them go, his gaze narrowing with concern on Saidh's protruding stomach.

"Surely she should no' be that large already?" Geordie murmured with a frown.

Niels shook his head. "I've never seen the like this early on."

"Aye, and ye ken what that means," Alick said gloomily. When the other two men merely looked at him in question, he rolled his eyes and pointed out, "We'll have to go to Drummond now. We can no' let Saidh try to ride there in her state. Hell, she was puffing and weary just from walking down the stairs and Greer carried her most o' the way."

Niels blew his breath out on a sigh, but nodded. "We'll make a detour that way on our return from McKay and—"

"Ye can no' wait that long."

That determined comment drew his gaze around and he saw that their brother-in-law was returning. Mouth thinning, Niels said, "We have a delivery to make, Greer. The McKays are expecting their woven cloth by the end of the week. We can no' just—"

"I'll have six o' me men make the delivery in yer stead," Greer said firmly. "But ye ha'e to head to Drummond straightaway else Saidh'll insist on going herself."

Niels pursed his lips as he considered the offer and then countered, "Twelve men."

"Twelve?" Greer scowled at the suggestion. "There were only going to be the three o' ye seeing it there yerselves."

"Aye, but 'tis expensive cloth, and one Buchanan is worth four o' yer average warrior," he pointed out. "O' course, if ye want to travel with them, then ye can get away with eight and yerself."

Somewhat mollified by the implication that he was as good a warrior as his brothers-in-law, Greer sighed and then nodded. "All right. Twelve warriors will escort the woven cloth to McKay."

Niels smiled slowly. He'd just traded a long, uncomfortable two-week journey to McKay and back, for a much quicker two-day jaunt to Drummond. Life was good when the heavens smiled on you like this.

Chapter 1

"BLOODY HELL! OPEN THE DAMNED GATE and let us see Lady Edith, ye whoremonger, or we'll set it alight and smash it down ourselves."

Alick's threat made Niels shake his head, because threats were all they were. Setting fire to the Drummond gates and smashing them down was the last thing they were going to do. Hell, with just the four of them there, he wasn't sure they even could. Though it would be fun trying, he acknowledged.

Still, they weren't here to start a war with the Drummonds. Their only task was to check on their sister's friend and report back to Saidh on how she fared. Unfortunately, nothing short of their actually seeing the lass was likely to keep Saidh from insisting on trying to ride out there to see her for herself. And he suspected even that wouldn't be enough. Once they'd agreed to come, she'd insisted on accompanying them. Only Rory's warning that the journey might harm her unborn babes had kept her at home. Well, that and Greer's threat to tie her to their bed and keep her there under guard until the babes were born if she even tried mounting a horse.

Niels shook his head again at the thought. Babes, as in plural. As in his sister was bearing more than one babe. Rory suspected it was twins. Alick and Geordie were sure it was going to be more and were betting on the size of the litter. Alick was guessing three, Geordie four. Niels thought they were both mad. Women did not have litters of three and four. Twins alone were a rarity. Three or four . . . well . . . he'd heard old wives' tales about some woman way back when, or from a distant land, having three bairns in one birth, but he was sure an old wives' tale was all it was. Still . . . Saidh *was* huge enough to be carrying three or four.

Raising his gaze to the men on the gate tower, he shouted out calmly, "We just wish to see yer lady. Our sister, her friend Lady Saidh MacDonnell, is concerned for yer lady's welfare. If ye do no' wish to open the gate, then jest have yer lady come to the gate and let us see her so that we can tell our sister she is well and healthy."

The men on the wall all glanced at each other, and then one said, "I thought it was Lady Edith ye were interested in, no' our lady?"

"Aye." Niels frowned. "Is Edith no' lady here? I understood her mother was dead and she was lady here now."

"She was," the man called back, "But Brodie, the youngest son, married and his wife, Lady Victoria is now lady here. And the laird ordered that the gate no' be opened to anyone until they return."

Niels's eyebrows rose at the news. He hadn't heard of the marriage, and was a bit surprised that the youngest son's bride would be allowed to step in and replace the daughter of the house as lady. Perhaps had the eldest brother and heir married, his wife as future Lady of Drummond would have stepped in, but the wife of the youngest son?

Still, that wasn't his issue to deal with here so he merely set that information aside to consider later, and said, "Well, 'tis Lady Edith we are interested in. Saidh has sent three messengers and received no response. She asked us to come and see her to be sure she is well." He paused a beat and then added, "She felt sure that, Scottish hospitality being what it is, ye'd no' turn away noblemen as ye have mere messengers."

The men above them began to argue back and forth. It seemed someone up there felt they should be allowed entrance. Others obviously didn't agree and he waited patiently as the argument continued. After a moment, however, he repeated, "We need not enter to please our sister. If ye would jest have Lady Edith come to the gate to assure us she is well we could be on our way."

"She can no'," the earlier speaker said and then admitted grimly, "She is too weak to make her way to the gate."

"She's still ill then?" Rory asked next to him, concern in his voice.

"Verra." The man sounded weary. "She's hanging on by a thread and lasted longer than her father and the two older brothers, but she's no' long fer this world. A shame too, she's provin' herself a fighter. Would have made a good clan leader."

Niels's eyes widened at the news that Ronald Drummond and his two elder sons were dead, but supposed it explained how the youngest son's wife could now act as lady of the castle.

Rory shifted restlessly in the saddle next to him, and Niels glanced over as he pointed out, "Saidh'll no' be happy if we leave with no more news than that the woman still ails."

Nodding, Niels raised his head to call out, "We'll no' be leaving here until the lass is either dead or back on her feet. Our sister would accept no less."

"We'll tell ye when she dies then," the voice called back.

Rory muttered under his breath.

Ignoring him, Niels said, "Or ye could let us in. Me brother here is the finest healer in Scotland. He may yet be able to save Lady Edith."

Silence reigned for a moment and then another hissed argument took place above.

Niels tried to wait patiently, but really, this wasn't done. He'd barely had the thought when Alick muttered angrily behind him, "This is a farce. A Scot does no' leave allies standing at the gate like beggars and refuse them entrance."

"No' if they want to keep them as allies," Geordie agreed in a growl.

"Geordie and Alick are right, Niels. This is beyond the pale," Rory said grimly. "I could be in there right now helping the lass, if they would but—"

Niels raised his hand to silence him and bellowed, "Quit yer bickering up there and use yer heads! Me brother can help her. Do ye care so little fer yer kin? What will yer laird, her *brother*, think when I tell him ye let her die? And I'll be sure to tell him too. Now open the damned gates ye lackwitted oafs, or I'll climb this wall meself, slit yer throats and open it mes—"

Niels paused midthreat as the gate began to rise. Eyebrows lifting, he murmured, "Hmm. Looks like they're opening the gate."

"I can no' imagine why," Rory muttered, rolling his eyes.

"Must be me natural charm," Niels said with a shrug, urging his horse forward before the men on the wall could change their minds and lower the gate again.

"Oh aye, for certain. The Buchanan charm wins out every time," Geordie agreed, following him onto the bridge.

"Brothers," Rory reprimanded, urging his mount between theirs, "if this is the kind of charm you display on a regular basis on your journeys, 'tis no wonder I'm always having to patch ye up on yer return."

"Nay, charm's nothing to do with that," Niels assured him. "Pity is the reason we return with wounds."

"Pity?" Rory asked with bewilderment.

"Aye, well we have to let our adversaries get at least a lick or two in, else they'd be demoralized at being bested so roundly," Niels said reasonably.

"And then there's you," Geordie added.

"Me?" Rory asked with dismay. "What have I to do with yer getting wounded in battle?"

"Well, ye need practice in healing, do ye no'? So along with helping our opposition feel less incompetent with sword, we give ye something to do when we return that makes ye feel important. No' that ye ever thank us fer it," Geordie added in a grumble.

"Thank ye?" Rory asked with disbelief. "Are ye mad? Ye—surely ye do no'—ye can no' be serious?"

"Nay," Niels said with amusement. "But we had ye believing it there fer a minute, did we no'?"

Rory snapped his mouth closed and scowled from one to the other.

"See all the fun ye miss when ye insist on staying at home with yer dusty old books and medicinals rather than travel with us?" Alick said cheerfully, urging his own mount up beside Geordie's as they started across the bailey.

Rory cast him a disgusted expression. "Ye mean eating the dust kicked up by the horse in front o' mine, sleeping on the cold, hard ground and being made fun of at every turn?" he asked dryly. "Oh, aye, I am sorry to ha'e missed that all these years."

"Sometimes, Rory, I'm sure yer a changeling," Geordie said sadly.

"Nay," Niels assured him. "'Tis more likely God just got things a bit confused when he was making Saidh and Rory."

"Ye mean mayhap he meant Saidh to be a lad and Rory a lassie?" Geordie suggested with a wide grin. "I think we may have discussed that very thing a time or two on our journeys."

"Aye, we have," Alick agreed.

"What?" Rory squawked with dismay.

"Well, think on it," Alick said as they neared the steps leading to the front double doors of the Drummond keep. "Ye like to stay home in the nice warm castle with yer herbs and such, while Saidh likes to travel and wrestle and would as soon skewer a man as look on him. 'Tis as if she was meant to be another brother, and ye the sister," he said reasonably as they all reined in at the steps.

Niels glanced to Rory to see how he was taking the suggestion and burst out laughing at his horrified expression even as Geordie and Alick did.

"Oh, aye, laugh it up the three o' ye," Rory said

sourly. "But I guarantee I will no' forget this the next time ye need yer wounds tended."

Still chuckling, Niels shrugged and slid off his mount with unconcern. Whatever petty punishment Rory chose to dole out later would be well worth the reaction their teasing had got.

"Are ye gonna save Lady Edith?"

Niels turned around at that soft question to find a small blond boy with earnest eyes standing behind him. Next to the lad was a deerhound with a red fawn coat. The beast was almost taller than the boy on all fours and certainly a good six stone heavier. Niels had never seen a dog so big.

"Are ye?" the boy asked, reminding him of his question.

"We're going to do our best," Niels said, shifting his attention back to the lad.

"Gran says no one can save her," the boy told them sadly.

"She does, does she?" Niels asked quietly.

He nodded. "Aye. She says 'tis just a matter o' time and she'll go just like the laird and his lads."

Niels frowned at the suggestion and then said, "Mayhap that would ha'e been true ere we got here, but ye see that man there?" He pointed to Rory as his brother finished dismounting and walked around his horse to join them. "That there is me brother Rory, and he is the finest healer in all o' Scotland. If there is anybody who can help yer lady get over what's ailing her, 'tis him."

The boy looked Rory over solemnly and then nodded. "I hope so, m'lord. Fer I'd be terrible sad did she die. She's ever so nice. Not like Laird Brodie's wife, Lady Victoria. If she'd been lady when we got here, we never would ha'e been allowed to stay."

"Hmm." Niels made the sound purely because he didn't know what else to say, and then straightening again, he asked, "What's yer name, lad?"

"Ronson, m'lord."

"Ye're no' from Drummond, Ronson?" Rory asked.

"Nay, m'lord. We're from the south. But when me ma died, the laird o' our old home threw us out. Gran and me, we traveled a long time to find a new home, but no one wanted us. They said Gran was too old and I was too young. But Lady Edith, she took us in and set Gran to work. Gave me a job too," he added proudly.

"And what job is that?" Niels asked, suspecting he already knew the answer.

"I look after Laddie here," he announced, chest puffing up as he threw a skinny arm over the huge beast. "He has to be fed and walked and brushed, but Lady Edith has no' the time fer all that what with all the work she has to do around here. 'Tis a most important job," he assured them.

"Aye," Niels agreed. "Most important. She's lucky ye came."

"Aye," Ronson said, and then frowned and admitted, "But I maybe will no' have the job much longer."

"Why is that?" Rory asked.

Ronson hesitated, his expression unhappy, and then confided, "I heard some o' the maids talking and they said as how even does Lady Edith survive, she's no' long for Drummond. They said as sure as spittin', Lady Victoria would see her sent off to the Abbey the first chance she gets and if that happens, we may have to leave." He worried his lip briefly and then asked, "Do ye think they're right? Will Lady Victoria send Lady Edith away?"

"I do no' ken, lad," Niels admitted. "But let's just tend one problem at a time and get Lady Edith well again before we start fretting on other matters. Shall we?"

"Aye," Ronson said, and then rubbed the deerhound's head between the ears. "Lady Edith's sure fond o' Laddie. I've been thinking maybe she'd feel better did he visit. He's most important to her. She might get better if he visited."

"Hmm," Niels said, biting back a smile. "Aye, well, mayhap later. I'm thinkin' we should just let me brother look at her first and see what he can do. All right?"

"Aye," he said with disappointment and then glanced past Niels and scowled. "Here comes Tormod and Cawley."

Niels peered over his shoulder to see two men approaching. Both were old, one was tall and slim with a limp, the other shorter and round.

"And who are Tormod and Cawley?" Rory asked as Niels turned back.

"They were the old laird's first and second, now they're Laird Brodie's first and second. Tormod's the tall one. He's the first . . . and he does no' like me," he added unhappily.

"I'm sure that's no' true," Rory assured him.

"Aye. 'Tis," Ronson insisted. "He told Lady Edith no' to let us stay. Said we'd be nothing but trouble and more mouths to feed."

"Ah," Niels said and almost sighed. He had no

doubt the man had said that. And probably right in front of the boy and his grandmother. Which was unfortunate.

"I'd best take Laddie in and brush him down now," Ronson mumbled.

Niels nodded and watched the boy lead the large dog away before turning to survey the approaching Tormod and Cawley. The pair appeared to be bickering and he wondered if they were the source of all the arguing that had taken place on the wall as they'd waited to be allowed to enter. If so, the bickering continued despite their being inside now.

"Enough," Tormod snapped as the pair halted in front of Niels and his brothers. He then turned his attention to them and announced grimly, "Cawley here will get someone to tend yer horses while I take ye to Lady Edith."

Niels narrowed his eyes at the less than polite greeting, but merely asked, "Are you the one in charge while Laird Drummond is away?"

"Aye. Sadly I am," he admitted, his mouth twisting with disgust and then he announced, "I'm Tormod Drummond, the man who'll be answering fer letting ye in here. And that's Cawley Drummond, who will no' be held responsible despite his nagging and harassing being the reason behind it."

"It's the right thing to do and ye ken it," Cawley said vehemently. "If they can save wee Edith—"

"Aye, aye," Tormod interrupted with irritation. "I let them in, did I no'? Despite the fact that Brodie'll probably have me flogged fer it."

Niels's eyebrows rose at both the lack of respect obvious in the man's not using Brodie's title, and the suggestion that Brodie would punish him for letting them in.

"Your laird'll hardly be complaining when Rory saves his sister's life," Alick said earnestly, stepping up beside Niels.

"Me brother Alick," Niels introduced him, and then added, "And that's Geordie, Rory and I'm Niels."

Tormod merely nodded and turned to respond to Alick's comment with a weary, "*If* he saves her life ye may be right. Unfortunately, I'm no' thinking that's likely to happen." On that grim note, he turned to lead the way up the stairs.

"Why? What ails her?" Rory asked with interest, hard on the man's heels.

Tormod shook his head. "Hell if I ken. No one does. It came on sudden. Hit Laird Drummond and his eldest sons Roderick and Hamish all at once. The old laird died the first night, but his health was already on the decline anyway. The two boys though, they were young and strong and lasted three or four days. Lady Edith nursed 'em," he added, not sounding happy about it. They understood why when he added, "I told her she should no', that she'd catch whatever it was they had and she should leave their care to the servants. But nay, she had to tend them herself, and sure enough I was right. We no sooner buried the second lad than she fell ill."

"And Brodie and his new bride?" Niels asked and noted the way the man's mouth thinned out.

"When Lady Edith's maid fell ill while tending her, Brodie panicked. Feared it would spread through the clan and take he and his bride as well. Decided they should leave for safer shores fer a bit." Pausing at the double doors, he glanced back as he opened one and added acerbically, "He could no' get out o' here quick enough. Packed up his new bride, her maid and some clothes, took a small escort of six men and rushed out o' here as if the hounds o' hell were on his heels."

"Leaving the rest o' ye here to handle matters," Niels surmised dourly as he led his brothers through the door the man held open for them.

"Aye. Just so," Tormod agreed with disgust. He followed them in and let the door slam closed behind him.

"And Lady Edith has been sick for more than four weeks now?" Rory asked as Tormod led them across the busy hall. That was what Saidh had told them, so they were surprised when Tormod shook his head.

"Just over three weeks," Tormod corrected.

"But our sister said her last letter from Edith was a month ago now and she mentioned feeling poorly then," Niels said slowly.

"Oh, aye." Tormod waved that away. "A week before this new ailment, Lady Edith had a bit o' a tummy complaint. She was over it though by the time this new illness struck three weeks ago."

"Ah." Niels nodded. "And her brothers died in a matter o' days from it, but she is still alive but ailing?"

"Aye. She's a fighter, she is. Would ha'e made a fine clan leader. Better than that useless brother o' hers. Howbeit Brodie's well and fine and somewhere safely away while she grows weaker every day." He rubbed the back of his neck with one hand as they reached the stairs to the second level. Leading the way up, he added, "I'm amazed she's lasted as long as she has, but she can no' last much longer."

"What are the symptoms?" Rory asked.

"With the father and brothers it was headache, dizziness, trouble breathing and hallucinations. From what I hear 'tis mostly the same with Lady Edith, except she's nauseous on top o' it, can no' keep anything down and weakening more every day."

They'd reached the top of the stairs and fell silent as they followed Tormod to the second door along the hall. Pausing there, the man turned to survey them, before settling his gaze on Rory. "Ye're the healer?"

"Aye," Rory said, standing proud.

Tormod nodded. "Ye can go in then. Ye other three can wait out here."

Niels merely nodded. He had no wish to go into a sickroom anyway. Hell, in truth, he'd rather be waiting down at the trestle table, preferably with some ale or mead. However, he hadn't been given that option so would wait in the hall to hear what Rory had to say on the subject of Lady Edith's health.

When Tormod opened the door, swinging it silently inward, Niels glanced inside with mild curiosity, his gaze sliding quickly over the room. A figure lay in the bed at one end, while at the other side of the room, a gray-haired woman, thin and bent with age, was pouring liquid from a footed vial into a large metal cup of what appeared to be mead. As he watched, she capped the vial, set it on the table and then turned to carry the concoction she'd made to the woman in the bed.

"Come now, time for your medicine," the woman crooned with an English accent. Pausing beside the bed, she sat on the edge of it.

Niels's eyes shifted to the woman in the bed then. She hadn't reacted at all to the woman's words. She lay still and silent, her face frighteningly pale. Her skin was as white as icy snow in the winter. In comparison, her hair was made up of red and gold strands, resembling fire around her face, he noted with interest, and then his view was briefly obscured as Rory moved into the room.

"What are ye giving her?" Rory asked approaching the bed. The old maid gave a start and peered around with surprise.

"Oh my, you startled me," the woman said, pressing a hand to her chest and shaking her head. She then frowned slightly and glanced from Rory to Tormod, who still stood in the hall with Niels and the others. Her gaze slid over them all with confusion and she asked Tormod, "Who are these men? Why would you let them into the lady's room, her being so sick?"

"These men are Buchanans," Tormod announced and then nodded to Rory even as he plucked the drink from the old woman's hand and raised it so he could give the contents a sniff. "He's a healer. Thinks he can help Lady Edith."

"Well, and thank heavens for that then," the woman said on a sigh and stood up. "Mayhap I can get a bit of rest. I'm not feelin' so well meself after tending Lady Edith night and day and—" Her words and footsteps ended abruptly and her eyes widened, her mouth forming an alarmed O as she wavered where she stood. Her hands started to rise up and to the sides as if seeking something to steady herself, and then she just collapsed.

Niels had started into the room the moment she first wavered. He caught the old woman as she fell and scooped her up into his arms. Noting the pallor of her face, he shifted his gaze to Tormod, eyebrows rising as he saw that the man had backed fearfully away from the door and now stood behind Alick and Geordie in the hall.

"Is there another room where we can put the maid?" Niels asked, watching as Rory began to examine the woman. His brother lifted her eyelids to see her eyes, and then opened her mouth for a brief look before lifting one hand and examining her nails. Niels watched silently, having no idea what his brother was looking for. It seemed to him like Rory was doing much the same thing Dougall did when examining a horse for soundness.

"Nay. This is the sickroom," Tormod said heavily. "She's got it now too and this is where she'll stay."

"Lay her down next to Lady Edith," Rory said grimly, releasing the woman's hand and letting it drop.

Nodding, Niels carried the woman to the bed and set her down next to Edith Drummond. His gaze slid to the younger woman as he straightened, and her fiery hair on the pillow caught his eyes. The woman might look like death warmed over, but her hair was something special, he thought, and then watched as Rory performed the same examination of Lady Edith as he had the maid just a moment ago.

"Do ye ken what illness it is?" Niels asked, his gaze shifting to her eyes as Rory lifted both lids at once. They were dilated, he noted, the black circles so large they nearly obliterated the bright green of her eyes, leaving just a thin border of the lovely color around the pupil. He had no idea what that meant.

Rory didn't respond at first, taking the time to check inside her mouth and then lift one delicate hand to peer at her fingernails. Finally, he set her hand back down and turned to pick up the drink the old maid had been about to feed her. Mouth tightening, he set the drink back and announced grimly, "'Tis poison, not illness."

"What?" Tormod started back into the room, but then hesitated at the door to ask, "Are ye sure? But Effie is sick too."

"Also poison," Rory assured him and walked over to the table to inspect the contents of the vial the woman had used. Shaking his head with a frown, he recapped the vial and set it back. "The maid must have had some of whatever the poison was in."

"Is it in the vial she added to the drink?" Niels asked.

"I'm no' sure," Rory admitted, returning to the bed. "There seem to be a lot o' herbs and such in it. Too many to be able to tell if that's the source or no'."

"But ye're sure 'tis poison?" Niels asked.

"Aye," Rory said firmly. "All the signs are there."

"Hmm." Niels peered at the pale woman again. "I guess 'tis good Saidh made us come then."

"Aye," Rory agreed solemnly.

"Will she survive?"

Niels glanced up with surprise to see that Tormod— now he knew he needn't fear catching anything—had entered the room and was standing beside him.

"Hopefully," Rory said with a sigh. "If she's strong enough to fight off the effects of what she's already taken and we keep her from getting any more."

"Ye do no' think the laird and his sons were poisoned too, do ye?" Tormod asked with a frown.

"Ye said they had the same symptoms?" Rory asked.

"Aye. But they were no' spewing up the contents o' their stomachs like the lass has been doing. Mayhap they were just sick."

Rory shook his head. "Spewing is no' a symptom

o' the poison. 'Tis more likely they were poisoned too and Lady Edith was still suffering some of the effects o' her tummy upset so that the poison did no' sit well and she could no' keep it down. That's most like what saved her life. She did no' keep enough o' the poison in her stomach to kill her. Just enough to make her weak and ill."

"Damn," Tormod breathed. "So someone set out to kill our laird and his heirs?"

"It would seem so," Rory muttered, eyeing the two women in the bed with concern.

"What do we do now?" Niels asked quietly.

Rory was silent for a minute, and then announced, "There is little I can do without kenning what the poison is."

"Surely there is something ye can give them," Tormod said. "A tonic that might help?"

Rory shook his head. "I daren't administer anything without kenning what they've been poisoned with. If I give them the wrong thing it could kill them. All we can do is try to get them both to take in liquids, watch over them, and then wait and see what happens."

Tormod headed for the door at once. "I'll have one o' the maids fetch up some broth and—"

"Nay," Rory interrupted at once. When the old man paused and looked back in surprise, he said, "I'll no' risk any more poison getting into their food or drink. I do no' think either would survive."

Niels's eyebrows rose. "Even the old woman? Surely she will be fine? After all, Lady Edith has been ailing for weeks and, unless I'm wrong," he added, shooting a questioning look at Tormod, "this is the first time the old maid has shown signs o' poisoning?"

"Ye're no' wrong," Tormod assured him. "This is the first time Effie's been the least ill since tending the lass."

"Aye, but Effie is old, and as far as I can tell, she does no' have the benefit o' throwing up the poison as Lady Edith does. If she got a large enough dose of it . . ." He peered at the old woman with a frown. "She could die as quickly as Laird Drummond did."

Niels peered at the woman solemnly. "That probably means she is no' the poisoner."

"Probably," Rory agreed.

Sighing, Niels turned to his brother. "Tell us what ye need to tend them, Rory, and we'll fetch it."

"Fresh water from the well, and the fixings to make broth." Turning to Geordie he said, "Mayhap that rabbit ye caught this morn on our way here, brother, and some vegetables."

Geordie nodded and turned toward the door. "I'll fetch the rabbit and fixings from me saddlebag."

"And I'll get the water," Alick said, turning as well.

"Make sure the water is fresh from the well, Alick, and make sure ye let no one near it on yer way back," Rory said firmly.

Nodding, Alick followed Geordie out of the room.

"What can I do?" Niels asked.

"We'll need mead or cider too. But I want a fresh cask to be sure no one has tampered with it."

"Come with me. I'll get ye what ye need," Tormod said abruptly and led him from the room. They walked in silence until they reached the stairs and then the man muttered, "I can hardly believe it. Someone murdered our laird and his sons."

Niels grunted in agreement, a frown curving his

lips. This was a problem he hadn't expected when he'd agreed to come here. And it *was* a problem. He couldn't just leave Rory here to nurse Edith Drummond back to health with a murderer wandering around Drummond poisoning people. He couldn't even bundle up Edith and transport her back to MacDonnell for Saidh and Rory to tend to there either, because if Edith survived, she'd have to return here . . . where again there was a murderer wandering around poisoning people.

Niels and his brothers had been raised with the belief that it was their place to protect the weak and in need when they could. Edith was definitely weak and in need, and with Greer taking care of his shipment, he could take the time to help sort out the situation here and keep her safe from further attacks.

Mouth tight, he considered everything Tormod had told them on their way above stairs and asked, "Ye said the laird and his older sons fell ill first?"

"Aye."

"And Edith did no' fall ill until the last of the three died?"

"Aye."

"So she was no' poisoned at the same time as her father and brothers," he said thoughtfully.

"Nay, she must ha'e been poisoned after," Tormod agreed solemnly and then pointed out, "As were the maids."

"Aye." Niels frowned.

"What are ye thinking?" Tormod asked.

"I'm thinking if she and the maids had been poisoned at the same time as the laird and his elder sons I would be looking to Brodie fer an explanation," Niels admitted dryly.

"Because he was the only one who would benefit from the deaths of his elder brothers and father while Lady Edith and the maids may ha'e merely been accidentally poisoned along with them," Tormod said with a nod, and then admitted, "When the three men died I did think it most convenient fer Brodie. Without that, he never would ha'e had a chance to be laird here."

"Aye," Niels agreed, and then shook his head. "But there was no need to poison Edith too. She is the youngest child, is she not?"

"She is. So he does no' benefit from her death," Tormod said, but added, "Except to get her out o' the way. Brodie's new bride did no' care fer Lady Edith much."

"Nay?" Niels asked with interest.

"Nay," Tormod assured him. "Their relationship was tepid at best ere this all happened, but when the old man died and the two elder sons looked to be going the same way, Brodie stepped up to act as temporary laird until the men died or recovered. Lady Victoria considered herself lady of the castle then and tried to boss the servants about, but they were no' having that. Lady Edith has been lady here since her mother's death and they all automatically turned to her fer guidance. Lady Victoria would give an order and the servants would go to Lady Edith to see if they should obey, and that infuriated Lady Victoria."

"Hmm," Niels murmured, but then shook his head. "Still, Brodie could easily ha'e sent Edith to the nuns to be rid o' her did his bride ask it. Besides, that does no' explain the maids being poisoned."

"Nay," Tormod agreed, his brow furrowing. "And

old Effie in there is Lady Victoria's maid. Lady Victoria is very fond o' her, I'm sure she'd no' poison her."

"Lady Victoria left without her maid?" Niels asked with surprise. While his sister, Saidh, had been known to do that, most ladies he knew would not travel without a maid to help her dress and such.

"Nay. She took her younger maid," Tormod answered and then explained, "Effie was Lady Victoria's nursemaid as a child and became her lady's maid once she was old enough to need one. Howbeit she's an old woman and no' as quick as she used to be so a second maid, a young girl, was taken on to help her with her tasks. The younger maid went with Lady Victoria and Effie was left here. Lady Victoria feared the trip might be too much fer the old girl after so soon arriving."

"Hmm," Niels muttered, and pondered that before asking, "Lady Edith's maid died?"

"Nay. She recovered," Tormod said solemnly. "She's down helping in the kitchens fer now." Mouth twisting with irritation, he added, "The lass has been fashing to tend her mistress, but the last thing Lady Edith said when she fell ill again herself was that Moibeal should be kept away from her. She did no' want the lass to get sick again too as she had. O' course, she had no idea they were being poisoned."

Niels nodded.

"Ye ken," Tormod said now, "it occurs to me that if 'twas the wine cask that was poisoned, then Lady Edith's falling ill may ha'e just been an unintended side result of the culprit's attempt to kill the laird and his elder sons."

"Aye," Niels agreed, but argued, "Howbeit the maids would hardly be drinking wine. At least they do no' at Buchanan. There the wine is fer the family only. The servants and soldiers drink ale, cider or water."

"Aye, 'tis the same here," Tormod agreed. "And they *should* no' have had any, but that does no' mean they *did* no' have any."

"Hmm," Niels murmured and decided he should probably have a talk with the maid.

Chapter 2

THE SOUND OF A TERRIBLE EXPLOSION WOKE
Edith. Blinking her eyes open, she glanced franti-
cally around the room, and then jerked her gaze to her
right as the sound came again. She gaped at the man
slumped in the seat next to the bed. He was the source
of the sound. Not an explosion at all, but a loud, snuf-
fling snort as the fellow snored in his sleep. Dear God,
she'd never heard such a loud, horrendous sound.

Edith stared at the man blankly, wondering who the
devil he was and why he was in her room, and then
she noticed the woman in bed next to her and peered
at her with mingled confusion and concern. She recognized her at once as Victoria's maid, Effie. But finding her in her bed was somewhat surprising. The fact
that the woman looked terribly ill just added to her
bewilderment. The old woman was extremely pale,
not an ounce of color in her thin, wrinkled skin and
she was completely unmoving too. Effie was so still
Edith wasn't even sure she was breathing at first. She
was beginning to worry the woman was dead when

she noted that her chest was rising and lowering the faintest bit with slow, shallow breaths.

Relieved, Edith let out the breath she'd been holding and then glanced around her chamber again. Her room was generally neat and tidy, but at present it looked like there really had been an explosion. An empty mug lay on its side on the bedside table, next to one standing up and two empty bowls. A bread crust and another cup and bowl were on the bedside table on the other side, and then a cask sat on the table at the far end of the room with several more metal cups and bowls between it and a small pile of browning vegetable peels. There was also what appeared to be a rabbit pelt, freshly skinned.

Wondering who had held the party in her room while she was sleeping, Edith glanced over the floor now, noting the sacks lined up against the wall. There were four in all with various items spilling out of them: cloth, vegetables, weapons. And the rush mats on the floor were both crushed and kicked aside, showing a lot of use and definite trails from the door to both the bed and table, and then from both the table and bed to the fireplace where a pot of something was bubbling over the fire.

Edith didn't have a clue what to make of all that, or the fact that there was presently a man at her bedside like some very loud guardian angel.

Or perhaps just a guard.

That last thought was a bit disturbing. Edith knew she'd been sick for a while. The mess in her room suggested it had been quite a while. What had been happening at Drummond while she was out of her head with illness? Had one of the clans they were feuding with learned of the deaths of her father and brothers and decided to take advantage and attack the castle?

The idea was an alarming one, particularly since she had not been awake to aid in defending against such a happenstance. Her brother Brodie, much as she loved him, was spoiled rotten and not the most capable of men. He would be useless in such a situation she was sure.

Biting her lip, Edith peered warily at the man slumped in the chair next to the bed. He was a big fellow, with wide shoulders and a youthful but not unhandsome face. He was also a complete stranger, not one of the Drummond men. Her gaze dropped to Effie again and she nudged her with her elbow, hoping the woman would wake and tell her what was going on and what had happened while she was ill. When the first nudge had no effect, she gave her a second, firmer poke, but that produced no response either.

Deciding to let the poor woman rest, Edith sat up, or tried. Honestly, it was an effort just to get herself into an upright position. She was as weak as a babe and had to turn on her side and slide her feet off the bed so her legs hung off it, and then push herself up into a sitting position.

Panting and sweaty from what should have been an easy task, Edith swayed where she sat on the edge of the bed and eyed the door with grim determination. Her chamber wasn't really that large. She knew from experience that the door was only six large steps or so from the bed. But after the struggle she'd had to sit up, even six steps seemed an awfully long distance to cross.

Unfortunately, while waking the snoring man in

her room would have been the easier option, Edith wouldn't even consider it until she knew if he was friend or foe. Which meant that if she wanted to find out what was going on in Drummond, and whether she was safe or not, she needed to slip out into the hall and get a look around. Preferably without waking her guard.

Determined to do it, Edith took a deep breath and then used every muscle at her disposal to get up. She pushed off with her hands and up with her legs and for one glorious moment she was upright and standing, and then she fell flat on her face on a rush mat just as the bedroom door opened.

"Bloody hell, Alick! Ye were supposed to be watching—Laddie! Nay!"

Edith pushed one eyelid up and then immediately closed it again as she spotted the huge tongue just inches from her eye. She barely got it closed before the side of her face was lashed with a very large slimy tongue from chin to forehead. Nose wrinkling, she listened to the pounding of feet quickly crossing the room. She noted that the snoring had ended abruptly just before a second male voice, sounding startled, cried out, "What? Hey! Where'd she go?"

"Idiot," the man now kneeling next to her muttered. Edith wasn't sure whom he was calling idiot, and didn't particularly care. She was too grateful to have Laddie's affectionate licking brought to an end and opened her eyes to see a man dragging the dog back toward the door by his collar.

"Ronson!" he bellowed.

"Oh, hey! Niels? How'd she get out o' bed?" Edith was quite sure it was the previously snoring man who asked that question since it came from the other side of the bed.

"How do ye think, Alick?" the first man growled and then bellowed again, "Ronson! Oh, there ye are. Get this mutt out o' here."

"Sorry, m'lord," Ronson cried, entering the room and hurrying to grab Laddie's collar. "He got away from me real quick. He's sneaky that way. But he's been missing Lady Edith and—Why is Lady Edith on the floor? What—?"

"Out," Niels growled. "Now!"

"Aye, m'lord," Ronson said, dragging Laddie with him as he shuffled backward toward the door. The boy beamed at Edith the whole way. "'Tis real fine to see ye awake, m'lady. Real fine. I'll bring Laddie back fer a visit when ye're feeling better."

The last word came muffled through the door as the man Alick had called Niels slammed it closed.

Edith could hear Niels muttering under his breath as she watched his large feet cross the room once more. It sounded like he was saying something about fools, lads and dogs who were really horses, and then he knelt next to her and she found herself turned and then scooped up off the floor and away from the nasty rush mat her face had landed on. It was dirty and beginning to mold, obviously in need of changing. She'd have to have the servants take them away and make new ones.

"Sorry about that," Niels growled, drawing her attention back to him. "The dog tends to follow me around, but usually stops in the hall when I come in here."

"Aye, Laddie follows Niels everywhere when he leaves the room," Alick told her solemnly. "So does young Ronson. They both seem to like him." Pursing his lips, he shook his head and added, "None o' us can figure out why."

Niels growled under his breath in response.

Edith glanced from one man to the other, unsure what to say. She had no idea if they were friend or foe. In the end, she merely nodded her head slightly. For some reason, that made the man carrying her smile and she blinked in surprise as his stern face suddenly turned very handsome. He had an incredibly appealing smile. It lit up his whole face and made his beautiful blue eyes twinkle. Edith couldn't resist smiling back as her eyes slid over his high cheekbones, straight nose, full lips and the wild, long hair framing it all. He really was very attractive.

"I'm Niels Buchanan," he announced, and Edith stopped gaping at how pretty he was and met his gaze as she recognized the last name.

"Not Saidh's—" That was all she managed to get out, and it was nothing more than a breathy sound. Her mouth was so dry she couldn't even work up spit in it. Fortunately, Niels didn't have the same problem and understood what she'd wanted to say.

"Aye, one o' Saidh's brothers," he assured her, turning toward the bed. Setting her down in it, he added, "And ye're Edith Drummond, one o' me sister's dearest friends."

"Aye," she agreed in a whisper as he tugged the linens and furs up to cover her. Edith's smile widened ever so slightly. Drummond hadn't been invaded by enemies. They were being visited by friends. "Is Saidh . . . ?"

"Nay, she's no' here," he said almost apologetically

as he straightened. "She was too far along with child to make the journey and sent us in her place."

Edith's eyes widened. "With child?"

"Aye, she is," the other man said, reminding her of his presence. Niels had called him Alick, Edith recalled as she glanced to him. Which meant he was the youngest of the Buchanan boys, Edith thought as she watched the younger man grin widely as he continued, "And we think she's carrying more than one babe. She's only four months along but already big as a cow. Greer will no' even let her go up and down the stairs on her own fer fear she'll lose her footing and roll down like a great ball."

Edith's eyes widened at the news. She couldn't imagine rough-and-tumble Saidh not being able to walk down a set of stairs let alone restricted from riding. She didn't imagine the woman was taking that well. But she didn't understand why Saidh hadn't mentioned being with child in her last letter. At least the last letter she'd read, Edith thought and wondered if she'd received others from her friend since falling ill.

"Alick, go tell Rory she's awake," Niels ordered, walking to the table where the cask sat.

"Aye," the younger man answered and then smiled at her reassuringly as he moved around the bed. "Our Rory's a healer, and the finest one around. Why, he's the one who sorted out that ye were no' ill but being poisoned. He'll have ye feeling right as rain in no time."

Alick Buchanan nodded at her cheerily and turned to hurry out of the room, leaving Edith staring after him with horror. Poison?

"Idiot."

That mutter drew her gaze to Niels. He'd finished

filling one of the cups with mead and turned to see her expression. Mouth tight, he shook his head and crossed back to the bed. "Forgive me brother. He has the tact o' a bull at the best o' times."

"Poison?" she whispered, her voice raspy.

Cursing, he settled on the edge of the bed and slid an arm under Edith to raise her up. "Aye. Poison. But drink this ere ye try to talk again, else ye may do yerself some damage," he said, holding the mug of liquid up to her mouth.

Edith hesitated, more interested in this poison business at the moment, but then she gave in and took a tiny sip. Once the cool, wet liquid hit her mouth, she would have taken more, but wasn't given the option. She barely had a half mouthful before he lowered the drink.

"Just a sip. Ye were no' able to keep it down when last ye woke so we'll go slow this time."

Edith's eyes widened at the claim. "I woke before?"

"Aye," he said dryly. "But ye were a might confused and no' really alert. Ye drank some mead and then tossed it right back up all over me and passed out again. I'd rather no' go through that again."

Edith groaned and lowered her head with embarrassment.

"There's naught to be embarrassed about," Niels said and she could hear the frown in his voice. "I've four younger brothers who I've had to care fer as they tossed up their stomachs . . . and they were no' poisoned. It was just too much drink fer them. With you, well at least ye had a good excuse."

Reminded of the poison, Edith jerked her head up on a frown. "Me father and brothers?"

Niels winced at her raspy voice and raised the

mead again. "Another swallow o' this, I think. This time swish it around real good and wet all the corners. Ye're obviously dry as a bone."

Edith dutifully took another mouthful of mead, but the moment she'd swished and swallowed, she asked, "Me father and—"

"Aye. Rory can no' be sure o' course, but he believes they were poisoned too. They had all the same symptoms. Except fer the . . . er . . . stomach issues," he said delicately. "But Rory suspicions that's what saved ye. Ye reacted to the poison and tossed it up each time ye had it. There was no' enough left in ye to kill ye as it did yer father and brothers."

Edith lowered her head on this news, her mind awhirl with grief and anger. It had been bad enough when she'd thought she'd lost her father and two brothers to illness, but to know they had been deliberately killed—Jerking her head up, she asked, "Brodie?"

"Well and fine, as far as we ken," he assured her. "He feared getting it himself and took his bride and left fer safer shores when yer maid got sick."

Edith didn't comment. Now that he mentioned it, she recalled Brodie's leaving. She'd been rather annoyed at the time, thinking it less than laird-like behavior to flee the keep and all its people when they might be at the start of a crisis. She noted that Niels sounded disgusted by his actions too, but merely asked, "Moibeal? She is—"

"Yer maid is fine," he assured her. "And fashing to see ye. I would be surprised does she no' ignore Rory's orders to stay away and show up here once she learns ye're awake."

Edith's eyebrows rose. "Why was she no' allowed—"

She broke off and glanced to the door when it opened. Alick was returning with another man and Edith found herself examining the three of them. They were all similar in looks with dark hair and those lovely blue eyes. But Niels was obviously older than the other two. He was also bigger, his shoulders wide, his arms thick and strong. Not that the other two didn't look strong, but Niels looked like a warrior used to wielding a broadsword, while Alick looked like he hadn't fully grown yet and Rory looked like . . . well, like he was a healer more than a warrior.

"'Tis good to see ye awake, Lady Edith," Rory said by way of greeting as he walked to the bed. "How do ye feel?"

"Thirsty," Edith admitted.

"I've only given her two small sips o' mead to see how she stomachs it," Niels announced, and much to Edith's disappointment, stood so that Rory could take his place. She wasn't sure why she was sorry he left, since she barely knew the man, but she *was* disappointed, and her feelings obviously showed on her face, Edith realized when Rory's eyebrows rose slightly and he glanced from her to Niels with a small smile.

Fortunately, he didn't embarrass her by commenting and merely asked, "How does yer stomach feel after the first couple o' sips?"

"Fine, thank ye," she whispered.

"Then Niels can give ye more in a minute," he said and leaned in to look into her eyes.

Edith stilled, fighting the urge to look away and simply waited.

"Yer eyes are back to normal," he murmured.

Edith had no idea what that meant, but looked away

with relief when he sat back again. She then frowned as her gaze fell on the woman in bed next to her. "Effie? Is she—?"

"She appears to have ingested the poison too," Rory interrupted, sparing her voice. "I think, like Moibeal, she did no' consume much o' whatever had the poison in it . . . else she'd be dead now. Howbeit she's old and frail enough that even a little might yet do her in."

"Ye ken what was poisoned?" Edith asked, her voice cracking in several spots. Her throat hurt it was so dry and the few sips she'd had of mead hadn't been enough to ease it.

"Niels, come give her more mead," Rory said, standing and moving around the bed to examine Effie now.

Edith frowned, thinking he planned to ignore her question, but when Niels settled next to her on the bed again and slid an arm under her shoulders to ease her to a sitting position, she forgot all about her question. Niels smelled like the woods in the springtime, a scent she'd always loved. Edith couldn't resist turning her head toward the curve of his neck and shoulder and inhaling deeply. When Niels stilled, she realized what she was doing and quickly turned her face back. Edith was quite sure she was blushing, but Niels merely smiled faintly and offered her the mug of mead.

"Thank ye," Edith murmured before taking a sip.

"Moibeal said she had a couple sips o' yer wine when ye did no' drink it the night she fell ill," Rory commented after she'd had several cautious sips.

Looking toward the other man, Edith saw that he had lifted Effie's eyelids and was peering at her eyes silently. His words hadn't been a question, but she nodded and responded as if it was anyway. "Aye. I said she could. I did no' have the stomach fer it after tossing it back up so many times, so she gave me her cider and I let her have me wine."

"She said she did no' drink much though. Is that right?" Rory asked, sitting up straight and turning his questioning gaze to her.

"Aye. She only had a sip. She did no' care fer it," Edith recalled, noting that her voice was getting stronger. The mead was making her throat feel better too.

"And did Effie have some o' yer wine too?" Rory asked.

"I—" Edith paused, her gaze dropping to the woman before she shrugged helplessly and admitted, "I'm no' sure. She may have. I do no' recall much o' the last week or so since I fell ill again." Frowning, she explained, "At first I could no' keep anything down, but felt better once I'd purged. That kept happening, and finally I refused the wine and broth Moibeal brought." Eyes narrowing as she thought on it, she murmured, "Once I stopped having those, I was able to keep down an apple and some bread Moibeal brought me and I started to feel better again . . . and then I wanted to build me strength so I had some stew and—" She grimaced with distaste. "It did no' seem to make much difference when that came back up. I was exhausted and weary and just wanted to sleep."

"Ye were weakening from no' being able to keep yer food down fer so long," Rory said solemnly.

"Mayhap," Edith admitted and glanced to the woman in bed next to her. "I have a vague recollection o' Effie trying to get me to eat or drink and saying I needed to build up me strength, but every time I did . . ." She grimaced with distaste and merely shook her head.

"Did ye ha'e wine with the stew while ye were tending Moibeal?" Niels asked, drawing her gaze his way.

Edith wrinkled her nose and shook her head. "Frankly, I fear I'll never want wine again after tossing it back up so many times. I did no' have anything to drink that night."

"So the poison was in both the wine and stew," Niels said grimly.

"It was?" Edith asked uncertainly.

"Aye," he assured her, his voice sounding angry. "Moibeal was poisoned from a couple o' sips o' yer wine, but ye fell ill again after eating stew. Both must ha'e been poisoned."

"Oh, aye," she said with realization and then noticed the grim looks Niels and Rory exchanged.

Still a bit fuzzy-minded, Edith wasn't sure what that exchange meant. Noticing her confusion, Rory explained, "We were hoping that perhaps the family wine had been poisoned in an effort to kill yer father and brothers, and ye merely had the bad luck to have some o' the poisoned wine. But if yer stew was later poisoned too . . ." He pointed out almost apologetically, "No one else fell ill from the stew that night."

Edith's eyes widened incredulously at those words. She understood what he was saying. After killing her father and brothers, someone had deliberately tried to poison her. Why would anyone want her dead? She was no one of import.

"Though," Niels added now, turning toward his brother, "the maids both being poisoned is most likely an unintended result o' trying to poison Edith."

"Aye," Rory agreed. "If Effie wakes up I'm quite sure we'll find she ate or drank something that was sent up fer Lady Edith."

Niels nodded, his gaze shifting toward the table where the cask, vegetables and rabbit skin sat. "So the liquid from the vial the maid was mixing into her drink is probably no' the poison."

"Nay. Probably not," Rory agreed. "Effie would hardly deliberately poison herself too."

"A little blue glass vial?" Edith asked, her ears perking up. She hadn't noticed it on the table, but it was small and there was enough mess with the mugs and whatnot that it might be hidden from her view.

"Aye," Niels said. "Effie was pouring the last o' it into yer drink to give to ye as we entered."

"Victoria gave it to Effie ere she left. She said it would help build me blood to aid in fighting the illness or some such thing," Edith murmured and grimaced. "It was foul. Just the smell o' it was enough to make me heave the first night Effie put it in me drink."

"Really?" Rory murmured, and the way he looked toward the table now with interest, convinced her the vial must be there somewhere.

"It can no' be the poison," Edith assured them quietly. "Victoria does no' like me much, but she's no' stupid. She'd hardly give Effie poison to give me in front o' others like that."

"Nay . . . o' course she would no'," Niels murmured, but neither he nor his brothers looked completely convinced by her words. "Here, have more mead."

Edith hesitated, but then let him feed her more mead. She didn't think for a minute the tonic Victoria had given Effie could have poison in it. Her sister-in-law simply wasn't that stupid. Mind you, she wouldn't put it past the lass to have poisoned them all, just not in something that would lead directly back to her. Victoria might have seemed all sweetness and batting eyelashes when she'd first arrived at Drummond as Brodie's new bride, but once Edith's father and brothers had fallen ill, her ambition had shown through. Victoria wanted to be Lady Drummond with all that entailed, and had been terribly frustrated that the servants were not simply falling in line with her vision while the older brothers still lived. The woman had shown her true colors then, throwing a temper tantrum of epic proportions. Even Brodie had appeared taken aback by her behavior and he was famous for his temper tantrums.

In truth, Edith had almost been glad to fall ill herself once her second brother, Hamish, had died. It allowed her to avoid watching the woman claim the position she was so greedy for. Edith was quite certain Victoria wouldn't have taken over graciously or kindly in an effort to secure the hearts of the people now under her charge. She had probably been spiteful and bitter as she'd barked her orders and demanded immediate obeisance. Edith couldn't have borne watching that.

Actually, she was no more eager to watch it now once her brother and his wife returned. Perhaps a visit with Saidh was in order so that she could sort out what she should do now. Edith was quite certain her days at Drummond were numbered. She had no doubt Victoria would want her out of there as quickly as possible, which probably meant a nunnery for her. If she wanted to avoid that, a visit with Saidh and the other girls who made up their group—Murine and Jo— might be helpful. If the four of them put their heads together, they might come up with an alternative future for her, and that would be . . . well, really it was the only hope she had. Although, it was a slim one at best.

Swallowing the mead, Edith asked, "Has there been word as to when Brodie and Victoria will return?"

Niels shook his head. "Nay. I asked Tormod that very thing this morning and he said no one has heard from them. He also said he did no' expect to, that Brodie comes and goes as he pleases without troubling himself to let others ken what he's about."

"Aye," Edith said on a sigh. "Brodie tends to be . . . impulsive. We did no' even ken he'd married until he arrived home with Victoria in tow. It seems he met her at court, fell madly in love and married her within a month."

"And her parents allowed it?" Niels asked with surprise.

"That was my first question," Edith admitted wryly.

"And his answer?" Rory asked with curiosity.

Edith grimaced. "He said they were perfectly fine with it."

"Do ye believe it?" Rory asked with interest.

"Nay," Edith admitted on a sigh. "And neither did me father. He sent a messenger to a friend at court, who immediately wrote him back with the true story as he knew it."

"Which is?" Niels prompted gently when she hesitated.

Grimacing, Edith explained, "Victoria was contracted to marry another when she met Brodie. My brother wooed her with tales o' his being heir to the laird at Drummond." All three Buchanan men stiffened at this news and she rushed on, "Her parents found out and her father took him aside and told him he knew he was the third son and would never be laird, his daughter was contracted to another, and to leave his daughter alone or else. But I do no' think they troubled to tell Victoria that Brodie had lied, because according to my father's friend, the next thing anyone knew Victoria and Brodie were gone." She grimaced. "It seems the pair fled court fer Drummond and stopped in a pub along the way to exchange consent in front o' witnesses."

"So they're no' really married?" Alick asked with a frown.

"Oh, aye, they are," Niels said heavily.

It was Rory who explained, "According to canon law all each party need do is give consent to be married. Ye need no' even have witnesses, although it helps if anyone refutes it."

"Then why is there always the priest prattling on and on? And what o' banns and—?"

"Not strictly necessary," Rory assured him. "Just preferred by most."

"Well . . ." Alick frowned, but seemed at a loss as to why anyone would want such bother.

There was silence for a minute, and then Niels said, "So he claimed he was to be laird."

"And now he is," Rory added darkly.

Edith sighed. She'd just known that was what they would focus on. "Look, I ken it sounds bad, and frankly, me brother is a selfish, unreliable and spoiled lad . . . but Father is the last person Brodie would hurt. He is the one who spoiled him so badly and let him go his own way so much growing up."

"And ye think he respected him fer that?" Niels asked curiously.

Edith stared at him blankly. "What?"

"Do ye think yer brother respected yer father fer spoiling him and letting him get away with so much as ye put it?" Niels asked, "Or do ye think he just felt like mayhap his father did no' care enough to be bothered to discipline him and teach him to survive in this world as a man?"

Edith frowned. She'd often seen her father's indulgence of Brodie as hurtful to her brother, knowing it was doing him no favors, but she'd never considered that Brodie might see it that way too.

"Yer brother got lucky with Victoria," Niels added quietly. "If he'd tried the like with our sister and we'd caught up to him ere they exchanged consent, we would ha'e beat him near to death."

"Aye, and probably cut off his ballocks and fiddle to boot," Rory said coldly.

Edith's eyes widened incredulously at the threat to Brodie's family jewels. "Nay."

"Aye," Alick assured her with a grin. "We planned to do all that and more to MacDonnell after he sent a message saying he'd ruined our Saidh and planned to marry her." Pursing his lips with displeasure, he added, "I'm still no' sure why we did no' do it."

"Because MacDonnell's a laird, and he ne'er lied to Saidh," Rory explained dryly.

"Besides, Saidh was no' contracted to another," Niels added. "She had no better prospects. In fact, MacDonnell was a fine choice to husband."

"And she loved him," Edith pointed out.

"Nay," Niels said at once, and when she frowned, assured her, "'Tis true. She lusted after him and liked him at first, but did no' yet love him. She said as much herself right in front o' us."

"Really?" Edith asked, her voice almost a squeak of surprise.

"Aye," Rory assured her with amusement. "Though, in truth, I think she probably was half in love with him when they married. She definitely loves him now."

"No' that it matters," Niels added quietly. "Had MacDonnell been a spoiled, lying third son unable to support her and any bairns they might produce, we would ha'e beat him to death rather than let him marry her . . . whether she loved him or no'."

"What?" Edith gasped, shrinking away from him with surprise.

Niels frowned at her reaction, but then asked, "Ye said ye do no' think Victoria's parents told her that Brodie had lied. Was it only because she ran off with him?"

"Nay," she admitted reluctantly.

"Then why?"

Edith blew her breath out unhappily, but then admitted, "Because she seemed shocked when they got here and Brodie introduced her to our older brothers."

"How shocked?" Niels asked.

Edith stared at him silently, suddenly suspecting he already knew the answer. If he'd talked to anyone here since their arrival he probably did, she realized, and wondered just how long the men had been here and what all they knew.

"She fainted," Edith admitted quietly, recalling the way Victoria had paled and then collapsed. Brodie had tried to brush it away as exhaustion from the trip as he'd scooped her up and carried her above stairs to his chamber, but they all heard the shouting coming from the room some ten minutes later when Victoria had apparently woken up.

Aware that no one had commented and the three

men were watching her solemnly, Edith sighed and asked, "How long ha'e ye been here?"

"Nearly a week," Rory answered.

"A week?" she gasped with amazement.

"Only six days," Niels corrected.

"But . . ." She glanced from man to man. "What ha'e ye been doing all that time?"

"Mostly taking turns guarding ye, hunting up game, making broth and dribbling it down yer throat while ye were unconscious in hopes ye'd recover enough to wake up," Rory answered gently.

Edith stared at them, her mind spinning slowly. While Brodie had fled the keep with its threat of illness, these three men, who did not even know her, had been here nearly a week. During that time, not only had they taken care of her, but they'd hunted and cooked her food, dribbling the broth down her throat in the hopes of getting enough nourishment into her to help her recover.

"Why?"

The word slipped out without her conscious intent, and for a minute it just hung there helplessly in the air. Then Niels shifted her slightly so that she was looking at him and said simply, "Because ye needed our help, lass."

Perhaps she was still exhausted and drained from her illness, or perhaps it was the deaths of her father and brothers that she had not yet had a chance to grieve, but Edith's eyes suddenly glazed over with the sheen of tears. Just as she felt herself beginning to crumble in Niels's arms, the bedroom door suddenly burst open. Edith turned to see another man enter the room, this one as big and brawny as Niels and holding up two dead birds by their feet.

"I got a nice pair o' pheasants this time, Rory. If ye only use one fer broth, we can maybe get Cook to roast up the other and—" The man stopped and blinked as he noted Edith half-upright in the curve of Niels's arm. "Oh, say, ye're awake! Well, is that no' fine?"

Chapter 3

$\mathcal{E}$DITH BLINKED HER EYES OPEN AND PEERED to the window, a smile claiming her lips when she saw the sunlight peeking through the cracks in the shutters. It was morning, finally, and today she could get up and go below. Rory and Niels had promised her as much.

It had been three days since she'd woken. Much to her dismay, the men had insisted she stay in her room, allowing her only to walk to a chair and back to her bed and usually with one of them hovering nearby in case her legs gave way.

To be fair to the men, Edith had been pathetically weak on first waking. Her attempt to get up from bed on her own the first time had been proof of that. Edith hadn't been much stronger the next day when she'd tried to rise again unaided. She'd managed three steps before falling.

Fortunately, Niels had woken up and quickly caught her before she hit the floor. That was when they'd insisted she shouldn't get up without one of them to help her, and to tell her that she was restricted to the room until she regained some of her strength. Edith had tried to argue with them, but it was hard to argue with four determined Buchanans. Honestly, they were worse than Saidh when it came to stubbornness. And the fact that, technically, they had no right to boss her about hadn't mattered to them at all. But yesterday she'd been determined, and the only way they'd managed to convince her to stay in her room was to promise she could leave it today without their trying to stop her.

Edith sat up in bed and glanced around. She was alone in her bed, which made a nice change. After two nights with Effie sharing her bed, Edith had insisted they move her to Brodie's old room next door yesterday. It wasn't that she minded sharing her bed so much as the woman's silent stillness and pallor made her feel like she was sharing it with a breathing corpse. It had begun to give her the creeps, and she'd found herself watching her to be sure she was still breathing.

Once the older woman was moved, Edith had become eager to clean up the chaos her room had fallen into. She'd assigned the men their own rooms, suggesting Rory take Hamish's room, which was next to Brodie's old room, so he could watch over Effie more easily. She'd then suggested Niels take Roderick's old room, which was next to that. Which left the two guest rooms across the hall from Roderick's and Hamish's rooms for Alick and Geordie.

That was when Geordie and Alick had packed up their bags and headed out for MacDonnell. Apparently they had been waiting until she was well on the way to recovery before taking news of her well-being to Saidh. It seemed they saw her ordering them about and cleaning up as a sign that she was definitely on the mend and not likely to relapse on them. The two men had left, intending to report to their sister on what had occurred at Drummond, and then would return to help them sort out who was behind the murders of her father and two older brothers.

Edith frowned at the thought. They'd talked about that a lot since her waking, but frankly no one seemed to have an idea of how to go about that task. Poisoning was a tricky business. They suspected someone was adding poison to the wine, which was more than possible. With her stomach still a bit delicate after her tummy ailment the week before, Edith had been avoiding wine. But anyone could have slipped poison in the wine cask, or the pitchers of wine on their way out to the table. The same was true of the stew she'd eaten while nursing Moibeal. Edith didn't even recall who had brought her stew that night, but even if she had, they didn't have to be the person who'd dropped poison in it.

Frankly, Edith had no idea how they could figure out who had poisoned her family members. The men hadn't really suggested anything useful either and she knew Niels had suggested Geordie and Alick ask Saidh and Greer if they had any ideas.

Edith pushed the linen and furs aside and slid her feet to the floor only to pause as her gaze landed on Niels, Ronson and Laddie on the floor to the side of the door. The trio was all wrapped up in Niels's tartan. Apparently Laddie had cuddled up in front of where Niels lay on his side, and Ronson had then cuddled up to the dog. The trio had then somehow wound up with

Niels's tartan blanketing them all. The sight made her smile.

Niels had been rather grumpy for most of the three days since she'd woken, giving her stern looks and insisting she not do this and not do that. But when Rory had finally allowed Ronson to bring Laddie up to visit the day before, Edith had seen an entirely different side of Niels. Oh, he'd still been grumpy and growly to a degree, but he'd been incredibly kind and patient with Ronson, and Edith had really appreciated it. The boy obviously hadn't had a lot of male influence in his life and appeared to look up to Niels quite a bit. Laddie also appeared taken with the man, obeying his orders promptly and behaving with better manners than Edith had ever seen.

Their visit had been a breath of fresh air in the sickroom. Ronson had chattered happily away, telling her everything that had happened since she'd fallen ill, which amounted to not much of anything, but was still entertaining when the boy told it. She'd also enjoyed having Laddie snuggling up to her on the bed, even when the dog had licked her face like crazy. There was just something about dogs that soothed the soul, and Edith's soul had needed soothing after the events of the past weeks.

She peered at the trio spooning on the floor and shook her head faintly, not sure how Ronson and Laddie had ended up staying in her room all night. She did know that Niels had insisted that she needed guarding still and was determined to sleep on the floor by the door. But the last she recalled, Ronson and Laddie had been curled up on the foot of her bed, sound asleep while she and Niels had talked quietly, she in the bed, he in the chair next to her bed. She must have fallen asleep, however, because she didn't recall the man, boy and dog moving to the floor.

Wishing she had some artistic talent so that she might paint this scene and never forget it, Edith eased out of bed, freezing when Laddie immediately lifted his head. She gave him the gesture to stay, and he did, but the dog didn't lower his head and simply watched alertly as she moved to the chest at the foot of her bed to retrieve a gown. Edith picked the first one her hand touched and quickly tugged it on over her shift. It would have been nice to be able to change her shift, but she wouldn't risk it with Niels and Ronson there. She was anxious enough just standing there in her shift even though Niels had already seen her in it.

Once dressed, Edith quickly ran a brush through her hair, washed her face and hands at the basin on the table and then moved silently toward the door, putting out her hand again to order Laddie to stay. Unfortunately, there was only so much a dog could take and the moment she reached for the door handle, he stood up and started forward, dragging the tartan with him. Ronson immediately stirred, but Edith hardly noticed, her eyes were widening on Niels as a good portion of the tartan was pulled away from him before it fell off Laddie and dropped to cover Niels's face. It also left the man bare from about midchest down.

It wasn't until Ronson popped to his feet, scrubbing his eyes sleepily, that Edith managed to drag her gaze from more than she'd ever expected to see of one of Saidh's brothers. Giving her head a shake, she opened the door and stepped out into the hall, followed quickly by Laddie and Ronson.

"Should we—" Ronson began, but paused at once when she hushed him.

Edith closed the door carefully, and then ushered the lad up the hall. They were at the stairs before she stopped to eye him and asked, "Does yer grandmother ken where ye slept last night, or has she been worrying herself sick wondering where ye were?"

"I told her," he said just a little too quickly, and then babbled, "Lord Niels told me to go below and ask would it be all right, so I did."

"Ye did what? Ask her or tell her?"

Ronson grimaced, but then sighed and admitted, "She was heading into the garderobe when I came down, so I asked her through the door and she did no' say no, so I came back up."

Edith clucked her tongue and shook her head. "She probably did no' even hear ye. Ye ken her hearing is bad, Ronson. Why did ye no' just wait fer her to come out and ask her then?"

"Because she takes *forever* in there," he complained.

"Aye well, I'm afraid when we get old we all take a little more time in the garderobe," Edith said.

"Hmm." Ronson scowled. "No' like Gran. Sometimes I think she falls asleep doing her business, she takes so long." Heaving out a heavy sigh, he shook his head and said woefully, "I'm never getting old, and that's the truth, m'lady. I'm no' spending all me time crapping in the gong."

Edith's eyes widened incredulously, and then, deciding a change of subject was in order, she asked, "What were ye going to say when we were leaving the bedchamber, Ronson?"

"I was just thinking mayhap we should wake Niels

so he can keep ye safe from the murdering, pimple-arsed whoreson who done poisoned yer father and brothers," Ronson said earnestly.

Edith blinked down at the boy several times as her brain tried to accept the words that had just come from his mouth. She'd never heard Ronson use such foul language, but didn't have to think hard to know where he'd learned the words. The Buchanans did have a very colorful way of speaking. Even Saidh had a mouth so foul it could make your ears pinken.

"Er . . . aye, well I'm sure I'll be safe enough from the . . . er . . . pimple-arsed . . ." Edith paused and then just shook her head and started down the stairs, saying, "I'm sure we'll be safe enough at table, do ye no' think?"

"But Laddie'll have to go outside or he'll be pissing everywhere like a warty prick," Ronson protested.

"Oh, dear," Edith breathed faintly. Goodness. A little time with the Buchanans was certainly a lot of time when it came to learning, it seemed.

"So I gotta take him out," Ronson continued anxiously, following her down the stairs. "And then ye'll be all alone. I can no' leave ye alone, m'lady. That murdering whoreson might get ye!"

"I'm—Oh!" Edith gasped with surprise when she was suddenly swept off her feet and into someone's arms. Turning her head, she gaped at Niels and protested, "I can walk, m'lord."

"Aye, but ye're too slow. Ye were blocking the stairs," Niels argued with a shrug as he continued down the stairs, and then he added grimly, "And ye should no' have left the room without me."

"I was just telling her that, m'lord," Ronson assured

him firmly, on their heels. "I told her as how we needed ye to keep her safe from the warty prick what poisoned her da and brothers."

"Actually, I believe he was the pimple-arsed whoreson, and Laddie would be pissing like a warty prick," Edith pointed out dryly, glaring at Niels as she did. When he just grinned at her, she whispered sharply, "His grandmother is going to kill me fer letting ye teach him such things."

Niels raised his eyebrows and then paused on the bottom step and turned to tell Ronson, "A man does no' use such words in front o' a lady."

Ronson looked confused and pointed out, "But *ye* do."

Niels pursed his lips and nodded. "Aye. I do," he admitted and then turned to cross the bailey floor, muttering, "I tried, m'lady, but by God's tooth he's right. I fear me brothers and I all swear something awful."

"Aye," Edith said on a sigh. "So does Saidh. I suppose there are worse habits."

Niels grunted what might have been an agreement to that as he set her on the bench at the table, and then glanced around and ordered, "Take Laddie outside, Ronson. His eyes are near floating he has to go so bad."

"Aye, m'lord," the boy said and hurried away, calling Laddie to follow just as the dog started to lift a leg by the end of the bench Edith sat on. Fortunately the dog obeyed and followed at once.

Niels watched them until they left the great hall and then dropped to sit on the bench next to Edith.

"He thinks much o' you," she said quietly.

"Aye. Well, I like him fine too," Niels said gruffly. "He's a good lad."

"He is," she agreed.

"It was good o' ye to take in he and his grandmother," Niels said softly enough not to be heard by others.

Edith shrugged. "Ye make it sound like charity. It was no'. I had positions fer both o' them."

"Aye. Ronson watches yer dog," he said with amusement. "Tell me the two o' them do no' simply follow ye around the keep all the livelong day."

"How did ye ken th—?" Catching herself, she stopped and clucked her tongue with irritation at giving herself away.

"Because they have been following me around in yer absence every time I left yer room," Niels answered her unfinished question, his tone dry. "'Tis obvious the lad usually follows ye around. Any question I asked about ye, he kenned the answer to."

Edith stiffened and turned to eye him suspiciously. "What kind o' questions?"

She was not soothed by the wide grin that suddenly claimed his lips.

"Ah, m'lady, I can no' tell ye how pleased I am to see ye up and about and well."

Edith turned quickly and smiled at Cawley as he claimed the spot on her other side and took her hand.

"I knew they could save ye," Cawley told her, squeezing the hand he held. "Thank God Tormod listened to me and *finally* agreed to let them in to tend to ye else ye'd have surely died."

"God's blood, Cawley," Tormod growled, dropping onto the bench next to him. "I was following orders. Once the lad pointed out that his brother might be able to save our lady, I let them in, did I no'? Despite the fact I'll probably be flogged fer it?"

"Oh flogged," Cawley said with disgust. "What's a little flogging when our lady is alive and well?"

"I do no' ken. Why do I no' take ye out front and give ye the floggin' I'll most like receive when the laird returns and then ye can tell what a little flogging is?" Tormod said grimly.

"Oh now, Tormod," Cawley said with alarm.

"I would no' do that and ye ken it," Tormod said on a sigh, and then asked, "Did ye talk to the cook, like I asked?"

"O' course I did," Cawley said at once.

"And?" Tormod asked.

"And he could no' remember who took the stew up to Lady Edith that made her sick," Cawley admitted unhappily.

"And?" Tormod repeated.

"And what?" Cawley asked warily.

"Is that it?" Tormod snapped. "I have been running meself ragged overseeing the men at practice and running the servants in Lady Edith's absence. I asked ye to do one thing, *one thing*—question the cook and his maids in the kitchen and find out what ye can—and that's all ye come back to me with?"

"Oh, well . . . I did try," Cawley said anxiously.

"No' hard enough," Tormod growled. "If we can no' sort out who put the poison in her food and drink then Lady Edith is still in danger. Get yer hairy arse into the kitchen and watch the food, make sure no one puts poison in anything. And ask questions while ye're there. Find out what ye can."

Cawley nodded eagerly and stood.

"And tell Cook he'd best make and bring out Lady Edith's food himself and never take his eyes off it while he does, because if she is poisoned again, I'll hang the two o' ye from the castle wall and let crows pick yer bones."

Eyes wide, Cawley nodded and waddled quickly off to the kitchens.

Tormod watched him go and then turned to the table with a sigh and muttered, "That ought to keep him out o' our hair for another day or two."

"Aye," Edith murmured and then glanced to Niels and noted his expression.

"Cawley is special," Tormod said when Edith hesitated to explain.

"Special?" Niels asked dubiously.

"Aye," Edith agreed. "He has a tendency to . . . er . . ."

"He tells tales," Tormod said mildly. "A lot. While he just claimed to Edith that he argued that you be let in, when Brodie returns he'll tell him just as earnestly, and right in front of her, that he tried to warn me against going against his orders and opening the gate to ye."

When Niels looked to her, Edith nodded solemnly. "It is what he's always done."

Niels pursed his lips and then asked Tormod, "So which is true? Did he argue you should let us in or keep us out?"

"Both," Tormod said with a scowl. "That is the hell of it. He never truly lies, he just . . ." He hesitated and then explained, "When ye first got here he argued we'd best no' let ye in, and reminded me Lady Victoria had said we were to let no one in. And then when ye mentioned yer brother was a healer and might save her, he argued I should let you in. But the moment I agreed, he began to argue that we should not."

Niels shook his head and asked with bewilderment, "Why is he the second here?"

"Because he is my father's half brother and he wanted to take care of him," Edith said quietly.

Niels eyebrows rose at the bald announcement, and then he asked, "Half brother?"

"'Tis a sad story," Tormod warned him, and then told it so that Edith didn't have to. "Ye see, the old bastard laird, Edith's grandfather, had banished Cawley and his mother when Cawley was but a lad. But Edith's father knew about it, and when the old man died he wanted to make up fer his behavior. He found Cawley, brought him here and made him his second, but then he made sure we all understood that it was in name only. When we say Cawley is special, we mean he's no' quite right in the head."

"My grandfather did no' just banish Cawley and his mother," Edith explained. "As a young boy Cawley somehow found out that my grandfather was his father. He approached him and told him he knew. I do no' ken what he was hoping to achieve. He probably just wanted a father, he was just a boy, no older than Ronson at the time, but Grandfather was enraged. He beat him horribly . . . nearly to death. And then he banished them both. Cawley's mother carried him away and did the best she could, but while his body healed, his mind was never the same again." She shrugged helplessly. "My father used to take them food and coins to try to help them get by, but could do little more than that until his father died."

"I see," Niels said quietly.

"The problem is that Cawley likes to be the center o' attention," Tormod said quietly. "If he is no' kept busy he will insinuate himself into everything and tends to cause confusion and strife."

"So, ye keep him busy," Niels said with understanding.

"Aye, and usually in the kitchens," Tormod said with a wry smile. "Because the one thing he likes best in the world is his food. In fact the minute he's in the kitchen he'll forget everything I told him and simply concentrate on eating."

"We think it is because he and his mother were nearly starving for so long," Edith said softly. "Now he eats all he can fer fear there will be no more tomorrow."

"Aye," Tormod said sadly. "Fortunately, Cook is a good-natured sort and simply sits him in a corner with bowl after bowl of food and lets him jabber away."

"So ye did no' mean it when ye said Cook had best make and bring out Edith's food himself and—"

"Oh, aye, I meant it," Tormod interrupted with a grim smile. "But it does no' matter if Cawley tells him, because I told Cook that meself last night, and again this morning."

"Ah," Niels said relaxing and even managing a smile. Then he glanced to Edith. "Is yer uncle Cawley the reason ye took in Ronson and his grandmother?"

"Nay," Edith said with surprise. "I took them in because they needed a home. Everyone should have a place to call home."

Niels stared at Edith and wondered if she realized just how much she'd said with those words. She had given Ronson and his grandmother a place where they could feel they belonged and that they could call home. She was giving them what she herself didn't

have. Her place here was temporary. Edith would lose
the only home she'd ever known and the rest of her
family along with it, all the soldiers and servants she'd
grown up with and considered her family, friends and
charges. She would even lose her damned dog since
he didn't think the Abbey would allow her to bring the
huge beast with her.

It was heartbreaking to him, and so unfair. Edith
was a good woman, a kind woman. She deserved better.

"M'lady."

Niels glanced around even as Edith did, his eyes
narrowing as he saw the skinny little man standing
behind Edith with a metal platter with pastries on it.

"I made yer favorite," the man said. "Pastry stuffed
with sweetened cherries."

"Oh, how lovely," Edith said smiling at the man.
"Thank ye, Jaimie."

"'Twas me pleasure," he assured her, beaming.
"We are all verra happy to see ye up and about again,
m'lady. And I promise ye, I did no' take me eyes off
these pastries from start to finish. I even stood and
watched 'em cook. No one got near them. So you
enjoy 'em. They're safe."

"Thank ye, Jaimie," Edith said again, and when the
man leaned past her to set them on the table in front of
her, she gave him a quick peck on the cheek of gratitude that had the man flushed and flustered. Bobbing
his head repeatedly, he backed away from the table
and then turned and rushed back to the kitchens as red
as the cherries in his pastries.

Niels eyed the pastries on the platter and caught her
hand when she went to grab one. "Mayhap I should try
one first in case they're poisoned."

Edith blinked at him with surprise. "Ye heard Jaimie, he watched them from start to finish. They are fine."

"But what if he is the one who poisoned the wine and stew?" he pointed out.

"What? He would no' . . ." Pausing, she narrowed her eyes. "Ye're just after me cherry pastries, m'lord."

"I am not, I—" he began to protest, but paused when she took a pastry off the platter and offered it to him.

"Try it then. They're very good."

Niels accepted the pastry, his mouth already watering. He was biting into it even before she turned to offer the platter to the other man.

"You too, Tormod," Edith said. "I can no' possibly eat all o' these by meself."

"Ah, ye're a fine woman, Lady Edith. A heart o' gold is what ye have," Tormod said, taking a pastry as well.

Niels saw Edith shake her head with amusement at the man's flattery, but he was busy trying not to moan at how good the pastry he'd just bitten into was. Dear God, if the cook at Buchanan made anything even near as good as this, he and his brothers would not be happily wandering far and wide making coin. They'd all be stuck at home, as big as Cawley and just as complacent.

"Pastries?" Ronson cried, rushing up to the table with Laddie on his heels.

"Aye. Cherry," Edith said and held the platter out to the boy. When he took one, she said, "Take two and sit next to Niels to eat. No sharing with Laddie though, ye ken they make him sick."

"I ken," Ronson said. "Thank ye, m'lady." Taking his booty, he climbed up onto the bench next to Niels and set to work at scarfing down the cherry delights.

"Well?"

Mouth full of pastry, Niels raised an eyebrow in question at Edith's question.

"Is it poisoned?" she asked dryly.

Chewing, he merely shook his head and Edith snorted and picked up three more pastries and set them in front of him, saying, "Enjoy."

It was in that moment that Niels Buchanan decided that Edith Drummond was one of the finest women he'd ever met.

"So, what are yer plans fer today?" Tormod asked.

Niels knew he was asking Edith but when she opened her mouth to answer, he quickly swallowed the pastry and said firmly, "Bed."

"What?" Edith turned on him with shock. "I am no' going back to bed. I just got up."

"Ye have to take this slowly. Ye've been ill fer weeks. Ye need—"

"I was poisoned, not ill," she reminded him grimly. "And I am fine now."

"Ye must no' overdo it. Ye're still weak," he argued.

"Aye, I am," she acknowledged. "But I'm no' going to get stronger lounging about in bed. Besides, there is much to do around here."

"Nonsense," Niels said at once.

"Oh really?" she asked with disbelief. "So ye did no' notice the horrid moldy stench to the rush mat ye slept on last night? Because I notice ye now carry that stink with ye, as do Ronson and Laddie."

Frowning, Niels sniffed himself and grimaced. He

had indeed noticed the smell when he'd first laid down last night, but so many hours with it in his nose had apparently made him immune to the scent. Now that she mentioned it though, he did carry the smell with him and it was quite putting him off his cherry pastries.

Scowling, he asked, "What has to happen to make the rushes smell better?"

"I shall have the women remove and burn the old rush mats and then I shall have to take the children down to the river to collect fresh rushes." She paused and then added, "And then the women will have to weave fresh mats to replace the old and we'll put them down and sprinkle dried flowers to make them smell nice."

Niels was silent for a moment, considering what she'd said. In the short time that he'd known Edith, he'd come to understand her well enough to realize that having the women remove and burn the old rush mats meant she'd help them do it, and taking the children down to collect fresh rushes probably meant she'd be performing the backbreaking work alongside them. It was just the kind of woman she was, leading by example and not simply standing back and barking orders. Niels also knew she felt fine just now, but the woman had spent the better part of the past month ill in bed. She would tire much more quickly than she realized.

However, he suspected he wasn't going to be able to talk her out of this rush business. In truth, he really didn't want to. Now that he was aware of it again, he found the moldy stench that had permeated his shirt and tartan unbearable. He was thinking a quick trip to the loch to bathe away the scent was a good idea, but it would do him little good if he then had to lie on the smelly mats again tonight. Since he had no intention of leaving Edith unprotected, that was where he was definitely going to be tonight, so fresh rushes were a necessity.

"Verra well, I suggest ye have yer maid Moibeal oversee the collecting and burning o' the mats while ye take the children down to collect fresh rushes," Niels said, and when she started to protest as he expected, added, "'Twill help speed things along and I think that may be necessary. Me leg was tender when I woke up this morn."

Edith blinked at him with confusion. "Yer leg? What has that to do with anything?"

"'Tis an old injury that usually only acts up before a rainstorm," he explained, which was true, though he was quite sure this morning's tenderness could be blamed on sleeping on the cold, hard floor and not a coming rain. "Ye'll want the rushes collected and the children back at the keep ere that happens else ye'll have a castle full o' sick children on yer hands."

"Oh, aye," she agreed with a frown.

"I'll oversee the collecting and burning of the old mats," Tormod said now. "I'll have the men help too. That way ye can take Moibeal along and a couple other maids to help with gathering rushes and corralling the children. They can be a handful."

"Oh, that's no' necessary," Edith said at once. "I can handle the children."

"Aye, but if 'tis going to rain, ye'll want the lads and lassies to be quick about their business, and ye ken how they dawdle and play. Moibeal and the others can help ye speed things along. In fact," Tormod announced, "I'm thinking mayhap ye should take all the maids and leave the collecting and burning completely to me men. It'll be done in no time then, ye'll beat the rain and ye ken it'll be like a day off fer them, a bit o' fun. After these weeks o' stress and tragedy, everyone could do with a little o' that."

"A fine idea, Tormod," Niels said with an approving nod, appreciating his aid.

"Laddie and I'll come with ye, m'lady," Ronson announced.

Niels grinned at the lad when he saw the cherry filling smeared all over his face. It looked like he'd got more around his mouth than in it.

"Thank ye, Ronson, that would be fine," Edith said with a smile.

Nodding, Ronson licked cherry filling from his hand and added, "Do no' ye worry none, Laddie and I'll keep ye safe from that boil-brained barnacle from Satan's arse what poisoned ye."

"Dear God, pray tell me Bessie did no' hear that," Edith breathed.

"Who's Bessie?" Niels asked with curiosity.

"Ronson's grandmother," Tormod explained.

Interested in seeing the woman who had helped raise the fine boy next to him, Niels glanced around. "Is she here?"

"Aye. That's her, mending by the fire. Do no' look," Edith gasped when he turned to peer over his shoulder, and then just as quickly asked, "Is she looking this way?"

"Nay. She appears to be asleep," Niels said, eyeing the old woman in the chair by the fire. Her hair was pulled up into a tight bun on the top of her head and her clothes were tattered, but clean. Her eyes though appeared to be closed and her hands lay unmoving in her lap on top of a shirt she'd apparently been mending.

"Thank God," Edith muttered. "Come on, Ronson. We'll go find Moibeal and the other maids, and then gather the children together and head out as soon as we can."

"Ye're no' letting her go out to collect the rushes by herself, are ye?" Tormod asked with a frown once Edith and Ronson had moved away to find servants to take with them.

Niels shook his head. "Nay. I'm going. And I'm taking some furs fer her to sit on, as well as some cherry pastries and me horse. She does no' realize it now, but she'll be exhausted within the hour."

"Aye, well, she's stubborn," Tormod warned him. "So do no' expect her to admit it when she tires. She'll work herself to the edge o' exhaustion and still force herself to press forward rather than admit defeat."

"Aye. I already suspected as much," Niels assured him. "She's a lot like me sister that way."

"Do ye have a plan?" Tormod asked with interest.

"Aye. I'll use the lad against her," Niels said simply.

The old man smiled and nodded. "That'll work. She frets about him enough ye'd think he was hers."

"Aye," Niels agreed and then asked, "Why is that?"

Tormod shook his head. "Lady Edith has always had a good heart . . . too good at times. Others take advantage." He sighed. "It breaks me heart to think what'll happen to her when Brodie returns. Most like she'll be on her way to the Abbey within an hour after he arrives. She deserves better."

"Aye," Niels murmured, wishing there was something he could do for her.

"Well, I guess I'd best go let the lads ken what they're doing today," Tormod said, getting to his feet.

"Will they mind?" he asked curiously.

Tormod snorted. "Not likely. Oh, they'll whine and complain about doing women's work while they drag the mats out, but once it comes time fer burning the rushes, they'll pull out the ale and drink and laugh around the fire."

Niels smiled faintly. It's what he and his brothers would have done too. Wishing the man a good day, he stood and headed above stairs to retrieve the items he wanted for this outing.

Chapter 4

"MAYHAP YE SHOULD REST, M'LADY."

Edith managed a smile for Moibeal at that suggestion, but merely shook her head. "I'm fine."

"Aye, but ye've been awful ill fer weeks," her maid said worriedly. "Ye do no' want to overdo it and fall ill again."

"I was poisoned, no' ill, Moibeal," Edith pointed out, bending to hack at the base of the next bunch of rushes with the sickle in her right hand.

Edith bit back a groan as she added the rushes to the bunch gathered in her left arm, and then glanced around in surprise when the whole stack was taken from her. Swallowing the "thank ye" that almost slipped out, she scowled at Niels instead and said, "I can manage, m'lord, ye—"

"Ronson's exhausted," Niels interrupted. "He did no' sleep well last night and is younger than most o' the other children here. He needs a break."

Pausing, Edith glanced around with a frown to see Ronson working wearily farther along the bank, the exhaustion clear on his pale face. "Aye," she murmured with concern and straightened. "I'll tell him to stop and rest now."

"I already did," Niels said with a shrug. "But he insists he'll work as long as ye do."

"Really?" She frowned.

"Aye. I was hoping to convince ye to take a wee break. Just long enough to get the boy to stop," he added quickly, and then tempted her with, "I brought some of those cherry pastries and furs to sit on. I already spread out the furs. I thought we could have a picnic. I suspect Ronson'll fall asleep soon as his belly is full and then ye can work some more or no' as ye wish."

Edith's mouth began to water at the thought of the cherry pastries, and her body was crying out for rest. Niels had been right. She had tired sooner than she'd expected, but she'd pushed on, determined not to give in.

Her gaze slid over the other children and maids working along the riverbank to collect the needed rushes and then lifted to the sky overhead. It was as blue as Niels's eyes. There wasn't even a hint of rain that she could see. They seemed to have plenty of time to accomplish their task. Her gaze moved next to the carts they'd brought down with them. One was full, the other just starting to be used and she nodded.

"Moibeal, have Sorcha lead the full cart back to the castle so that the older maids who stayed behind can start on weaving the mats. Have Bryce accompany her," she added, choosing the oldest boy. "Give them an apple each to take with them and then pass out the apples to the children and the rest o' the maids. Everyone can sit down and rest for a few minutes."

"Aye, m'lady," Moibeal grinned gratefully, not at her, Edith noticed, but at Niels. As if he'd accomplished a miracle in getting her to stop.

Shaking her head, Edith started to turn and nearly toppled over when she tried to move away from the shore. The mud was sucking at her feet, sapping her strength. If Niels hadn't caught her arm, she would have fallen over. Mumbling a "thank ye," she let him lead her toward the trees where he'd set out the furs.

"Ronson!" Niels called as he saw Edith seated. "Bring Laddie and come sit a spell."

"Aye, m'lord."

Edith grimaced at the relief in the boy's voice, and bit her lip when she saw him struggle out of the mud along the river and then drop his stack of rushes and head toward them. The boy was dragging his feet something awful until Laddie moved to his side. Throwing his arm over the dog, Ronson leaned on him and managed to pick up his pace a bit. The moment he reached the furs, though, he released the dog and collapsed to sit on them.

"This rush collecting is a buggering business," Ronson gasped, flopping onto his back on the furs.

Edith sighed and just shook her head, too exhausted to comment on his language. Honestly, Niels and his brothers had been at the castle for only ten days, most of that time spent in her room from what she could tell, and already had the lad sounding like a soldier. Only the soldiers tried not to swear so much in front of the women, or at least not in front of her.

"Muddy feet off the fur, lad. And make sure Laddie

does no' get on them. He's soaked from trying to catch fish in the river," Niels said mildly as he sat down and opened the sack he'd brought to begin digging inside.

"Aye, m'lord." Ronson shifted to make sure his muddy feet were not on the fur, and then patted the grass next to his feet and said, "Come on, Laddie. Lay down."

The huge dog moved over to sniff Ronson's hand, obviously hoping for a treat. When he didn't find one, he huffed, and then gave himself a good shake, sending water flying everywhere.

Ronson squealed in surprise and covered his face, but Edith merely smiled and closed her eyes against the smattering of water drops spraying over her. She was too content to move, the sun felt fine on her face and lit up her eyelids so that all she saw was a bright red vista.

"Lass?"

Edith opened her eyes to see Niels holding out a cherry pastry and a skin of liquid.

"Thank ye," she murmured, accepting the offering. Taking them both, she sniffed at the liquid in the skin, relieved when it turned out to be cider.

"I did no' bring wine because ye mentioned ye did no' care fer it much," he murmured, handing Ronson a cherry pastry as well before taking one for himself.

"Thank ye." Edith said sincerely and sipped some of the sweet liquid before passing back the skin.

Raising her pastry, she bit into it and moaned softly with pleasure as the sweet center exploded in her mouth. No one made pastries like Jaimie did. Edith ate the first quickly, but took more time with her second, half-distracted as she watched Niels peel an apple in one long strand that dangled from the edge of his knife.

"How'd ye do that, m'lord?" Ronson asked, eyeing what Niels was doing with fascination.

"Just keep going round," Niels said and stopped to retrieve another apple. Handing it to the boy he said, "Get out yer *sgian-dubh* and I'll show ye."

"Ronson does no' have a *sgian-dubh*," Edith said gently.

Niels frowned and then handed him his own. "You can use mine then. I'll use me dirk."

Ronson accepted the black-handled, short knife, his eyes wide and reverent.

"Watch ye do no' cut yerself," Niels cautioned as he retrieved his dirk and slid it under the apple peel he'd started. "Now just start at the top by the stem and go around, but ye do no' want to cut too deep else ye waste the meat o' the apple. Do no' cut too thin though either, else it'll tear."

Edith watched silently as he instructed the boy, fascinated by how gentle and encouraging he was with him.

Lying down on her side to watch, she smiled as she noted how Ronson had his tongue out and curved to the side as he worked. His concentration was such that one would have thought he was learning the most important task in the world, she thought with amusement, and then glanced toward Laddie when he suddenly leapt to his feet and hurried off. The dog had rushed down to the water to join the others. They'd finished their apples and were returning to gathering rushes, she saw with a frown, and turned back to Ronson and Niels. Ronson was still near the top of his apple, working slowly and carefully to peel it in one long strand.

She'd wait until he'd finished and eaten his apple and then suggest they go back to work with the others, Edith decided. In the meantime, she'd just close her eyes for a minute and enjoy the sun warming her skin, and the breeze cooling it.

IT WAS THE TRUNDLE OF THE CART'S WHEELS that woke her. Blinking her eyes open, Edith peered at the furs in front of her face and then lifted her head and peered about. Her eyes widened incredulously as she saw the maids and children following the over-flowing cart of rushes out of the clearing. They'd finished while she slept, she realized with dismay. Good Lord, how long had she slept?

Her gaze shifted to the sky to see that the sun was high overhead. It looked to be about noon to her. Sighing, Edith sat up, her eyes returning to the departing party again, just in time to see Moibeal look back and note that she was awake. The maid smiled and gave her a wave and then continued to usher the children away.

An excited bark caught her ear then and Edith looked toward the river where Niels, Ronson and Laddie were. The dog was leaping around excitedly on the shore, looking like he wanted to chase after whatever it was Niels and Ronson were throwing into the water. It took a moment before she realized Niels was showing Ronson how to skip stones on the river's placid surface. The realization made her smile faintly. It was something she and her brothers had done as children. This was the only spot on the river where the water slowed enough to allow it.

She watched briefly, marveling again at how good

he was with the boy, and then glanced down. All evidence of their picnic was gone, just the furs left for her to sleep on. Edith got up and quickly gathered and stacked them in a small pile. She then headed down toward the water's edge to join the men, smiling and giving Laddie a pet when he rushed excitedly to her side in greeting.

"Laddie!" Niels barked when the dog tried to jump on her. The deerhound obeyed the sound at once and kept his feet on the ground as Edith petted him.

"How do ye feel?" Niels asked softly as she continued forward, the dog now at her side.

"Like I slept while everyone else worked," she said with self-disgust.

"Aye, ye did," Niels agreed easily. "Which means yer ready fer the second part o' yer day."

Edith eyed him suspiciously. "Why am I quite sure ye do no' mean weaving mats?"

"Because yer an exceptionally intelligent woman," he said solemnly, and then glanced to Ronson and Laddie who had moved farther down the shoreline. "Come on, lad, 'tis time to go."

"Aye, m'lord. Come on, Laddie," Ronson said and ran toward them.

"Ye still have no' told me where we are going," Edith said when Niels took her arm and turned to walk her toward his horse.

"What would be on yer list o' things to accomplish? After weaving the mats that the women will have done in no time even without yer help," he added quickly.

Edith reached down to scratch Laddie behind the ear when he moved up to her side and nudged her leg. But her mind was on anything that might need doing at the keep. She'd need to talk to Jaimie about the menu for the next little while, although he'd apparently done well enough without her input these past weeks. She did need to find out what he needed her to buy for him on market day in the village though. But she could do that tomorrow or the next day. Market day was held in the village every week on Saturday. It was now only Monday.

Other than that, things seemed to have progressed nicely in the keep despite her illness. The servants were well trained and knew what to do. They'd also apparently been good about doing the day-to-day tasks without supervision, although she suspected Tormod had something to do with that. She didn't doubt for a minute that he had run herd on them in her absence, which she appreciated. So while she was sure there were other things to do, she wouldn't know what needed doing until she had a good look around. Really, the rushes had been the only thing that had needed urgent attention. The smell of them was unbearable.

Mind you that had made bathing Laddie a rather urgent issue . . . and Ronson . . . as well as finding the boy a clean tartan. Niels could use a bath and fresh tartan too after his night on the moldy rushes, but she could hardly order him to bathe. And then Edith would like to bathe herself. She'd wanted a bath since waking but hadn't ordered one because she refused to bathe in front of the Buchanan brothers and they had seemed to have taken root permanently in her bedchamber. At least Niels had. Rory had spent as much time in Effie's room as her own. And Geordie and Alick had left to ride to MacDonnell, but Niels still insisted she needed his protection and refused to leave her alone, even in her chamber.

"I'd like to bathe and see to it that Ronson and Laddie do as well," she admitted as she watched him quickly roll up the furs and secure them to the side of the horse in a rope sling. He then quickly mounted.

"Perfect," Niels pronounced and Edith gasped as he suddenly leaned down, caught her under the arms and lifted her onto his mount before him.

"Why is that perfect?" Edith asked as she settled sideways in his lap.

"Because we are all going to the loch for a bath," he announced, and then turned and held a hand out to Ronson. "Take me hand, lad."

Ronson hesitated, but then held his hand up and Niels swung him up and around behind his back on the horse. "There's no' a lot o' room with all three o' us on here. Wrap yer arms around me, lad, so ye do no' slide off the horse's arse."

"Ai, yi, yi," Edith breathed. She would never get Ronson to stop swearing as long as Niels kept using such words in front of the boy. His grandmother would surely blame her for this.

"That's right, lad. Hold on tight," Niels instructed, reaching around Edith to grab the reins.

"Mayhap ye should put him in me lap," Edith suggested, shifting to try to look around him at the boy.

"He'll be fine," Niels said soothingly. "'Tis no' far."

Edith nodded, but she also slid her hands around his waist to clasp Ronson's arms and make sure he stayed in place. For some reason that made Niels chuckle. At least that's what she thought he was doing. She felt his stomach move and his breath brush the top of her head, though there was no sound behind the laugh.

"What is so funny?" she asked, lifting her head to peer up at him.

"Nothing." Niels smiled faintly and shrugged. "I was just thinking ye will make a fine mother."

Edith smiled sadly. "I'd like to think ye're right, but I fear I'll ne'er get the chance to find out."

When Niels frowned at her words, Edith lowered her head and rested it against his chest.

"Ronson, make sure Laddie follows us," Niels instructed, urging his horse to move forward.

As Ronson called out to the dog, Edith closed her eyes and tried to clear her mind of the worrisome issue of her future. There was enough on her plate at the moment without thinking about that. They still had to figure out who had killed her father and brothers and tried to kill her. She suspected if Brodie found out they'd been poisoned, he'd find some excuse or other to not return to the keep until the culprit was found. Which meant she had to stay and run the castle in his absence.

Edith couldn't in good conscience leave Tormod to run things alone. He was a fine first, and knew what he was about, but he was getting on in years, and she knew it had been a burden on him to run both the soldiers and the household servants while she was ill. Unfortunately, Brodie was just selfish enough to spend all of his time at court, sending home only for coin if the culprit was never found. He'd drain Drummond of all of its wealth, and leave his people miserable and starving without a second thought. Which left her in a bit of a precarious position. She needed to resolve the matter of who was behind the poisoning so that it was safe enough that Brodie wouldn't have an excuse not to return. But she also needed to be gone before he returned if she wanted to avoid being sent to the Abbey to live out the rest of her days.

Today, in truth, had been a bit of an indulgence. Changing the rush mats in the castle had been a way to briefly escape the keep and delay dealing with the real problem. Edith had felt she deserved the time out after being ill for so long. But tonight she would have to sit down with Rory, Niels and Tormod and try to come up with a plan to sort out the matter. She'd also pack a bag with what she would need for her visit with Saidh, so that she could leave at a moment's notice should the matter be resolved quickly.

That was the other reason she'd put off tackling the matter right away. She'd sent a letter with Geordie and Alick for Saidh, outlining her problem and her hopes of visiting with Saidh and the other two women who made up her friends to try to find a way to avoid life as a nun. She wouldn't just show up on the woman's door, begging admittance.

But Geordie and Alick needed time to ride to Mac-Donnell and back with Saidh's answer. If they weren't back before the issue was resolved, she wasn't sure what she'd do. Perhaps trade in her fine dresses for the plain garb of a servant and go in search of a position in another castle under another name. Surely she'd have a better chance at happiness as a housemaid or lady's maid than as a nun?

Edith grimaced at the thought. She wasn't a fool and knew the dangers inherent in such an undertaking, but she had few options available to her.

"Here we are."

Edith lifted her head and glanced around as Niels drew his mount to a halt. They'd entered a small clearing by the loch that she knew well. It was on the edge of the loch, and where she often came with Laddie when she wished to swim in private. Most of the castle used a larger stretch farther down the shore and closer to the castle, but here the land curved sharply inward and then back out, creating a tiny cove that offered privacy.

"Down ye go, Ronson," Niels said, and Edith released the hold she'd kept on the boy's arms as Niels reached back to grab him by the back of his shirt and tartan and swing him down to the ground. Laddie was immediately there to greet the boy, licking his face excitedly.

Edith sat upright then, retrieving her arms from around Niels and shifting her bottom so that she slid forward and began to slide off the mount. The moment that happened, she twisted her upper body and caught at his leg to ease her drop. As her bottom cleared the horse, it followed in the turn and she landed on the ground facing the horse and clasping Niels's leg. Edith was rather proud of herself for disembarking on her own without the need to be lifted down like a child . . . until she noted Niels's odd stillness and the unreadable expression on his face.

Realizing she was still clasping his leg, she released it at once and stepped back, then turned and moved around the horse to where Ronson and Laddie were as Niels started to disembark. Laddie immediately moved toward her and Edith petted him, using the action to keep him from jumping up on her.

"Good boy," she murmured. Running her hands

along the dog's side, she glanced back to see what Niels was doing. He'd removed the rolled-up furs from the sling he'd made to hang from his saddle, as well as the sack that had held the cherry pastries and apples and a much larger sack too, and was now moving to the center of the clearing with Ronson trailing him.

"What can I do to help?" Edith asked, following now as well.

"Ye can take this and go bathe in the loch while Ronson and I set up a little picnic," he answered and dug around in his bag before producing a small square of Aleppo soap. Handing it to her he added, "I was hoping to find ye some with lavender oils in it or such, but this smells nice too."

Edith smiled faintly. "Ye'll find no lavender at Drummond."

Niels's eyebrows rose. "I thought women liked lavender?"

"Most do," she admitted with a smile. "And I think 'tis fine, but it was never allowed in the keep at Drummond."

"Why?"

"Father refused to have it," she said simply.

"Did it give him the sneezes or something?" Niels asked with amusement.

"Nay." Edith shook her head. "He had an aversion to it. I remember a visitor coming who smelled o' it once when I was a child and me da got all quiet and glum. When I asked Mother why, she said that lavender reminded him o' his mother and his sisters Ealasaid and Glynis and made him sad and gloomy. They all three favored the scent," she said, and explained, "They died when he was young. From the sweating sickness I think mother said. All three died quickly and 'twas a shock to him." Realizing she was babbling nervously, Edith shut her mouth and took the precious hard bar of laurel soap he held out, but then just stood there uncertainly. She had brought Ronson down to swim on occasion and had no problem stripping down to her shift in front of him, but Niels was not a five-year-old boy.

"Ronson'll make sure I do no' look," he assured her gently, and then smiled at the boy and said, "Will ye no' lad?"

"Aye," Ronson said at once, and then frowned and asked, "But why can ye no' watch Lady Edith swim? I swim with her all the time."

"Lucky you," Niels said under his breath, but didn't explain. Instead, he assured Edith, "I'll be right here setting up. And when I finish I'll sit with me back to the water. Once ye're done ye can dry off and dress." He produced a clean, dry folded strip of linen and a fresh gown from the larger sack he'd brought and held them out to her. Once she'd accepted the offerings, he added, "And then ye can sit and have some lunch while Ronson and I bathe Laddie and ourselves."

Edith stared down at the dress he'd pulled from the sack. It was one of hers, and he'd rolled it to help keep it from wrinkling, but of course it hadn't completely prevented them. "Where did ye—?"

"Moibeal fetched it fer me," he admitted with a wry smile. "I originally intended to fetch it meself, but then it occurred to me ye might keep things in yer chest ye'd no' like me seeing, so I hunted her down and she helped."

"Oh." Edith nodded slowly. Moibeal had chosen

her finest gown, one Edith had never even worn yet
except during fittings. A deep forest green, it was
Moibeal's favorite. The maid swore it brought Edith's
eyes and hair to life, showing her off to perfection and
would make any man fall in love with her. Her choosing the gown for Niels told Edith the maid saw him as a
prospective husband for Edith, and approved. That was
not something that she'd even considered before this.

"Go on. I promise we'll no' look," Niels said gently.

Swallowing, Edith nodded and turned to move to
one of the trees at the edge of the clearing. Half of its
branches stretched out over the water, but half were
over dry land. Edith hung the gown and strip of linen
from one over land that was low enough to reach, but
high enough that the clean gown did not reach the
ground. Then she turned to glance back to the boys,
finding both Niels and Ronson chattering quietly as
they unrolled and laid out the furs.

Turning her back to them, she set down the bar of
soap and quickly undid and stripped off her gown,
then snatched up the soap again and hurried into the
water in just her shift. The water was cold at first, and
she had to bite her lip to keep from squealing as she
hurried out until it was waist deep. Edith then dove
under the water and swam for a bit until her body adjusted to the temperature.

The setting was beautiful and Edith usually took
her time and enjoyed the peace of the cove and the cool
water when she came here. Today she did not. Edith
was quick and businesslike as she washed herself and
her hair, but the whole time her mind was poking and
prodding around the idea of Niels as a husband.

Now that she was thinking about it, the idea was an

interesting one. It would certainly solve her worry of ending up in the Abbey. As for Niels himself . . . well, she quite liked him. He was handsome, and seemed clever, and competent. More importantly to her, he was also extremely good with Ronson, showing both kindness and patience. Edith felt sure he would make a good father.

From Saidh's letters, she knew that Niels had taken over as his older brother Aulay's first at Buchanan when Dougall had left with Murine. Which made her curious about how he was able to be away so long. But she supposed with so many brothers, another was filling in for him at Buchanan while he was here. At any rate, she knew that Niels would never have a keep of his own, but that didn't matter to her. She would be quite content to live in a little cottage in the village, bearing and rearing bairns.

That last thought made her glance toward Niels again as she considered the practicalities of getting those bairns. Edith's mother had been a skilled healer and had taught her a good deal. She'd also taken her along to help as she'd sewn up wounds and helped birth babies. Edith knew the basics of how those babies got into the woman, and now considered having to do that with Niels.

It was hard to imagine what led to the man planting his seed, and how unpleasant it might be. Her mother had told her it was painful the first time, but her friend Jo had shared a bit of her own experience with them and assured them there was a lot of pleasure to be had too. Edith found that hard to believe. Really, it sounded like such an odd act.

Her hand slid under the water and between her legs,

finding the spot where the man "plowed the field with his fiddle" as Jo had called it. She poked around curiously, but then shook her head. Nope, she couldn't imagine wanting a man to do that to her, even Niels, handsome as he was. Still, if it was necessary to get bairns . . .

Realizing that in her mind she already had the two of them marrying and making babies, Edith gave her head a shake. Niels might not be the least interested in her in such a way. She might have to resign herself to marrying some nasty old baron with bad breath or something.

Sighing, Edith ducked under the water to rinse the soap from her hair and body and then straightened and glanced toward the boys. Niels sat facing away from the water, leaning back on his arms with his legs out in front of him and crossed at the ankles. Ronson was sitting the exact same way, obviously copying him. The sight made her smile as she hurried out and snatched the linen from the tree to quickly dry herself.

It was only then that she realized that while Moibeal had given Niels a fresh gown, she hadn't thought to send a new, dry shift too. Which meant she either had to pull her gown on over the now soaking shift, or go without. The decision was an easy one. She was not sitting around in a soaking wet shift and gown.

Muttering under her breath, she cast a glance over her shoulder to be sure the boys weren't looking, and then quickly tugged the wet shift off and even more quickly tugged the gown on in its place. Of course, in her panic not to be caught naked, she didn't think to dry herself first. It made pulling the dress on a bit difficult since the soft cloth tended to cling to her damp skin. Edith managed it after a bit of a struggle and then huffed out an exasperated breath and quickly used the linen to dry her hair as much as she could.

Once that was done she recognized her next problem. She had no brush to tame the wild strands of hair that were now no doubt a ruffled mess. Slinging the linen over the tree branch to dry, she quickly ran her fingers through her hair, trying to tame the mess the red strands were no doubt in. She then snatched up the soap, her wet chemise and the discarded gown she'd been wearing when they arrived and made her way to the furs where the men waited.

"Yer turn," Edith said brightly as she reached them.

Niels was immediately on his feet, but paused as he turned to look at her. When his eyes widened slightly and his lips twitched, Edith knew her hair was probably a terrible mess. Sighing inwardly, she dropped to sit on the furs and waved them away. "Go take yer bath. The water is fine."

Ronson was off at once, stripping off his braies and shirt as he went. Niels was a little slower to leave, but after saying, "Go ahead and start eating, we'll no' be long," he scooped up fresh clothes for Ronson, and a neatly folded shirt and fresh tartan for himself and turned to make his way down to the water's edge.

She saw him reach to his tartan and then it suddenly dropped away. Niels was left standing in nothing but a shirt that didn't quite cover his bottom. Edith gaped briefly, following the curves of his behind, and then promptly turned her back to the water to give them the privacy they'd afforded her. But it was hard. While she'd bathed in absolute silence, Ronson and Niels did not. The boy was laughing and chattering away and then squealing when Niels apparently splashed him.

Edith was hard-pressed not to turn and see what was happening.

It was only when Niels called for Laddie that Edith glanced around and noticed that the dog was still lying curled up beside the furs and hadn't followed them to the water. The dog opened one eye and then closed it again and pretended not to hear. She wasn't surprised. Laddie hated baths. At best he suffered them and then went wild, shaking the water off and rubbing himself up against anything and everything he could to try to dry off afterward.

"Laddie," Niels growled in a warning tone, and the dog huffed miserably, but stood and moved slowly and reluctantly toward the water, his head and tail down. Chuckling to herself, Edith resisted the urge to turn and watch what would happen next, and simply listened. If he were true to previous baths in the loch, she knew Laddie would stop at the water's edge and have to be dragged in, and then would need to be held there else he'd rush out at the first opportunity. But that he'd then try to climb onto whoever was bathing him to get out of the water.

Judging by Ronson's laughter and Niels's curses that was exactly what the dog was doing, she decided moments later, and risked a glance over her shoulder. Laddie was on his hind legs, with his front paws on Niels's chest, trying to lick his face. Niels was twisting, trying to avoid the dog's tongue and then staggered and fell under the water, taking the dog with him.

Edith started to rise, concerned the dog would unintentionally drown Niels. But he popped up at once and stood, water pouring down his sculpted chest to return to the river where it reached his waist.

Edith swallowed and sank back to the ground, her wide eyes traveling the same hard curves as the water. Had she really thought him just *handsome enough*? She wondered. The man was magnificent. He surely wasn't the first man she'd seen bare-chested, she had three brothers, and there were hundreds of soldiers at Drummond, but none of them looked as perfect as Niels Buchanan did in that moment with the sun making the drops of water on his naked chest sparkle like diamonds. He was beautiful.

"Come here, Laddie," Niels ordered and actually patted his chest. He also braced his feet though. Edith could tell that by the way he shifted just before Laddie lunged upward, bracing his paws on his chest. He normally would have tried to climb out onto Niels then, but Niels grabbed the dog's paws on his chest and growled, "Stay."

When the soaking dog just looked at him pitifully, Niels took the soap Ronson had been holding and began to lather the beast. He glanced her way as he did, and Edith quickly turned her back once more, her face heating up at getting caught looking.

Sighing, she peered over the food laid out on the furs. Apparently the cherry pastries hadn't been all Niels had brought from the castle. The picnic he'd packed was an impressive layout. There was a whole roast chicken, cheese, bread, apples and more cherry pastries. Despite Niels's suggestion she start eating, Edith hadn't. She'd planned to wait for them to join her, but when her stomach growled hungrily, she decided an apple wouldn't hurt while she waited.

Edith was nearly finished with her apple when a nearly ten-stone, soaking wet Laddie suddenly rushed her and crawled into her lap. Squealing, she fell back and then tried to push him off as the dog attempted to dry himself on her dress.

"Laddie," Niels barked.

The dog froze at once and then rushed off back toward the water. Edith twisted her head slightly to look after him and gaped when she spotted Niels on his knees in naught but his shirt, folding pleats into his plaid by the water's edge. Ronson was busy pulling on his braies, but Niels caught her looking again. When he winked at her, she snapped her mouth closed and sat up abruptly so that her back was to them again.

Edith then busied herself looking for the remains of her apple. It had landed beside the furs. She picked it up, wrinkled her nose at the grass and dirt on it, and then set it down next to the furs again with a little sigh.

Chapter 5

"Ye did no' eat."

Edith glanced around at that comment and managed a smile as Niels led Ronson and Laddie back to her.

"Nay. I thought to wait fer the two o' ye," Edith murmured as Ronson rushed ahead to join her on the fur.

Laddie tried to follow, but Niels barked, "No!" bringing the dog up short. "Sit," he ordered, and Laddie sat down beside the furs where he'd been earlier.

"Good boy," Niels praised, petting the dog as he walked past to claim a spot on the furs.

Edith shook her head slightly. Laddie was a good dog, but rarely obeyed anyone as quickly and well as he appeared to listen to Niels. She usually had to repeat an order at least once or twice before the dog obeyed her, and he hadn't listened to her father and brothers at all. It was why he'd ended up her dog instead of one of the hunting dogs.

Niels picked up the bag he'd brought all the food in and dug out a large bone for Laddie. The dog stood up at once, immediately drooling.

"Sit," Niels said firmly. Laddie sat, and Niels gave him the bone with another, "Good boy."

The dog grabbed it and dropped to lie on the ground, holding it between his front paws as he began to gnaw on the end.

"So that's how ye make him behave," Edith murmured with amusement. "Ye bribe him with bones."

"Nay. He's a good dog," Niels said, turning to survey the food between them. He reached for the chicken, broke off a leg and offered it to her. "There's mead in the skin there. Help yerself."

"Thank ye," Edith murmured, accepting the leg.

The three of them ate in a companionable silence and Edith found herself imagining that they were a family, sharing a meal after a swim: mother, father and son. After they ate, they would ride back to the keep and—

She stopped herself there, because the keep would not be her home for much longer. And Niels wasn't her husband or ever likely to be, and Ronson was not her son. Laddie was the only one of the three that belonged with her, and that might not be true for much longer. Not if she ended up at the Abbey.

"What's making ye frown, lass?" Niels asked suddenly.

Edith quickly forced a smile to her lips. "I was just thinking, m'lord."

"About what?" he asked.

"Nothing of import," she lied with a shrug and then changed the subject. "So, Saidh is happy and huge with child. But neither ye nor yer brothers said much about Murine and Dougall. Is all well there?"

"Oh, aye," he smiled faintly. "They seem very happy

now that everything is settled. Although Dougall's complaining about all the travel they have to do."

"Travel?" she asked with surprise.

"Aside from Carmichael, they have her brother's castle and people in England to oversee," he said and explained, "She inherited Danvries when he died."

Edith's eyebrows rose. "So she went from fearing she'd have no home to two castles to run?"

"Aye," he grinned. "But it means a lot o' travel back and forth until they decide on what to do about Danvries."

"What do ye think they'll do?" she asked curiously.

Niels considered the question, and then said, "Probably get one o' me brothers to run it fer them. At least until Dougall has a son old enough to take over."

"Not you?" Edith asked curiously. "Ye're the next oldest are ye no'?"

"Aye, but I've plans o' me own for the future," Niels said solemnly. "At the moment, I'm helping Aulay at Buchanan. Well, no' right this minute, obviously," he added wryly. "But when matters are settled here I'll go back to Buchanan and my position as his first."

"It was good o' him to let ye come check on me fer Saidh," Edith said quietly. "I shall have to write and thank him."

"There's no need. He does no' ken I'm here," Niels said with amusement, and then explained, "We kenned when we were young that Aulay would inherit Buchanan and the rest o' us would have to make our own way. But me parents did no' leave us beggared. They left us each some land and some coin, and helped us decide what endeavor we wanted to pursue to earn more. For Dougall it was horses. He always loved the great beasts and he had an eye for 'em. He was always able to tell which would sire the best colts and which mare would birth the best and so on."

"And what was yer endeavor?" Edith asked curiously.

"Dogs," he answered with a smile. "I breed fine hunting dogs. Train them too."

"Ah," Edith murmured. That explained how good he was with Laddie.

"But there's no money in that," Niels added wryly. "I do breed and sell some to lairds in search o' good hunting dogs, but I make the real money with sheep."

Edith blinked. "Sheep?"

"Aye. Well, wool, really. I bought sheep with me money and have grown the herd o'er the years. Most o' the wool they produce is exported to Flanders for profit, but I keep a portion and it is spun and made into what many consider the finest woven cloth in Scotland. Because we produce so little, I'm paid an exorbitant fee fer what is made. Between the wool and woven cloth I make a tidy sum."

He paused briefly and then returned to the original subject. "And that's where Aulay thinks I am now, delivering a shipment o' me woven cloth to the Mc-Kays. It was contracted before Dougall left and I took over as Aulay's first, and I had to honor the contract. Geordie and Alick were accompanying me, and we only stopped at MacDonnell to see Saidh and escort Rory safely there so that he could check on her. We were supposed to head straight to McKay from there."

"And instead ye're here," Edith said and frowned. "Niels, I do no' want to interfere with yer business. If ye have to deliver yer woven cloth—"

"Nay," he assured her. "Greer had his men escort it north in exchange fer our coming here to check on ye on Saidh's behalf."

"Oh." Edith smiled crookedly. "Good."

"Aye." He glanced down briefly and then looked to Ronson when the boy suddenly got up and moved over to wrestle with Laddie.

"The lads are getting restless," Edith murmured, beginning to pack up the remains of their picnic. "I suppose we should head back before everyone starts to worry."

"Aye," Niels murmured and then reached in the large sack and retrieved a hairbrush.

"Oh," Edith reached up self-consciously to her hair. "I suppose I look a fright."

"Nay," he assured her and then grinned and added, "But if I take ye back looking like that, they'll think it was more than swimming we got up to."

Edith's eyes widened incredulously and she felt herself blush. She snatched the hairbrush from him and began to drag it quickly through her knotted hair, wincing as she did.

"Edith, lass," Niels murmured, shifting to his knees to move around behind her. "Give me that ere ye brush yerself bald. Yer hair is too beautiful to abuse it so. 'Tis obvious ye're use to yer maid doing this."

Edith glanced around at him in surprise at the compliment and then turned forward again when he took the brush and began to run it gently through her hair. At first she merely sat silent, watching Ronson play with Laddie. The pair seemed caught up in a game of chase now, Ronson running after the dog and then whirling and running away as Laddie started to chase him. Edith smiled as she watched, but said to Niels, "Ye've done this before."

He chuckled, his breath brushing her ear and sending a shiver down her back. "It shows, does it?"

"Aye, ye're very gentle," she said, and then asked, "Saidh?"

"With nine children and the keep to run, Mother often gave us chores to help out and I usually ended up brushing Saidh's hair fer her in the mornings. I learned to be gentle quite quickly," he added dryly. "Saidh was no' above a swift kick to the nether regions on whoever was unfortunate enough to have the chore that day."

"Nine," Edith murmured. "Saidh mentioned that she had eight brothers when we first met, but then she named only seven o' ye and I thought I'd misheard. But there *were* nine o' ye?"

"Aye," Niels admitted, sounding reluctant. "Ewan died in the same battle that scarred our brother, Aulay," he explained quietly. "The family does no' talk about it though."

"Why?" Edith asked.

"I think because we were unable to claim his body and bring him home," Niels admitted slowly, the brush stilling briefly. "Dougall, Conran and I saw Ewan fall under a broadsword, but after the battle we could no' find his body."

"Mayhap he did no' die," Edith suggested hopefully.

"He died," Niels assured her heavily. "He was cleaved in half, Edith. Our brother could no' have survived that. No one could."

"Oh," Edith murmured, and then didn't know what to say. In the end she merely whispered, "I'm sorry."

"Thank ye," was his solemn response.

They both fell silent then and Edith found herself wracking her brain, trying to think of something to say to lighten the moment. A squeal from Ronson distracted her, however, and her gaze focused on the lad as he tackled Laddie, throwing himself over the dog's back. When the dog merely dropped to the ground and rolled to remove the boy, Niels chuckled softly behind her and Edith felt herself relax. She smiled faintly as they watched the pair play.

"Has Ronson no friends among the children?" Niels asked after a moment.

Edith's smile faded. "I'm afraid his grandmother has discouraged him from playing with the other children."

"Why?"

She could hear the frown in his voice, but admitted, "Bessie said that his circumstances will soon change and there was no sense in his making friends with lads he'd soon have nothing to do with." Clearing her throat, she added, "I do no' really blame her. She's probably right. Brodie will listen to Victoria and throw the pair of them out once she convinces him to send me off to the Abbey. Ronson's grandmother is just trying to ensure he's hurt as little as possible when that happens. This way he'll only lose a home and no' friends along with it."

"Victoria does no' like Ronson and his grandmother?" Niels asked quietly.

Edith sighed. "In truth, Victoria does no' like much of anything at Drummond. If she could replace all the servants, she would."

"Because they did no' automatically obey her over

you when Brodic took on the temporary mantle of laird while ye're brothers were sick?"

"Aye," Edith murmured. "I suspect she'll try to be free o' every one o' the maids that did that as soon as I'm gone. She may even succeed. She's a smart woman. She'll find an excuse to manage it."

"I'm sorry," Niels said quietly.

"So am I," she admitted. "They deserve better."

"I meant fer the pain it's causing you," Niels said solemnly. "'Tis obvious ye care fer yer people, and their uncertain future distresses ye."

Edith turned to meet his gaze and nodded solemnly. "They are me family. Every last one o' them. I grew up with them here, caring fer me and . . ." She lowered her head on a sigh. "I feel as if I'm failing them by not being able to protect them."

"Lass, they ken ye'd help them if ye could, but ye can no' even protect yerself," he pointed out, and then frowned with displeasure.

She started to turn forward again, but paused when he said, "Edith?"

"Aye?" she asked.

Niels opened his mouth, closed it and then simply shook his head and put the brush back in the bag. "Yer hair is done."

"Thank ye," Edith said softly, but eyed him with curiosity. There had been purpose in his eyes for a moment. She was quite sure he'd meant to say something else, but had no idea what. And apparently he'd changed his mind.

Shrugging, she pushed herself to her knees and helped gather up the rest of their picnic items to pack away, then helped him roll up the furs as well. She carried the food sack while he carried the furs and the larger sack with the wet linens and their soiled clothes and they walked to his horse. While he set the furs in their sling and hung the large bag from the saddle, she reached up to try to affix the smaller bag as well and was still struggling with the task when he finished his own chores. Seeing that she was having problems because she wasn't quite tall enough to attach the bag to the pommel, he stepped up behind her to help.

Edith stilled the moment she felt his chest against her back. There was something so intimate about it, and then she realized that Niels had gone still as well. They both stood there for a moment, back to chest, both holding their breaths, and then he lowered his hands to her waist. He clasped her so lightly that she could have escaped if she'd wanted to, but Edith found her feet unwilling to move and simply stood there waiting. An era seemed to pass and then he murmured, "Yer hair is so beautiful."

"Thank ye," Edith breathed, swallowing when he brushed her hair away from her neck. When he then bent to nuzzle her there, she bit her lip to stifle a soft gasp, and found herself leaning back into him. Niels let his arms drift around her then, to cross under her breasts, and Edith clasped them lightly, her head tilting as he nibbled at her ear. When he lifted one hand to catch her chin and turn her face up and back to his, Edith went willingly, even eagerly, and closed her eyes as his lips covered hers. His tongue slid out to nudge its way between her lips, and she opened with surprise and then stilled as his tongue swept in. Edith met the invasion with a moan as a cacophony of sensation burst to life inside her. She was vaguely aware of his hand drifting down her throat and then her chest, but didn't really pay attention until it stopped to cover one breast and squeezed lightly.

Edith gasped into his mouth as her body responded, her back arching instinctively to push her breast more fully into the caress as his other hand suddenly rose to claim the other one. She had no idea she was pushing back into him with her bottom until she felt the hardness that met her, and then one of his hands slid inside the neckline of her gown to touch her without the cloth between them and Edith cried out into his mouth as he began to pluck at the already hard nipple.

Edith was so distracted by that she definitely didn't notice his other hand leaving her breast to drift downward until he cupped her between the legs through the cloth and almost lifted her off her feet. This was nothing like it had been when she'd been poking at herself earlier out of curiosity. Even with the cloth between them, this aroused an unbearable excitement in her that she'd never dreamed possible. And it made her want more. The problem was, she wasn't quite sure what more she wanted. But her body seemed to have ideas of its own and was shifting against his hands, writhing into first one caress and then the other in search of something she didn't quite understand, and then a high-pitched scream made them both freeze.

In the next moment, Niels was breaking their kiss to mutter, "Ronson," and then his lovely hands were leaving her and he was gone. For one moment, Edith simply stood there, her brain slow to put everything together, and then she turned and peered around the empty clearing. Even Niels was gone.

Confused, Edith took one staggering step away

from Niels's horse, and then steadied herself before continuing in the general direction she'd thought Ronson's scream had come from. When she reached the edge of the clearing, she pushed her way into the underbrush in search of both males. The scream they'd heard had been panicked, even terrified, she thought as her brain began to function again and one urgency was traded for another as she began to worry about the boy.

"Are ye all right, lad? What—? Dear God."

Edith heard Niels's words just as she pushed through more bushes and nearly trampled both Niels and Ronson before catching herself. Ronson stood frozen with Laddie at his side, while Niels knelt examining something on the ground in front of the boy.

"It's Lonnie," Ronson said, sounding scared, and Edith glanced over his shoulder to see a man lying facedown in the dirt, an arrow protruding from his back.

"Who's Lonnie?" Niels asked, glancing back at Ronson and pausing briefly when he spotted Edith.

"One o' the soldiers at Drummond," Edith answered for the boy. "He usually stands guard on the wall."

"Aye, he does. But he left with the laird when he and Lady Victoria left the castle," Ronson told them.

"Did he?" Edith asked with a frown, peering down at the man. Lonnie's face was turned their way, his mouth open, his eyes too, and she had to look away. The man had obviously been dead awhile. He was unrecognizable to her.

"Aye. He does no' look like Lonnie, but I saw Magda give him that kerchief when he left. She said 'twas to remember her by," Ronson said.

Edith glanced back to see the bit of cloth the boy spoke of tied around Lonnie's arm.

"Come." Niels stood abruptly and began to usher them back through the woods to the clearing. "I'll return ye both to the castle and then bring back men and a wagon to get Lonnie."

"We can no' just leave him here. Maybe we should take him with us," Edith said with concern.

"Lass, we've only the one horse. Besides, he's been out here for a good week at least. A few more minutes will no' make much difference," Niels said grimly.

"Aye," Edith murmured as they reached the clearing and crossed to the horse. This time, Niels mounted, lifted her into his lap and then lifted Ronson into hers. She was sure it made it harder for him to handle the reins, but Niels didn't complain, and she was glad she could hold the boy. He was shivering slightly after his discovery. She closed her arms around him and leaned silently against Niels's chest for the return journey to the keep.

"WELL?"

Edith glanced up from the food she was mostly pushing around her trencher at that question from Niels, and saw Rory joining them at the table.

"Well," Rory said, "it looks like he died from the arrow wound."

"And the other injuries?"

Edith's eyebrows rose slightly. She hadn't noticed any other injuries, but then she'd only got two quick looks at the man and had focused mainly on his face the first time and the kerchief the second.

"Animals," Rory said quietly. "After he died."

Edith grimaced and set down the silver goblet of mead she'd been about to drink from.

"Can ye tell how long he's been dead?" Niels asked after a pause.

Rory shook his head. "A week at least, but it could be more. I can no' tell."

"Poor bastard," Tormod said grimly. "His horse, weapons and boots were gone, so I'm guessing it was bandits. Must ha'e caught him on his way back to the keep. We've had trouble with them in the area before."

"Aye," Edith agreed, and then frowned. "But Ronson said Lonnie left with Brodie and Victoria. Why was he returning alone?"

Tormod's mouth tightened with anger. "Yer brother probably sent him back to see if it was safe to return. Or mayhap, after setting out it occurred to him that he should have someone who could ride out and let him ken it was safe to return so sent the lad back to be his eyes and ears here."

It seemed the most likely answer so Edith merely nodded unhappily and absently turned the silver goblet of mead in a circle, her gaze on the liquid inside as she wondered what they should do now. They had no way to let Brodie know what had happened to Lonnie. They didn't even know where he had taken Victoria. It could be court, or the castle of one of his friends. While Brodie was spoiled and selfish, he could also be extremely charming when he chose and had made many friends among the younger lairds. Before marrying Victoria he'd often spent his time visiting one after the other, hunting here, hawking there and just drinking, gambling or wenching at another. They could be anywhere.

Sighing, she sat up straight and glanced to the three men at the table with her. "We have to devise a plan to sort out who the poisoner was so that Brodie can return and I can leave."

"Leave?" Tormod asked with a frown.

Edith eyed him solemnly. "He'll send me away to the Abbey the minute he gets back, Tormod. I know that and so do you."

"Aye," Tormod growled unhappily. Bowing his head he added in a mutter, "I just did no' think ye'd give in and go to the Abbey so easily."

"I do no' plan to," she assured him and managed a smile when his head came back up and he eyed her questioningly. "I can no' make him let me stay here," she said gently and saw the disappointment in his face. "But I may be able to avoid spending the rest o' me days in the Abbey. I may even manage to marry some kindly old laird who would be willing to take in anyone Victoria convinces Brodie to be rid of."

"That'd be something at least," Tormod said with a frown.

"Aye. But I'd have to leave before Brodie returns to avoid the Abbey. I'll stay as long as I can, but when we ken he's returning, I'll have to go to MacDonnell."

"MacDonnell?" Rory asked with interest.

"I asked Saidh if I might visit. That was in the letter yer brothers took with them. My hope is that Saidh and perhaps Murine and Jo can meet up with me there and help me sort out what to do. One o' them may ken a kindly old laird looking fer a wife. I have a healthy dower, so 'tis no' as if I'm penniless."

"I see," Rory murmured and glanced to Niels, but then asked, "So ye're determined to marry a laird?"

Edith smiled faintly. "Nay. I'd be happy with a cottage and half a dozen bairns. But time is me enemy. If I marry, me full dower goes with me. If Brodie sends me to the Abbey, he could probably get away with giving them half my dower or less. Finding an old laird, or even a young one in need o' coin seems more likely than anyone falling in love with me in the time I have," Edith said quietly, avoiding looking at Niels. She could still taste his kiss, and feel his hands on her body, but she wasn't foolish enough to think that meant he would suddenly offer her marriage and save her from her fate.

She wished it did. Edith would like to experience more of those kisses and caresses, and she doubted very much if she'd be lucky enough that she was attracted to whatever desperate laird she could get to marry her. But Edith had always been pragmatic about such things.

"So . . ." Tormod glanced at each of them in turn. "How do we sort out who the poisoner is?"

Silence reigned for a moment and then Rory said, "I'm no' sure. We are no' even sure how the old laird and his two older sons were fed the poison."

Niels turned to him with surprise. "I thought we'd decided the first dose must ha'e been in the wine because Edith did no' drink it."

"Aye, but surely Brodie and Victoria would ha'e had the wine that night," he pointed out, and then turned to Tormod and Edith and asked, "Did they not?"

"I'm no' sure," Tormod said with a frown. "That was weeks ago now and so much has happened." He now looked to Edith. "Do ye recall?"

Biting her lip, she sat back in her seat, trying to

remember thc night in question. As he'd said, it had been three and a half weeks ago now. And she'd been sick for much of that time. Finally, she said, "I think that might ha'e been the night they fought over Victoria's dower."

"Her dower?" Niels asked curiously.

Sighing, Edith nodded. "Apparently, Brodie assumed that once he'd married her, Victoria's father would hand over her dower."

"But he did no'?" Rory asked.

Edith shook her head. "Nay. He sent her maids and some dresses to Drummond, but the dower had to be given up to the man she'd been contracted to marry. It was in the contract. If she refused to marry him for any reason, he got the dower anyway." She grimaced. "The maids arrived that morning with the message and Brodie and Victoria were arguing about it all day."

"Aye. That's right," Tormod said dryly. "He ripped up the message and threw it at her, accusing her o' tricking him into marrying her with promises o' her huge dower, and she—" He paused and grinned. "I thought she'd brain him with a pitcher o' ale she was so furious at that accusation. '*I tricked you?*' says she with disbelief. 'I was the one who was tricked, my *laird*.'" He shook his head. "She was fair furious. They both were. So much so they did no' care who heard them. They started here in the great hall, and then he followed her to the kitchen when she tried to escape him there, and then up to their room." He shook his head. "The maids were so busy listening ye could no' get a lick o' work out o' them that day."

"Nay," Edith agreed wryly. "Anyway, they ended up in their room, hollering half the night until I sent a maid to tell them to shut up, that Father was deathly ill." She sighed. "I did no' ken that our brothers were too yet. They had retired early, probably because they were feeling unwell, but I did no' ken they were sick too until the morning when I went to tell them each that Father had passed."

"So Victoria and Brodie did no' drink the wine at table that night," Rory said thoughtfully.

"And they were in the kitchens at some point," Niels pointed out.

"But they were no' here when I fell ill the second time and that was from the stew no' the wine," Edith reminded them firmly.

"But they left that day," Niels pointed out. "They must ha'e somehow poisoned the stew ere leaving. Brodie is the only one who benefited from the deaths of yer father and brothers."

"They left that morning," Edith said patiently. "Moibeal felt ill in the night, but no one kenned until I woke up and found her on her mat in my room, clutching her stomach and delirious. Brodie feared an outbreak, panicked and packed up Victoria and left right away. They could no' have poisoned my serving o' stew later that day at sup. They were long gone. And the stew itself was no' poisoned else everyone in the castle would be dead," she said with exasperation.

"Mayhap Victoria had Effie put some o' the tonic in yer stew that night ere it was brought up to ye, and the poison was in the tonic," Rory suggested.

"Effie would hardly then take the poison herself," Edith pointed out.

"Nay, but mayhap Effie did no' ken 'twas poison," Rory said reasonably. "Yer brother may no' even ken what his wife was up to. It may ha'e been Victoria alone. Perhaps she was determined to be the Lady o' Drummond as yer brother had promised and was willing to murder to achieve it."

Edith nodded slowly. That actually seemed possible. She certainly liked it better than the suggestion that Brodie might be behind the deaths. Which meant they had a problem. "Then there is nothing we can do," she pointed out. "There is no way to prove Victoria poisoned the wine or the stew . . . unless ye can say unequivocally that the tonic had poison in it," she said and raised an eyebrow in question.

Rory shook his head regretfully. "Nay. There are so many herbs in the tonic, it would be impossible to sort out what poison had been used, or if it was in it."

"Then unless Effie wakes up to say she put it in me stew, and drank or ate it herself that last day, Victoria will get away with murder," she pointed out wearily.

"How is Effie doing?" Tormod asked abruptly.

"No change," Rory said, and then frowned and added, "No change at all in fact, and I would expect there to be. But she seems exactly as she was when we first got here. No stronger but no weaker."

"Aye, well, ye're dribbling broth down her throat all the time," Niels pointed out. "No doubt that's helping prevent her weakening further."

"Hmm," Rory muttered and then merely shook his head and stood. "Speaking o' which, I suppose 'tis time I went up to do that again."

"Now?" Tormod asked with surprise. "But what about our coming up with a plan to catch the poisoner?"

"Have ye got a plan?" Rory asked with interest, and

when Tormod grimaced, he said, "I'm afraid Edith is right. There's really no way to prove Victoria did it. At least nothing any of us has come up with yet. I suggest we all think about it tonight and then meet again tomorrow morn and see if anyone has ideas."

"Agreed," Edith said.

When Tormod grunted unhappy agreement, Rory nodded and turned to leave the table.

Edith glanced to Niels then, but found him looking toward the fire. Following his gaze she saw Ronson curled up with Laddie next to his grandmother's feet, sleeping. The trio was surrounded by several women all busily making mats with the last of the rushes that had been collected that day. They were almost done. There weren't many rushes left now.

Her gaze slid over the fair-haired boy curled up against the large dog and she sighed to herself. Ronson had rushed to his grandmother the moment they'd returned, seeking comfort from his only remaining family member after the trauma of seeing Lonnie dead. Edith hadn't been surprised. He'd been awfully quiet on the return journey to the keep, merely clutching her tight and shivering. Edith supposed it was the first dead body he'd seen. It surely wouldn't be his last, although hopefully not under the same circumstances. Tripping over a dead man in the woods had to have been disconcerting for the boy. Besides, he'd known Lonnie a little. The young man was one of the few soldiers who had troubled himself to be nice to the new lad after he and his grandmother had arrived.

"Ye should lay down and rest awhile ere the sup."

Edith met Niels's gaze briefly and then glanced shyly away and back to the women by the fire. There was no sense in her bothering to walk over to help them. Judging from experience, it looked to her like they barely had enough rushes to finish the mats they were presently working on.

"Aye, I think I will rest before dinner," she decided, standing up. Ronson hadn't been the only one shaken up by the discovery that day and she'd actually like a chance to push it from her thoughts.

"I'll see ye up and keep an eye out fer trouble," Niels murmured, taking her arm.

Edith stilled briefly, but continued forward, her heart thudding now in response to the innocent touch. It made her think of his touching her elsewhere, and his kisses as he'd done so, and she wondered if he'd kiss her again once they were in her room. Would he kiss her? Caress her? Would he do other things?

He shouldn't, her sensible side said staunchly, and Edith knew that side was right, but she wanted him to—she just wasn't sure what it was she wanted him to do. She'd like more kissing and caressing certainly. Her breasts were already tingling at the thought of his hands on them, his fingers plucking at her tender nipples. And heat was again building between her legs at the thought of him pressing there as he had in the clearing.

Edith could hardly believe they'd behaved that way with Ronson there. Although, he'd fortunately been off running through the woods with Laddie and missed their indiscretion. Still, if he'd returned and caught them—

"Here ye go."

Edith pulled herself from her thoughts and glanced around with surprise to see that while she'd been distracted, they'd ascended the stairs and arrived at her room.

"Thank ye," Edith murmured and led the way inside.

When he closed the door softly, she turned to offer him a nervous smile that turned into an O of surprise. She was alone. It seemed there would be no more kisses after all.

Chapter 6

$\mathcal{N}$IELS ROLLED ON HIS SIDE, GRIMACED AS HIS forehead banged into the wall and then abruptly opened his eyes and sat upright. He'd fallen asleep on the job. He was supposed to be guarding Edith, but had dozed off at some point during the night and had apparently ended up lying down and sprawling on the floor without waking.

Giving his head a shake in an effort to wake up, Niels peered along the hall to the stairs. He could hear the sounds of activity floating up from the great hall below, and wondered what time it was. It must be early yet, he decided, because no one had come out of their rooms. Not Edith, and not any of his brothers. He would have heard if Edith's door had opened, and his brothers would have made sure he knew they were up by kicking him awake and taunting him mercilessly for falling asleep. So it had to still be quite early.

Niels had barely had the thought when movement drew his gaze toward the stairs. He saw Rory moving up the hall toward him with a bowl in hand. Restraining a groan, Niels wiped his hands over his face and tried to look more alert. It seemed one of his brothers was up and had witnessed his failure in guarding Edith. It made him wonder why Rory hadn't stopped to wake him up on the way below stairs.

"Good morn, brother," Rory said cheerfully, stopping beside him.

Drawing one knee up, Niels rested an arm nonchalantly on it and grunted. It was as much of a good morning as he could manage just then.

"Is all well?" Rory asked. "Edith is safe and fine?"

"Aye," Niels growled.

"Hmm. And how would ye ken that when she's below stairs breaking her fast with Geordie and Alick and ye're here?" Rory asked mildly.

Niels's head whipped toward his brother. "What?"

"Aye, she's been up and about fer a good hour now, along with everyone else," he informed him with amusement.

"Well, why the devil did ye no' wake me?" he snarled, launching himself to his feet.

"Edith would no' let us. We came out just as she was heading for the stairs and she insisted we no' wake ye. She said 'twas obvious ye were exhausted what with yer no' waking when she *tripped over ye*," Rory finished acerbically.

Cursing, Niels raced for the stairs, ignoring Rory's laughter.

Last night had been Niels's third night guarding her door from the hallway, and he couldn't believe he'd failed so miserably at it. Although, perhaps he should have expected as much since he hadn't slept at all the two nights previously. Niels hadn't been able to find restful sleep since kissing Edith in the clearing. Kissing her had been a huge mistake. Niels had known it even as he'd done it, but hadn't been able to resist her. She'd been temptation incarnate to him in that clearing. Her hair had looked almost aflame with the sun shining on it, and it had smelled sweet from her bath in the loch. Once his body had brushed against hers as he reached up to help her hang the sack from his saddle, he'd been lost.

Edith hadn't helped matters much. She'd been like fire in his hands, her mouth clinging eagerly to his, her body responding passionately to his caresses. God, her nipple had been hard before he'd even slipped his hand inside the neckline of her gown to catch and pinch it. And the way she'd thrust into his touch when he'd cupped her between the legs . . . The memory was enough to have him hard even now. At the time Niels had wanted nothing better than to drop to his knees, push her skirt up to her waist and lap up the wet heat he was sure waited for him between her legs. He might even have done that had Ronson's shriek not brought them both to their senses.

That thought made Niels grimace. At the time, he'd actually managed to forget all about the boy being with them. He had no idea when the lad had left the clearing with Laddie, or what he'd seen before leaving. But Niels thanked God he hadn't tugged Edith's neckline down in front of the boy, baring her breasts for easier access as he'd wanted.

Sighing, he stopped at the top of the stairs and peered down over the great hall, looking for his brothers. Geordie and Alick had arrived back from MacDonnell last night after the rest o' the keep had gone to bed. Exhausted from their journey though they were, Alick had still offered to guard Edith's door for him to give him a break, but Niels had refused and sent the younger man to bed. Now he thought perhaps he should have accepted the offer. He had been less than useless snoring away outside her door, especially if her tripping over him hadn't woken him. If that were true, then anyone could have just stepped over him, entered the room and killed Edith. Not that that was a real concern anymore. They were pretty sure Victoria was the culprit and she wasn't here. Still, pretty sure wasn't positive and it was better to be safe than sorry.

Niels's gaze slid over the people bustling this way and that in the busy great hall below, and then he suddenly relaxed against the railing as he spotted Edith. She stood out in the crowd, a bright figure in pale green with fiery hair. She was chatting with Tormod, Geordie and Alick, he saw, and smiled when she laughed. The sound was like a bell in the room, clear and sweet, and Niels found himself wanting to hear more of it.

"She does no' understand why ye're acting as ye are toward her."

Niels glanced over to see that his brother had followed him and now stood at his side, peering down at Edith.

"Acting how?" Niels asked, though he knew the answer. He'd been pretty grumpy and grim around Edith since the clearing. He'd also been placing Tormod or Ronson at the table between him and Edith at meals, and keeping his distance. Guarding her, but at more than an arm's length, never close enough to touch. Niels would like to say his exhaustion was the reason, but it wouldn't be true.

"Acting like she disgusts ye," Rory said quietly.

Niels almost laughed at the suggestion, disgust was far and away from how he felt about the woman. That was the problem.

"I think she likes ye," Rory added when Niels didn't comment.

He stiffened at the suggestion, but said nothing.

"I think ye like her too," Rory added.

"O' course I do, she's a lovely woman. Smart, pretty, funny, beautiful, good-natured, lovely, kind to her people and beautiful."

"Ye said beautiful twice," Rory said with amusement. "Four if ye count *lovely* and *pretty* as the same word as *beautiful*."

"Leave off, Rory," Niels said wearily. "Ye ken there can never be anything between us."

"And why is that?" Rory asked with interest.

"Because I'm a third son with no prospects just like Brodie with Victoria. Only I'd ne'er lie to claim her. She deserves better."

"Ye're the fourth son actually," Rory said quietly.

Niels turned to skewer him with a glare. "Would ye bring up our Ewan at a time like this?" Before Rory could respond, he added grimly, "He's dead and gone, let him rest."

"Fine." Rory glanced back to Edith, but added, "Howbeit she can no' possibly deserve better than you. Ye're one o' the finest men I know."

"The other finest men being our brothers," Niels suggested with amusement.

"Aye," Rory acknowledged without apology. After

a moment, he added, "Besides, Edith has no prospects. Saidh said her betrothed died years ago while still a lad, and ye ken as well as I do that Brodie'll ship her off to a nunnery the minute he gets back."

"Aye, well, ye heard her the other day. She has plans to avoid that by marrying a nice wealthy laird with a castle and people fer her to run," he reminded him.

"It will no' happen," Rory said with certainty, and when Niels frowned at him, shrugged and said, "Do you ken o' anyone who fits that description?"

"Aye, one or two," Niels said unhappily.

"Any ye'd recommend to her?" Rory added.

"Nay," he said at once. Neither man was husband material. One was notoriously violent, having beaten two wives to death. Hence the reason he could not even buy a wife at this point. The other could no' pull himself out o' the wine barrel long enough to sign a contract. Neither was good enough for Edith. Hell, he wouldn't even recommend them to the likes of Victoria, who might very well be a murdering witch.

"Exactly," Rory said firmly. "She'll no' find a husband and will end up a nun."

Niels's hands tightened on the rail. The very thought of Edith as a nun made his stomach twist. It seemed to him to be a sacrilegious suggestion; vibrant, fiery Edith as a nun, never experiencing love or loving, never having children or a home.

"I think ye should marry her," Rory said.

Niels closed his eyes briefly and then shook his head. "I have nothing to give her. According to me plan it will be four more years ere I could give her a home or—"

"She'd be welcome at Buchanan with ye, Niels, and ye ken it."

"Aye, but she—"

"Is no' Victoria," Rory said solemnly. "Ye heard her as clear as I did when she said she'd be happy with a cottage and bairns."

Niels hesitated and then said, "What if she does no' want to marry me?" he asked, and then admitted, "I want her. But I do no' want a wife who only marries me to save herself from having to become a nun."

Rory laughed softly at the suggestion. "Brother, the woman has been eating ye alive fer days with her eyes. She tracks yer every move, kens where ye are every minute and does no' miss a word ye say. And judging by the look in her eyes as she does it, the nunnery is the last thing she thinks o' when she looks at ye." He peered down at Edith now almost wistfully, and admitted, "In truth I'm terrible jealous. She looks at ye the same way Saidh looks at Greer, and Murine looks at Dougall. I can only hope that someday a woman will look at me like that."

"Really?" Niels asked hopefully. He'd been so busy trying to keep from looking at Edith, he hadn't noticed how she looked at him.

"I'd never lie to ye about something like that, Niels," Rory said solemnly.

Edith's laughter rang out again and Niels turned to peer at her. He then found his feet taking him down the stairs to join her, when if he had a lick of sense he knew he'd take himself off to his room and get some much needed sleep. He should really be well rested to consider such a serious decision, he knew. Unfortunately, he didn't appear to have the sense God gave him at the moment. All he could think was that he wanted to be with her.

"It's no' true!" Edith was protesting on a laugh as he reached the table.

"What's no' true?" Niels asked with a smile, stopping next to Tormod and wondering if it would be rude to ask the man to move over so he could sit next to Edith. He was supposed to be guarding her after all. Well, technically, his guard duty was over, still—

"Niels," Geordie and Alick said together.

He glanced to his brothers and nodded and then spotted Edith's smile and returned it as she greeted him with a cheerful, "Good morn, kind sir. I hope ye slept well."

Niels stilled and it was Alick who said on a laugh, "Oh, that's just cruel, that is."

"What?" Edith asked with a frown, and then her eyes widened with dismay. "Oh, I never meant—'Tis just a greeting, I did no' mean to—"

Waving away her apology, Niels dropped to sit on the bench on the other side of Tormod and leaned forward to look past him to see her. "Ne'er fear, I'm no' offended," he assured her, and then added with self-disgust, "'Tis no less than I deserve fer sleeping on guard duty."

"Aye, well, asleep or no, I'm sure just yer presence there at my door was enough to keep anyone from poisoning me in my sleep," she told him firmly.

Niels bit his lip and held back the smile that wanted to claim him at her words. Poisoning her in her sleep? That would be a new trick. Did the woman think he'd sat outside her door all night to prevent her being poisoned? It was in case the poisoner wasn't Victoria and decided to move on to other tricks now that poisoning was not on the table.

"Besides," Edith added with a concerned expression, "ye must ha'e been exhausted to sleep so soundly. Why, ye did no' even stir when I fell on top o' ye."

Niels stiffened and asked sharply, "Fell on me? Rory said ye only tripped."

Edith grimaced, but admitted, "Aye, well, I tripped and then fell on ye." She shrugged. "I suppose I'm still recovering and a little clumsy."

"So, ye're saying ye actually fell *on top o' me* and I did no' wake up?" he asked with dismay. His brothers were forever teasing him that he could sleep through a battle raging around him, but good God, if he'd actually slept through Edith's falling on him . . .

"Aye, I was most concerned I'd hurt ye, and mentioned me worries to Geordie and Alick when they came out o' their room, but they assured me ye were fine, just a sound sleeper. And as they escorted me below they began regaling me with tales o' other times ye'd slept soundly."

Niels stiffened, dismay sliding up his back. Clearing his throat, he asked warily, "They did?"

"Aye, like the time when ye were sixteen and yer brothers shaved ye bald while ye slept," Edith added.

Niels felt his jaw tighten and glared at his brothers for telling such embarrassing tales about him.

Looking uncomfortable, Geordie muttered, "Aye, well to be fair, it was no' that he slept through that so much as he was unconscious," he admitted. "'Twas a wedding, and the first time he was allowed to drink. Niels was in his cups and that's really why he did no' wake up."

"Really?" she asked with a frown. "Ye shaved him bald while he was unconscious?"

"What other tales did they tell?" Niels asked dryly.

Edith was still frowning at his being shaved bald, but finally said, "They told us about another wedding when they were able to cart ye, bedding and all, out to the bull's pen. They said they even dropped ye a time or two and yet ye still did no' wake up, and they left ye lying there in the pen til morn." Turning back to Geordie and Alick she asked, "Was he in his cups that time too? Is that really why he did no' wake up?"

"Aye," Geordie admitted, looking uncomfortable when Niels stared at him.

"Oh, aye!" Tormod said suddenly. "I recall this tale now. I thought it sounded familiar." Turning to Edith he explained, "Yer father, Laird Drummond, was at the wedding and told it to me when he got back." Glancing past Edith to Geordie and Alick now he added, "But ye left out the best bits."

"What did they leave out?" Edith asked with curiosity.

"Well." Tormod glanced past her again to eye Geordie and Alick as he asked, "Did ye boys no' then wait around for hours until he finally *did* wake up and then let the bull loose as Niels tried to drag his bedding out o' the pen?"

"Ye did no'!" Edith gasped with horror and his two brothers nodded guiltily.

"Aye." Sitting back, Tormod shook his head. "Laird Drummond said ye laughed yer fool heads off as ye watched it chase yer brother about . . . until Niels ran straight fer ye lads and leapt over the fence right in front o' ye. The bull chased after him, smashing the fence to pieces, but Niels was still running while the rest o' ye were standing there with yer fiddles in hand, making perfect targets. He said as how the bull would have mown ye down had Niels no' turned and run back at yer screams. He said the lad jumped on the bull's back, grabbed him by the horns and steered him back into the pen and away from harming anyone until the older men could get there and get a couple o' ropes around the bull. Once they had it under control, Niels got off and out o' range and they repaired the fence."

Edith frowned on hearing the end of the tale and turned to Geordie and Alick to say heavily, "Ye did no' mention that part."

Both men avoided her gaze and Geordie muttered, "Aye, well . . ."

"What about the story about the piglet ye dressed in a lady's gown and placed in his bed with him?" Edith asked now, her tone suspicious. "Ye said ye thought it would wake and startle him, but rather than trample all over him as ye expected, the piglet settled right down and cuddled up to Niels and the two slept for hours with him blissfully unaware he was sleeping with a pig." She raised her eyebrows. "What perchance did ye leave out o' that tale?"

Niels watched both men squirm briefly, but then decided to put them out of their misery and change the subject. However, as he opened his mouth to do so, Alick blurted, "We'd painted the piglet's lips and cheeks red, and Conran wrote the name Annie on the pig's forehead."

"Annie?" Edith asked curiously. "Why?"

"Because, at the time, Niels had a fancy fer our neighbor, Annie," Alick admitted reluctantly.

"So ye put *her name* on a piglet?" Edith asked with dismay. "What if she and her family had come to Buchanan and seen it? Aside from insulting the lass, you would have humiliated yer brother in front of her." Mouth flattening out, she shook her head and said firmly, "Ye ken, now that I think on it, ye boys were very unkind to yer brother."

Niels's mouth had been tightening with each example she'd given of what his brothers had shared with her. But now, as Geordie and Alick began to look dismayed, he began to smile. His brothers were actually looking shamefaced, their heads hanging . . . and it nearly made Niels laugh out loud. He'd done or been a party to tricks as bad or worse against each one of his brothers. They all had. But he'd never had anyone stick up for him like Edith was doing. She was lecturing Geordie and Alick like they were a couple of young lads, still wet behind the ears.

"Shaving off his beautiful hair the way ye did was bad enough," Edith said now with disgust, and Niels sat a little straighter, his ears perking up at her description of his hair as she continued, "But ye could have killed him with that bull nonsense. And ye're verra lucky that he troubled himself to save ye from that bull the way he did too. I would have let it tear ye to shreds were it me and I knew ye'd set out to get me gored, fer surely ye must have realized that could happen."

"Oh, nay, we would no' have let the bull hurt Niels," Geordie said at once.

"Aye," Alick assured her. "Niels was always the fastest runner of us all. We knew he could outstrip the bull, and we surely would have rushed in to save him if the bull had even gotten close to goring him."

Edith glowered at them for a moment, and then sighed and nodded. "Aye. I ken that. Saidh has told me enough stories of her childhood that I ken how close ye all are. Still, his beautiful hair?" she asked with a wince.

Niels was about to ask her what she liked about his hair when she suddenly peered past Tormod and smiled.

"Any change?" she asked Rory as he approached the table.

Rory shook his head grimly. "Nay. Her color is a bit better, her eyes are back to normal, but she still sleeps. I begin to fear she may never come out of the sleep the drug put her in and may just fade away and slowly die."

Edith frowned at this news and then whirled toward the kitchen as a scream sounded. When it was followed by a great ruckus of shouting and shrieks, she stood up, obviously intending to investigate, but Niels caught her arm and steered her toward Geordie and Alick, who had also stood up.

"Watch her," he barked, and hurried toward the kitchen on the heels of Tormod and Rory. He quickly caught up to the pair and surpassed them, reaching the door to the kitchens first. Pushing inside, he frowned at the group of people blocking the entrance, with their backs to the door, unaware that they were in the way. All of them too were now silent, he noted as he began to make his way through the crowd to get to what held their attention. He had to weave through the people to the far end of the kitchen to find the source of the upset, and then he stopped dead and simply stared at the man lying prone on the ground.

"Cawley?"

Niels glanced around sharply at Edith's voice and scowled at the two men on her heels as she slid past him and rushed to her uncle.

"I told ye to watch her," he snapped.

"We are," Geordie said at once. "But as she pointed out, ye did no' say *where* we had to watch her, so we watched her all the way in here and we're watching her still."

"Speaking o' which," Alick said now. "I'm watching her about to get blood all over herself do ye no' move her away from the body."

Niels swung back to see that she'd knelt next to her uncle and was indeed about to get her gown bloody. A pool of the dark liquid was now visible, spreading out from under the body. Cursing, he moved to Edith and lifted her away.

"Nay, Niels! Cawley's hurt," Edith protested, trying to break free of his hold.

"He's no' hurting anymore, lass, he's dead," Niels said quietly, scooping her into his arms to carry her from the room.

"But what happened?" she asked sounding bewildered.

"I do no' ken, lass. Rory'll examine him and find out," he assured her.

"But there was blood," Edith pointed out as if he might have missed that fact.

"Aye," he murmured, and carried her to the chairs by the fire where Ronson's grandmother was busy with her mending. The old woman glanced up at their arrival, started to peer down to her needle again, but then blinked and raised her head again to stare at them with surprise as Niels settled in the chair with Edith in his lap and began to chafe her hands.

Frowning, she set down her mending and asked, "What's the matter? What's happened? Has she had a fall?"

Niels stopped chafing and peered at the woman with some surprise of his own, amazed that she appeared to be oblivious to the chaos taking place behind her. And then he noted that she had spoken quite a bit louder than necessary, and he realized that the old woman had some hearing issues.

"Nay," he said finally. "She's just upset. Cawley's dead."

Uncertainty crossed her face briefly, and then Ronson's grandmother nodded. "Aye. Cawley upsets everyone at some point or other I think. He's no' right in the head," she said, pointing at her own head. Leaning forward, she patted Edith's knee. "Do no' let whatever Cawley said upset ye, lass. He does no' mean it."

Edith stared at her blankly for a minute, and then turned and buried her face in Niels's chest. Quite sure she was crying, although she was doing it silently, Niels patted her back helplessly.

"There now, see?" Ronson's grandmother crooned, patting her knee again. "Have a good cry and forget about whatever nonsense Cawley was spewing. 'Twill all be fine."

Niels's eyes widened in alarm when he heard a smothered wail against his chest and he began to pat her back with both hands.

"Yer that Lord Niels fella my grandson's taken such a shine too, are ye no'?" the woman asked suddenly.

Niels nodded distractedly, quite sure he could feel dampness on his chest now.

"Yer no' the one teaching him all those cuss words, are ye?"

Freezing, he turned guilty eyes to the woman. Noting the sudden tension in her face and the unpleasant squint she was eyeing him with, he swallowed and said, "Er . . ."

"Good," the old woman said, her body relaxing and a smile wreathing her face. "I suspected a fine lord like yerself would no' sink to using such foul language as I've heard come out o' me sweet boy the last few days. Still, I'd a taken a switch to ye fer teaching him such and the like anyway if that were the case, lord or no'," she said firmly. "So it's glad I am it was no' you."

Sitting back in her seat, she poked the tip of the thread she held through the eye of a needle as she added, "It was probably that Cawley. I'll have to have a talk with him later about it. I'll no' take the switch to him though," she reassured them when Edith wailed louder into his chest. "He's no' right in the head that one and does no' ken better. But I'll tell him in no uncertain terms to watch his tongue around the boy from now on, I will."

Still patting Edith's back, Niels stared at the woman in bewilderment, not sure what to say, and then turned with relief when he spotted Geordie and Alick rushing toward him. Arms tightening around Edith, he stood and moved to meet them.

"What did Rory find?" he asked as soon as they paused.

"He's dead," Alick murmured, dragging his gaze from Edith in Niels's arms.

"Nay! *Really*?" Niels asked with feigned surprise.

Geordie choked on a laugh, and then coughed to clear his throat and said, "He's thinking we all need to have a little sit-down and a chat, but somewhere we'll no' be overheard."

Niels nodded grimly and then shifted his attention to Edith as she sniffled and hiccuped into his shirt.

Sighing, he said, "Edith's room then, and tell Rory to bring something to make Edith sleep. She's overset."

For some reason, that set her to crying again. Frowning, Niels pressed her to his chest and began to bounce her lightly in his arms as he rubbed her back now, trying to soothe her.

"I'll tell him to bring enough fer the both o' ye," Geordie said dryly and when Niels appeared surprised, he pointed out. "Yer bouncing her around like a bairn what needs burping, Niels."

Niels stopped bouncing her and scowled. "Just tell him to bring Tormod too," he muttered and then turned to head for the stairs.

He'd carried Edith up the steps to the upper landing and along the hall to her room before she said anything, and then she pushed away from his chest and peered up at him through deep green pools of sorrow.

"I'm sorry, m'lord. I do no' ken why I'm crying. I did no' even cry when me father and brothers died. There was so much to do and . . ." She shook her head helplessly.

"Then that's probably why, lass," Niels said, pressing her face back to his chest and reaching to open the door to her room. "Ye never got the chance to grieve properly and now it's all just hitting ye at once."

"Mayhap," Edith agreed on a sigh and shook her head against his chest. "Poor Cawley. He was such a gentle soul. And there was so much blood. What happened?"

"Rory'll tell us when he comes," Niels murmured, kicking the door closed and crossing to sit on the side of the bed with her in his lap again. He had spotted the hilt of a knife in the man's chest, just peeking out from the folds of his tartan, but had no intention of telling her that until he had his brothers to back him up. Niels had no idea what to do with a crying woman. Saidh had never cried growing up. Well, except when their parents had died. She'd cried then and, come to think of it, none of them had known what the hell to do about it then either, so they'd just left her to sort it out herself and waited for her to come find them once the storm was over so they could distract her, and themselves, from their sorrow.

That was it, Niels realized. He needed to distract Edith from her sorrow, he thought and immediately had an idea about how to do it. Well, he knew how he'd like to do it anyway. He'd wanted to kiss her again ever since the incident at the loch. Unfortunately, his better side was asking if that was really suitable to the moment. Unleashing his lust on her when she was grieving might not be the most—

"Niels?"

"Hmm?" he asked, glancing down distractedly when she leaned back to peer up at him.

"Will ye please kiss me again?"

Niels blinked and then shook his head and marveled, "'Tis as if ye're reading me mind, lass."

"It is?" Edith asked with confusion.

"Oh, aye, 'tis," he assured her and then lowered his head to claim her mouth, only to freeze before their lips met as a loud "ahem" filled the room.

Pausing, they both turned to stare blankly at Moibeal.

Blushing to the roots of her hair, the young maid began to sidle toward the door. "I'll just finish cleaning the room later and leave now, shall I?"

"Aye," Niels growled even as Edith whispered the word.

Nodding and bobbing, the maid reached the door, opened it, smiled and then slid quickly out.

Sighing, Niels turned and smiled at Edith, then started to lower his head again, only to pause as a knock sounded at the door.

"Moibeal," Edith complained.

"Moibeal just headed below," Geordie announced, opening the door and sticking his head in. "Should I call her back?"

"Nay." The word was a near squeal as Edith scrambled off Niels's lap.

Niels sighed to himself. He had no idea why she was so embarrassed to be caught in his arms. He'd been carrying her around downstairs and holding her in his lap in front of all and sundry just minutes ago and it hadn't seemed to bother her then. Now, however, she was reacting as if they'd been caught being naughty.

Mind you, a couple of more minutes and they might very well have been caught being naughty, Niels acknowledged. Because he knew without a doubt that a simple kiss would not have been enough for him. Given another five minutes alone with Edith and her sweet mouth, and Geordie would have really interrupted something. Niels would have had her on her back on the bed and his hands would have been all over her.

Unfortunately, they'd never even managed the kiss, and it seemed obvious he'd have to wait until later to distract Edith with them.

Chapter 7

"STABBED?" EDITH SAID SLOWLY, HER MIND unable to comprehend what Rory was saying. "Someone *stabbed* Cawley?"

"Aye. With this," Rory said and held up a black-handled dirk.

"That's my father's," Edith gasped, moving quickly forward to stare at the ornate ruby-topped handle. She could hardly believe it.

"Are ye sure?" Niels asked, moving to her side to peer at the weapon.

"O' course. 'Tis one o' a kind. I'd no' mistake it fer another," she murmured, her gaze sliding over the weapon again. She'd always thought it beautiful, but now, with Cawley's blood still on it, the beauty was somehow tarnished.

Turning, she walked to the bed and sat on the end of it. "Who did it?"

The men all glanced at each other silently, and then Tormod said, "No one kens."

"What?" she asked with dismay. "But there were a ton o' servants in the kitchen."

"Aye, and every one o' them was watching the food to be sure no one poisoned it," Tormod said grimly. "No one was paying attention to Cawley. They just left him to sit in his corner eating the pastries Jaimie made fer him and . . ." He shrugged helplessly. "No one saw a thing until Cawley tumbled off the barrel he was sitting on and began to bleed on the stone floor, and they said no one was near him when that happened."

"How could no one have been near him?" she asked with disbelief. "Someone had to have stabbed him."

"He was stabbed in the heart, Edith," Rory said softly. "He died almost at once. He may have sat in a stunned state for a count of three or ten before dying and tumbling from the barrel, or may have died leaning up against the wall and only tumbled from it afterward. Either way would have given whoever stabbed him a chance to slip away."

"Aye," Edith breathed the word out and then rubbed her forehead before asking, "But why would anyone kill Cawley? He was harmless."

There was silence and then Niels said, "He was yer father's brother?"

"Half brother, aye," Edith admitted. "Technically, he was me uncle, though me brothers and I never called him that," she murmured and then narrowed her eyes on him. "Ye're thinking this is connected to the poisonings?"

Niels pointed out almost apologetically, "Well, 'tis another family member dead."

"Aye, but Cawley was no' officially family," she said with a frown.

"Ye said everyone at Drummond kenned he was yer father's brother," Rory reminded her quietly.

"Well, aye, but—"

"Could he have inherited Drummond?" Geordie asked.

Edith shook her head. "Nay. Brodie is next in line."

"But if Brodie returned and died, and you died," he added quietly. "Could Cawley have inherited then?"

"Well, I suppose," she admitted, her brow furrowing. "If all of Father's children died without heirs, I suppose it could have passed to Cawley as his half brother and closest living relative."

"And who would inherit after that?" Rory asked.

Edith pursed her lips and thought briefly and then shrugged helplessly and said, "Tormod I think. Yer father and me grandfather were brothers, nay? Ye were me father's cousin?"

"Aye," he admitted reluctantly.

Edith nodded and then turned to Niels and said, "But Tormod is no' the one who killed Cawley. He was sitting with us fer a good hour before ye came below and he came from the bailey when he joined us. I saw him go nowhere near the kitchens. There is no way Cawley sat there dead in the kitchen for an hour without anyone noticing."

"Nay," Rory agreed. "The blood would have run down his body and there was no sign of that. I do no' think he was dead more than a minute or so before tumbling to the floor. If that. Tormod could no' have killed him."

"Thank God," Tormod muttered with feeling.

Edith moved over to pat the man reassuringly on the arm, but said, "Mayhap it has nothing to do with inheriting Drummond. Mayhap 'tis one o' the clans we're feuding with getting us out o' the way, or someone seeking revenge against the family for some unknown injury. Or mayhap Cawley's death has nothing to do with the poisonings," she added.

When her words were met with silence, she threw her hands up with exasperation and headed for the door.

"Where are ye going?" Niels asked with concern, following her.

"Well, 'tis clear we ken no more now than we did after the poisonings," she said impatiently. "And I am sick to death o' thinking about it. I am going to take Laddie fer a walk."

"No' by yerself, ye're no'," Niels said firmly, catching the door as she started to pull it closed behind her. He followed her out of the room and trailed her to the stairs before asking, "How long has it been since ye took yer mare fer a run?"

Edith stopped at the top of the stairs and admitted unhappily, "Too long."

"Then mayhap we should go fer a ride," he suggested gently. "It might do us both some good to feel the wind in our hair and run fast through the woods."

Edith hesitated and then nodded. "Aye," she breathed.

Smiling, Niels took her hand and started eagerly down the stairs.

Ronson was sitting on the floor with Laddie by the fire. Both started to rise when they saw them, but Niels waved them off and picked up speed as they stepped off the stairs and started across the great hall.

By the time they got outside and headed for the stables, Edith was almost running to keep up with him. She didn't mind so much, she had a lot of pent-up energy she needed to spend. It was something that had seemed to trouble her ever since their trip to the loch. She'd been restless and almost dissatisfied as she'd gone about setting to rights the small things that had been neglected at Drummond while she was ill. But her mind had constantly been on Niels and what he'd made her feel, and her eyes had repeatedly sought him out with a sort of yearning.

Unfortunately, while she'd wanted to be closer to him, he'd seemed to be avoiding her just as eagerly. At least he'd been avoiding touching her, even in the most random manner. There had been no polite holding of her arm as he'd escorted her below in the morning, no brushing of arms or other body parts as he reached for something at the table. In fact, he hadn't even sat next to her. Instead, she'd found herself between Tormod and Ronson, or Rory and Ronson, or Rory and Tormod with Niels on the other side of one of them. She had no idea why. But it appeared whatever had made him keep his distance had been resolved, because he was holding her hand as he led her into the stables.

"The stable master's no' here," Niels murmured as they entered.

"What can I do to help?" Edith asked as they approached the stalls where her horse was housed next to his.

Pausing, Niels turned and caught her by the waist to set her on the rail of one of the stalls and instructed, "Sit here and look pretty. I'll no' be a moment."

Edith blinked at him as he moved off to begin saddling his horse, and then slid off the rail and moved to collect her mare's saddle. No one had ever instructed her to sit and look pretty. She didn't even know how to do that. Edith had never even thought of herself as pretty. Smart? Yes. Hardworking? Yes. Kind? Yes. But no one had ever said she was pretty. Certainly not her brothers, and Edith didn't have a lot of experience with men besides her father and brothers.

"Ah, lass. Ye never listen to me," Niels said with amusement, moving to help with her horse once done with his own.

"I've never taken instruction well," she admitted wryly. "Me brothers always said I was difficult and contrary."

"I'd have said intelligent and independent," he countered lightly, finishing with the saddle. Once done, he set her on her mare and then led the animal out of the stall as he added, "And I happen to like that about ye."

Edith found herself beaming at the words.

"I'll be right back," Niels assured her once he had her out of the stables. He went back in, but returned a moment later leading his stallion and Edith found herself admiring the lines of both males as Niels mounted. Catching her looking, he grinned briefly and then nodded toward the gates. "Ye ken the area better than me. Lead the way."

Edith hesitated briefly, and then knew exactly where she wanted to go and steered her horse out of the bailey at a trot. The moment they'd crossed the bridge, she urged the mare to a run down the hill and into the woods. Edith didn't look back to see if Niels was following. She had no doubt he'd be able to keep up. His horse was a fine beast.

The spot Edith had decided on was a good distance away, but not so far as to be dangerous. Still, her mare was winded from a combination of the distance and the speed they'd traveled at by the time she reined in.

Pausing on the edge of a field of heather, Edith peered over the small meadow and breathed out a little sigh of pleasure. This was exactly what she'd needed. Her favorite spot when the world seemed to be crowding in on her. This was where she'd come when her mother had died, when she'd learned the man contracted to be her husband had died and where she wanted to be now.

"Beautiful," Niels murmured, reining in next to her.

Edith smiled. She'd known he'd like it. Sliding off her mount, she tied the reins around a branch on the nearest tree and then started along a trodden path through the meadow of waist-high heather as Niels tied up his own beast. Bees and other insects immediately began to buzz about, but Edith ignored them, knowing they'd settle again once they'd passed.

Niels caught up with her and followed silently until she'd reached the large, flat boulder in the middle of the clearing. It was only about knee-high, and hidden from view by the tall heather until she got close to it. But it was also wide enough for three people to lie on side by side, and nearly completely flat, though it was slightly slanted.

"I did no' even see this from the edge o' the meadow," Niels said with surprise as Edith stepped up onto the rock and moved to the center to sit down.

"Nay, but ye would have had we ridden much farther," she assured him.

"Aye." Niels settled beside her and peered out over the meadow of flowers, a wry smile twisting his lips. "I should have brought a picnic."

"We just broke our fast," Edith said with amusement and then frowned and added, "At least I did. Ye've no' eaten yet, have ye?" Shaking her head, she started to get up. "We should go back so ye can eat."

"Nay," he caught her arm to stop her rising and shook his head. "It's fine. I'm no' hungry."

"Are ye sure?" Edith asked with concern. When he nodded, she hesitated, but then relaxed and glanced around at the sea of flowers surrounding them.

Seated, they were only head and shoulders above the flowers. But she knew from experience that lying flat on the rock they would disappear from the view of anyone passing the meadow. Closing her eyes, she lifted her face to the sky and inhaled deeply. The air was redolent with the smell of heather and after a moment, she lay back on the sun-warmed stone surface and peered up at the clouds overhead.

"Oh, look, 'tis Laddie," she murmured with a smile.

"Where?" Niels asked, glancing around with confusion.

Edith grinned and pointed up at the cloud shaped vaguely like a running dog. "Right there, next to the ducky-looking cloud."

"Ah," Niels said relaxing. His gaze slid over the clouds and then back down to her and she was aware that he was watching her, but she simply continued to stare up at the shifting clouds until his head suddenly blocked her view.

Blinking, Edith refocused her gaze on his face and simply waited, knowing he would kiss her now. It was why she'd brought him here, to get that kiss he'd been about to give her in her room before they'd been interrupted.

Niels didn't disappoint her. He lowered his head until his mouth covered hers and at first that was all he did, brush his lips lightly over hers. But when Edith raised her hands to slide them up his arms, his mouth opened over hers and his tongue slid out to trace the crease between her lips. Edith instinctively opened to him on a little sigh and he caught her lower lip between his, and drew on it lightly, almost teasingly. It made her smile lazily, and then he released her lip and tilted his head as his tongue swept out to fill her mouth, and the sweet tempo suddenly changed.

With her breath catching in her throat, Edith clutched at his shoulders and held on tightly as his mouth ravished hers. It was as if the passion they'd shared by the loch had been merely restrained when they'd been interrupted, and now he'd unleashed it. Edith's own desire immediately rose up to meet it and she slid one hand into his hair, her fingers knotting in the strands and urging him on as she slid her tongue forward to meet his.

The soft hum of the insects feasting in the field around them faded, drowned out by the pounding of her heart, and the sweet honey scent of the heather was replaced with Niels's more musky, woodsy smell as he slid one arm under her to raise her to sit next to him. Edith went willingly, clinging to him with both arms and lips. When he broke the kiss to trail his lips to her ear even as his hand shifted to find and squeeze one breast through her gown, Edith tilted her head back and to the side on a moan and arched into the caress. Her eyes opened to the sky briefly and then she lowered and turned her head to find his mouth again as she felt him tug at the neckline of her gown.

Niels kissed her at once, but continued to work at the lacings of her gown as he did. She felt the material loosen and then it was just gone and his warm hands were covering both her breasts. Edith jerked in reaction as excitement jolted through her, and then moaned into his mouth as he began to squeeze and knead the mounds of flesh. When he broke their kiss again, she muttered a protest and then cried out and tightened her fingers in his hair when he suddenly ducked to close his mouth over one eager nipple.

"Niels," she gasped, shaking her head as he drew on the sensitive nub and then closed his teeth lightly on it. He didn't leave the other nipple wanting, his fingers were rolling it lightly and plucking by turn and Edith was writhing in response, her back arching and legs shifting restlessly as liquid heat pooled low in her belly and began to ooze down to the spot between her legs.

When he finally let her nipple slip from his lips and raised his head to kiss her again, Edith was ready for him and she was the one who did the devouring, kissing him almost violently and pressing as close as she could manage. She felt his hand on her ankle and then sliding upward along her outer leg, pushing the cloth of her gown ahead of it. When her lower body twisted toward his as he reached her hip, his hand immediately took advantage, sliding around to cup one round cheek of her bottom and squeezing firmly. In the next moment, he was shifting to his knees and urging her to hers.

Edith followed the direction almost mindlessly, her mouth clinging to his as she moved to kneel between his spread knees. The moment she did, Niels's hands slid down and curved under to brush across her most sensitive skin. Edith broke their kiss, her head going back on a startled cry of pleasure, and Niels turned his head and nipped at her shoulder, growling, "Christ, lass, ye're so wet fer me."

"I'm sorry," Edith muttered with confusion, and a startled laugh slid from Niels's lips.

"Do no' be sorry," he said breathlessly. "Ne'er be sorry fer that," he added more firmly and then kissed her again and bore her down to lay sideways with him. The moment Edith stretched her legs out from their folded position, Niels rolled her onto her back and broke their kiss to claim one nipple again. But she hardly noticed, because now his hand had pushed her skirt up to her waist and was urging her legs apart. Edith bit her lip, but let her legs fall open, and then cried out his name and bucked as his clever fingers slid between them to find the core of her again. Her legs snapped closed around his hand in an instinctive response, but he merely used both hands to press them open and then slid down her body to place his mouth where his fingers had been.

Edith froze, her eyes open and staring at the rolling clouds overhead as he began to do things her mind couldn't even track. He licked and he suckled and did things with his tongue that had Edith crying out and grabbing his head. Tugging at his hair, she tried to close her legs, but he held them open and in the next moment she was digging her heels into the stone and raising her hips into his mouth almost violently, but again he was in control, holding her down and open for his attention.

Helpless and half-crazed with the excitement mounting in her, Edith released his head and grabbed at the rock they lay on, but the mostly flat surface offered no purchase. She ended up grabbing her own breasts instead, her nails digging into her skin as she tried to find a way to ground herself. But it was too late, there was no stopping it. Edith screamed, half-terrified and half-shocked as her pleasure exploded and rolled over her in a thundering, mindless wave. When she recovered enough to regain her awareness of where and who she was, Niels was cradling her in his arms and murmuring soothing words as he rocked her gently.

With all that lovely passion fading, shame and embarrassment were quick to claim Edith as she realized her gown was a twisted mess around her waist and she was as good as naked in his arms. Closing her eyes, she turned her face into his neck and pressed closer, trying to hide as much of her body as she could.

Niels paused in his rocking and soothing murmurs at once, and pulled his head back, trying to see her. "Edith?"

"Aye?" she muttered, ducking her head self-consciously and crossing her arms over her breasts to try to hide them.

"Are ye all right, lass?" he asked with concern.

Edith nodded, but shifted her arms so that one crossed over her breasts, leaving her free to try to pull the top of her gown up to cover herself.

"Don't," Niels protested, catching her hand. "Ye do no' have to hide yerself from me."

"I . . ." Edith shook her head helplessly and tried to pull her hand free.

"Marry me."

She froze at those words, her head finally coming

up so that she could stare at him with amazement. "What?"

"I ken ye were hoping to marry a laird with a castle ye could run, and I do no' have that yet, but I'll be able to start building one fer ye at the end o' another four years. In the meantime, we can live at Buchanan, either in the keep or a cottage in the village if ye prefer. And I'll happily give ye as many bairns as ye wish fer," Niels assured her and then repeated gently, "Marry me, Edith. Be me wife and share yer life with me."

Edith simply stared at him, hardly believing he'd asked her, but then she frowned and asked, "Are ye only asking me because ye think ye have to now ye've ruined me?"

The question made Niels chuckle and Edith scowl.

"'Tis no' funny m'lord," Edith said stiffly, pulling away from him and beginning to try to untangle her twisted dress. "If ye're only offering out of guilt over what we've just done, then ye'll surely come to regret it and resent me fer it and I could no' bear ye coming to hate me."

"Edith, lass," Niels said gently, catching her hands to stop her again. "I am no' laughing because I think yer being ruined is amusing, I'm laughing because . . ." He hesitated and then simply said, "Ye're no' ruined, Edith. Yer maidenhead is still intact."

She blinked and then stared at him doubtfully. Edith did know the basics and that a man generally inserted his fiddle in a woman to breach her maidenhead. However, she found it hard to believe anything had survived the explosion of pleasure she'd experienced. Besides, she'd felt something push into her at the end. That was what had set off the explosion. Of course, his head had been between her legs with his fiddle nowhere near that part of her, she realized, flushing. "But I felt something—"

"Me finger," he interrupted gently. "Yer virginity is still intact."

"Oh." Blushing, Edith lowered her head.

"I do no' want to marry ye because I've ruined ye. I want to marry ye because . . . well, frankly, because I *want* to ruin ye," Niels admitted on a wry laugh and then shrugged apologetically. "I want ye something fierce, Edith."

When she frowned and began to lower her head again, he added quickly, "But I like ye too."

Pausing, she glanced back up at him uncertainly.

"I'll no' lie and say I love ye, lass," he added solemnly. "'Tis too soon fer that, and I do no' wish there to be lies between us, but I do like ye. I think ye're a fine woman, beautiful and smart. More importantly, ye're kind too. Ye care fer the well-being o' yer people, and ye take in strays who need a home. Ye've a good heart, Edith, and I like that about ye." Smiling again, he added, "And the fact that I want ye too jest makes it all the sweeter. I think we could be happy together."

Edith stared at him for several minutes, replaying his words through her mind. She liked that he wouldn't lie and claim he loved her. And she liked him too. She liked how kind and patient he was with both her and Ronson, and she liked how he managed Laddie with firm affection. And she too wanted him, desperately. No one had ever made her feel even a small percentage of the passion he'd roused in her, which perhaps wasn't saying much since she'd never even been kissed before him, but she knew enough to understand that the passion he inspired in her was rare and she'd be lucky to have it in her marriage bed. Even more importantly though, she liked and respected Niels and she also thought they could be happy together.

Releasing the breath she'd been holding, Edith let her gown drop and leaned up to press her lips to his, but her mouth barely brushed his when Niels pulled back and asked, "Is that an aye, ye'll marry me?"

Blushing, Edith nodded and whispered, "Aye."

"Thank God," Niels growled and finally kissed her.

Much to her amazement all the earlier passion she'd thought sated immediately leapt back to life inside Edith. Moaning, she twined her arms around his neck and pressed against him, her nipples tingling as they brushed across the cloth of his shirt and tartan. Wanting to please him as much as he'd pleased her, Edith didn't simply hold him this time, but allowed her hands to move over his chest, exploring, as she sucked on his tongue and then let hers wrestle with his. But when she found the large pin holding his tartan in place and undid it, Niels stiffened and then caught her by the shoulders and urged her back, ending their kiss.

"Nay, lass, I do no' think—"

"Please," Edith moaned breathlessly, her hand reaching for his shirt-covered chest as the tartan dropped to pool in his lap. "I just want to see."

When Niels hesitated, a battle taking place in his eyes, she reached for his shirt and tugged it up from under the folds of his tartan so she could slide her hands beneath. Edith then let them glide over the hard expanse of his stomach and then his chest as she pushed the cloth upward, revealing inch after inch of his perfect chest. When the cloth rose high enough to expose one of his nipples, she bent and closed her lips over it and Niels's hands tightened on her shoulders in surprise.

"Lass," he growled as she suckled and then flicked at the hardening tip with her tongue, not sure she was doing it right, but trying to emulate what he'd done to her. She thought she might be doing it right when he growled under his breath and let one hand slide into her hair to cup her skull as she worked. Still, he said, "Lass, we should no—"

The words died abruptly when Edith slid one hand down to find the hardness covered by the bunched-up tartan. Unsure what she should do with it now that she'd found it, Edith merely clasped it through the cloth and squeezed lightly. The next thing she knew, she was on her back on the stone and Niels was on top of her, his hips between her legs and pressing into her as he kissed her almost violently.

Groaning into his mouth, Edith spread her legs farther, raised her knees and dug her heels into the stone so that she could press back up into the hardness rubbing against her through the cloth of his tartan. She also slid her hands around his hips and grasped his . . . bare bottom, she realized with surprise. Eyes blinking open, she broke their kiss to glance down and saw that the tartan had slid off him to lie between them. It left her a lovely view of his bottom.

"What's wrong?" Niels growled and lifted himself slightly to peer over his shoulder as if he thought she'd seen someone. He was caught completely off guard when Edith immediately stopped pressing upward, let her hips drop to the stone and reached into the space she'd made between them to wrap her fingers around his hard erection.

Sucking in a sharp breath, Niels turned back to stare at her wide-eyed and Edith used her free hand to try to pull his head down for another kiss, but he resisted. Actually, he seemed kind of frozen, she realized and worried that she'd hurt him. She didn't think she was squeezing too tightly, but didn't know how sensitive he was.

"Am I doing it wrong?" she asked uncertainly.

"That depends what ye're trying to do," he said between clenched teeth.

Edith bit her lip, and then admitted, "I want to pleasure ye like ye did me."

Niels swallowed and closed his eyes. "Lass," he said finally. "Ye're playing with fire. Jest leave off and let me catch me breath and we'll return to the keep and—" His words died abruptly again when she moved her hand. Edith's eyes widened as he jerked in response.

"Tell me what to do," she begged, moving her hand again.

It was apparently too much for Niels. Cursing under his breath, he caught her wrist and squeezed until she released him, and then was immediately off her, taking his tartan with him.

Biting her lip, Edith sat up and watched as he laid his tartan out on the path and began to fold pleats into it in the narrow space.

"Did I do something wrong?" she asked uncertainly, easing to the edge of the rock and standing up.

"Nay, I just think we should—" Niels paused as he glanced her way and saw that while her skirt had dropped back into place, the top of her gown still lay around her waist leaving her breasts bare. Glancing down, she saw that her nipples were puckered as if cold, and blushed. She also immediately started to grab the material, intending to cover herself, but he caught her arm to stop her and then drew her closer.

"God, I want ye," he whispered, his breath a warm rush across her sensitive nipple. "I've no' stopped aching since the day at the loch," he admitted.

"Then why were ye avoiding me?" Edith asked, and flushed as she heard the hurt in her own voice. She hadn't meant to let him hear it, but she had been hurt by how distant and cold he'd been toward her after kissing her. She was also starting to worry he might act like that again now despite asking her to marry him.

Niels studied her expression with a frown and then said, "I'm sorry, lass. I did no' mean to hurt ye."

"Ye're no' going to act like that again once we're back at the keep, are ye?" she asked.

"I probably will," he said apologetically. "But only til we're married. 'Tis only because when I'm near ye, I want ye so bad I . . ." He shook his head.

"I want ye too," she confessed. "So bad 'tis an ache."

"Aye." Niels smiled wryly. "I ken the feeling well."

"Mayhap if ye bed me, it would no' be so bad and we could—" Her voice died on a gasp as his mouth suddenly closed over her nipple.

"Niels," she said uncertainly, staggering against him and grabbing for his shoulder as he suddenly slid a hand under her skirt to run up her leg.

"I'll no' bed ye til we're wed, lass," he muttered, releasing her breast and lifting his face to watch her expression as his fingers found her center again. "But I'll take away yer ache, fer now."

"What about you?" Edith groaned.

"Aye, I'll take away mine too," he assured her, and she glanced down to see that he had his free hand wrapped around his erection. "Lift yer skirt, Edith. I want to see while I pleasure ye."

Edith reached down shakily to pull her skirt up hand over hand until she had it gathered at her waist.

"Beautiful," Niels muttered, sliding a finger inside her. "Come closer, love. I want to taste ye." He urged her closer with the finger inside her, and Edith staggered forward.

"Spread yer legs more," he instructed and she widened her stance, although she wasn't at all sure her legs would hold her much longer as his fingers slid in and out and he tilted his head up and leaned in to lap at her. Bracing herself with both hands, Edith closed her eyes briefly and then opened them and peered down at what he was doing to himself, noting the way he was holding himself and the rhythmic motion he used. She wanted to touch him too and be more involved, but didn't have much choice in the matter until her legs began to shake.

Apparently noticing, Niels straightened and growled, "Kneel."

Edith sank to her knees beside him and he kissed her, his thumb now caressing the sensitive nub that was the center of her excitement as he slid his finger in and out of her in the same rhythmic motion as he was using on himself. She kissed him back at first, but soon didn't seem to have the presence of mind to even manage that and simply kept her open mouth pressed to his as her body began to quake.

When she cried out and bore down on him, her hands clutching at his shoulders as she found her pleasure, Niels responded by thrusting into her one last time and then shouting into her mouth as he found his own release. When it ended, they were both panting and sagging against each other. Niels retrieved his hand and held her close as they regained themselves.

After several moments, he kissed her forehead and murmured, "We need to dress and head back."

Edith sighed and nodded with regret. She didn't really want to dress and return to the troubles at Drummond. She wanted to run away with Niels, find a big, soft bed somewhere and have him teach her all there was to know about the bedding. Unfortunately that wasn't an option, she acknowledged, and began to move.

Chapter 8

$\mathcal{E}$DITH WAS LEADING THE WAY AS THEY RODE back into the bailey. Going faster than she probably should have, she nearly ran over Laddie when he appeared suddenly before her. Only fast reactions and instincts born of years of riding saved the huge beast as Edith caught the right rein higher up and pulled. The horse immediately turned, just avoiding trampling her poor dog. The mare then stopped and Edith turned to scowl at Ronson as he came running up.

"I'm sorry, m'lady! He got away from me! I'm sorry!" the boy cried, slipping a hand under Laddie's collar as if to hold him back when the beast was now sitting happily in the path, apparently completely oblivious to how close he'd come to death. "I really am, m'lady. 'Twill ne'er happen again. I swear. Please do no' throw me and me gran out. I'll do better."

All of Edith's anger, born mostly of the scare she'd had, slid out of her at those words and she sighed and shook her head. "Come here, Ronson."

He hesitated briefly, but then moved forward, dragging Laddie with him, fear plain on his face. The moment he stopped beside her mare, Edith bent to put her face closer to his. She thought she heard a hiss above or behind her as she did, but ignored it to say solemnly, "Ronson, I will never—"

The rest of the reassurance died in Edith's throat as she was suddenly tackled and dragged off her mount by two hundred pounds of male muscle.

"Niels?" Edith said with bewilderment as she found herself lying on her back on top of his chest on the ground. She started to turn her head to look at him, but paused in surprise as her gaze slid over the front of the castle and she thought she spotted someone standing in her bedchamber window. Before she could get more than an impression of the person, however, she was suddenly rolling and Edith found herself facedown in the mud with a heavy weight on her back. She didn't have to think hard to guess who it was on top of her, and squawked, "Niels!"

"Stay down," he barked, pushing her head into the dirt with his hand. "Ronson. Get over here, lad."

Edith lifted her face out of the mud and glanced around to see that Ronson was already almost to them, dragged by Laddie who thought this was a fine game and began to lick her face and head the moment he could reach her.

"Laddie, no," she ordered, or tried to. The moment she opened her mouth to say the words, Laddie decided to check and see if she had any treats in there for him, and it was difficult to speak with two tongues in her mouth. Turning her head away, Edith pressed her lips closed and then dropped her head back into the dirt and tried to hear what Ronson was saying.

"'Twas an arrow, m'lord! I saw it fly past her when she bent to speak to me! Someone tried to shoot Lady Edith!"

"What?" Edith squawked, and jerked her head up to look around, only to have Niels push it back to the ground.

"Stay down, lass. I'm no' losing ye now," he growled and then added, "Ronson, get over here, lad, else ye might get hit by accident do they shoot again."

In the next moment, Edith found Ronson squeezed up beside her under the shelter of Niels's body.

"Are ye all right, m'lady?" the boy asked earnestly as Niels began to bark orders at the people now shouting and running about the bailey. "That was sure close. Someone nearly shot ye!"

"Did they?" she asked weakly, her head bobbing as Laddie licked the hair on the back of her head. She had no idea why the dog was doing that, but managed to get one hand out from under her and cover the spot in hopes he'd stop. Instead, he turned excitedly to licking both her hand and her hair, dragging the now wet strands over the back of her hand, and she suspected, pulling some out. It certainly felt like some of her hair was being ripped out by the roots.

"Aye," Ronson told her. "If ye had no' bent to talk to me right when ye did, I wager the arrow would ha'e hit ye in the chest and killed ye deader than a spent whore."

"Deader than a what?" she asked with disbelief.

"Than a spent—" Ronson began, but his words ended on a startled gasp when Niels suddenly rose, taking them both with him.

"Keep the shields over them," Niels barked. "The

arrow came from above! Did ye send someone to check the upper chambers?"

Edith blinked up at the six shields six soldiers were holding over them like a roof, and then down at the arm that was like a steel band around her waist. Niels was holding both her and Ronson up off the ground and tight to his chest as he jogged toward the keep with the men surrounding them to protect them from arrows.

"Aye. I sent four men. They should be up there now. If there is anyone there, they'll find them," the man beside her said, and Edith turned to see that it was Tormod holding the shield on that side. Catching her looking at him, he nodded as he jogged and murmured, "M'lady."

Smiling weakly, Edith turned to peer at the other men now, noting that Alick was beside Tormod, grinning at her as if this was a walk in the park. He jogged sideways toward the keep, holding a shield high over their heads just as Tormod and the others were doing. Geordie, she noted, was on Niels's other side with yet another shield. He too smiled at her reassuringly when he saw her looking. And Cameron, one of the Drummond soldiers, was next to him, trying to give her what she thought was supposed to be a reassuring smile as well. She couldn't see the two men behind them, but knew they were there.

Edith looked over the men she could see again and thought it was like some kind of bizarre dream she'd fallen into. Perhaps they were still at the stone in the meadow and she'd dozed off.

When they reached the steps, Niels didn't slow but jogged quickly up them, the men managing to keep pace despite mounting the stairs sideways. Edith expected the first two men would have to lower their shields to open the doors, but someone must have been watching for them, because the moment they neared, the doors swung open. Their party jogged right on in, shields not lowering until they were well inside the great hall.

Niels set down both Ronson and Edith, but then turned to survey her, his hands traveling over her body as if searching for a hidden *sgian-dubh* as he asked, "Are ye all right? Were ye hurt at all? Is anything broken or—"

"I'm fine," Edith said with embarrassment, catching his hands as he began to pat her behind and upper legs. "Truly. I was no' hurt. I'm a little thirsty, and even hungry, but completely unharmed," she assured him.

Releasing a pent-up breath, Niels nodded and then took her arm to usher her to the table.

"I'll go tell Cook to fetch out the nooning meal fer ye, m'lady," Tormod said, nodding at Rory as the man came from the kitchens and the two men passed each other.

"I'll fetch down a pitcher o' mead," Geordie said, heading for the stairs.

"Here, sit, lass," Niels murmured, urging her to the high table. "Ye've had a scare."

"What happened?" Rory asked, reaching them then. "Some servants came rushing into the kitchen saying there were screams and people running in the bailey. What—"

"Someone shot an arrow at Edith, and I'm marrying her, dammit!" Niels snapped.

Everyone went completely silent at that. Edith suspected it was probably because they were trying to sort out the information that he'd just blurted in one furious burst and decide if he was angry only about the arrow, or about the marrying part too. No doubt they were stumped as to whether they should be offering congratulations or condolences, she thought wryly.

"M'lady?" Moibeal appeared at her side, and suggested tentatively, "Mayhap we should go above stairs and clean ye up."

"Nay. I'm fine. I'll change after I eat," Edith murmured, frowning at Laddie and pushing the dog away when he began to nose around her lap.

"Did ye find anyone up there?" Tormod's voice drew Edith's gaze as he reappeared from the kitchens and headed to meet four grim-faced men who were now descending the stairs.

"Nay. We searched every room. Other than old Effie, the rooms were all empty," the first man said.

"But we think they shot the arrow from Lady Edith's room," the second man added. "Her shutters are the only ones open."

"They were closed when I left me room this morning," Edith said when Niels glanced to her. Turning to Moibeal, she asked, "Did ye open them to air the room?"

"Aye, while I cleaned up," she admitted, and then added, "But I closed 'em when I was done. They should no' be open now."

"The bastard shot at ye from yer own room," Niels growled, dropping to sit on the bench next to her, his fist thumping the table in frustration.

"Bastard," Ronson echoed, thumping the table and dropping onto the bench as well.

Eyes widening, Edith looked swiftly toward the chairs by the fire, relieved to see that old Bessie appeared to be asleep and had not witnessed her grandson's use of foul language.

"We shall have to post men at the windows during the day to prevent something like this happening in the future and—Leave off, Laddie!" Niels interrupted himself to snap at the dog trying desperately to lick his hand. When he pushed the dog away again, Laddie gave up and moved back to Edith.

"M'lady, I really think ye'll want to clean up before ye eat," Moibeal suggested in slightly pained tones.

Edith shushed her, and again pushed Laddie away from her lap as Tormod frowned and turned to Rory to ask, "Ye're sure Effie's no' conscious?"

"Aye," Rory assured him. "I test her morning and night to be sure."

Tormod nodded as if he understood what Rory meant by testing the old woman, but Edith didn't understand herself. Before she could ask what kind of test it was, Niels cursed, drawing her attention again as he cupped Laddie's face in one hand and told the dog firmly, "Enough. No more licking."

The dog stared at him wide-eyed and then let his tongue loll out, trying to lick the hand that was holding him.

A small laugh slipped from Edith before she could stop it. Shaking her head, she said, "I do no' ken what's the matter with him. First he's licking me head, then yer hand and he keeps poking around me skirts as if he thinks I ha'e a treat hidden in me pocket fer him."

"He probably smells ye on me," Niels said with a sigh as Geordie returned with a pitcher of mead in hand.

Eyeing it with interest, Edith shrugged and said distractedly, "Aye, well ye were laying on both Ronson and me out there, but he's no' licking—" Her words died abruptly and her gaze and full attention slid to Niels's hand as she recalled exactly where it had been. Her gaze dropped to her own lap as Laddie returned to nose around curiously, and then she recalled Niels pushing her head down with his hand, and she stood abruptly. "I'd best go clean up before we eat."

"Thank the good Lord fer that," Moibeal muttered, but Edith hardly heard the maid, her attention was on the slow, sexy smile that was now claiming Niels's lips and chasing away his anger. He did have such a lovely smile, but Edith wasn't thinking about that so much as the things he'd done to her in the meadow. Just the memory of his hands and mouth on her body made her nipples harden and wet heat pool between her legs. Edith wanted nothing more than to drag the man above stairs with her, strip off her clothes and—

"Are ye coming, m'lady?" Moibeal asked when Edith just stood there staring at Niels. "Ye really need to—"

Edith sighed as the imaginings in her mind bumped up against reality. She couldn't drag Niels anywhere, and she certainly couldn't try to seduce him into giving her pleasure again with Moibeal there, nagging at them. Turning on her heel, she headed for the stairs, muttering, "I am coming, Moibeal. I do no' ken what ye're all upset about though. 'Tis just a bit o' mud on me skirt."

"And all over yer face, and in yer hair," Moibeal said with some exasperation of her own as she fell into step beside her. "And yer hair's sticking up every which way too. I do no' ken how ye managed that. It looks like ye're standing in the middle o' a confused storm."

"Laddie was licking me head when we were on the ground in the bailey," Edith explained, reaching up to her hair to feel around, and then sighing as she felt that Moibeal was right. Dear God, her hair was wet and almost stiff from Laddie's licking. It was also standing up every which way. How could Niels look at her with those hungry eyes when she must look like an utter idiot?

"So."

Niels tore his gaze from Edith's retreating behind and turned warily to his brother. "What?"

"Ye asked and she said aye?" Rory asked with a grin.

Niels smiled and relaxed for the first time since the arrow was loosed. Turning to face the table, he nodded. "Aye."

"Aye to what?" Geordie asked with confusion.

"I'll second that," Tormod said, settling on the other side of Ronson. "What did we miss?"

"Me brother's marrying yer Lady Edith," Alick told the older man with a grin.

"Oh." Tormod's eyes widened and then he smiled and reached past Ronson to thump Niels on the back. "Well, say, that's fine, that is."

"Aye, congratulations," Geordie said smiling widely. "This calls fer a celebration. Does anyone want a drink?" he asked, holding up the pitcher of mead he'd just fetched.

Niels nodded, but paused when Tormod stood up with a grimace.

"Aye, I'll have a drink. But no' of mead," the man said heavily. "I'll have one o' the maids fetch us some ale."

"Even better," Niels decided.

Geordie set the mead aside with a shrug. "We'll save the mead fer Edith then."

Niels nodded absently, his thoughts turning to the problem of keeping Edith safe. Men at the windows during the day, guards on her at all times . . . Keeping her inside would not hurt either, he thought.

"The ale'll be out shortly," Tormod announced as he claimed his seat again a moment later. He then turned to eye Niels with approval. "Well-done," he said. "She's a good woman. Ye're a lucky man. When do ye plan to wed her?"

"Where's yer priest?" Niels asked for answer.

Tormod grinned. "That soon, eh?"

"Sooner," Niels said firmly.

Tormod nodded and stood up. "I'll go have a little chat with our Father Tavish, then. If he's in a good mood ye may be married by the sup."

"Should we no' discuss what to do about this latest attempt on Edith's life?" Rory asked with a frown.

Tormod paused and turned back with interest. "Have ye any ideas about who may ha'e shot the arrow at our lady, or how to catch them?"

"Well . . ." Rory frowned, but finally admitted, "Nay."

Tormod nodded slowly, but his expression was pensive and he didn't move away at once.

"Do you have any ideas, Tormod?" Niels asked, eyeing him curiously.

"I may," he said slowly, and then grimaced and added, "Of a sort."

"And what would that be?" Geordie asked at once and then patted the bench seat he'd just stood up from. "Sit down and tell us. I think I can safely speak fer everyone when I say we'd be happy fer any ideas at all."

"Aye," the others murmured together.

Tormod hesitated, but then sat down at the table and cleared his throat before saying, "Well, I ken the three o' ye planned to guard her in shifts, but it occurs to me that if we get ye and the lass married, Niels, she'll be that bit safer with ye snug in her bed."

"Aye," he agreed with a nod.

"And then I could send men out to find Brodie," he added. "I can send a couple to court and others to each keep belonging to one o' his friends until we find him and can pass along the news that there is no fear o' illness anymore."

Rory shook his head. "Brodie can no' be behind the poisonings and attacks, Tormod. They are no' here."

"Nay, I ken, but if he comes back, we can pretend we're no' concerned about him and only guarding Edith. But we watch him anyway, real sly like, and when the killer tries to kill him, we can hopefully catch them in the act," he pointed out.

"Ye want to use yer laird as bait?" Rory asked with disbelief.

"Well, better him than Edith," Tormod said gruffly. "She was at death's door fer three weeks, and then was nearly killed today. He can take a turn and help solve this, the cowardly bastard. 'Tis his place as laird anyway."

"Aye, 'tis," Niels agreed solemnly. He wasn't too worried about Brodie. He didn't like the man on principle alone, but liked him even less for leaving Edith here alone and ailing. He also didn't like that the man would have apparently tried to ship her off to the Abbey did he not plan to marry her first. Besides, in his experience, cowards were usually the last ones to be injured in any endeavor. The man would no doubt survive if they went through with their plan. What had his interest was that Tormod was willing to risk him that way. What's more, he suspected the man would no' be torn up if Brodie died as they caught the killer "in the act."

Niels wasn't really surprised. He'd heard the man say more than once that Edith would make a better clan leader, and as far as Niels was concerned, he was right. Still, a laird was supposed to be able to depend on his first to have his best interests at heart, and Tormod appeared more interested in Edith's well-being than his laird's.

"Anyway, I'd best go talk to Father Tavish," Tormod muttered, getting to his feet.

"Would ye tell Brodie that 'twas poison, no' illness and that the killer had no' yet been caught?" Niels asked before he could slip away.

"Aye," Tormod said on a sigh. "I'd ha'e to put that in the message I send. 'Tis me place. I'd also ha'e to tell him I hope he'll return and help find the culprit who killed his father, brothers and uncle." Tormod shrugged. "He'll probably no' return until we sort out this business, but I thought it could no' hurt to try."

Niels relaxed, relieved to hear that Tormod was up-holding his position as first. He would have lost respect and trust in the man otherwise. Nodding, he said, "If nothing else, 'twill tell us where he's run off to."

"Aye," Tormod said dryly and headed for the doors to the bailey.

"I'm glad ye asked that," Geordie said quietly. "I was beginning to worry he was willing to sacrifice his own laird."

"He is," Niels said with amusement. "But no' without warning Brodie o' what he faces, and I suspect he'd protect him with his life as well. It does no' stop him from hoping something happens to free him from the man as laird though."

"I can no' blame him, really," Geordie admitted. "By all accounts, Brodie will drain this place dry and leave his people in misery."

"Aye," Niels murmured, his gaze sliding to Ronson. The boy had been listening attentively to every word said, he saw with a frown. The lad was a smart one, and Niels thought now that perhaps he should talk to Edith about taking the boy and his grandmother with them when they left for Buchanan. He didn't think Aulay would mind, and they'd take them on to their own home afterward when it was built.

"Well," Alick said now. "First Saidh, then Dougall, and now you." He shook his head. "At this rate we'll all be married and raising babies o' our own soon."

Geordie snorted at the suggestion. "The hell we will. I've a lot o' living to do ere I settle down and have some woman start whelping," he said with disgust, and then added, "And what poor, brain-addled woman is it that ye think would want ye fer a husband?"

Niels smiled faintly at the insult and then glanced to Rory when he tapped his arm.

"Does Edith ken the wedding will take place today?" his brother asked.

Niels shook his head. "We did no' talk about when we should marry."

"Well, then mayhap ye should go warn her so she can prepare herself," Rory suggested.

"Prepare herself fer what?" he asked with a frown. "All she has to do is repeat the lines the priest says."

"Aye," Rory agreed patiently. "But she'll want to look pretty fer the occasion."

"She is always pretty," he said with a scowl. Actually, she was always beautiful. At least to him. Shrugging, he said, "'Twill be fine."

"Fine," Rory said with exasperation, getting to his feet. "I will go warn her meself. I need to get this broth to Effie anyway. 'Tis probably ice-cold, but she is no' likely to notice or care in her current—Where are ye going?" he asked with surprise.

"To tell Edith we're marrying today," Niels growled, heading for the stairs and adding under his breath, "Damned if I'm letting ye do it."

"Mayhap I should take a bath," Edith said, peering at herself with a frown now that her gown was off. She was filthy from rolling around in the bailey, her hands and arms and the lower part of her legs were all covered in mud. If her face was as bad, a bath was definitely in order.

"I ordered one soon as I saw the state ye were in," Moibeal assured her, looking over the mud stains on the gown Edith had been wearing.

"Oh." Edith smiled at the girl. "What would I do without ye, Moibeal?"

"Walk around all muddy with yer hair in a mess I should think," Moibeal said affectionately.

"No doubt," Edith agreed with amusement, moving to the basin of water on the bedside table to wash away the worst of the mud on her hands.

"I heard Lord Buchanan say that ye were to marry him," Moibeal commented after a moment. "Is it true?"

Edith stopped and glanced around at the question, something in the maid's voice catching her attention. But there was nothing in the girl's expression to explain the queer feeling she suddenly got.

"Aye," she said finally and turned back to the water.

"When is it to happen? Before or after Brodie returns?"

Edith paused in her scrubbing and frowned as she admitted, "I do no' ken. We did no' really talk about that."

She felt sure they should have talked about that. They really needed to marry ere Brodie returned or he might not allow it, and as much as she'd want to tell her brother to go stuff himself, she wouldn't be able to. He was now her laird, his decisions as good as law . . . if he was there to make them, she added the thought grimly.

Nay, they definitely needed to marry before he returned, she decided and whirled to hurry toward the door. "I should go talk to him about that."

"M'lady!" Moibeal squawked. "Ye're no' dressed."

"Oh," Edith muttered with exasperation, and then returned reluctantly to the water basin. Talking to Niels would have to wait until she was clean, dressed and looking less a wreck. He might have second thoughts about marrying her in her present state.

"If ye marry soon," Moibeal said after a moment, "do ye think we'll leave fer Buchanan right away?"

Edith stopped scrubbing at her skin again, her brow furrowing. "I . . . no, I'm sure we . . . Ye do no' think he'd want to leave right away, do ye?"

"If he wants to keep ye safe, aye," Moibeal said firmly. "And ye should want to go too. Ye were nearly killed today, and that poisoning business . . ." Her hand slid to her throat and she grimaced. "I only got a small dose o' it, and was ill fer only a day or two and 'twas miserable. Ye were in agony and seeing things and throwing up fer weeks. 'Tis a wonder ye survived. The sooner we leave here the better."

Edith turned to peer at the younger woman. Voice gentle, she said, "I can no' just abandon Drummond and all o' its people, Moibeal. And I can no' leave Brodie to return all unknowing to a murderer. Besides, who is to say the murderer would no' follow us?"

"What?" the maid squawked, apparently not having considered that.

Edith shrugged and pointed out, "Well, if they are determined to kill me too, they'll probably no' just give it up because I move house. At least here, we ken to expect it and can guard against it. At Buchanan we may ne'er see it coming."

Moibeal's mouth tightened and then she muttered, "A fat lot o' good it did kenning about it today when ye were nearly shot with an arrow."

"Aye," she admitted on a sigh and turned back to the water. "But we did no' expect that. The other attacks were poison, which is a sneaky, cowardly way to kill."

"Cawley was stabbed," Moibeal pointed out.

Edith grimaced. "Aye, but I suspect the killer snuck up on Cawley too. Probably while he was distracted, eating."

"Cawley was always distracted, eating," Moibeal said sadly.

"Aye." Edith swallowed. She really had been fond of the old man. Everyone had been really. At least she thought they had. Most of the people at Drummond had been kind to him, forever finding excuses to send him off to the kitchens, his favorite place. Jaimie hadn't seemed to mind his being there else they would have sent him elsewhere. A good cook was hard to find in Scotland, and Jaimie was one of the best. They wouldn't have risked losing him, but he'd always seemed fond of Cawley, smiling at his chatter as he worked.

"Anyway," Edith said now. "We've learned a lot about the killer already."

"Oh, aye," Moibeal agreed dryly, "To watch out fer poison, stabbing and flying arrows."

"That they are skilled at all three," Edith corrected solemnly.

Moibeal was silent for a minute and then asked, "And how does that help?"

"I should like to ken yer thoughts on that, meself."

Edith whirled to see Niels standing in the open door and instinctively squealed and tried to cover herself. Only realizing after she'd done it that it was a perfectly stupid thing to do. She was wearing her chemise, and he'd already seen every part of her without it. Good Lord, she'd stood bare inches from him, with naught but her gown twisted around her waist while he—

"Lord Buchanan!" Moibeal said with exasperation, hurrying to wrap Edith's gown around her shoulders. Moibeal, of course, did not think her modesty stupid, since she had no idea what they'd been up to.

Scowling, the maid moved in front of Edith once she'd grasped the edges of the gown and snapped, "Ye can no' jest enter a lady's bedchamber without knocking."

"Even if she's to be me wife?" he asked, closing the door and then crossing his arms over his chest as he leaned back against it.

"Ye're no' married *yet,* m'lord," Moibeal pointed out with some asperity.

"So, 'twill be all right in a couple o' hours, but no' now?" he asked with amusement.

"Exactly," Moibeal said, and then blinked and asked, "A couple o' hours?"

"A couple o' hours?" Edith echoed, stepping around Moibeal to better see him.

"Aye." He gave her a slow smile, his eyes sliding over her body. "Tormod's gone to talk to the priest. He said we'll be married by sup."

Recalling that her face was filthy and her hair a terrible mess, Edith turned quickly and began to splash water over her face and head. She would have liked to just stick her head in the basin of water, but while it was wide enough for the effort, it was not deep enough that she'd be able to submerge her face past her ears.

"Are ye going to tell me how it helps us that we ken the killer has used all three methods to try to kill yer family members?" Niels asked, taking away the small scrap of linen Edith had just picked up and begun to scrub her face with.

Of course, she jumped in surprise at both his words and his action. She hadn't even heard him cross the room.

"Hmm?" he asked, dipping the cloth in the basin

and then wringing out the worst of the water before starting to rub soap on the wet linen.

"Oh, aye," Edith murmured as he began to wash her face for her. Where she had scrubbed roughly, he was surprisingly gentle, but since the linen was quickly covered with mud, she supposed it must be working.

"Edith?" Niels queried and when she met his gaze in question, reminded her, "How does it help us that the killer has used the three different methods?"

"Oh," she sighed and then explained her thinking. "Well, it eliminates a lot o' people at Drummond as the culprit," she pointed out.

Niels smiled slowly and nodded, but Moibeal immediately asked, "How?"

Edith glanced to the girl and asked, "How many servants do you ken who know about weeds? Or where to stab to hit the heart? And who can shoot arrows straight enough to hit someone by the gates from this window?"

Moibeal moved to the window to peer out and pursed her lips. Turning back, though, she said, "I'll grant ye, few would be skilled enough to make a shot like that. But there are plenty about who ken enough about weeds to poison someone. And everyone kens the heart is in the center o' the chest."

"'Tis actually to the left o' center," Edith corrected. "It starts about midchest, but then goes left, with only a little on the right of center."

"Oh," Moibeal said with a frown. "Still, they may ha'e just got lucky in hitting the heart."

"Nay," Niels said, his voice slightly distracted as he worked at cleaning Edith's face. "The ribs are in the way. Ye have to strike at just the right angle to avoid their stopping the blade. Or slide it up under the ribs as happened with Cawley," he added grimly. "And the culprit kenned enough to leave the blade in."

"What difference does that make?" Moibeal asked curiously.

"The heart continues to beat at least for a little bit after being stabbed," Edith explained. "And doing so, it wounds itself further on the blade and there is no saving them."

"Oh," Moibeal said faintly.

"Ye ken a lot about such things, lass," Niels commented, dipping the linen in the basin to rinse it before returning to his work.

"Me mother was a healer," Edith said quietly. "She tended the people here as much as possible and taught me what she knew ere she died."

"And ye now heal those ye can?" Niels asked.

"Aye," Edith murmured, and then grimaced and added, "At least with birthings and wounds or injuries. I ken about healing weeds, but know little or nothing about the use o' poisonous weeds else I would have recognized that we were all poisoned and no' ill."

Niels nodded and then set the linen on the table next to the basin before cupping her face and meeting her gaze solemnly. "Are ye a'right with marrying me so quickly?"

"Aye," Edith said shyly, and then asked with concern, "Are you?"

"Oh, aye, m'lady. I am looking forward to it," Niels assured her in a voice that told her just what he was looking forward to.

Flushing, Edith tried to duck her head, but he held

her face in place and bent to kiss her. She was quite sure he meant it to be a swift, sweet meeting of lips, but the moment his mouth brushed across hers, Edith opened to him and he couldn't resist deepening the kiss. Sighing, Edith immediately released her hold on the gown wrapped around her shoulders like a shawl and slid her arms around his neck. She rose up on her tiptoes as she did, her body pressing eagerly against his.

Niels responded by letting his hands drop to clasp her bottom and lifting her slightly as he slid a leg between both of hers, so that she rode his thigh as he let her drop down a bit and then lifted her again. It brought a hungry groan from her and a loud, "Ahem!" from Moibeal.

Edith wasn't at all surprised when Niels broke their kiss with a small sigh and set her away from him.

Smiling crookedly, he promised, "Tonight."

"Aye," Edith breathed and then watched him leave the room.

"Gor!" Moibeal breathed, fanning herself as she closed the door behind him. "That man, m'lady!"

"Aye," Edith sighed, sinking to sit on the side of the bed.

"What I would no' give to be in yer slippers tonight," Moibeal said, shaking her head as she crossed back to collect the discarded gown from the floor. Straightening, she assured her, "That man is going to show ye pleasure like ye've never known."

"Aye," Edith agreed, and thought to herself that he already had. Niels had pleasured her twice already that day, while she had done nothing at all in return. She'd tried, but not knowing what she was doing . . .

"Moibeal?" she said, eyeing the girl determinedly.

"Aye, m'lady?" the maid asked, distracted as she began to brush at the dried mud on her gown, trying to remove the worst of it before actually washing it.

"Ye must tell me everything ye ken about pleasing a man," Edith said firmly.

Chapter 9

"WHAT?" MOIBEAL ASKED WEAKLY.

"Ye must tell me everything ye ken about pleasing a man," Edith repeated firmly, quite sure the girl would be shy about such a conversation.

"Me?" the maid asked with dismay.

"Well ye're more experienced than me, Moibeal. I ken ye and Kenny are . . . er . . . friendly," she said lamely.

"Aye, but . . ." The maid hesitated, and then nodded with a sigh and walked over to sit down next to her. "All right then, I'll tell ye what I ken. Which is no' much," she warned.

"It's still more than I ken," Edith pointed out.

Moibeal nodded acknowledgment of that and then looked thoughtful. "Well," she said finally, "men seem to like it standing up."

"Do they?" Edith asked with surprise. No one had mentioned that to her. She'd just assumed since it was called bedding that it was done in the bed. Lying down.

"They all seem to do it standing up," Moibeal pointed out. "Kenny is forever urging me up against a wall or tree, even a fence the one time."

"Hmm," Edith murmured and supposed it might be true. After all, animals did it standing up, well on all fours, but still on their feet. And the servants, serfs and soldiers she'd caught in the act on occasion seemed to be up against a wall or such too. And then there was Niels. In the meadow when he'd been touching her down *there*, he'd wanted her standing. He'd only had her kneel because her legs were shaking so badly and had obviously been about to collapse.

That thought made her frown as Edith wondered now if he'd been disappointed that she hadn't been able to remain standing.

"They seem to prefer it dark too," Moibeal added after a moment, obviously struggling to help her.

"Dark?" Edith straightened where she sat.

"Aye, well, when it's done, it seems always in a dark corner so I assume they prefer it that way," she pointed out.

"Oh, aye." Edith nodded and even sort of understood it. Niels's manhood had been a bit intimidating when she'd seen it . . . and kind of odd-looking at the same time, really. She supposed it was best not to have to see it. Although, he hadn't seemed to mind looking at her naked, she recalled. But perhaps he was just being polite and trying not to hurt her feelings, Edith thought and then glanced to Moibeal expectantly. When the maid merely stared back blankly, she asked, "What about kissing him and such below?"

"His bottom?" Moibeal asked with surprise.

"Nay, below in front," Edith said, blushing.

"Oh. *Oh!* Ye mean—" she raised her eyebrows up and down "—*there.*"

Edith hesitated. "I'm no' sure. By there do ye mean . . . *there*?"

"I mean his fiddle," Moibeal said with exasperation.

"Aye," Edith agreed, brightening. She should have thought to call it that herself. She'd heard her brothers refer to it as such. Saying things like, "The oafbrained bastard just stood there with his fiddle in hand and naught to say," and such.

"Well," Moibeal said, and Edith returned her attention to the maid to see that she was frowning. Expression apologetic, the girl admitted, "I've ne'er done that meself."

"Oh," Edith said with disappointment and admitted, "He did it to me and I thought to please him back that way, but was no' sure how."

"He did?" Moibeal asked breathlessly and then demanded, "When? Where?"

"In the meadow today," Edith admitted, flushing brightly, and then assured her, "He did no' take me innocence though."

Moibeal snorted. "Well, that's debatable."

"Nay. He said so. He said me maidenhead had no' been harmed," Edith assured her firmly.

"Hmm." Moibeal bit her lip and then asked, "What was it like?"

A small smile tugged at her lips as she recalled the experience and then Edith breathed, "It was heavenly. A revelation. I did no' ken such pleasure existed."

"Gor," Moibeal breathed.

"Aye," Edith said on a sigh. "And that's why I was

hoping to please him back the same way, but I do no' ken how."

The maid glanced down with a frown, and then sighed and said, "Well, while I've no' done it meself, Magda and Agnes were talking about it one day."

"Aye?" Edith asked hopefully, recognizing the names of a couple of the maids who worked in the kitchens.

"Aye. Agnes was complaining to Magda that her Donald was too big and she could no' get him all in her mouth without gagging, but he was always pushing in deep when he got excited," Moibeal explained.

Edith's eyes widened incredulously at the thought of putting Niels's manhood in her mouth. The man was huge. She'd surely gag too. She'd thought she would only be expected to kiss and lick him there as he had her. It seemed there was more to it than that though.

"So, Magda says as how Agnes should wrap her hand around him in front o' her mouth so as he can no' go in so far, but still feels like he is."

"Hand in front o' her mouth," Edith murmured, trying to imagine it.

"Aye, like this." Moibeal jumped up and grabbed the hairbrush from beside the basin, wrapped her hand around it just above the bristles and placed the uncovered handle in her mouth and then moved it in and out.

"All right." Edith nodded, she could do that.

Tossing the brush back on the table by the basin, Moibeal dropped onto the bed again and added, "And then Agnes said as how she'd try it, but she did no' like doing it anyway, as Donald's seed tasted bitter, especially when he drank too much."

Edith's eyes widened. She would get his seed in her mouth? That was not something she'd expected. And what if Niels's seed was bitter too? She wouldn't want to offend him by spitting it out. That thought made her worry about what she'd tasted like to Niels. Had she tasted bitter too? Worried now, she asked, "Did Magda ha'e any advice about that?"

"Aye." Moibeal nodded. "Magda said as how a dollop o' Jaimie's fruit preserves would fix that right up."

"I see," Edith breathed, wondering if it would work for the woman's taste as well . . . just in case.

"And that's all I ken on that subject," Moibeal said apologetically.

"'Tis fine." Edith patted her hand. "'Tis more than I kenned before."

They both glanced to the door when a knock sounded.

"That'll be yer bath," Moibeal said, standing up.

"Aye." Edith stood as well, but caught the maid's arm before she could go answer it and said, "Do no' do it now, but ere the bedding, mayhap ye should bring up some o' Jaimie's preserves for me."

"Aye." Moibeal nodded solemnly. "I'll no' forget."

"Thank ye," Edith murmured and released her so the girl could answer the door.

"WOULD YE CARE FER SOMETHING ELSE TO DRINK, lass?" Niels asked Edith gently, noting that she'd hardly touched her mead and was simply sitting there looking lost in thought. And fretful thoughts too, it seemed, if one was to guess by her expression as she looked over the great hall full of people celebrating their wedding.

"Nay. Thank ye." Edith managed a smile, and then said, "Actually, m'lord, I think I might like to go prepare fer bed."

"As ye wish," Niels said and stood up at once, more than happy to retire, early as it was.

"Nay." She patted his hand, her smile a little strained. "Finish yer ale, m'lord. I would have a moment alone to prepare meself anyway."

Niels hesitated, wanting to assure her there was no preparation necessary, but it was her wedding night and if she wished a moment alone, he would grant her that, he decided, and nodded. "Go along, then. I'll no' be long . . . wife," he tagged on at the end with a smile.

Edith returned his smile and squeezed his arm, and then murmured, "Thank ye . . . husband."

They grinned at each other briefly, and then she squeezed his arm again and turned to head for the stairs as Niels sank slowly back onto his seat. He watched her until she'd disappeared along the upper landing. He then elbowed Rory to get his attention.

Breaking off his conversation with Tormod, the younger man turned to him in question. "What?"

"Did Edith look pale to ye?" Niels asked with a frown. "She seemed quiet and a touch pale to me." When Rory raised an eyebrow and glanced around for the woman in question, Niels added, "She's gone above stairs to prepare fer bed."

"Oh." Rory peered toward the stairs, but said, "I did no' notice her looking pale. She did seem a bit quiet though," he admitted and then shrugged. "But 'tis her wedding day. She's most like nervous about tonight . . . unless ye already—"

"Nay," Niels interrupted firmly. "I have no' bedded

her. I wished to wait until I had her wedded all good and proper."

"Well, then there ye have it," Rory said reassuringly. "No doubt she is simply nervous o' what is to come tonight. She is fine."

"Aye," Niels muttered, and Rory turned back to Tormod, leaving Niels to fret. He supposed it could just be nerves Edith was suffering, but she'd been fine during the ceremony. It hadn't been until they'd sat down to eat that she'd seemed to go quiet and pale. Besides, he'd rather hoped that what they'd done in the meadow might have lessened her anxiety about the bedding somewhat. Although, as he'd told her himself, he hadn't taken her maidenhead that morning, so there was still that to contend with and he knew that could hurt greatly for some women. She probably knew it too, he supposed. Niels took another drink of ale, and then eyed the liquid in his goblet, measuring how many more swallows he would have to take before he could go above stairs. By his guess, he had six or seven swallows left. Not so much, he assured himself, setting down the goblet briefly.

"Oy!" Alick said, slapping his back as he dropped to sit on the bench next to him. "When do we get to cart ye up to the bedchamber, strip ye and throw ye in bed with Edith?"

"Yer no' doing that," Niels assured him firmly.

"Oh, come now, brother," Geordie chided, settling next to Alick. "A wedding is no' a wedding without a bedding ceremony."

"Mayhap, but out o' respect to her father and brothers who have no' been dead a full month, Edith and I decided to bypass the bedding ceremony," Niels announced, lying through his teeth. He hadn't talked to Edith about the bedding ceremony. He hadn't even thought about it until Alick had just brought it up, but recalling Edith's quiet, pale face, he had no intention of putting her through that.

"Oh, aye," Alick said now, sounding much more subdued. "In truth I forgot about that."

"'Tis easy to forget," Geordie said quietly. "Other than the way she fell apart when Cawley died, Edith has handled everything like a soldier."

"She's no' had the chance to grieve," Rory said, turning to join the conversation now. "They died and Edith immediately was terribly ill, and then she recovered only to have to nurse her maid, and then was ill and recovered again to discover her family was murdered. In truth, the lass has had little opportunity to deal with any o' the upsets to her life o' late." Eyeing Niels seriously, he said, "She'll need to do that soon, Niels. Else it will all hit her at once and may crush her."

"Aye," Niels muttered, frowning. He couldn't imagine anything crushing Edith. Her strength in dealing with everything was one of the things he admired most about her.

"Well, if we're no' having a bedding ceremony, why are ye still down here?" Geordie asked, changing the subject.

"Because Edith asked for a moment to prepare herself fer bed ere I join her," Niels admitted, and then added, "Unfortunately, I'm no' sure how long that is."

"Well, since her maid is coming down the stairs, I suspect that would be this long," Rory murmured, looking past Niels toward the stairs.

Turning abruptly, he spotted Moibeal halfway down the stairs and stood at once. The moment he did, the maid glanced to him, smiled and gave a slight nod. Taking that as an indication that Edith was ready for him, Niels grabbed up his ale, gulped down the last of it and slammed the goblet down on the table.

"Good sleep," he muttered to everyone in general and then headed for the stairs. He wanted to run, but didn't. He made himself move at a sedate pace that was in total contrast to the rapid beating of his heart as he finally allowed himself to think on all the things he planned to do to Edith tonight. Niels had been refusing to allow himself that luxury all afternoon and evening through the talk with the priest, the ceremony and the meal. Mostly because he'd feared if he thought too much on it, he'd have dragged Edith straight from the ceremony to her bedchamber, and he'd wanted her to enjoy the celebration of their marriage.

Now, though, that danger was past and he let himself contemplate all the things he could do to her in an effort to select the ones he would do that night. He wanted to taste her again, the lass had been sweet as honey on his tongue and he wanted that again. He'd give her pleasure that way, he decided, and then caress her to pleasure a second time to ensure she was good and ready for when he breached her. Hopefully, that might minimize the pain for her somewhat. He'd have to be careful with her, o' course, this being her first time. He'd take her in the bed in the traditional manner first, and then if it did no' pain her much as he hoped, and if he did no' spill his seed right away as he feared he would when her sweet heat closed over him, he'd try different positions to find the one they both liked best.

For some reason Niels was liking the idea of having her in front of him, his hands clasping her breasts as he slid in and out of her. That image had him going hard as stone so that his plaid suddenly had a notable bulge. Ignoring it, he thought that he'd let Edith try riding him as well, to see if she liked it . . . mayhap on the bed, or even on one of the chairs in the room . . . or both. Then, if it was no' yet morning, he might take her on the fur in front of the fire, the flames warming them and casting shadows in the room as he explored her body and then claimed her again, this time with her feet on his shoulders so he could plunge deep inside her while caressing the nub at her sweet center until she was begging him for her release.

Niels had reached the door to the bedchamber they would share now, and raised a hand to knock, but then lowered it and simply reached for the handle. She was expecting him after all.

Opening the door, he took one step into the room and then paused as he saw that it was nearly completely dark with naught but dying embers in the fireplace.

"Edith?" he said uncertainly.

"Over here, m'lord husband."

Turning in the direction of her voice, he squinted and could just make out her figure in the darkness. After the briefest hesitation, he closed the door and then started to move cautiously toward her. "Why is it so dark in here, lass?"

"Do ye no' like it?" she asked, sounding anxious. "Moibeal said men seemed to prefer to perform the consummation in the dark."

Niels blinked at her use of the formal term for the bedding, but asked with confusion, "Moibeal?"

"Me maid," she explained. "I wanted to pleasure

ye this night as ye did me in the meadow so asked her advice. She's more experienced at these things than me," she explained almost apologetically.

"Ah," Niels murmured, shifting to the right as his hip bumped into what he thought was one of the chairs in the room. Touched that she wanted to please him, but a little concerned by the advice she may have been given, he asked, "And what else did she say?"

"That men prefer to perform the bedding standing up," she admitted. "I thought this was a good spot. That way if me knees go weak again like they did in the meadow I can lean against the wall and brace me hand on this table so ye'll no' be disappointed."

Niels stopped walking and frowned at her words. She had in no way disappointed him that day and he didn't like that she thought she might have. He also didn't like not being able to see her as they talked.

"Ye did no' disappoint me in the meadow," he said firmly, changing direction and moving toward the glow of the dying fire. "And I do no' prefer to love ye in the dark. I would see yer face while I pleasure ye."

Dropping to his haunches by the fire, he grabbed several pieces of wood and began to build up the fire. Fortunately, the embers were hot enough that he soon had it roaring back to life. Straightening then, he grabbed the candles from the small ledges built into the wall on either side of the fireplace and lit them from the flames. Setting them back on their respective ledges, he finally turned to find Edith and nearly swallowed his tongue. The woman made quite a sight standing next to the small table she'd mentioned, completely naked but for the shadows cast by the dancing flames.

Blushing now that he was looking at her in the

light, Edith tried to cover her breasts and the thatch of hair between her legs with her hands.

Already hard from his imaginings on the way up here, Niels grew harder still at the sight of her and was hard put not to cross the room, yank up his tartan and take her there against the wall as she had apparently expected. Forcing himself to remain still, he cleared his throat and said, "And the reason most o' the men take their women standing up in dark corners is because 'tis the only privacy they can find no' having a bedchamber."

"Oh," Edith said, blinking, and then she asked uncertainly, "Would ye prefer the bed then?"

"Aye," he growled.

Nodding, she turned and hurried to the bed, but stopped abruptly before climbing onto it and swung back to wave him over.

Niels hesitated a moment, but then walked over to join her. The moment she could reach him, Edith grabbed his arm and urged him to turn with his back to the bed, then quickly began to work on the pin that held his tartan in place.

"Lass," he said catching her hands. "What are ye doing?"

"I want to please ye," she said shyly, shaking his hands off and returning her efforts to his pin.

Niels frowned and almost told her it wasn't necessary, but she managed to undo the pin just then and his tartan fell away at once to drop to the floor. When Edith then caught the bottom of his shirt and began to tug it up, Niels helped lift it off and even tossed it aside. He started to reach for her then, but gasped instead and reached behind him as she suddenly shoved him in the chest and he fell to sit on the bed.

"There," she said with satisfaction. "Now I can pleasure ye as ye did me."

Niels's eyes widened when Edith spread his legs and dropped to kneel between his still-booted feet, but then she just as quickly popped back to her feet and rushed away, muttering, "I almost forgot."

His eyes followed her curiously, but then dropped to her behind and got caught there as he watched the full round globes shift as she walked. His gaze did not lift when she stopped briefly at the table by the fire and then turned to head back. Instead, it focused on the spot between her legs that he was eager to explore and stayed there, until she suddenly stopped in front of him and dropped to her knees again. Her breasts were immediately in his line of vision and he sighed as he tried to decide what he wanted to touch, caress, lick and taste first. Should he suckle her breasts first or throw her on the bed and dive between her legs where her sweetness waited? Or perhaps he should just lick her all over and—

His thoughts died on a gasp and his gaze shot down to himself as Edith suddenly took his fiddle in hand. It was not a tentative caress or touch, it was a firm, no-nonsense grasping and pulling his erection down so that it pointed straight between her breasts. Even more surprising though, was the fact that even as he looked down she began to pour what looked like some kind of cooked fruit in a sauce on his fiddle.

"Er . . . Edith?" he said uncertainly. "What are ye doing?"

"Agnes does no' like to pleasure Donald with her mouth because she says his seed is bitter," she said.

"Ah . . ." Niels's face scrunched up as he tried to understand what that had to do with what she was doing.

And then she continued, "But Magda said a dollop o' Jaimie's preserves would take the taste away, so I thought I'd try it. No' that I think ye might taste bitter," she added earnestly, lifting her pale face to look at him. "But just in case. Ye ken?"

Lowering her head, she added, "I could no' ask ye if I taste bitter because ye were no' here, so I put some on meself as well in case I tasted bitter to ye earlier."

Niels simply stared at the top of her head, a confusion of responses rolling through his head. First, he suspected Magda, whoever she was, had meant that Agnes, whoever *she* was, should *eat* a dollop o' preserves to rid herself of the taste. He highly doubted there was a fellow named Donald walking about Drummond with preserves on his fiddle. Second, he was having trouble getting past the idea that Edith was presently kneeling in front of him with preserves smeared all over her quoniam. He would definitely have to lick every last drop of that off her ere doing anything else he wanted to do, so it was good he'd decided to start by pleasuring her with his mouth and tongue first, Niels decided.

Above all of that, however, was the image in his mind of Edith's face when she'd lifted it and he'd seen it by firelight. While he'd thought her pale below stairs, she was dead white now and he'd caught a flicker of discomfort on her face before she'd ducked it to continue to dump cooked fruit on his cock.

Concern struggled briefly with desire for the upper hand, but won easily and Niels leaned forward intending to catch her chin, lift it and ask if she felt all right. But before his fingers could reach her, she finished dressing his fiddle in fruit and popped the tip into her mouth to begin licking and sucking the sweet off.

Niels froze, his mouth opening and closing and his body almost lifting off the bed as he was hit by sensation after sensation. By Satan's warty prick! The woman was—God's teeth! Did she—? By the Virgin, she—

Closing his eyes briefly, he tried to regain control of himself, but he simply couldn't and opened his eyes again almost at once. Edith obviously didn't have a lick of skill at what she was attempting, but she was enthusiastic as hell as she conscientiously removed every last drop of the preserves she'd just applied. And damned if just the sight of her kneeling there with his cock in her mouth wasn't near to killing him with excitement.

Niels had barely had the thought about her lack of skill when Edith stopped removing the preserves she'd put on and began to move her mouth up and down his length in a rhythmic manner with her hand leading. It was a rhythm he recognized, three strokes and a slight pause and then three more repeated over and over. Niels recognized it because it was how he played the fiddle as a rule, and how he'd played it that morning in the meadow as he'd given her pleasure the second time. He'd noted her watching a time or two, but apparently, the clever minx had been paying more attention than he'd realized.

And unless Moibeal had advised her on the mechanics of grasp and whatnot, Edith appeared to be a natural, he noted as a groan slid from his lips. She was holding him firmly with both lips and hand, but not too tightly. She was also being careful to avoid grazing him with her teeth, which he would thank God for later, Niels decided as he drew close to the point of exploding and his body began to tighten and strain toward it.

Niels was about to warn her that he was about to spill his seed so that she could remove her mouth if she wished, when Edith suddenly froze. Blinking his eyes open, he glanced to her just in time to see the confusion and panic on her face as she began to heave and then puke up preserves all over his prick.

Jaw dropping, Niels gaped at her briefly, and then reached forward with concern when she suddenly toppled over and lay on the floor convulsing and heaving and bringing up the rest of what she'd eaten that day.

"Edith!" Niels cried, lunging off the bed to kneel beside her. Grabbing her shoulders, he held her until she'd finished purging and then rolled her on her back. Peering at her pale, unconscious face with both concern and confusion, he brushed her hair away from her cheeks, and then did what he'd seen Rory do several times and lifted her eyelids. His head jerked back at once as if from a blow as Niels noted that her eyes were dilated. It was how they'd been when they'd first arrived at Drummond and Rory had seemed to see that as an indication that she'd been poisoned. Recalling that, Niels felt his heart lodge itself somewhere in his throat.

Scooping her up off the floor, he carried her around to lay her in the bed, and then turned and rushed to the door, his boots thumping as grimly as the thoughts in his head at that moment. Tugging the door open, Niels rushed out and up the hall to the top of the stairs, bellowing for Rory.

Chapter 10

"AYE. POISON. AS YE THOUGHT," RORY SAID grimly. Straightening from examining Edith, he turned to Niels and opened his mouth to say more, only to pause briefly with his mouth open and eyes wide, before saying with disgust, "Put some clothes on, brother, or at least clean the puke off your cock. Good Lord!"

Glancing down at the mess covering his groin, Niels scowled and then turned sharply and moved to the basin to begin cleaning himself as he asked, "Is she going to be all right?"

"I'm hoping so, aye," Rory said, turning back to Edith.

"When we first got here ye said was she poisoned again she could die," Niels reminded him grimly.

"Aye. If she'd been poisoned again at that time she surely would have died," he assured him. "But she's been eating well and rebuilding her strength since she woke up. And she seems to have tossed up the poison. Or at least I think she has. She certainly tossed up everything I know her to have eaten today. And some I did no' ken about," he added dryly before asking. "Did Jaimie make more pastries with preserves in them? I do no' recall her eating cooked fruit."

"Nay. She had that up here," Niels muttered as he finished cleaning himself and moved to grab his shirt and pull it on over his head. Walking to the foot of the bed now, he bent and picked up the goblet the preserves had been in and handed it to Rory. "Was the poison in this?"

Rory took the goblet, sniffed it delicately and then stuck a finger in and licked it to taste the preserves. After a moment, he shook his head.

"I do no' think it was in this," he said, setting the goblet on the bedside table as a knock sounded at the door.

Niels moved to answer it, his eyes widening when he saw that it was Tormod, Geordie and Alick. When he saw that his brothers carried Edith's trencher and drink from their celebratory dinner, he frowned and asked, "What's that for?"

"I recalled ye mentioning that Edith seemed quiet and pale at dinner and wondered if the poison might have been in her food or drink at sup," Rory explained, moving to join him at the door.

Niels frowned as he watched him sniff at the remains of food in the trencher and pointed out, "We ate out of the same trencher and I'm no' ill. It can no' be the food."

Nodding, Rory handed the trencher back to Geordie and took the mead from Alick to sniff. The way he immediately stiffened made Niels narrow his eyes.

"Poison?" Tormod asked grimly.

"Aye, this smells like the tonic Victoria left behind," Rory murmured, sniffing again.

"I thought that was all gone," Geordie said with a frown.

"Aye. 'Twas," Rory said grimly. "Obviously, someone made more."

"So Victoria's tonic was the source of the poison?" Niels asked grimly.

"I think so. But now as then 'tis hard to tell. The smell is very faint this time, but still carries the scent of several herbs," Rory said, and then peered at the nearly full glass and said, "It does no' appear Edith drank much of this. That is something anyway."

"But how did it get in the mead?" Geordie asked. "'Tis from the pitcher I got from the cask here in this room. The fresh cask we opened on arriving. 'Twas supposed to be safe. And I watched the pitcher I fetched every moment until ye and Edith went above stairs."

"Except when we were at the wedding down at the church," Alick pointed out. "Ye left it on the table then."

Geordie shook his head. "Nay. If I could have taken it down to the ceremony outside the church I would have, but I could no' so I dumped that pitcher and fetched fresh from the cask in here when we got back."

"The cask in here," Niels said slowly, turning to look at the cask in question. It sat on the table along the wall where Edith had been waiting for him naked in the dark. As Rory walked toward it, Niels reminded them, "The killer shot an arrow at Edith from this room just before noon."

Geordie stared at him blankly and then turned to watch Rory sniff the liquid in the open cask. When he set it down, turned a grim face to them and nodded, Geordie cursed. "I'm sorry, brother. I did no' think about the killer being in here and what they may ha'e done."

Niels shook his head wearily. "Nay, neither did I. And I should ha'e. I guess I was just so distracted with the wedding and everything . . ."

He turned to peer at Edith in the bed. She looked so small and frail under the linens and furs Rory had pulled over her. And it was his fault. He'd failed to protect her. He wouldn't do so again.

"I'm taking her to Buchanan the minute she wakes up," he announced firmly, moving to the bed to sit on the edge of it and brush her hair away from her face.

"Aye. Mayhap 'tis for the best," Tormod said sadly. "I shall be sorry to see her go, but ye may have a better chance o' keeping her alive there. Even does the killer follow . . . well, surely yer people would ken if a stranger was in their midst. So there ye'd only have to worry about stray arrows when she went outside."

Niels stiffened at the words, knowing they were true. She wouldn't be completely safe even at Buchanan. Not if the killer was determined to get at her. But she'd be safer at least . . . if he could get her to stay inside the keep. Somehow, he suspected that wasn't likely.

"I should go below and see if any more o' the men I sent out have returned with news o' Brodie," Tormod muttered, moving toward the door. "Only one has returned so far and two o' the keeps I sent men to were close enough they should have got there and back today." Pausing at the door, he glanced back and said, "Let me know when she wakes, or—" Mouth tightening, he changed his mind about whatever he'd been about to say and said instead, "Just let me know when she wakes."

He didn't wait for a response before leaving the room. Niels heard his brothers talking in soft murmurs by the door, but didn't bother trying to listen. He suspected they were discussing who would return to Buchanan with him and who would stay. He already knew Rory would be unwilling to leave just yet with Effie still unconscious. He suspected Geordie and Alick would escort Edith and him home to Buchanan to help him make sure she arrived there safely, but then would return until Rory was ready to give up on the old maid and leave.

When the door closed softly, he glanced around to see that Geordie and Alick had left. As Rory walked back toward him, Niels asked, "Should I be making broth to dribble down her throat?"

"Nay. Wait and see if she wakes up come morning," Rory said. "There is naught to do fer now . . . except perhaps to clean her up."

"Clean her up?" Niels asked with bewilderment, turning to peer at Edith's pale but clean face. He'd washed away the mess as he'd waited for Rory to reach the room. Edith was clean.

"She was naked and uncovered on the linens when I came in earlier," Rory reminded him.

"Aye?" Niels said with bewilderment. Not understanding what that had to do with anything.

"Well, her legs were no' quite closed and I noticed she has what appears to be preserves seeping out from between her legs. Ye may want to clean that up so she does no' wake up and find her thighs stuck together with the sticky mess," he said as if he was talking about the time of day. Giving up his insouciance then, he asked, "It was on ye too when I entered. What the devil were the two o' ye doing up here to get preserves on her quoniam?"

Niels merely shook his head and moved to fetch the

basin and damp linen from the table to wash the preserves away. This wasn't how he'd imagined removing
it when Edith had mentioned that she'd applied it. But
then nothing about his wedding night had gone as he'd
planned.

EDITH WOKE TO LOUD SNORING AND SOMETHING
heavy across her chest. Opening her eyes, she looked
around with confusion, only to still as her gaze landed
on Niels. He lay on top of the linens and furs in only
his shirt and boots, while she was naked beneath the
warm bed coverings.

She stared at him for a moment as the memories of
the night before slid over her, and then grimaced and
closed her eyes again, quite sure she simply could not
face the day ahead. Or at least her husband. Dear God,
her efforts to please him had ended in a miserable failure, and the poor man must now wonder if marrying
her had not been a huge mistake.

Another snore sounded beside her and Edith opened
her eyes to survey the room as it occurred to her that if
she continued to lay there she would definitely have to
face Niels sooner rather than later. Whereas, if she got
up and found some chore to attend somewhere else,
like say down in the village, well, she might be able to
avoid the humiliation of having to face him for hours.
Perhaps even until the sup.

That thought was enough to have her sliding sideways in the bed, easing her way out from under his
arm and hand. Niels stirred only once during this op-
eration and Edith froze and waited a heartbeat until
he issued another snore, and then continued sideways
until she was free to sit up and get out of bed.

Hurrying to her chest, she took the first gown she touched and tugged it on over her head as she rushed to the door. Edith eased it open, and then slipped out. She was careful to pull it silently closed, and then began to walk away before bothering to do up the gown's laces.

"M'lady!"

Edith stopped abruptly and glanced around to see her maid rushing toward her.

"What are ye doing up, m'lady?" the girl asked with exasperation, grabbing her arm and turning her back toward the room. "Ye should still be abed. Ye were very sick last night. Ye nearly died . . . again," she added on an irritated note.

"I am fine," Edith assured her, digging her heels in as the girl tried to drag her back to the room she'd just escaped. "'Twas just a bit o' a stomach upset. But I feel fine this morning," she assured her maid, tugging her arm free.

"Stomach upset?" Moibeal asked with amazement and then shook her head. "Nay. 'Twas poison again, m'lady. Did yer lord husband no' tell ye?"

The maid sounded vexed that Niels had failed to impart such important information, so despite Edith's shock at yet again being poisoned, she said faintly, "Nay, he is still sleeping."

Moibeal blinked and, just like that, the irritation at the man turned instantly to compassion for him. "Oh, aye, and no doubt. The poor man was up most o' the night watching over ye," she said sympathetically. "He was still pacing about at dawn when I came to yer room to check on ye. He looked exhausted then and I said as how he should lay down, that ye'd surely rouse him when ye woke up." She scowled at Edith now. "Which ye obviously did no' do, so ye can just turn around and march back in there and—"

"Nay!" Edith snapped, tugging her arm free when the girl tried to strong-arm her back the way she'd come. "If he is exhausted I should let him rest," she added less sharply, and was relieved to see the words make the maid pause. Hoping to distract her further, she asked, "Are ye sure 'twas poison? My stomach was bothering me at the sup, but I thought it just nerves about the bedding to come," she admitted.

"Oh, nay, 'twas no' nerves," Moibeal assured her. Frowning as she noted that Edith's laces were undone, the maid began to untangle them as she explained. "They sorted out that it was poison in yer mead. They figure the killer must have dosed the cask in yer room when they were in there shooting arrows at ye."

"'Twas only one arrow," Edith muttered.

Ignoring that, Moibeal added, "And Lord Rory said 'twas just a good thing ye only had a couple sips at sup, as he thinks the killer has changed the poison and increased the dosage in the hopes o' finishing ye off. He thinks if ye'd had more than a couple sips, ye'd ha'e died ere ye could bring it back up. 'Tis lucky ye've such a sensitive stomach and puked it all out."

"That is debatable," Edith said under her breath, recalling the event. If she'd been truly lucky, she would have done it after pleasuring Niels, not all over him in the middle of it.

Ignoring that as well, the maid said quietly, "This latest attempt upset Lord Niels something fierce, and he said as how he plans to take ye away from here today when ye wake."

"Away?" Edith asked with surprise. "To where?"

"To Buchanan," she said solemnly. "'Tis obvious he cares fer ye and wants ye safe . . . and so do I, m'lady," she added quietly.

Edith frowned. "But Brodie is no' back yet."

"Not yet," Moibeal agreed mildly. "But Tormod sent men out yesterday after the incident with the arrow. Each carried a message from him about what has been happening here, telling him that 'twas no' illness but murder, and asking him to return."

Edith bit her lip at this news, wondering why no one had bothered to mention it to her. She supposed what with the unexpected wedding and everything it might have been forgotten. On the other hand, it didn't really matter anyway. She wasn't at all sure Brodie would be any more likely to return if he knew there was a murderer at Drummond killing off members of their family than he had been willing to stay when he'd thought it just illness.

"There, 'tis done," Moibeal said quietly, finishing with the laces and stepping away.

"Thank ye," Edith murmured and turned back to continue toward the stairs.

Her maid sighed at once and followed. "Ye ken if yer lord husband wishes to leave today, we need to pack yer chests and—"

"We'll worry about that when he wakes up," Edith interrupted. "If he was up all night fretting over me, he needs his sleep."

"Besides which, yer thinking o' refusing to go, are ye no'?" Moibeal asked dryly, and then pointed out,

"But he's yer husband now, and ye ken the choice is no longer yers."

Edith stopped walking and turned to stare at her. "What?"

"I feared ye had no' thought on that," Moibeal said with a sigh, and then straightened her shoulders and said, "Me lady, yer father was as kind and indulgent with ye as he was with Brodie. He let ye run the keep as ye wished, and allowed ye to visit Lady Saidh and Jo as the mood struck ye, but—"

"Are ye suggesting I'm as spoiled as Brodie?" Edith interrupted with dismay.

"Nay," Moibeal said at once. "Ye've always been a hard worker and concerned with the welfare o' the people here, while Brodie cared only fer himself and his pleasure. But yer father gave ye freedoms many women do no' have," she added solemnly. "If ye did no' wish to do something or go somewhere, he did no' make ye. But he could have. It was his right . . . and now 'tis yer lord husband's right. If he wishes ye to go to Buchanan, ye've no choice but to go."

Edith narrowed her eyes at those words, knowing they were true, but not pleased by them. Giving an annoyed "hrrmph," she turned to continue on to the stairs, her mind racing with ideas of how to get her own way and stay until Brodie returned. She was half-way down the stairs to the great hall when it occurred to her that thinking that way might be more like her brother than she'd like to admit.

The idea brought her up short, but then her mind immediately rejected that suggestion. Her brother would not have cared about the well-being of the people here, and that was the reason she was wanting to stay until Brodie returned. It wasn't for herself, she pointed out and released a relieved sigh and started walking again.

"Yer up. How do ye feel?"

Edith looked up at that comment and forced a smile when she saw Rory approaching from the kitchens. It wasn't that she wasn't happy to see him . . . but she wasn't. She was afraid that, knowing that Niels wanted to take her away from Drummond today, the man might go wake his brother, and she wasn't ready for that. She needed a plan to avoid having to follow through with her husband's plan.

"I feel fine, m'lord. Thank ye," Edith murmured.

"Please, call me Rory," he said with amusement. "We are family now."

She blinked in surprise at that. Silly as it seemed, it hadn't occurred to her that marrying Niels meant she now had six new brothers. And Saidh was her sister now, at least in law, she realized and beamed at the man. "Thank ye, Rory. And ye must call me Edith."

He smiled and nodded, and then glanced toward the stairs. "Where is Niels?"

Edith hesitated, but then took a deep breath and said, "He is sleeping, and I thought it best to let him rest since he was apparently up most o' the night worrying over me."

"Aye, he was, but . . ." Rory looked toward the stairs again and then to Moibeal. When his eyes narrowed on her maid, Edith noted the disapproval on the girl's face. Apparently, he had no trouble sorting out what might be behind that disapproval, because when he finally turned his gaze back to her, he said solemnly, "I'm guessing Moibeal mentioned that Niels wants to take ye away to Buchanan today."

Edith hesitated, trying to marshal a sensible argument for why they shouldn't do that.

Before she could, Rory continued, "And I ken that must be frightening."

She blinked at the suggestion.

"Leaving the home ye've always known fer a new one full o' strangers is no doubt a daunting prospect," he said solemnly, "But 'tis fer the best. 'Twill be safer fer ye, as well as the people here."

"The people here?" Edith asked with surprise.

"Well, we've been fortunate so far. At least somewhat. Moibeal survived the poison meant fer ye, and is healthy and well again. Effie I begin to think will no' survive, however, but at least we got lucky yesterday and no one was behind ye when ye bent over and the arrow sailed past ye missing its mark. Had Niels or Tormod or anyone else been behind ye, they may have taken the arrow in yer stead. Even Ronson could have if ye'd picked him up on the saddle with ye, or if the shooter's aim had been off."

Edith was sagging under the realization that he was right when Rory added, "And then there is last eve's mead incident."

She glanced at him sharply. "What of it? No one else drank it, did they?"

"Nay. But we almost did. Geordie fetched it right after the arrow incident and was going to pour each o' us some when ye went above stairs to clean up. But Tormod said he'd rather have ale, and the rest o' us thought that sounded fine and we'd leave the mead fer you. Had we no' done that, Geordie, Alick, Tormod, Niels and I would all probably be dead now."

"Dear God," Edith breathed, dropping to sit on the bench at the table.

"Aye," Rory said grimly. "We got lucky. Next time we may not. 'Twill be safer fer everyone once Niels gets ye away from here. It may even help reveal the killer."

Blinking at that, she glanced up. "How?"

"Well, if they are determined to finish what they've started and kill ye too, they'd have to follow ye to Buchanan," he pointed out. "They'd reveal themselves did they do that."

"Oh, aye," Edith breathed and shook her head. Yesterday, she'd argued to Moibeal that leaving Drummond wouldn't leave her any safer since the killer could follow. Now Rory had turned that argument against her. If the killer followed, they'd surely be recognized as the killer. And if she stayed, she could be putting others at risk.

Edith couldn't believe that hadn't occurred to her. Or perhaps she could, because while she hadn't realized it before Rory had suggested it, she was anxious about leaving Drummond. It had been her home all her life. It was the only home she knew, and these were her people. She'd grown up with them around her and couldn't imagine her life without them. But she would have to. All girls had to grow up, marry and move away from the people they loved. Well, not all she supposed, thinking of Murine. She now lived in her childhood home with her husband, Dougall, but few women got that lucky.

"Well," Moibeal said brightly. "Then I suppose I should go up and start in packing fer the trip."

"I had best go wake my husband first," Edith said on a sigh and stood.

"Nay," Rory said at once. When Edith glanced to him with surprise, he grimaced and said, "Niels can be a bit hard to wake in the mornings and cantankerous when he's tired. I shall stop in and wake him on my way to feed Effie some more soup. The two o' ye can go up and start packing once he comes down. That way ye can break yer fast while ye wait," he added, and then cautioned. "Only eat what yer cook says is safe. And make sure they open a fresh cask o' whatever ye want to drink."

"Aye," Edith muttered, but as she watched Rory turn to head above stairs, she thought it might be better if she simply not eat or drink anything until they'd left. She was sick of being sick.

NIELS WOKE TO A LOUD CRASH AND LUNGED upward in bed, glancing wildly to Edith, only to find she was no longer beside him. Turning his gaze around the room in search of her, he found his brother Rory instead. The man was leaning against the closed door, a satisfied smile on his face.

"Where's Edith?" Niels growled by way of greeting, and Rory pushed himself away from the door with a smile and started across the room.

"She's below, waiting fer ye to wake up so that she and her maid can start packing."

"Packing?" he asked with surprise.

"Aye. Her maid told her ye planned to take her to Buchanan and I convinced her it was fer the best."

"Ye did?" Niels asked with surprise. Last night as they'd sat by the bed, he'd mentioned his worries that Edith would argue leaving or even refuse, but he hadn't expected his brother to intervene.

"Aye," Rory said, sounding pretty pleased with himself. "And then I helped ye further by convincing her to let me wake ye when she said she would."

"How was that helping me?" he asked with bewilderment.

"Because I'm quite sure had she come up here to wake ye, the two o' ye would have ended up rolling around in bed all day and not left until tomorrow," he said dryly.

Niels stilled at the suggestion, his mind captured by the idea. They hadn't yet even consummated the wedding, he realized. Technically, that meant they were not even married, did it not? He wasn't sure, but really, should they take the risk? After all, if they encountered Brodie before consummating, he might be able to have the marriage annulled or something. Nodding, he began, "Mayhap—"

"Nay," Rory said firmly.

"Nay, what?" Niels asked with surprise. "I have no' said anything yet."

"Ye were about to point out that the wedding was no' consummated and suggest that ye should stay another day so ye could see to it," Rory said without a lick of doubt. "Ye probably e'en managed to put together some argument that her brother may have the wedding called invalid did ye encounter him before ye consummated it."

"Damn, brother, ye ken me well," Niels said with amusement.

"Aye," Rory agreed. "And I ken that ye'd never forgive yerself did ye stay that extra day and end up widowed all fer a chance to swive yer wife."

"Aye, I would," Niels agreed unhappily, and tossed the linens and furs aside to get out of bed.

"Besides, Brodie could no' prove the marriage was no' consummated," Rory commented suddenly.

Niels snorted at the suggestion as he grabbed his shirt off the floor and pulled it on. Once his head cleared the collar, he said, "I think the fact that she was poisoned and sick as can be would probably give that away."

"Aye, but the bedsheet suggests she may have been sick *after* the consummation. Or that the wedding was consummated this morn ere getting up," Rory pointed out and Niels turned to peer at the bed, his eyes widening when he saw the dried red-brown stain on the bottom linen. It was from the preserves Edith had smeared on herself thanks to the advice of the unknown Magda, but it did look like blood. A slow smile claimed his lips.

"I'll take it and hang it over the banister while ye pleat yer plaid, shall I?" Rory asked, moving toward the bed.

Niels started to nod, but then frowned and asked, "What if someone investigates and realizes 'tis just preserves?"

Rory paused and then relaxed and said, "I'll only leave it up until the nooning meal and then take it down and burn it. That way all will see it, but Brodie'll no' be able to examine it when he returns."

"Good," Niels said, looking around now for his tartan. "Thank ye."

"Me pleasure, brother," Rory said lightly, stripping the stained linen off the bed. "I'm always happy to aid in the course o' true love."

Niels glanced to him sharply. "Love? I do no' love Edith. I like her, but that is it."

Rory gave him a pitying look as he straightened with the linen in hand. "Sometimes, Niels, I swear ye're a dolt with naught in yer head but boiled brains . . . and this is one o' those times if ye truly believe ye do no' love the lass. The way ye were fretting over her last night made it pretty clear to one and all that ye love her."

"One and all?" Niels asked with wide eyes. "How would one and all ken anything? Only ye, Tormod, Geordie and Alick were up here."

Rory's eyebrows rose. "Do ye truly no' recall running to the top o' the stairs in a panic, wearing naught but yer boots and puke and bellowing like a wounded bear fer us to come quick, that yer Edith was stricken?"

"Oh," Niels muttered, vaguely recalling that now.

"Aye, oh," Rory said dryly. "Trust me, everyone in this keep is now convinced ye love their lady. You are the only one who apparently does no' realize it yet."

On that note, he turned and carried the linen out, leaving Niels to pleat his plaid and ponder the fact that he might just love his wife. Dear God, how had that happened?

"Нмм."

Edith glanced to Moibeal at that comment. The maid had sat down to discuss what all they would have to pack for the journey as Edith broke her fast. Both women had quickly realized that it was going to be a much larger endeavor than they'd thought. Aside from her chests of clothes, Edith had two chests of linens and such that her mother had started when she was but a babe. She'd said they were for her to take with her when she married. There was also her bow and arrow and countless other personal items that would need to be packed.

"What?" Edith asked Moibeal with curiosity when the woman didn't comment further.

"It appears yer husband is awake, or at least out o' bed," Moibeal said with amusement, nodding toward the stairs.

Edith turned to follow her gaze, expecting to see her husband coming down the stairs. Instead her eye was caught on the huge strip of white linen Rory was hanging over the upper bannister. Her jaw dropped as her gaze zeroed in on the huge dark stain in the center.

"And here I worried that what with ye being ill and all, ye had no' consummated the wedding," Moibeal commented, and then added, "At least we needn't worry Brodie could have the wedding voided should he arrive before we leave."

Edith merely stared at the sheet. As far as she could recall, they hadn't consummated the marriage. But that definitely looked like blood on the sheet. Perhaps Niels had worried that Brodie might annul the marriage if given the chance and had consummated her while she was unconscious to ensure that didn't happen. Her gaze dropped to her lap at that thought and she simply sat for a moment, trying to see if she felt any different down there.

Nope, Edith decided finally. She didn't feel different at all . . . which was kind of disappointing. She really would have expected to feel different somehow, although she wasn't sure how or even why she'd have thought that. His kissing her and thrusting his tongue into her mouth hadn't left her mouth feeling different afterward. But then there was no maidenhead in her mouth to bleed, and judging by the amount of blood on the linen, the breaching had not been a small thing. Edith almost wondered if she shouldn't find some blood moss and change into the dark red gown she usually wore during her menarche to minimize visual signs of bloodstains. If she was still bleeding . . .

Standing abruptly, Edith headed for the stairs, intent on checking on the issue, but paused at the bottom of the stairs when Niels appeared at the top and started down. Embarrassed and shy, Edith ducked her head and started up, but paused when Niels drew even with her and caught her arm.

"Good morning, wife," he murmured, bending to press a kiss to her forehead.

"Good morning, husband," Edith whispered. Flustered, she glanced up and then away when she saw he was eyeing her oddly.

"Where are ye going?" he asked.

Edith opened her mouth, and then immediately closed it, not comfortable discussing her body's needs with him yet, but then said, "To pack."

"Ah." He smiled and squeezed her arm. "Just pack a couple gowns for now. Geordie and Alick are returning after seeing us to Buchanan to collect Rory and have agreed to bring a cart to bring back Ronson, his grandmother, Laddie and anything else ye need from Drummond."

Edith forgot all about her possibly still bleeding at that and glanced up with surprise. "Ronson and his grandmother?"

"Well, if Bessie is willing," Niels said wryly. "I

thought you might like them to come to Buchanan with us. Was I wrong?"

"Nay. That would be wonderful, husband," she assured him quickly, a smile curving her lips. "I was worrying what might become of them after I left. Victoria does no' care for either o' them."

He smiled. "Then if his grandmother is willing, Geordie and Alick will bring them. They'll bring anything else ye might need too." Niels frowned briefly, and then added, "Although it might be best do ye leave Moibeal here until then. She can tell me brothers what all ye want brought. That way, they'll no' accidentally leave anything behind." He hesitated and then added, "If ye can do without yer maid fer a week or—"

"Oh, aye," Edith interrupted him quickly. A week without a maid was little enough to give up in exchange for making sure nothing was left behind.

"Good. Then go pack a few gowns and essentials and we'll leave as soon as ye're ready," he suggested.

"Aye, m'lord, husband," Edith said and turned to go, but then paused and swung back to throw her arms around his neck and press a quick, enthusiastic kiss to his lips. "Thank ye, husband," she said happily as she then withdrew her arms, but he stopped her by slipping his arms around her waist and holding her close.

"That is no' much o' a thank ye kiss, wife," Niels murmured, his voice growing husky. "We can do better than that, do ye no' think?"

"Aye," Edith whispered and closed her eyes as his face lowered and he claimed her mouth. When one of his hands rose to cup the back of her head and tilt it to a better angle as his tongue slid out to caress her lips,

Edith opened to him and moaned into his mouth as he deepened the kiss. That was all it took for her body to come alive with excitement and ache with need. She could feel the hardness growing between them and pressing against her belly, so wasn't at all surprised when Niels suddenly scooped her up into his arms and started up the stairs without breaking their kiss. She was even looking forward to his assuaging the ache he'd created, so was startled when he suddenly broke the kiss and stopped walking.

Peering up at his face, she saw that he was staring past her looking slightly vexed. Edith turned to see that Rory now stood at the top of the stairs, arms crossed over his chest and one eyebrow raised.

Sighing, Niels set Edith down on the step above him. He held her briefly until he was sure she had her footing and then urged her up the stairs saying, "Go pack. I'll send Moibeal to ye so ye can tell her the plans, and then I'll go find Geordie and Alick and let them ken we're leaving soon."

Hiding her disappointment, Edith nodded and continued up the stairs alone.

Chapter 11

"GEORDIE!"

Blinking away the raindrops clinging to her eye-lashes, Edith glanced to her husband on the horse ahead of hers at his shout and then looked past him to the man riding at the front of their group. Alick rode behind her, but Geordie was leading the way, riding ahead to watch for trouble. He slowed now and then turned to ride back at that call from his brother.

Bringing her horse to a halt behind her husband's mount when he stopped, Edith waited patiently as the two men began to converse. She couldn't hear what they were saying over the storm thundering around them, but hoped it had something to do with stopping to wait out the downpour. It had started around noon, two hours after they'd left Drummond. It had just been a light drizzle at first, but Niels had immediately dug a plaid out of his bag and dropped back next to her to suggest she wrap the water-repelling cloth around herself. She hadn't really thought it necessary at first, but had accepted the offering and drawn it around herself, appreciating the gesture.

The drizzle had continued off and on through most of the afternoon as they'd ridden, but half an hour ago it had suddenly turned into a downpour. It was growing harder and windier with every passing moment and Edith was now cocooned in the plaid, with just her eyes peeking out for all the good that did. It was now almost as dark as night, though she knew it could only be late afternoon, but between that and the wind blowing the rain into her eyes it was getting hard to see.

Dashing the water out of her eyes, Edith sat up a little straighter in the saddle and watched when Niels suddenly turned his horse and sidled up next to her so that their horses each faced opposite directions.

"We're thinking we should stop and wait out the storm," he announced, leaning out of his saddle and leaning close to be sure she heard.

Edith nodded with relief.

"We need to find high ground though, or someplace that'll offer a bit o' protection. Ye ken this area better than us, lass. Do ye know a likely spot?"

Biting her lip, Edith glanced around, searching for anything that might look familiar. The truth was while this was Drummond land, she didn't often stray far from the castle. The loch and the meadow were as far as she usually went unless traveling to visit Saidh or Jo or something of that ilk, and she could count on one hand how many times she'd done that.

Unless she included childhood trips, Edith thought suddenly as her gaze landed on a tree ahead and to her right.

"The lodge!" she blurted with excitement.

"The lodge?" Niels asked.

Edith nodded with the first smile she'd managed since it had started to rain. "Ye see that tree there? The big one with carving on the trunk."

Niels turned to look where she was pointing and then nodded. "Aye."

"Me da did that years ago when we were children. He used to bring me, my mother and brothers out to the lodge a couple times a year when we were young," she explained, shouting to be heard over the rain. "We were supposed to be hunting, but mostly we played games and had picnics and swam and such. He carved that on one o' the trips. It means we're close to the lodge."

"Can ye find it?" Niels asked at once.

Edith peered at the tree for a moment and then nodded, "Aye, I think so."

"Then lead the way and we can get in out o' the rain," Niels said with a smile.

"Aye." Edith nodded, and then urged her horse forward, searching the ground for the path she recalled. It had been years since her father had brought them all out here, not since her mother died, and at first she worried the path might be completely gone by now. But after a surprisingly short search, a crow of triumph slid from her lips and she turned her mare onto the path. Someone had obviously been using the lodge for the path to still be there, Edith thought as she led the men into the trees. Probably one of her brothers. Both Roderick and Hamish had liked to hunt.

It took twenty minutes or so to reach the lodge. Edith didn't remember it taking that long, so was starting to worry she'd followed the wrong path or something when the trees suddenly gave way to the clearing where the small stone building and stables were. Relief coursing through her, Edith steered her mare straight for the small stable, slowed her as they approached the closed door and then quickly slid off and rushed forward to open it herself rather than wait for one of the men to do it for her. She was so eager to get out of the cold, damp rain, that even the stables looked attractive to her at that point.

She eagerly pulled the door open, and then staggered back, bumping into someone as the stench of rotting meat rolled out over her.

"Edith, what—?" She heard Niels say as hands clasped her shoulders, and then he must have caught the scent that now had her covering her mouth with her hand and heaving. Cursing, her husband urged her away from the stable and toward the lodge, only to stop and lead her to a tree that would offer cover instead.

"'Tis okay. Ye can take yer hand away now. 'Tis better here," Niels said.

Edith lowered her hand to take a cautious sniff and then sighed with relief and took several deep breaths to clear her nose and lungs and soothe her stomach. Once she was sure she wasn't going to be sick, she glanced toward the stables and was just in time to see Geordie and Alick come out. Both had the cloth of their tartans over their faces, but their eyes were grim as they collected the reins of the horses and led them to the tree.

"What'd ye find?" Niels asked solemnly as he helped them tie the horses to a low branch in the tree they stood under.

"Dead horses," Geordie said grimly. "Starved to death would be my guess. It looks like they tried to eat their stalls, or perhaps they were just trying to get out to find food."

"How many?" Niels asked when Geordie paused.

"Seven in all."

Edith stiffened and eyed him sharply. "Seven?"

"Aye." Geordie nodded.

"Husband," she said anxiously, grasping Niels's arm. "Brodie took six men when he and Victoria left, and Lonnie was killed in the woods, his horse presumably stolen. Ye do no' think . . . ?"

Mouth flattening, Niels urged her toward Alick. "Stay here with me brother, I'll be right back."

He turned to head for the lodge with Geordie on his heels. Edith bit her lip as she watched. She felt like she should be going with him too, but simply couldn't bring herself to do it. Her mind was painting an image of what they would find inside and it wasn't a pretty one. No man would willingly leave horses to starve to death, they depended on them too much. The owners certainly must be dead too, and had been for longer than the horses who had starved to death. If it was Brodie, Victoria and their escort . . .

Swallowing, Edith watched Niels open the door to the lodge. The way both men immediately jerked back and then drew a bit of tartan up to cover their noses and mouths before entering, told her there was definitely something dead inside.

Apparently, Alick thought so too, because he suddenly placed a supportive arm around her shoulders, and said, "It may no' be yer brother and his wife."

She knew he was trying to reassure her, but even

he didn't sound like he believed it, and Edith found herself unable to see through the sudden well of tears in her eyes. Dashing them away, she bit her lip and simply waited. It seemed a long time before the two men came back out. Geordie immediately walked off into the woods and she could hear his heaving even over the rain.

While Niels was as gray-faced as his brother, he went in the opposite direction. He walked straight to the well. He didn't even have to draw water, the rainstorm had apparently left the bucket that sat on the well wall full of water. Niels dipped his hands in and appeared to be cleaning them. When he finished, he dumped the water on the ground and then walked over to the tree to join them.

"Is it them?" Edith asked quietly, already knowing the answer.

Niels opened his mouth, closed it and then sighed and admitted, "'Tis hard to tell. They've been dead awhile, but 'tis six men and a woman. The woman is wearing a gold gown."

Edith frowned. "Victoria was wearing a gold gown when they left."

Niels merely nodded, not seeming surprised, and then he held up his hand and said, "And the man beside her was wearing this."

Edith glanced down at his hand when he held it out. For a moment she just stared at the gold ring resting on his palm. It was a man's ring, gold with the Drummond family crest on it. It was the signet ring her father had worn up until the day he'd died. He'd pressed it into the wax on any messages he sent as proof they were from him. When he had died, Tormod had removed it and taken it to Roderick, and then he'd taken it to Hamish when Roderick died. The last she'd seen it Brodie had been wearing it as he left Drummond. He'd been wearing that ring, and Victoria had been riding beside him, her gold gown glowing in the sunlight.

It was them. The woman was Victoria, and the six dead men were Brodie and the five remaining men from his escort. She had now lost every last member of her family. She was alone, Edith realized dully and wondered where that high keening sound was coming from. She realized it was coming from her just before darkness closed in around her and she began to fall.

CURSING, NIELS CAUGHT EDITH BEFORE SHE could land in the mud, and then simply stood there, holding her and staring at her pale face, wondering what to do. They couldn't stay here. Even did they drag the dead out of the lodge and put them in the stables until they could arrange to return them to Drummond, the smell in the lodge would be unbearable. Besides, he didn't want Edith waking in the place where she knew her brother had taken his last breath.

"Do we ride on?" Alick asked hopefully as Geordie returned from the woods.

"Nay," Niels said grimly, and then sighed miserably and turned to carry Edith to his mount.

"I'll hold her while ye mount," Geordie said quietly.

Nodding, Niels handed her over and put a foot in the stirrup.

"But where are we going?" Alick asked with a frown. "We can no' take her back to Drummond. She's no' safe there."

"Nay, she's no'," Geordie agreed solemnly, and then pointed out, "But she is the last o' the old laird's children. She's now clan leader. She'd no' thank us did she wake up to find we'd made her as much a coward as Brodie by taking her to safety at Buchanan and leaving her people unprotected."

Niels's mouth tightened as his brother put words to his own thoughts. Much as he'd like it otherwise, they would have to return to Drummond. And then they'd have to keep Edith safe while he smoked out the killer. He just hoped to God he could do it before the killer could finish what he'd started and kill the last of the Drummond clan, his wife.

"THEY'RE LIFTING THE GATE."

Niels tore his gaze from Edith's pale, sleeping face in the moonlight and glanced toward the keep to see that the gate was indeed rising. Now that the storm had finally ended, the night sky was as clear as could be with a large full moon and countless stars making visibility pretty good now that they were out from under the cover of the trees.

Sighing, Niels urged his horse forward to cross the open area between the castle and the forest that surrounded it. He set the pace at a slow walk to avoid jolting Edith.

Niels had sent Geordie ahead to warn the men on the wall that they were returning and to get them to open the gate. While he did that, Niels and Alick had waited at the base of the hill, just outside the trees. He'd wanted to avoid getting too close and risking Edith being woken up by the shouting back and forth. She'd woken up several times on the return journey, and each time had cried herself back to sleep. The only reason he knew that was because, hidden under the tartan he'd wrapped around them both, she'd soaked his shirt with warm tears each and every time she'd woken.

Niels knew all Edith's tears weren't solely for Brodie and Victoria. Edith was finally mourning the passing of her entire family. She'd let a little out when Cawley had died, but that had merely been a drop in the bucket of the sorrow she must feel. He couldn't even imagine how he'd feel were he to lose all of his brothers as well as his sister in a few short weeks. But he did know it would be devastating. Niels wanted to spare her from that as much as possible for now. He knew that he was just delaying the inevitable. Edith needed to let her pain out and cry, and if she didn't do it now, she would just do it later. But between getting little more than an hour's nap last night after her poisoning, and their very long, very useless journey today, Niels was too exhausted to be able to offer her the comfort he felt she would need. He was hoping he could get her inside and to bed without waking her. Once he'd had a nap, even a short one, he could hold and comfort her as she spent her tears.

Geordie was dismounted and waiting at the gate with Tormod, Rory and several soldiers as Niels reached it. When Geordie moved out into Niels's path, he stopped his horse and raised an eyebrow in question.

Whether he could see that or not, Geordie explained. "The men are waiting to shield her from arrows," Geordie said solemnly as the group of men rushed forward with various items Niels didn't understand until they put them together next to his horse. A barrel, a crate and a bucket, one next to the other, made up a set of makeshift stairs for him to dismount without jolting Edith.

"Thank ye," Niels almost whispered the words. Bracing his left foot on the barrel, he lifted and shifted his right leg over his mount's head and stood up with Edith in his arms. He then walked down the crate and bucket as if they were stairs to reach the ground.

As Alick dismounted and their horses were led away, Tormod said, "This way," and stepped aside so that Niels got his first look at what they'd arranged. The sight made him stop in surprise.

With the raging storm slowing them at first, the return journey had taken longer than the journey out had. It was late now, closer to dawn than the dusk that had just past. Everyone but the men on the wall should have been inside sleeping, and they probably had been before Geordie's arrival. But now it looked like every last man and woman at Drummond, from the soldiers down to the kitchen maids, were lined up two by two from the gate to the keep doors, each of them holding a shield high in the air so that they formed a tunnel Niels could safely carry Edith through without the fear of arrows from overhead.

Swallowing, Niels turned to Geordie and murmured, "Thank ye."

"It was no' me idea," he said with a crooked smile. "The word that we found Laird Brodie dead and Lady Edith was returning spread while we waited fer ye to cross from the woods to the gate and the men just started lining up with the shields. Before I knew it servants were pouring out o' the castle to help protect their lady. Her people think a lot o' yer wife."

Niels stared at him blankly for a minute, and then simply nodded and started into the tunnel Edith's people had made to offer her safe passage. But he was touched beyond words at this show of caring and concern for his wife. To him it indicated that they cared for her as much as she cared for them. He was quite positive they would not have done this for her brother.

Niels walked quickly, but kept his head up and tried to make eye contact with every person he passed to let them know that their actions were noted and appreciated. Many nodded as if understanding, others simply straightened a bit with pride, but some did not notice because their sorrowful eyes were on their sleeping lady.

Despite the tunnel of shields, Niels was relieved to get Edith inside the keep. After the hours spent cold and damp, the heat in the great hall was welcome.

"I sent Moibeal up to build a fire in m'lady's room," Tormod announced as they followed him inside.

"Thank ye. Grab a cask o' ale and some goblets and come up," he added as he headed for the stairs.

"Who?" Geordie asked uncertainly.

"All o' ye," Niels said grimly. He wanted Tormod and his brothers all there. He needed to talk to them, but was unwilling to leave Edith alone. They'd have to talk quietly around the table by the fire . . . which only had two chairs he recalled, and as he started up the stairs, Niels added, "Ye may want to grab some chairs from the other rooms. There are only two."

"Are ye sure we'll all fit?" Rory asked, and something about the amusement in his voice made Niels pause and half turn to look back. His eyes widened incredulously when he saw that every last man and woman who had lined up to ensure Edith's safe passage had followed them inside and across the great hall, and were either on the stairs behind him, or waiting patiently for their turn to follow them up the stairs. It seemed his "all o' ye" had been heard and taken literally when he'd meant only his brothers and Tormod. Niels almost explained that he hadn't really meant everyone in the castle, but then changed his mind and simply said, "We'll talk down here."

As soon as everyone started backtracking down the stairs, Niels glanced to Alick and asked, "Would ye fetch some furs from the bed to lay Edith on by the fire?"

"O' course." Alick slipped past him and hurried upstairs as Niels followed everyone else back down. It was slow enough going with so many before him that Alick was back just as he stepped off the stairs and started toward the fire. It looked like his brother had grabbed every last fur off the bed, and a few from another room, he noted with a weary smile as the younger man ran ahead to lay out and stack the furs to make a comfy bed. He then laid the last couple over Edith once Niels had set her gently down on the others.

The moment they stepped back, Laddie appeared and curled up in front of his mistress. Edith stirred then, and Niels held his breath, afraid she'd wake up, but she merely curled her arm around the dog and buried her face in his fur.

"Laddie and me'll keep her safe, m'laird," Ronson said solemnly beside him.

Niels glanced down into his serious little face and nodded. "Thank ye, lad."

Ronson nodded in response and then sat down on the edge of the furs to stare at his lady with eyes too old for his years.

Sighing, Niels turned and headed to where the men were silently setting up the trestle tables again. They were disassembled each night to make room for sleeping, and then reassembled every morning, but morning was coming early this day. Or perhaps night had been extended, Niels thought, since he planned to retire as soon as he'd finished talking to their people.

"So ye found Brodie?" Tormod said finally, once Niels was seated with ale in hand.

"Aye," he said grimly. "At the family's hunting lodge. Brodie, his wife and the five remaining men in his escort were all there and dead. And their horses were all in the stables still and also dead."

"Starved to death," Geordie put in.

"Could ye tell how Brodie and the others died?" Rory asked. "Were there wounds or—?"

"I think it was poison," Niels interrupted. "They were all at table with bowls o' what looked like dried-up stew in front o' them and half-drunk goblets o' ale. The ale cask had a hint o' that smell from the poisoned mead, so I'm guessing they were poisoned, but that this time enough was put in that it was fast-acting. Unlike Laird Drummond and his sons, they did no' even finish their meals or get up from their seats ere they died. And they had been dead quite a while, long enough they were unrecognizable."

"The maid," Tormod muttered.

Niels glanced to the warrior uncertainly. "Moibeal?"

"Nay, Lady Victoria's maid, Nessa. Ye said there was one woman and six men, but Lady Victoria took her young maid and left Effie here. There should have been two women and six men."

"Oh, aye," Niels said with a frown. "I recall Edith mentioning that, or mayhap it was you, but I only saw the one woman." He turned to Geordie in question, but his brother shook his head.

"I did no' see another woman either. Just the one," he said quietly.

"Mayhap it was no' them then," Tormod said. "Ye said they were unrecognizable."

"Aye. That's why I took this off the finger of the one next to the woman." Niels slid the ring out of his pocket and held it out for Tormod to see.

The old man's mouth tightened and he nodded. "Aye. Brodie had that when they left. It's the laird's ring." He ran a weary hand through his grizzled hair and said, "I'll take some men and go fer the bodies at first light. We'll check the area for the maid too. Mayhap she didn't have as much as the others and managed to drag herself outside to die."

Niels grunted at the suggestion, but then cleared his throat and said, "Just so ye're prepared, they're a terrible mess. Bloated and their skin slipping. I had to cut off Brodie's finger and remove it so I could take the ring to Edith for identification."

"Then they've been dead quite a while," Rory said quietly.

"My guess would be probably since the night they arrived at the hunting lodge," Niels said solemnly. "The horses would have taken three or four days, perhaps a week at most to die without food and water, and they were far from freshly dead too."

"What now?" Tormod asked quietly.

"Now I keep Edith safe and find the culprit behind the deaths o' her whole family," Niels said grimly, rubbing the back of his neck. He was so damned tired, but said, "We're going to have to find a way to keep the food and drink from being poisoned."

"I can restrict access to the kitchens to just meself and me three most trusted workers."

Niels glanced around until he spotted the speaker, and recognized the Drummond cook, Jaimie, among the crowd of people who had been standing and sitting nearby listening. The man stepped forward and continued, "We can set up tables outside the kitchen. The three lasses I choose can deliver the food out onto that table as 'tis ready, for the other servants to carry to the trestle tables. But I shall personally bring Lady Edith her food to ensure no one gets near it."

"We'll move several casks o' ale and cider out o' the buttery and store them here in the great hall until this is resolved. That way we can keep whatever Lady Edith wishes to drink locked up in the buttery," Tormod added. "I am the only one with a key. I shall personally fetch her drinks when she wants one."

"That covers poisoning," Rory said quietly. "But it means ye'll have to watch fer attack."

"Aye," Niels nodded. "She'll need a guard with her at all times, at least two men. And she can no' go in the bailey unless she has shields around her and over her head to guard against arrows."

"I'll arrange her guards in shifts before I leave," Tormod said quietly. "I'm sure we'll have no shortage o' volunteers."

A murmur of agreement went around the crowd at

that, and Niels nodded wearily, but then stood. "Thank ye. I'm to bed."

"I'll see ye and Edith up. I'm ready fer bed meself," Geordie said, rising as well.

"Aye," Alick got up. "'Tis been a long day."

Niels started to turn away and then paused and swung back. "Tormod, if ye're riding to the lodge, ye will no' be here to tend to Edith's drink. Mayhap ye should give me the key until ye return."

"Oh, aye." Tormod searched through a ring of keys for the right one. Removing it, he held it up but then said, "There are things I'll need to talk to ye and Lady Edith about when I get back. Things ye should ken now Brodie is dead."

Nodding, Niels took the key. "We'll talk when ye return," he assured him and then added a solemn, "Safe journey."

"Aye, and ye all stay safe here too, m'lord." Tormod said grimly. "It bears considering that now that ye've married our lady, ye may be a target as well."

Niels stiffened in surprise at the suggestion, but then nodded slowly and turned to walk over to collect Edith. Ronson glanced up sleepily as they approached. Seeing them coming, though, he prodded Laddie to wake him and then grabbed his collar to urge him up and off the furs and out of the way.

Edith murmured sleepily when Niels carefully picked her up, but didn't fully wake.

"I'll bring the furs up," Niels heard Alick whisper behind him as he turned to head for the stairs.

Niels wasn't surprised when all three of his brothers followed him above stairs and to Edith's room. He laid her in the bed, covered her with the bed linens and then helped Alick arrange the furs over that before moving to the door with them.

"Tormod is right," Rory said pausing at the door and turning back to face him worriedly. "Ye could be a target too now that ye married Edith."

Niels shrugged. "And as we learned from Moibeal and Effie, just being here could get a person poisoned or killed."

Geordie scowled. "We really need to come up with a better plan than just to try to keep Edith safe. We need to catch this bastard."

"I am open to suggestions," Niels said quietly. "But no' until after I've slept. I am too tired to think straight just now."

"Aye, get some rest," Rory said, turning to open the door. "We'll all talk once ye've had some sleep."

Niels grunted in agreement, held the door as his brothers left and then closed it quietly and moved back to the bed. He'd intended to remove Edith's gown after the men left so that she might sleep more comfortably, but in the end he didn't even bother to remove his own clothes. He simply lay down on top of the furs and was asleep the moment his head hit the bed.

Chapter 12

$\mathcal{E}$DITH OPENED THE BEDCHAMBER DOOR, AND then paused and stared at the two men lying on mats on the hall floor. Geordie and Alick. They were lying head to head, directly in front of the door. Movement caught her attention then, and she glanced up to see two more men standing against the opposite wall. They were Drummond soldiers she'd known for years. Two of Tormod's most trusted men, Cameron and Fearghas. Even as she noted that, Cameron stepped forward and offered her a hand.

After a hesitation, Edith accepted and gripped it as she lifted her skirt high enough to clear the heads of the men on the floor and stepped over them.

"Thank ye," Edith said the words on a whisper of sound to avoid waking Geordie and Alick, but Cameron appeared to hear it. Nodding, he leaned past her to pull the door silently closed and then straightened and simply stood there, waiting.

Smiling uncertainly, Edith turned to head up the hall, and immediately heard a soft shuffle that suggested the men were following. She waited until she was halfway to the stairs before stopping to turn around though. Both men stopped at once, waiting.

Hoping that distance was far enough not to disturb the two men still sleeping, she raised an eyebrow and asked softly, "I am guessing ye're meant to guard me?"

"Aye, m'lady," Cameron answered.

"Tormod has arranged for two men to guard ye day and night," Fearghas added. "We're to stay with ye until the sup when we'll be replaced by two others."

"Ah." Edith sighed. She should have expected as much, she supposed, and then frowned when she heard movement back down the hall. Leaning to the side, she saw Geordie shifting on his mat and decided she'd best get moving or they'd wake the pair. Smiling at the men crookedly, she nodded and then turned to hurry the rest of the way to the stairs, aware that they followed at once.

"What are ye doing up? Where's Niels?"

Jumping in surprise at those booming words as she reached the top of the stairs, Edith grabbed the rail to steady herself and turned to scowl at a sleepy-looking Geordie and Alick as they rushed toward her and her guards. She'd managed to slip out of bed and make it to the door without waking her husband, and would not now have his brothers do it with their bellowing.

"My husband is sleeping. Something he has done little enough of o' late, so keep yer voices down," Edith said in a quiet hiss.

"Aye," Geordie acknowledged more quietly. "I'd wager he's no' slept a handful o' hours since we got here last week."

Edith frowned at this news. She knew Niels hadn't

slept much since her waking, but hadn't realized it had started before that. Sighing, she changed the subject and said, "I was just going below to break me fast. Ye're welcome to join me do ye wish, but as ye can see I already have men to guard me so ye may rather find yer beds and get some proper sleep."

"Nay. We'll go with ye," Geordie said firmly.

"Aye." Alick nodded.

Shrugging, Edith turned and started down the stairs. She'd given them an out had they wished to sleep. It seemed they wouldn't though, and while Tormod had ordered two men to guard her, she really had a guard of four.

Ignoring the thump of their feet behind her, Edith glanced around the great hall as she descended. The trestle tables were set up, but most of the castle inhabitants had apparently already broken their fast and gone about their business. There were only a couple of people at the table, and they appeared to be finishing and preparing to leave. Bessie was seated by the fire as usual, mending in hand, but her fond gaze was on her grandson, Ronson, as he slept curled up next to Laddie between her and the fire.

That was unusual—the boy would normally be up and about by this hour, running about the keep and bailey. Edith supposed their late return last night had disturbed everyone's sleep, although she'd apparently slept through it. She wasn't terribly surprised. She'd spent most of the ride back from the hunting lodge curled up under the plaid Niels had wrapped around them, trying not to weep and then giving in to sobs as her mind ran around in circles replaying the past several weeks over in her head. Her father and broth-

ers dying, Cawley dying and now the fact that Brodie
was dead too. It had been a relief to finally fall asleep
and escape her misery. She wasn't at all surprised that
her wounded mind had clung to sleep once they'd returned home.

In fact, Edith had almost simply rolled over and
gone back to sleep when she'd woken this morning.
But she knew she couldn't escape what had happened
through sleep, and indulging in the dark feelings trying
to claim her could be dangerous. It could be hard to
climb out of a hole once your mind dug its way in.

What she needed was some semblance of normalcy,
Edith thought. To her that meant returning to her usual
routine of tending to Drummond and its people. With
that thought in mind, Edith crossed the great hall to
the door to the kitchens, eyeing with curiosity the two
men standing guard there. Both nodded solemnly in
greeting and one opened the door for her while the
other stepped forward and put a hand out to bar the
path of the men.

"Lady Edith may enter, but no one else," the man
said almost apologetically, and Edith glanced around
in surprise to see annoyance flash across the faces of
all four men.

"But we're to guard her. We were ordered to no' let
her out o' our sight," Cameron pointed out.

"And we were ordered no' to let anyone pass but
Lady Edith's husband," the guard said firmly.

"Ye're letting her pass," Geordie pointed out.

"Well, aye," the man said as if the reason for that
should be obvious. In case it wasn't, he added, "She's
our lady. We can hardly bar her from going wherever
she wants in her own castle, can we?"

Fearghas glowered at the man. "She's our lady too and we are meant to keep her safe, so get out o' the way, ye warty canker, ere I—"

"Perhaps ye should let at least one o' me guards accompany me into the kitchen," Edith interrupted, afraid they were going to start a brawl. "That way he can keep me safe and help me carry drinks fer everyone."

There was silence for a moment as the men glared at each other, and then the kitchen guard relented and stepped to the side. "All right, but just one o' ye, and I'll accompany ye too, to be sure all is well. The rest o' ye will wait out here with Arnie."

"Fine," Edith said quickly before anyone could protest. Glancing at Geordie's and Alick's scowling faces, she smiled reassuringly. "I'll only be a moment and I'll bring us all something to break our fast."

Turning away then, she hurried into the kitchen, intent on preventing further protest or problems. Edith didn't bother looking around to see whether Cameron or Fearghas was the guard to accompany her, but simply headed toward Jaimie as soon as she spotted him chopping up a large side of beef.

"Oh! M'lady," he greeted, dropping the large cleaver and quickly wiping his hands when he saw her approaching. "Good morn. How are ye feeling? Are ye ready to break yer fast?"

"Aye, Jaimie." She smiled at him gratefully. "Geordie and Alick are up too and ready to break their fast as well, and . . ." She glanced back to see that Cameron was the one who had followed her inside with the guard from the door. When she raised her eyebrow in question, he shook his head.

"Fearghas and I already broke our fast, thank ye, m'lady," he murmured.

Turning back to Jaimie, she said, "Then mayhap just a pitcher o' ale fer the men. That way Cameron and Fearghas can have some if they like. But I'll have cider this morning, I think." After the incident with the mead on her wedding night, she was now as loathe to drink that as she was wine. Hopefully, her new distaste of the two beverages wouldn't last long, for if this kept up, there'd be nothing she'd want to drink, Edith thought, and then noticed that Jaimie had gone quiet and was looking toward her guards with alarm. Raising her eyebrows, she asked, "Is there something amiss? Are we out of cider?"

"N-nay," Jaimie stammered, and then shook his head and explained, "But I can no' fetch ye aught to drink, m'lady. Tormod locked up the buttery to ensure no one could poison ye again."

"Oh," Edith said nonplussed, and then smiled wryly. "I suppose I shall have to find Tormod then so I can have a drink."

"Ah . . ." Cameron said behind her and when Edith turned to him in question, he explained apologetically, "Tormod took a wagon and some men to ride out to the lodge at first light. He gave the key to yer husband ere leaving though."

"But he's sleeping," Edith said with a sigh.

"I could send Fearghas to go wake him and ask fer the key," Cameron suggested, but she shook her head.

"Nay. He's had very little sleep o' late and needs it." Forcing a smile, she turned back to the cook and said, "I suppose I'll just have an apple or something for now,

Jaimie, and then eat something more filling when me husband wakes and I can have a drink with it."

Nodding, he turned and rushed to the pantry, barking at the women cutting vegetables to get food and drink together for the men.

Sighing, Edith walked idly around the kitchens as she waited and smiled wryly to herself. She'd never seen it so empty. Usually there were loads of people rushing around and she wondered if having his staff so restricted would make things harder on Jaimie.

"Here ye are, m'lady. I got ye two. The finest o' the bunch," Jaimie said as he rushed back to her.

"Thank ye," Edith murmured, accepting the apples he offered.

He nodded and smiled crookedly, but there was worry in his eyes and Edith raised her eyebrows in question and asked, "Is something wrong, Jaimie?"

"Oh, nay, nay," he assured her, and then frowned and added, "Well, aye, I was wondering . . ."

"What?" Edith asked encouragingly.

Sighing, Jaimie shook his head and said apologetically, "'Tis market day in the village, m'lady."

"Is it?" Edith asked with surprise. They had market day in the village on every Saturday. The priest had wanted it to be on Sundays to encourage parishioners to attend mass ere visiting the merchants who lined up with their wares, but their neighbors, the Lindsays, had theirs on Sundays and some of the sellers were traveling merchants who traded at both places, so Saturday it was.

Edith supposed it was a sign of the stress she'd been under that she'd managed to lose track of what day it was and nearly forgot all about market day. She always went to buy cheese, eggs, capons and spices or whatever else Jaimie might need. It saved him the trouble, and gave her a chance to get out of the castle. Besides, she liked looking at everything on display. Sometimes she found some nice cloth, or some quality soap imported from Spain or the hotter countries. It depended on what merchants managed to make it to market day.

"Aye, 'tis," Jaimie said now, twisting his apron between his hands anxiously. "And ere yer return I planned to attend meself to get the things we need, but with the new restrictions reducing me staff, I fear I've no' the time and—"

"Nay, of course not," Edith interrupted, patting his hand. "I'll go. Just tell me what ye need and I'll fetch it back fer ye."

"Oh, thank ye, m'lady," Jaimie said with relief.

"There's no need to thank me, Jaimie," she assured him solemnly. "I am just sorry ye had to remind me o' me duty. I fear I did no' even realize 'twas market day until ye mentioned it."

"Aye, well, 'tis no small wonder that," the cook said sadly, sympathy on his face, and then bit his lip and offered, "And if 'tis too much trouble this time, I'm sure I can make do with what we have and—"

"Nay," Edith assured him and then smiled wryly and admitted, "In truth, 'twould be nice to go to market and forget what's been happening around here fer a bit."

Jaimie brightened at once. "Oh, well, that's fine then," he said and began to rattle off a list that made her realize just how painful his offer to do without had been. With her being sick for weeks, and Jaimie's having a limit on how much coin Tormod would give him to take to market, they'd run out of a great deal of things in the castle. It made her wonder how he'd managed to produce the delicious meals he'd come up with. But now that she was thinking on it, most of the meals she'd eaten since waking had been stews and soups. If that's all they'd had to eat recently, then she imagined everyone would be heartily sick of them.

As his list continued, Edith began to be grateful for having her guards. In fact, she started to hope that Geordie and Alick insisted on accompanying her too, because she would need the help bringing everything back. Mayhap she would take Ronson and Laddie with her as well . . . and a cart. Nay, a wagon.

"M'LADY, DO YE NO' THINK WE SHOULD HEAD back to the wagon now?"

Edith turned to respond to Cameron's pleading words, and blinked in surprise when she bumped her nose on the shield Ronson was struggling to hold up behind her as he followed her around.

"Sorry, m'lady," Ronson said earnestly, stepping back a pace.

"That's fine, lad," she said with a smile, and then glanced to Cameron, opened her mouth and then closed it again with a frown as she saw that while his hands were free, one of them was on his sword. In the meantime, Fearghas, Geordie and Alick were all juggling overflowing armloads of the items she'd been passing back as she bought them. She hadn't realized she'd bought so much. And she was only halfway through the list.

Biting her lip, she said, "Mayhap we should take

everything back to the wagon. Then one o' ye can wait with our goods while the rest o' us continue shopping."

"M'lady," Cameron said wearily. "Ye really should no' be here."

"Aye," Geordie agreed. "Niels did no' even want ye out o' the keep, let alone down in the village."

"That's as may be, but as lady at Drummond there are certain things that need doing, and if ye all want to fill yer bellies on something other than stew fer the next week, then we need to finish getting the items on Jaimie's list," Edith said firmly. This was the argument that had convinced them to reluctantly relent and let her leave the castle to begin with. Which was just utter nonsense to her. She was the Lady of Drummond and simply could have ordered her guards to make Geordie and Alick get out of the way and accompany her to the market and they would have had to do it. But she didn't think that was likely to win her any points with her new in-laws, so she'd reasoned, wheedled and begged until the men had caved in.

Although, in truth, Edith suspected that in the end it was the threat of stew all week again that had won her argument. It certainly had turned the tide for Cameron and Fearghas, which had helped with the reluctant Geordie and Alick. It seemed stew had pretty much been the meal of choice the past three weeks and her people were heartily sick of it.

"How much more is there to get?" Geordie asked finally after the men all exchanged glances.

"Several spices, capons and cheese," Edith responded at once, and then frowned and added, "And we are nearly out o' soap too."

Geordie shook his head, but said, "Carry on then.

But one o' us'll soon have to start taking items back to the wagon. We can no' carry much more."

"Two o' ye will have to carry items back and then one will have to watch the goods in the carriage while the other returns to carry more."

Edith whipped around at that dry voice and smiled brightly at Niels as he pushed his way between Geordie and Alick to reach her. "Husband! Ye're up."

He grimaced at the words, but bent over Ronson and the shield to kiss her on the forehead before growling, "Ye should have woke me when ye got up."

"Ye were tired and—"

"And ye should no' be out here. 'Tis no' safe," Niels interrupted grimly.

"I have me guards, and yer brothers and even Ronson here," she said, smiling down at the boy.

"Sorry, brother," Geordie muttered. "But yer wife can be fair persuasive when she wishes, and it seems the cook has run out o' a lot o' items while she was ill and whatnot."

"And I was thirsty," Edith added, trying for a pitiful look. "But it seems all the drink at the keep has been locked up. Even the cider. So we came down and had a drink at the inn before starting to shop, else we'd surely be done and back by now."

"No' likely. We'll be here until the market closes at this rate," Alick said under his breath, earning a scowl from Edith.

"Ye let her drink at the inn?" Niels asked with dismay.

"Well, o' course they did," Edith said, scowling at him now. "Why would they not? The innkeeper could hardly be the one poisoning me at the keep."

"Nay, but what if whoever is poisoning ye has followed ye from the keep and managed to drop poison in yer drink at the inn?" he asked sharply.

"I watched fer that, m'lord," Cameron said at once and Edith glanced to him with surprise. She hadn't even thought of that happening. It seemed her guards had, however. She supposed that's why they were some of Tormod's most trusted men. They thought of things like that.

"Wife," Niels said now, drawing her gaze back his way. "The drink being locked up and yer having guards are to keep ye alive. But ye make that harder to do by putting yerself out in the open where ye're an easy target. Ye should no' have left the keep."

Edith narrowed her eyes on him briefly and then asked, "Where are yer guards?"

"What?" he asked with surprise.

"Well, ye may be a target too now that ye've married me," she pointed out, and added, "After all, Brodie's Victoria was killed. Ye should have to stay in the keep too, and ye surely should no' be riding around without a guard. So . . . where are they?"

"She's right about that, brother," Geordie said and reminded him, "We were talking about it last night. Ye *could* be a target now too."

Niels scowled at his brother for his trouble, and then took Edith's arm and tried to steer her away. "Fine. Let us both return to the keep right now."

"Nay," Edith gasped, digging in her heels. "There are still things Jaimie needs."

When Niels paused and turned to frown at her, she added, "'Tis our job to supply what our people need, husband. Surely ye ken that? If I do no' get what he needs, he can no' properly do his job, and 'twould be because o' my failure, no' his."

Cursing, he released her and threw his hands up in the air. "Fine. We will get what the cook needs, but no dawdling, Edith. Get it done quickly so we can return to the keep."

Edith smiled at him brightly and nodded. "Aye, husband. And look, now ye're here, none o' the men need return to the wagon. Ye can help carry the spice and soap."

Edith then turned away and hurried to the spice merchant with Ronson and the men rushing to keep up and bumping her on every side.

"AND NOW YE KEN HOW WE ENDED UP HERE shopping with yer wife."

"Hmm," Niels muttered at that comment from Geordie as they followed Ronson and the other three men hovering around his wife.

"Although," Geordie added, "I will say she has brightened considerably since leaving the keep. She was sad-looking and dragging her feet there, but perked up once we got here."

Niels frowned at the news that Edith had looked sad and slow when she woke up, but supposed it should be expected considering all that had happened. While Edith had avoided talking about her father and brothers, he knew from things he'd heard from Saidh and Tormod that Edith had loved her father dearly, as well as her brothers . . . even Brodie, who by all accounts was a wastrel. She'd been quite fond of Cawley too. And all had died in short order. In his opinion, she was handling it all incredibly well.

"So I'm thinking her getting out and about today may be a good thing despite the risk," Geordie concluded.

"Aye," Niels muttered. Certainly Edith seemed animated and less pale than usual as she haggled with the spice merchant.

"Niels?" Alick said, sidling closer to him as he paused behind Ronson.

"Hmm?" he asked, glancing to his brother and noting that most of what the lad held were bolts of fabric. One was a fine green cloth the exact color of Edith's eyes that he hoped she planned to make a dress from. She'd look lovely in the material.

"We've nearly circled back around to the wagon," Alick pointed out. "Why do Geordie and I no' carry our items to the wagon, and then I'll wait there to watch over everything while Edith finishes and Geordie'll be able to help carry everything else she buys."

"Aye, if ye do no' mind that would help," Niels said with a nod.

"Trust me, I do no' mind at all," Alick assured him.

"O' course he does no' mind, it means he can sit and flirt with all the pretty girls here rather than traipse around after Edith with his arms full," Geordie said dryly, and then heading for the wagon with Alick, added, "I'll be back directly."

Niels smiled faintly as he turned back toward Edith and then glanced down with surprise when several items were piled on top of his crossed arms.

"Thank ye, husband," Edith said as she stacked the spices on top of each other on him. "Fearghas can no' carry any more, Ronson is busy with the shield and Cameron insists at least one o' them must keep their hands free to defend me should the need arise."

When she turned away quickly then, and hurried off to the next trader, Niels shook his head and shifted his arms slightly to hold the items now cradled against his chest. He then followed the others trailing after his wife. She was at the cheese trader now, he noted, and when his wife had selected several hunks of cheese and showed no sign of slowing, Niels glanced to Fearghas and suggested, "Mayhap ye'd best take that to the wagon and tell Geordie to hurry back."

"We might do better just to bring the wagon here," Cameron warned as Edith continued picking cheese. "The soap trader is next, but the capons come after that and with the whole castle to feed she'll want a lot o' them."

"Aye," Niels agreed.

"I'll take this to the wagon, and have Alick bring it here," Fearghas announced and turned to hurry away.

Niels turned back to his wife then and blinked as he saw that she'd moved on with just Ronson trailing her while they were distracted. She was now in front of the soap trader, examining the wares laid out on a plaid on the ground.

"Oooh, this smells nice," she was saying as she picked up and sniffed one of the soaps.

"Aye, m'lady, that one has oil o' rose in it," the trader said with a smile.

Pausing beside his wife, Niels waited until she had selected the soap she wanted and paid for it before asking, "Edith, did ye no' get any cheese?"

"Aye. I selected so much, Duer said he'd deliver it to the castle," she said, turning to begin piling soap on his arms, and then stopping with a frown as she eyed the spices he already held. Apparently, concerned the soap might affect the spice, she started to turn to Cameron, but paused suddenly and smiled as she peered past the two men. "Oh, good they're bringing the wagon."

"Aye. We thought ye'd need it fer the cheese and capons," Niels said dryly.

Edith shook her head and moved forward to dump the soap she held in the back of the wagon as it stopped next to them. "Nay. I always get so many capons that once I place the order and pay, Iain delivers them to the castle as well."

Niels merely grunted and moved up to pile the spices he held in the wagon as she backed up. When he finished and turned around, she'd bustled off to the capon man and was bartering with him. Ronson, Geordie, Fearghas and Cameron were with her, so he walked up to the front of the wagon and said, "The capons are the last o' it, but they'll be delivered. Ye can head back to the keep do ye wish."

Nodding, Alick took up the reins and headed out, leaving Niels to approach the others. He'd spotted the horses by the inn as he arrived and had tied up his horse there as well, so that was where they all went when Edith finished her bartering. Niels took Edith up before him on his horse, and then suggested, "Geordie, why do ye no' take Ronson up before ye?"

"Oh, nay, m'lord," Ronson protested at once. "I must ride with ye. I have to keep the shield in front o' Lady Edith when we get to the bailey."

Niels had been going to take the shield from the lad to give him a break—he'd started to look weary toward the end—but nodded now. "Very well, lad."

Geordie immediately caught the lad and lifted him

up onto Edith's lap, but held on to the shield and said, "I'll give it to ye once we reach the gate. It tended to get in the way a bit on the way down."

"Aye," Ronson agreed. "Was a most troublesome whoreson."

Shaking his head, Geordie turned and mounted with the shield and they were off. Niels let Cameron lead the way. Fearghas followed behind and Geordie remained at his side. They rode at speed until they neared the gate and then Cameron began to slow. He came to a full halt as they reached the gate. Reining in his own mount, Niels glanced to Geordie as he drew up next to them and then watched as his brother slid the heater shield across the horse's back sideways in front of Ronson and waited for him to get a good grip on it, before releasing it and easing his horse away.

"Ready?" Cameron asked.

Niels nodded. The shield was two feet high laying on its side the way it was. It left his head and part of his chest above it so he was able to see, yet completely hid Ronson, and covered all but the top of Edith's head. When Cameron started forward, Niels followed at once through the gate and into the bailey, glad the man picked a fast walk to cross to the keep stairs.

They were halfway across when Edith suddenly leaned to the side to peer around the shield. Frowning, he nudged her back. She went willingly and remained behind the shield for the rest of the distance to the keep stairs.

Aware that she was vulnerable from overhead now, Niels took the shield from Ronson and held it over his wife and the lad until Cameron dismounted and came to remove the boy. Once the lad was down, Niels tightened his grip around Edith and dismounted, taking her with him, then hustled her up the stairs to the keep doors. He didn't lower the shield until they were inside.

Handing the shield to Cameron then, he took Edith's arm and headed immediately for the stairs.

"Wait, where are we going?" Edith asked with surprise. "I was hoping ye'd unlock the buttery so that I might have a drink."

Niels paused at once, but then just stood there frowning. He'd intended to urge her upstairs and seduce her into consummating their marriage. He'd intended to do that on waking, only to find her gone, and now he was coming up against a new obstacle. What kind of churl would refuse his wife a drink when she was thirsty? Still . . . Aye, he thought and turned to ask politely, "What would ye like to drink, wife?"

"Cider," she murmured and then added, "But I can get it meself do ye but unlock the buttery."

"Nay. 'Tis fine. I shall get it," he assured her, and then turned to Cameron and Fearghas. "Escort yer lady above stairs to her room. I shall fetch the cider and follow directly."

Edith looked surprised at the request, but didn't protest when Cameron and Fearghas urged her away. Satisfied that he could still continue with his plan to bed his wife, Niels started across the great hall for the kitchens only to pause as his name was called. Glancing back, he saw Rory coming down the stairs even as Edith and her guards walked up them and briefly debated ignoring his brother, but then sighed and waited to see what he wanted. He would give him two minutes, Niels decided, but then he would fetch that drink and go upstairs to consummate his marriage . . . finally.

Chapter 13

"ARE YE ALL RIGHT, M'LADY? YE SEEM TO BE moving a bit stiffly," Cameron pointed out about halfway up the stairs.

"Aye." Edith grimaced. "I am a bit stiff, but fine."

"'Tis no wonder what with yer walking about most o' the day today . . . and after riding all day and night yesterday. In the rain, no less," Fearghas said sympathetically.

"Mayhap a hot bath would help with that," Cameron suggested. "Yer da always swore a nice hot bath chased away his aches and pains."

"Aye, he did," Edith said with a soft smile. Her father had suffered terrible pain in his bones and joints the last few years of his life and swore the only thing that eased his discomfort was a steaming hot bath.

"Shall I order ye one then?" Cameron asked.

"Aye, please. Thank ye, Cameron," she murmured. Nodding, the man stopped—she thought to go back down and order a bath for her—but he turned on the step he stood on and bellowed, "Fetch yer lady a bath! Lady Edith wants a bath!"

For one second, the shout was followed by a brief silence from everyone in the great hall except for her husband, who groaned. At least she thought it was Niels who groaned, and Rory's cheerful, "See, ye do have time after all!" seemed to back that up.

Wondering why he'd groaned, Edith glanced back as she stepped onto the upper landing. All she saw, though, was Rory leading Niels out of the keep. It seemed her drink would be delayed.

Moibeal was in the bedchamber when Edith entered. The maid was unpacking the chests she'd packed after Edith, Niels, Geordie and Alick had set out for Buchanan. When they'd both thought they would be living out their lives there.

Well at least until Niels was ready to build that home for them he'd mentioned. Four years, he'd said. Edith hadn't bothered to mention then that her dower was quite generous and, depending on how much money he had gathered on top of what his father had left him, that he might be able to build it at once. There hadn't been the opportunity really, and she'd thought there was plenty of time for such things. Now, not only could he have her dower, but he had a home too. He was now Laird of Drummond.

Edith considered that more seriously. She hadn't really given that much thought. She was lady here now, and Niels was laird. She wondered if he'd considered that. And what he thought about it. She hoped he was happy. He hadn't married her expecting to get the castle and title, but had.

"I've started to unpack. But just before ye came in I started to wonder if I should be doing it here."

Edith glanced to Moibeal uncertainly at those words. "We'll no' be moving to Buchanan now."

"Nay." Moibeal hesitated, and then said, "But I was no' sure whether I should be doing it here or in . . . the big bedchamber."

In the big bedchamber, Edith thought and then realized it was Moibeal's way of avoiding saying the laird's chamber. Her father's room, Edith realized. Moibeal didn't want to make her think of her father and the loss of him.

Sighing, she shrugged. "I suppose we shall have to move there eventually. But Niels shall have to see it first. He may no' like it as it is. We may have to change things. He would no' sleep in Hamish's room after I gave it to him," she pointed out. "So I can only assume he did no' like that one."

Moibeal snorted at the suggestion. "'Tis more like he did no' like leaving you. He slept in the chair by yer bed, on the floor and even in the hall across yer door-step every night even before ye married," she pointed out dryly. "'Twas no' that he did no' like Hamish's room. I do no' think he even ever saw it."

"Oh," Edith murmured, and then turned and headed for the door. "Well, we may as well go take a look at the laird's chamber and see what shape 'tis in then. 'Twill pass the time while we wait for my bath to come."

"Aye, I heard Cameron shout for a bath," Moibeal said with amusement, following her to the door.

Edith nodded. "I am a bit stiff and he suggested it to ease my aches."

Cameron and Fearghas straightened abruptly when Edith opened the door and stepped out.

"We are just taking a quick look at me father's room," Edith explained as she stepped into the hall. The two men nodded and fell into step behind her and Moibeal as they walked up the hall.

The laird's chamber was twice the size of the rest of the rooms, taking up the whole end of the hall. Edith opened the door, entered and then paused abruptly. She'd expected the room to feel empty. Not literally. But the few times she'd traveled for any length of time, she'd returned to find her room feeling cold and empty, and smelling stale. She'd always assumed it was because the fire had been unlit for so long and no one had lived in the room. But her father's room had been empty for near a month, yet smelled of smoke and . . . was that lavender?

"Why is the room warm?" Moibeal asked. "And what is that smell? Is it flowers?"

"Lavender, I think," Edith murmured, and then glanced to the floor to see bits of the dried flower strewn about.

"Yer father's room never smelled o' lavender ere this," Moibeal pointed out, even as Edith thought it.

Cameron and Fearghas had been standing at the door, but now moved into the room. Cameron went straight to the fireplace and grabbed the poker. Dropping to his haunches then, he poked around in the hearth.

"Someone has been sleeping in the bed," Moibeal said grimly, drawing her attention. The maid was peeking through the closed curtains around the bed, but now tugged them open to reveal the disordered linens and furs.

"Are ye sure they were no' just left like that after me father was removed?" Edith asked, moving to the bed.

"Nay. I stripped the bed meself while ye tended Hamish," Moibeal told her. "The bed was bare and the bed curtains open when I last saw this room."

"Someone has obviously been sleeping in here," Cameron said grimly. "And quite recently. These are no' ashes, they're embers, m'lady. Someone had a fire in here and 'tis just dying."

"The old laird's ghost," Fearghas said in a fearful whisper.

Seeing Cameron's eyes widen at the suggestion, Edith scowled at Fearghas. "Nay. Me father never liked lavender. He said it made him sad. Besides, Fearghas, there is no such thing as ghosts, and if there were, they'd hardly need a fire. The person sleeping in here is a living one. Probably Geordie or Niels moved in here fer some reason."

"If that were the case, the fire would no' be hot. They slept outside yer door this morn," Cameron reminded her.

"Well, Rory then," she said with exasperation and took one last look around before heading for the door. "Come along, me bath is probably on its way by now, if no' already waiting."

Her bedroom door was open and servants were busily pouring in buckets of steaming water when Edith led the trio back to her room. She expected Cameron and Fearghas to wait in the hall, but they entered and stood on either side of her until the servants had finished and left. Only once she and Moibeal were all who remained did they nod and return to the hall, pulling the door closed behind them.

"Ye do no' really think yer husband's brother has been sleeping in yer father's room, do ye?" Moibeal asked as she helped her undress.

Edith sighed at the question, but didn't answer right away. The truth was, she didn't. She doubted very much if Rory would trouble himself to spread flowers on the floor to scent the rushes. However, she didn't want the castle to suddenly fill with tales of her father's ghost inhabiting his old room either. She didn't need maids afraid to clean the room once she and Niels moved to it. Especially when it wasn't true. It couldn't be. There was no such thing as ghosts, she told herself. Besides, her father really had hated lavender. It would be the last thing his ghost would scent the room with.

"M'lady."

"Hmm?" Edith glanced to Moibeal and sighed as she realized the girl was still waiting for her answer. Sighing, she stepped into the hot water, wincing at just how hot it was, and then eased to sit down. It was so hot it stole her breath for a moment, but once she'd adjusted, she sighed and said, "'Tis no' me father's ghost, Moibeal."

"Oh, I ken that," she said at once, a little too quickly. "But do ye really think 'tis Lord Rory?"

"I do no' ken," she said rather than admit she doubted that. Much as the girl denied it, Edith knew Moibeal was as superstitious as the next person. "I shall ask him later."

"Aye," the maid said and asked. "Shall I wash yer hair first?"

"Aye, please," Edith murmured.

Moibeal helped to wash her hair, then left her to her bath and quickly collected her discarded clothes.

Edith scrubbed herself up, and then relaxed in the water for a bit. The aches and stiffness were gone, and she was just considering getting out when the bedchamber door opened. Glancing over her shoulder, Edith smiled when she saw that it was Niels. Her smile widened when she saw the pitcher and two goblets he carried.

He smiled in return and then glanced to Moibeal and opened the door wider. The maid understood the silent request at once and hurried out of the room. Niels closed it silently behind her and then carried the pitcher and goblets to the bedside table and poured two glasses.

"I apologize fer taking so long," he said, setting down the pitcher and crossing the room to collect the large strip of linen Moibeal had left to warm over the chair by the fire. Opening it as he walked toward her, he said, "Rory wanted to speak to me."

"'Tis fine," Edith said, gathering her courage to stand up. She knew she shouldn't be so flustered at the thought of it. He was her husband. And she'd been as good as naked with him in the meadow. She also must have been when they consummated the wedding. However, she felt as shy in that moment as if he'd never even glimpsed a naked ankle, and they'd not even kissed.

Pausing next to the tub, Niels held the towel open for her and said, "Remind me to tell ye about it after."

"After what?" Edith asked, trying to distract herself as she stood quickly and stepped out of the tub and into the linen. Much to her relief, he closed it around her at once, but much to her surprise, he then picked her up and carried her back to the table and set her on the edge of it right in front of one of the chairs.

Eyeing him with confusion, she opened her mouth to ask him what he was doing, only to find his hands cupping her face as his mouth suddenly covered hers. Hands rising tentatively to his arms, Edith started out simply holding on as he kissed her. But she was quickly clutching at him and kissing him eagerly back.

When his hands slid away from her face and glided down to the top of the linen to unwrap it, Edith gasped. She then moaned into his mouth as his hands found and cupped her breasts so that he could toy with her nipples using a thumb and finger of each hand.

Edith reached for him then, not his plaid, or his shirt. Her hands went straight for the gold, one lifting his plaid so the other could find the hardness waiting beneath. The moment she did, Niels jerked in shock and then was suddenly gone.

Opening her eyes at once, Edith blinked at him as she saw that he'd dropped to sit on the chair and was urging it closer to the table. Her legs had been open with him standing between them, but she started to close them self-consciously now. She never finished the action. Niels caught each under the knee, tugged her closer so that she was half-off the table and had to lean back on her arms to keep from teetering off it. He then pulled her legs farther open and bent to bury his face between them.

Edith cried out at the first flick of his tongue across her eager flesh, but it was followed by many more such cries as he feasted on her. She tried to muffle the sounds she was making, first by covering her mouth with her hand, and then by biting on her middle finger too, but the sounds kept coming. Some were breathless cries, some were pleading gasps, some were almost screeches, but Edith was quite sure the men in the hall probably heard every last one. She was equally sure that everybody in the castle heard her final, delirious scream as her body exploded with pleasure to leave her a stunned, trembling mass lying limp on the table-top with her head turned toward the fire.

Edith was aware of it when Niels stood and removed his tartan and shirt, but other than roll her eyes toward him to watch, she didn't seem to have the strength to move. When he then scooped her up, carried her to the large fur in front of the fire and knelt to lay her on it, she caught his arms and then his hands as Niels straightened to kneel beside her. She was trying to hold him to her. But she couldn't.

"Ye're a feast fer the eyes, wife," he murmured, simply sitting on his haunches looking at her. "Ye're hair looks afire and shadows are painting yer skin."

Her energy was slowly returning now, enough for her to start to feel embarrassed at just lying there with him looking at her, and Edith slid one hand up his leg, toward his groin. She never made contact. Niels immediately shifted to lie next to her on his side.

Bracing his head on his hand with his elbow on the furs, he smiled. "Recovering, are ye?"

Edith nodded, and touched his face gently.

"Would ye like more?" Niels asked, running one hand lightly along her thigh.

Breath catching in her throat, Edith hesitated, but when his hand stopped just before it would have found her, she gave a jerky nod.

"Aye," Niels breathed, letting his fingers glide between the protective folds to touch her. He ran one finger gently over her and Edith closed her eyes and moaned.

"I love it when ye let me hear yer pleasure," he said softly, strumming his finger over her again and bringing about another one. "And I love how wet ye get fer me. As if yer body's weeping fer me to love ye."

"Aye," Edith groaned, her hips beginning to shift into his caress, and then she stilled as he pressed a finger into her. Her eyes flew open, and she peered at him. "Niels, please."

"Please what, love?" Niels asked, sliding his finger back out and then caressing her with his thumb as it slid back in. "Do ye like this?"

"Aye," she gasped, writhing under his touch.

"I do too. I like how yer body clings to me, it wants me in ye."

"Aye," Edith groaned.

"Do ye want me in ye, love?"

"Oh, God, aye!" she cried, thrusting violently up into his caresses now.

"Find yer pleasure fer me, love, and I'll take ye." This time he didn't give her a chance to reply, but leaned forward to claim her mouth with his and began thrusting his tongue into her in time with the finger below. The hand that had been holding up his head then dropped to caress and knead her breast at the same time and finally pinched her nipple. And that was when Edith began to shudder, her body quaking as she screamed into his mouth.

And suddenly Niels was on top of her. She didn't notice the shift until he was thrusting into her and she felt the difference. This wasn't his finger. This was much bigger. She felt the slightest pinch and then he was in, filling her and forcing her body to accommodate him. Edith cried out again and clutched at his shoulders, her hips still thrusting as her pleasure continued to pulse from her core, clinging and squeezing him.

Niels groaned through his teeth and thrust back repeatedly, and then he suddenly rose up, caught her legs by the ankles and drew them over his shoulders. Edith gaped up at him in surprise and then cried out when he reached down to where they were joined to continue to caress her; it prolonged her body's response as he rode the wave he'd caused. For Edith it seemed to go on forever and she was sure she couldn't take it, that her heart would stop or she'd simply die there underneath him, overwhelmed by so much sensation.

Just when she thought that, Niels stiffened above her, his body plunging so deep she cried out with it, and then she scored his back with her nails and screamed as her pleasure intensified and then shattered.

EDITH WOKE TO FIND IT WAS DAYLIGHT AND SHE was lying with her head on Niels's chest as he lazily caressed her back. She lay still, simply enjoying it for a moment, and then let him know she was awake by blurting, "I felt a pinch when ye—" She paused abruptly, unwilling to put words to what they'd been doing.

Fortunately, Niels seemed to understand exactly when she'd felt the pinch without her saying so, because he hugged her briefly and said, "Sorry, wife. They do say the first time is painful for the lass."

"The first time?" Edith asked with surprise, lifting her head to peer at him. "But I thought—There was blood on the linen and . . ." Her voice trailed away to silence as he began to chuckle. Eyebrows rising, she asked, "What is so funny, my lord husband?"

"What ye thought was blood on the linens was the preserves, lass," he explained with amusement.

"The preserves?" she echoed, and then her eyes widened as she recalled Magda's advice and what she'd done with Jaimie's preserves.

"Aye," he said with a faint smile. "It got on the bed when I laid ye in it after ye lost consciousness. By morning it had dried and looked enough like blood that we hung the linen. That way ye'd be protected did Brodie return ere our marriage was consummated and try to have it annulled."

"Oh," she breathed and lowered her head to his chest, her mind whirling with thoughts. She'd thought he'd consummated the marriage while she was unconscious, but he hadn't. Niels had found another way to protect her.

"'Tis morning," he murmured suddenly.

Smiling, Edith shook her head slightly where it lay, and let her hand glide down to his hip. "Nay. 'Tis still night, husband," Edith said as she let her hand slide to claim his semi-erect manhood.

"Again?" He sounded amused, but his voice was also husky. She was beginning to recognize that as a sign that he wanted her. Although she would have known anyway since he immediately hardened fully in her hand.

"Aye. Again," Edith said, caressing him.

"Greedy," he accused, but sounded pleased and the hand at her back drifted down to squeeze her bottom, before drifting between her legs from behind to tease her.

Edith moaned and kissed his chest appreciatively. They had been in bed ever since he'd walked in on her bath the afternoon before. Well, really they had not been in the bed the whole time. She'd been on the table, then they'd been on the fur, then he'd carried her to the bed and made love to her again before they'd drifted off. They'd woken up several times in the night, each time reaching for each other again.

In truth, Edith couldn't seem to get enough of him. The pleasure he gave her was heady, and she just wanted more and more. She wanted to learn more too. Edith hadn't known there were so many positions and so many different things to do. And with each new position, her confidence grew and she became bolder.

"We need to talk first," Niels growled, but his fingers continued to fondle her, and he didn't stop her caressing him.

"Aye. Talk," she murmured, shifting her head so that she could lick and then nip at his nipple.

Niels groaned, but then caught her hand and dragged it from his erection before grabbing her by the shoulders and forcing her up and away from him. Expression serious, he said, "We really do need to talk, Edith. 'Tis important."

She considered his face for a moment, and then sighed and nodded.

"Thank ye," he murmured and then shifted to sit up in bed with his back against the wall.

"What for?" Edith asked uncertainly, shifting to sit next to him.

"Had ye pressed the issue, I could no' have resisted loving ye again, and this is important," he promised her.

For a moment, Edith was tempted to press the issue

after all, but he'd said it was important and his expression had turned grim, so she behaved herself and tugged the linens up to cover herself as she waited for him to begin.

"Rory came to me yesterday afternoon," he began in a soft voice.

"Aye, when we returned from the market," she said.

Niels nodded. "He had something o' a plan to catch the killer."

"Really?" she asked with interest. "Tell me."

He hesitated, and then sighed and said, "His plan was fer ye to die."

"What?" Edith squawked, jumping to her knees to gawk at him with disbelief.

"Aye, that was me reaction," Niels said dryly. "But his thinking was that we fake ye dying, lay ye out here as if ye've been cleaned and prepared fer burial and then see who steps forward to try to claim Drummond."

Edith shook her head. "That will no' work. We already ken that Tormod would be the next in line and I am quite sure he is no' the one behind all o' this. So if the killer is really after Drummond, they may be just trying to make him look guilty so that he is blamed for everything and hung, leaving them to make a claim for the title." She frowned and added, "And if we fake me death and then do no' accuse Tormod the killer may just kill him to get him out o' the way."

"Aye," Niels grimaced. "Well, that was no' me argument, but 'tis all true."

"What was yer argument?" Edith asked curiously.

"That I'd no' risk ye that way," he said solemnly. "I pointed out that the murderer might slip into yer room while we had ye laid out pretending to be dead and stab ye or some such thing when they realized ye were still breathing."

"Oh, aye," she said weakly. "That would be unfortunate."

"Most unfortunate," Niels agreed dryly, and then sighed and admitted, "But as we talked I came up with an idea o' me own."

"Oh?" Edith asked with interest. "What is that?"

"To give them the opportunity to poison ye, and catch them at it," he answered.

Edith raised her eyebrows. This did not sound much better than Rory's idea on first blush.

Noting her expression, he explained, "Ye would no' be poisoned."

"Oh, good," she said on a laugh.

Niels grimaced, and said, "We will go below to break our fast. Ye'll notice that Alick is no' there and ask after him," he instructed.

"All right," Edith agreed solemnly.

"When ye do, I'll say I sent him to Buchanan and then on to MacDonnell with messages to let them ken we're no' coming after all and what is happening here."

"But ye did no' send him anywhere," she guessed.

"Nay, I did no'. He's in his room right now, waiting to come in here and hide."

"Hide?" Edith's eyebrows rose and she glanced around. "He could hide under the bed, or in the larger chest there. Moibeal has mostly emptied that one out, I think, and we can transfer whatever is left to the other chests."

"Under the bed may be better," Niels said glancing around the room as well. "We'd have to put holes in the chest so that he could see out otherwise and I do no' want his view obscured in any way."

Edith nodded and then turned back to him as he continued.

"Anyway, after I explain about Alick being away, ye should rub yer forehead and complain that ye've a headache. I'll suggest ye go lay down fer a bit, that it may help. You then say that ye'll just fetch some cider to take up with ye and I'll say, nay, I'll take care o' it. Ye go ahead."

"Then I come up here where Alick is hiding," she suggested.

"Nay, ye wait out o' sight on the upper landing," Niels said firmly. "I will fetch the cider or mead or something else, but rather than take it up meself, I'll tell Moibeal to take it up to you and then return to the table to talk to me brother. And then ye come downstairs before Moibeal can get to the top and tell her to put it in yer room, and then to return and find ye in the kitchens, that ye want a word with her and Jaimie ere ye lay down. Ye must say it loudly enough that all can hear," he added, and then continued, "And then ye go to the kitchens."

"So, Moibeal will take the drink up and put it in the bedchamber where Alick is hiding, and then come below, leaving it alone," Edith said slowly.

"Aye. I'm hoping our killer will risk slipping up here to poison the drink ere ye return and Alick will see who 'tis."

Edith nodded and said cautiously, "It may work. If they're desperate enough to risk coming up here when everyone is in the great hall and they might be seen."

"Aye." Niels frowned and then sighed and said,

"We shall just have to hope they are desperate enough fer the title o' laird to risk it."

"If they are even after that," Edith said glumly.

"What else could they be after?" Niels asked with surprise.

Edith shook her head. "I'm no' sure, but the killings . . ." Swallowing, she said, "Roderick and Hamish suffered horribly before dying, and me father would ha'e too had he no' already been weakened by his heart complaint. I suffered too," she added, "And I ken Rory thinks I survived because me body kept rejecting the poison, but the last time me drink was poisoned, he said that the killer had increased the poison and I surely would have died had I drank more."

"Aye, I recall," Niels said when she paused.

"Well, why did they no' give a stronger dose the first time they poisoned us?" she asked quietly. "Why put in just enough to kill them after great suffering? From what ye said, Brodie and the others died quickly, so the killer kenned how much to use, and simply did no' do that for the wine that killed me father and brothers and made me sick."

"Ye think they wanted ye to suffer," he said thoughtfully.

"They could ha'e doubled the dose in any o' the drinks or stew I had during those three weeks I was sick," she pointed out. "But they did no'. They drew it out."

"Mayhap," Niels said thoughtfully. He was silent for a minute and then asked, "Is there anyone ye can think o' who may wish ye ill like that?"

Edith lowered her head and thought briefly, but finally shook her head, and then, trying to lighten the mood, said, "Apart from yer Annie, nay."

Niels blinked in confusion. "Who?"

"Yer neighbor in the pig story yer brothers told me," she said with a small smile. "If she's a brain in her head she must love ye madly and will surely wish me a slow, painful death fer marrying ye."

A chuckle slipping from his lips, Niels drew her against his chest for a hug and murmured, "Ye do make me happy, Edith."

"Well and sure I would," she said lightly. "I'm the perfect wife. One who comes with a castle and title and dies quickly after ye marry her, leaving ye free to marry another. That is the perfect wife, is it no'?"

"Nay," he said sharply. "And I'm no' letting ye die, Edith. I love ye."

Chapter 14

 I LOVE YE.

Those words echoed in Edith's head and she sat as if frozen for a minute, her eyes locked on her husband's, and then a knock sounded at the door.

Niels tore his gaze from hers and glanced toward the sound. Tossing the linens aside, he muttered, "That'll be Alick coming to hide."

"Husband," Edith said, scrambling off the bed, but it was too late, Niels was opening the door.

A squeak of alarm slipping from her, Edith dove back into bed and pulled the linens over herself. But Niels just murmured a few words and then closed the door. Turning around, he frowned when he saw she was back in bed, and asked, "What are ye doin'? Why are ye no' getting dressed?"

Edith hesitated for a moment, just staring at him, and then she slid out of bed. Hurrying to her chest, she rifled through for a gown and chemise and then quickly ran a brush through her hair before pulling her clothes on. She knew Niels was dressing even as she did, still it was something of a surprise to her when she turned and saw that he had finished already too. The man was fast at pleating his tartan when he wanted to be, that was for sure, Edith thought.

"We'll talk later," Niels said quietly as she joined him by the door.

Nodding, she let him take her arm and lead her from the room.

Edith didn't see Alick anywhere in the hall as they stepped out, but Cameron and Fearghas were there waiting to escort them below. Supposing Alick was waiting in one of the nearby rooms to hide in the bedchamber after they left, Edith nodded absently at the two soldiers and then promptly forgot about them as Niels led her up the hall. Her mind was too muddled with the thoughts rolling around in her head for her to think about much else. She kept seeing Niels's face as he'd said he loved her.

His declaration had caught her completely by surprise. She had never even dared dream she might hear words like that from him . . . at least not so soon.

When he'd asked her to marry him, Niels had said he wanted her something fierce, but that he liked her too. He'd said he thought her fine and smart and liked that she had a good heart. He'd said he thought they could be happy together. Those were all things Edith was thinking of him too. She too had wanted him something fierce, and she had thought him fine and smart. She'd liked his patience with Ronson and Laddie, and his caring and concern for her. And she too had thought they could be happy together. She still did.

If she were honest with herself, Edith had hoped

that from all of that, love would someday grow. She hadn't even really acknowledged that to herself, but the hope had been there, like a seed taking root under the dirt before pushing its way through to the light. The possibility had seemed a hopeful one to her since she felt their mutual liking and admiration were a solid basis for it to grow in.

And I'm no' letting ye die, Edith. I love ye.

Could he really love her already? And if so, might the feelings churning inside her be love for him as well?

"Wife?"

Edith blinked her thoughts away, noted the bench before her and gave her head a shake. While she'd been lost in thought they'd descended the stairs and crossed the great hall to the trestle tables.

"Oh," she breathed, and immediately sat down, vaguely aware that Cameron and Fearghas were moving off to claim seats farther down the table where they could keep an eye on her without intruding.

"Good morn, m'lady."

Edith smiled automatically at the man on her left as Niels settled on her right, and then blinked as she saw that it was Tormod. "Ye're back."

"Aye," he said and then tilted his head quizzically. "Are ye all right, m'lady?"

"Fine," Edith murmured and then glanced past him to Geordie.

"Tormod was just telling us that they found no sign o' Victoria's maid, Nessa, at the hunting lodge," her brother-in-law said.

Edith sat up straight, her eyes widening. "I forgot about Nessa. She went with them too."

"Aye," Niels said, and explained, "But Geordie and

I did no' find her in the lodge with the others. Tormod was going to look fer her when they went to collect yer brother and the others."

"But she was no' there," Tormod finished. "We searched the entire lodge and then a good way into the woods around the lodge, but there was no sign o' her at all," he assured them solemnly and then added, "Yet none o' the horses were missing. She rode with one o' the soldiers on the way out because Brodie did no' want a cart to slow them, and there were seven dead horses there in the stalls. Only Lonnie's was missing, so she did no' ride away."

"Not on her own," Niels agreed, and then added, "But she could have left the lodge with Lonnie to return here."

There was a moment of silence as everyone considered that, and then Tormod sighed. "If so . . ."

He didn't finish his thought, but then he didn't have to. They all knew the rest of what he hadn't said. If Nessa had been with Lonnie when he was killed, and if the man *had* been killed by bandits as they'd assumed, then the maid had most likely been taken by them. Nessa had been a pretty little thing. If bandits *had* taken her, she'd probably been sorely used and then left dead in the woods somewhere. If not on Drummond land then wherever the bandits traveled after Drummond.

Shaking his head, Tormod said into the silence that had fallen, "Between Effie being poisoned and possibly dying, Victoria poisoned and dead and Nessa taken and probably murdered by bandits, Victoria and her maids did no' make out well here."

"Nay," Edith murmured, but frowned and stared

down at the tabletop, her mind racing as she tried to put together the bits of information those words had suddenly sent bouncing around inside her head. None of them made sense, or meant anything on their own, but she was sure they would if she could put them together properly.

"What are ye thinking, lass?" Tormod asked.

Edith shook her head, but then grasped at one bit of information that kept flashing through her mind and said, "The murders started after Victoria and her maids got here."

Dead silence met her words and Edith glanced around to see her husband, his brothers and Tormod all staring at her wide-eyed. It seemed obvious that hadn't occurred to them. It also seemed obvious they weren't sure what to make of it either.

Sighing, she said, "It just seems to me that we have been asking who and why without being able to sort it out. But we have no' once considered when it started as possibly being important, and yet why would it start all o' a sudden like that? One day all was well at Drummond, and then the next me father was dead, me brothers dying and I was ill, and it all happened shortly after Victoria arrived. The day her maids got here, actually."

"I had no' thought o' that," Tormod said slowly.

"But Nessa is missing and Effie was poisoned too," Rory pointed out with a frown.

"Aye, we can no' find Nessa," Edith said thoughtfully.

"But that does no' mean she's dead necessarily, does it?" Niels said now, following her train of thought.

"Nay, I suppose not," Rory acknowledged. "But Effie is definitely poisoned and likely to die eventually."

"When?" Edith asked.

Rory stared at her blankly.

"I mean is she showing signs of weakening?" Edith asked, and then pointed out, "Ye said the other day that she was looking better and had more color. That ye'd almost think she was getting food other than the soup ye dribble down her throat."

"Aye, but I test her daily. She is no' conscious and can no' be eating," he said firmly.

"How do ye test her?" she asked at once. It was something she'd wanted to ask since Niels had mentioned this testing business to her. Because she suspected she knew how. At least, she knew how she would test, and if Rory was testing Effie the same way—

"I stick a needle in her foot," Rory said, his eyebrows slightly raised at the question, and then he added, "Quite deep too. There is no way she could pretend to sleep through it."

"Ah," Edith breathed out the word, her head going back slightly at this news, and then she turned to stare down at the tabletop again, more pieces connecting in her mind.

"Lass?" Tormod asked. "What are ye thinking?"

Edith was silent for another minute, and then admitted, "I'm thinking that twice now I've seen what looked like a woman in one o' the windows o' the upper chambers, and—"

"When?" Niels asked at once.

"The day the arrow was shot at me was the first time," she admitted. "I landed on yer chest on me back, and just before ye rolled me under ye, I saw someone in the window o' me room. 'Twas just a quick glance, and I only got an impression o' the person, but now that I'm thinking on it, it could have been a woman."

"And the second time?" Geordie asked.

"Yesterday on the way back from the market," she admitted. "As we started into the bailey I remembered what I'd seen the day the arrow was shot at me and I leaned out around the shield to look toward the window."

"Aye, I remember," Niels said quietly. "I pushed ye back behind the shield."

Edith nodded. "But in the quick glimpse I got, I thought I saw a woman there again." She shrugged as if it wasn't important, and added, "But again I only got a quick look."

"So, ye're thinking Nessa is here somewhere?" Tormod asked grimly.

"That or the woman I saw was Effie," she said on a sigh, quite sure they would reject it at once.

"Nay," Rory said firmly as she expected. "I told ye, I poke her feet with a needle twice daily. And I poke it deep, Edith. She could no' feign sleep through it."

"Effie has no feeling in her feet," Edith told him baldly.

"What?" Rory asked sharply.

"Are ye sure?" Niels asked.

Edith nodded. "Victoria told me so herself. 'Tis why she brought Nessa to help her. Effie has no feeling in her feet and her legs are weak—she can no' walk far or stand long. It makes doing her job difficult."

Cursing, Niels started to rise, but Rory caught his arm.

"Wait," he said. "Think on this, brother. Why would Effie kill everyone? Had she stopped at Edith's father and brothers, I might believe she was trying to give Victoria all that Brodie promised her when he talked the girl into marrying him. But then she would hardly kill Victoria and Brodie. And now that Victoria is dead, she gains nothing from killing Edith."

"Victoria, and not Effie, could have been the one who was truly poisoned by accident," Tormod said solemnly, and explained, "Victoria did no' care fer ale. Mayhap Effie put the poison in the ale, thinking Victoria would no' drink it." His mouth tightened and he added, "And I'm sure Lady Victoria would no' have drunk it had she had something else, but Brodie rarely considered others and did no' this time. There was nothing else for Victoria to drink."

"So she drank the ale," Edith murmured with a nod. That made sense, she supposed, but there were still pieces that didn't fit, she thought, and then glanced around as Niels suddenly headed for the stairs. Tormod and Geordie were hard on his heels.

When Cameron and Fearghas stood and moved to stand behind her, Edith got up to follow as well, but she was moving much more slowly. So was Rory, she noted as he fell into step beside her. She was silent for a moment, aware of Cameron crowding her from behind. He was right on her heels, eager for her to move more quickly so that they could get to where the action was, but Edith ignored him and as she started up the stairs with Rory, said, "Ye do no' think 'twas Effie."

Rory grimaced. "Perhaps 'tis just because I have been nursing her for so long, trying to get her to live that I do no' want to believe it, but nay. I do no'." He glanced at her sharply then and said, "And you?"

"I do no' ken," she admitted. "There are still things that do no' fit."

"What do ye mean?" Rory asked with curiosity.

"Well, Effie could be awake, and she could have enough knowledge o' poisonings to be behind *those* deaths," Edith acknowledged.

"But how could she ha'e got down to the kitchen to stab Cawley without anyone noticing her?" Rory suggested.

"Aye," Edith said on a sigh. "And I find it hard to believe that Effie could hold the bow steady enough to shoot an arrow so straight. Aside from her feet being numb, she had the palsy in her hands and arms. "

"It was no' her," he said with relief.

"Ye were afraid ye'd been working so hard to keep a murderer alive," she said with understanding.

"I would ne'er have forgiven meself," Rory admitted as they stepped onto the landing.

Edith nodded, and then glanced up the hall as Niels strode out of the room Effie had been put in, his face set in harsh lines.

"She's gone," he announced grimly.

"Gone where?" Rory asked with surprise. "She was in bed when I went below to break me fast and some-one would have noticed had she come down the stairs."

"She must be up here somewhere then," Geordie growled.

"I'll search all the rooms," Tormod said grimly.

He started to turn away, but paused when Cameron stepped up beside Edith and asked, "Could she be the one who started the fire in the laird's room?"

"What?" Niels asked with surprise.

Before Cameron could speak again, Edith explained, "Yesterday as we waited fer me bath to come, Moibeal, the lads and I went to take a look at the laird's chamber to see what would need doing should we decide to move there. But when we got there we found evidence that someone has been using the room."

"Aye, the room was warm, so I checked the fireplace," Cameron announced. "I thought all there was in the hearth were ashes, but they were warm, some still embers."

"And the bed is made up with linens and furs and had obviously been slept in," Fearghas added.

When Niels immediately turned and headed up the hall, Edith followed. She didn't realize everyone else was trailing her until Tormod barked, "Fearghas, get back to the stairs and guard them. Let no one up or down."

The man sighed at missing out on all the excitement, but stopped at once as the rest of them continued to the door to the laird's bedchamber.

"Is that lavender?" Rory asked, sniffing the air as he followed Edith and Niels into the room.

"Aye," Niels said, running a boot over the dried petals strewn over the rush mats.

"'Tis warm," Tormod commented.

"Aye, there are embers in the hearth again," Cameron said, kneeling by the fireplace to poke around at them as he had the day before. Straightening, he looked to Tormod and assured him, "I saw no one enter or leave the room while Fearghas and I stood guard."

"Tearlach and Wallace stood guard in the hall last night. They'll be abed—go wake them and fetch them back here, Cameron," Tormod ordered, moving to Niels's side as he tugged the bed curtains open to reveal the disarranged linens and furs.

"Moibeal opened those yesterday, and we left them

that way when we returned to me bedchamber," Edith said solemnly. "Someone must have been here since."

"Ye should have told me about this," Niels said with a scowl as he turned to glance at her.

"I intended to," she assured him, and then blushed. "But I did no' really get the chance, and then quite forgot all about it until Cameron brought it up."

"It did sound as if ye distracted her quite thoroughly," Geordie said with amusement when Niels continued to glower.

"Aye, well, mayhap we should let some light in here," Tormod muttered, hurrying to the nearest window to open the shutters.

Happy for the excuse to hide her face for a moment, Edith opened the shutters on the second window, and then glanced up with surprise when Niels was suddenly beside her.

"I'm sorry. I should no' have snapped at ye," he apologized, rubbing her back soothingly.

Edith smiled crookedly. "Ye did no' really snap, m'laird."

"Ye just growled like a bear," Rory added as he passed them on the way to examine the water in the basin on the table between the two windows.

Scowling after him, Niels added heavily, "And I apologize for me brothers' embarrassing behavior."

"*Our* behavior?" Geordie asked with a hoot. "We are no' the ones who kept everyone in the castle up half the night with our howling."

Groaning, Edith closed her eyes and leaned her head on Niels's chest, muttering, "Sorry. I'll try to be quieter in future."

She'd meant that for Niels and had said it low

enough that she thought only he'd hear it, but Geordie said, "Oh, lass, ye've nothing to apologize fer. Yer voice was like a bird singing. 'Twas wondrous to hear. Now Niels on the other hand . . ."

"He sounded like a wounded bear," Rory finished dryly. "Scared the little ones sleeping in the great hall near to death."

"I'll just wait in the hall and watch fer Tearlach and Wallace," Tormod said loudly, obviously uncomfortable with this conversation.

"Now, see what ye've done," Niels growled. "Ye've embarrassed me wife *and* Tormod."

"Aye," Rory said with a sigh and turned from the water to meet Edith's gaze as she lifted her head and glanced toward him. Grimacing apologetically he said, "I'm sorry, lass. But truth to tell, we'll probably do it again repeatedly over the years. Yer family now."

"Aye," Geordie agreed. "And that's how we are with family."

Much to Edith's dismay, their words brought a sudden lump to her throat and tears were quickly filling her eyes.

"Oh, lass, do no' cry," Geordie said with alarm. "We'll try to behave better."

"It'll probably no' work, but we *will* try," Rory assured her with concern.

Pulling back abruptly, Niels caught her chin in his hand and raised her face. He scowled when he saw the tears threatening to overflow her eyes, and Edith found herself suddenly pressed firmly to his chest as he began to thump her back as if burping a babe.

"I hope ye're proud o' yerselves," he snapped. "Grown men making a wee lass weep."

A burble of laughter slipped from Edith's lips, and she pushed away from his chest. Shaking her head, she said, "'Tis fine. I'm no' crying."

"Actually, aye lass, ye are," Rory said gently as she dashed away the tears that had spilled over onto her cheeks.

"Unless yer eyes are just leaking," Geordie said hopefully. "But it does look like we made ye cry."

"Nay," she assured them, and then added, "Well, aye, but only because I was touched by yer considering me family."

"Ah," Rory said with understanding. "Well, I'm afraid yer stuck with us. Ye *are* family now that ye married our brother."

"Aye," Geordie growled, and then teased, "But the fact that ye agreed to marry him proves yer touched."

Niels glowered at his brother, but Edith chuckled and then glanced toward the door as Tormod stepped back into the room to announce, "The men are coming."

The first didn't return to the hall then, but paced briefly in the center of the room as they awaited Cameron's arrival with the guards who had been in the hall outside their chamber during the night.

Edith bit her lip and eyed the two men sympathetically when they hurried into the room on Cameron's heels. Both men had obviously been rousted from a deep sleep and looked a bit panicked, as if they thought they were in trouble. It appeared Cameron hadn't explained things and had simply rumbled them from their beds in the garrison and rushed them back here.

The moment they paused in front of Tormod, he asked, "Did ye see anyone coming or going from this room last night?"

"Nay," they said in unison, both obviously surprised by the question. That more than anything said they hadn't.

"Fine." Tormod nodded. "Ye can find yer beds again."

The two men looked more bewildered than when they'd entered, but nodded and turned to leave.

"That fire did no' start itself," Niels said now. "There must be a secret entrance. We should search the room."

Tormod hesitated and then said, "There's no need to search. I ken where it is."

Edith glanced at him with surprise. "There's a secret entrance?"

"Aye."

"Where?" she asked, glancing around curiously.

Tormod hesitated and then said stiffly, "Only the Laird and Lady o' Drummond ever ken where 'tis."

"And you," Niels added.

"Aye. Laird Drummond told me when Lady Drummond died. He felt someone besides him should ken in case he died unexpectedly before passing the secret on to his son," Tormod explained.

Niels nodded solemnly and said, "If ye'd rather only tell Edith, my brothers and I can leave."

She glanced to him with surprise at that, and opened her mouth to protest, but before she could, Tormod said, "Nay. Ye're laird here now. Ye should ken."

Edith relaxed and beamed at Tormod. The man had just given most definitive approval of her husband. Her people must have accepted him. It wasn't something she'd even worried about ere this, but she was glad not to have to.

When Tormod still hesitated to speak, Niels said quietly, "I trust me brothers with me life."

Sighing, the man nodded and turned to Cameron. "Close the door on yer way out."

The soldier nodded smartly and slipped from the room, pulling the door closed behind him.

The moment it had shut, Tormod walked to the candle ledge to the left of the fireplace and pressed on the smallest stone in the middle. The wall on the left of the fireplace immediately shifted, a portion of it about seven feet tall and three wide sliding open about an inch. Tormod caught the raised edge and pulled the hidden door open into the room.

"Where does it go?" Niels asked as he, Geordie and Rory crowded into the opening to peer into the darkness revealed to them.

"This one leads to hidden stairs."

"Stairs to where?" Edith asked, fascinated.

"They go both up to the wall and down to a passage at ground level with several hidden doors. There is one in one of the garderobes off the great hall, one in the pantry off the kitchens, one from the gardens and then another to a tunnel that runs out under the bailey and outer wall to a cave in the woods at a spot about halfway between where the woods start and where the loch is."

Niels considered that and then turned to ask, "So around where we found Lonnie?"

"Aye," Tormod admitted, surprised to note that. "Quite close, in fact. About twenty feet to the right and ten feet farther out from where ye found Lonnie if yer back were to the castle."

Niels nodded and then raised a questioning eyebrow. "Ye said *this* one leads to the great hall and the kitchens. There is another?"

Tormod turned to walk to the candle ledge on the right of the fireplace. This time he pressed the largest stone in that ledge and a second secret door slid inward an inch.

"This one leads to the bedchambers along the outer wall," Tormod announced, pulling it open as the three brothers moved over to look into this new, dark passage. "The rooms Lady Edith and her brothers occupied and that you're all in now."

"What about the windows?" Edith asked with a frown and when Tormod glanced to her in question, she pointed out, "Surely the windows in each room are in the way. Do ye have to crawl under them?"

"The passage slopes down from each entrance to clear the windows and then back up to the next entrance. In truth, as much o' it is between the upper part of the great hall wall and the outer wall as the wall o' the upper chambers and the outer wall. And there are peep holes drilled every few feet so ye can look down on the great hall."

Frowning, Edith asked, "There are no' peep holes into the bedchambers, though, are there?"

Tormod's eyes widened at the suggestion and then his brow furrowed and he admitted, "I'm no' sure, m'lady. Yer father merely took me to each bedchamber, showed me how to open each entrance, explained about the passage dropping down between each secret door and told me ye could see into the great hall through peep holes. He did no' mention being able to see into the bedchambers and I've never had occasion to actually go inside the passages."

Grunting, Niels looked around the room and then said, "Wait here," and slipped out into the hall. He opened the door just enough to slide through so that the open passages would not be revealed to anyone in the hall.

They all stood silently, lost in their own thoughts, Edith supposed. She was certainly thinking. She was fretting about those peep holes. Worrying over whether there were any looking into the bedchambers, her bedchamber specifically. And if so, had the mystery person who'd been sleeping in this room watched them in their private moments? The possibility was distressing enough that Edith was grateful for the distraction when the door opened and Niels slipped back into the room carrying a lit torch.

Holding it high, he crossed the room, pausing by Edith to kiss her on the forehead, and then said, "I'll be right back," and slipped into the passage. Frowning, Edith moved to the opening and watched him raise his torch, but then peered back when Geordie asked, "Are there any passages to the bedchambers on the inside?"

"Nay. Just the outer rooms. That's why the family members were all given those rooms and the inner rooms were made guest rooms," he explained.

The men all nodded. It made sense. The passages were first and foremost an emergency escape should the castle be invaded. Visitors would not be here all the time and were the passages needed for an emergency escape, the family would be the first concern.

"There are torches in holders along the passage."

Edith gave a start at that announcement directly behind her, and stepped out of the way so that Niels could come back into the room. Smiling at her distractedly, he crossed to the second entrance and disappeared briefly inside that one.

"This one too," he announced as he came back out a moment later, and Edith noted the glow in the passage now. Apparently, he'd lit at least the first torch, she thought and then saw the same glow at the other entrance too.

"So this must be how someone has been getting in and out of this room without anyone seeing them," Rory commented, walking over to peer into the passage Niels had just come out of.

"Most likely," Niels agreed, but Edith noted that the suggestion made Tormod frown.

"It may even be how Effie has managed to disappear," Geordie pointed out.

"Nay," Tormod said, shaking his head firmly. "Effie could no' have kenned about these passages."

"Victoria could have told her," Edith pointed out.

"Victoria could no' have known either," he assured her.

"Brodie probably told Victoria the minute he found out about them," she assured him dryly.

"That's just it, he did no' ken about them, so could no' have told her," Tormod explained.

"What?" she asked with surprise. "But he was laird once Hamish died."

"Aye," he agreed, and then pointed out, "Fer two whole weeks ere fleeing the castle. And I would ha'e got around to telling him eventually. Probably," he added in a mutter, and then clucked with irritation and admitted, "I apologize, m'lady, but yer brother was a selfish, coddled, beef-witted idiot. I could hardly believe we were stuck with him as laird, and was hoping we would no' be. O' course, had he bothered to ask what he should ken to run Drummond, I would have told him. But he did no'. So . . . I decided to just wait until things settled down before sharing all the secrets o' this place with him."

"And would ye have done the same with us had this no' come up?" Niels asked in a deceptively mild tone.

"Hell no," Tormod said seeming truly shocked at the suggestion. "Yer a hundred times better man than Brodie was. A good match fer our lady. I'm glad to have ye and ken most everyone here at Drummond is relieved to have ye both as laird and lady rather than Brodie and Victoria. When I gave ye the key to the buttery I did tell ye I had things I must talk to ye about once I returned from collecting the bodies at the lodge," he reminded him and then gestured to the secret passages. "These were on that list."

Nodding, Niels relaxed and asked, "If Brodie did no' ken about these passages, who does besides you?"

"That's the hell o' it," Tormod said looking suddenly weary. "As far as I ken, I am the only living person who knew about these passages until just now when I told all o' you. But I swear to ye that I'm no' the one who's been sleeping in this room."

"Someone else must ken about the passages then," Edith said simply. She believed Tormod. He looked so frazzled by all of this that she simply couldn't believe he was the culprit. Besides, if he were the culprit, he'd hardly tell them that he was the only one who knew about the hidden entrances and secret passage. He'd claim he'd told Brodie who may have told Victoria who shared it with the maids. Or he might even have claimed several people knew about them. But he hadn't, and she believed him, she just wasn't sure anyone else would so was relieved when her husband nodded thoughtfully.

"Aye. So, someone must have discovered them on their own," Niels reasoned. "Mayhap Effie while cleaning."

Edith twisted her lips dubiously. "Effie did no' clean as far as I ken."

"Then mayhap yer brother Brodie accidentally found it himself while playing as a child, told his wife about it and she told the maid," Rory suggested.

She supposed that was possible. Edith had always kept a safe distance between herself and any fire. As a child, she'd been present when one of the young maids had got too close to the fireplace in the great hall. The girl's skirt had caught on fire and she'd been horribly burned before Edith's mother had covered her with a fur and smothered the flames. That incident had made her cautious of getting too close to any kind of fire or fireplace. Her brothers had never had the same problem, and as she recalled, Brodie had liked to play soldier around the fireplace, setting his little carved wooden men onto the candle ledges and then knocking them off one after the other, sometimes even throwing them into the fireplace to watch them burn. She supposed he could have leaned against just the right stone one time and discovered the secret passage.

"However and whoever discovered it, we need to search the rooms and the passages," Rory said quietly. "Effie is somewhere."

"Aye." Niels nodded and then glanced to the two passages and frowned. "We need to search each room and the passage at the same time. Otherwise we risk someone using the passage to slip by us as we are in each room."

"There are five bedchambers off the right passage

if ye include this one, and there are five o' us," Edith pointed out. "We could leave someone stationed here to be sure no one slips away using the passages and the other four could go to each o' the other bedchambers, search them and then all make our way back here via the passages to be sure there is no one there either."

"Except only Tormod kens how to open the other passages," Geordie pointed out.

"Aye, but I could take Lady Edith's room," Tormod said slowly, and pointed out, "'Tis the furthest away. After a quick search, I could slip into the passage, ensure no one is in it between that room and Brodie's and then open the hidden entrance to Brodie's room from the passage."

"Then you and whoever searched Brodie's room could continue on to the next hidden door, and the next, ensuring no one slips past ye and no one is in the passage," Niels said, nodding, and then smiled at Edith and complimented her. "Good idea, wife . . . Only the fifth person will be Alick. You will be safely down at the trestle tables with yer guard."

Edith's eyes widened. She'd quite forgotten about poor Alick hiding under the bed in their chamber. The young man must be wondering what the devil was happening at this point. Still, six people were better than one, she thought. But when she opened her mouth to say so, Niels silenced her with a quick kiss.

Lifting his head, he raised a hand to brush his knuckles lightly across her cheek and said, "I need to ken yer safe, wife. Else I'll be distracted with worry and may make a mistake that could get meself or Tormod, or one o' me brothers killed. 'Tis a murderer we're hunting."

Edith's brow furrowed, but after a moment, she sighed and gave a reluctant nod. It wasn't likely she would win this argument anyway. Men could be incredibly stubborn when it came to women treading on their territory, and she had no doubt Niels saw catching the killer as his job.

Besides, she didn't think they would find anything in the chambers or passages anyway. Effie would hardly be hiding in there when she had so many exits to choose from. Most of which weren't presently full of the men hunting her.

On top of that though, Edith also wanted a quiet moment to think. A good many things weren't making sense to her and she felt sure if she could just sort through them slowly and logically, she could untangle this mystery.

Chapter 15

"*M*'LADY?"

Edith stopped pressing on the stones in the wall behind the loo bench and glanced toward the garderobe door with a frown. "Moibeal?"

"Aye, m'lady," her maid said, her tone wry. "Cameron fetched me over to see that ye were all right. It seems ye've been in there awhile and they were beginning to worry."

"I'm fine. I'll be out directly," she called with exasperation and then peered at the wall again and sighed. She'd pressed every stone on the garderobe's back wall and as far as she could tell nothing had happened. There was no click, not even a breath of sound, and certainly no hidden door slid inward to reveal the entrance to the passage from here. Neither had that happened in the first two garderobes. This was the third and last one she'd checked since leaving her husband and the others to search the bedchambers and passages above as Cameron and Fearghas escorted her below stairs.

Now, she eyed the wall and considered that there was probably more of a trick to the entrance in the garderobe than just pushing a stone. Otherwise, with so many people using it, anyone could accidentally lean against the correct stone and discover the hidden door.

But what would the trick be? she wondered, reaching out to try to turn a stone rather than push it.

"M'lady?"

"I'm coming!" Edith called with exasperation. Stepping down off the bench, she walked to the door and pushed it open. Despite being happy to escape the stench of the garderobes, she scowled at Cameron, Fearghas and Moibeal as she stepped out, and then focused on her maid and asked, "What?"

"I was just going to ask ye if ye wished me to fetch one o' yer tonics," Moibeal said patiently. "The men said as how ye've stopped at every garderobe since coming below, spending an awful lot o' time in each, yet were immediately stopping at the next, so I thought mayhap ye had the flux and—"

"Nay, I'm fine," Edith said, flushing as she realized how her behavior had been interpreted by her guards. Shaking her head, she stepped around the trio and headed for the kitchens, muttering, "I need to have a word with Jaimie."

She wasn't at all surprised when all three trailed after her. The men had to, and it wasn't as if Moibeal had anything better to do at the moment. No doubt the guards had stopped her at the landing and refused to allow her to go clean the bedchamber as she normally would.

"Halt."

Edith glanced up with surprise and eyed the man who had stepped in front of her as she approached the kitchen door. Two new soldiers were guarding it today, she saw, her gaze sliding from the stern face of the man before her to his wincing partner still by the door.

"Move, Sholto," Cameron growled before Edith could speak. "Yer lady wants to enter the kitchens to speak to Jaimie."

"Tormod ordered us no' to let anyone pass," the man said firmly.

"Well, yer lady trumps Tormod," Fearghas said impatiently. "So move."

"Sholto," the second man said worriedly. "Mayhap ye should—"

"Shut up, Roy. I have this," Sholto snapped, and then propped his hands on his hips and scowled at the lot of them. "I have me orders and—"

"Sholto," Edith interrupted pleasantly.

Snapping his mouth shut, he eyed her warily. "Aye?"

"I am lady here. Tormod works fer me. Which means you work fer me. I want ye to move out o' the way." When he scowled and looked like he might refuse, Edith added, "And I suggest ye do it now or I'll tell yer wife ye were messing with the ale wench and I had to treat ye fer the drip."

"Ye mean the clap?" Moibeal gasped as Sholto paled and jumped to the side.

"Hmm," Edith muttered, leading the way into the kitchens now that her path was clear. She did hate that name for the ailment. It just reminded her of what often had to be done for it. Quite frequently, the patient's fiddle got clogged up with the discharge drip-

ping out of it. When that happened, her mother had
said one must clap it hard with your hands from both
sides to try to unclog it. She'd also said, though, that a
hand and a book might be used instead.

Sholto was such an annoying character, however,
that Edith had used two books. The man had howled
endlessly afterward. She doubted very much if he'd be
visiting the ale wench again anytime soon. Come to
think of it, he probably wouldn't come back to Edith
with any healing needs either, she acknowledged with
a grin as she glanced around the kitchen for the cook.

"He's no' here," Moibeal said with surprise as they
surveyed the almost empty kitchen. Honestly, four
people were like a drop of water in a bucket in this
huge room.

"I'll ask one o' the maids where he is," Fearghas
murmured and hurried off to do so.

Edith watched him go, but then found her gaze sliding to the back of the room as a memory of Cawley
lying bleeding on the floor flashed through her mind.
Her gaze slid over the large rush mat now lying where
he had been and it didn't take a lot of hard thinking to
work out that it was covering the stain his blood had
left behind. Cleaning it out of the cracks and crevices
of the stone would have been impossible.

"M'lady?"

Edith blinked and looked around at Moibeal's
voice, startled to find that in her distracted state she'd
crossed the room and now stood staring down at the
mat where Cawley's body had been. "Aye?"

"Fearghas says Jaimie is out in the gardens picking
some herbs," the maid told her gently.

Nodding, Edith peered back at the rush mat, and

then at the barrel behind it. That would have been where Cawley had been sitting when he was stabbed, she thought, and then shifted her attention to the door next to it. The pantry. Tormod had told them that there was another hidden entrance in there, she recalled. If the killer had used it, they might not even have had to come out of the room to stab him. Just crack the door open and—

"M'lady?" Moibeal said gently.

"Aye," Edith sighed, turning away. She would check the pantry later and see if she could find the hidden entrance. Or perhaps she'd just let Tormod show both her and Niels where it was later.

Heading for the back door out of the kitchens, she asked, "Out in the gardens, ye said?"

"Tormod said ye were no' to leave the keep," Cameron reminded her as he and Fearghas caught up to them.

"It is only the gardens, Cameron," she said on a sigh. "There are no windows on this side of the building for anyone to shoot arrows at me from. 'Twill be fine."

"But—"

"I'll just step outside the back door," she said soothingly. "Ye can bring Jaimie to me. 'Tis far too hot in here to stand about waiting fer ye to find him. At least by the back door it will be cooler."

Whether he would have argued the point or not, she didn't know. They'd reached the back door and she was already pushing her way out.

"I'll go fetch Jaimie," Fearghas said, sounding annoyed as he hurried ahead of her.

"There," Edith said cheerfully, ignoring the way Cameron was glaring at her. "Is this no' nice?"

"Nicer than the flogging we'll take fer letting ye out o' the keep," Cameron groused.

"We'll only be a minute. Tormod will never ken," she assured him. When he merely eyed her with disbelief, she raised one hand to her chest, the other to the air and said with amusement, "May God strike me down if I'm wrong in this."

Cameron glanced upward as if expecting to see lightning hurtling down toward them, and then horror crossed his face and he threw himself at Edith and Moibeal.

Edith gasped in surprise as she was caught about the waist and propelled forward, and then grunted in pain as she crashed to the ground just as a loud thump sounded behind them. For one moment, she lay there on her stomach, almost certain lightning *had* struck, but then reason returned and Edith realized that what she'd heard behind her was the thud of something heavy hitting the ground, and not the crack of lightning.

"Are ye all right, m'lady?" Cameron asked anxiously, getting to his feet beside her.

"Aye," Edith said, and peered past him to her maid. "Moibeal? Are ye all right?"

The maid rolled to her side and looked back at where they'd been, muttering, "Better than her."

Frowning, Edith started to get up, but had only managed to get to her hands and knees before Cameron caught her under the arms and lifted her to her feet.

"Thank ye," she murmured, brushing at her dress as she turned to see what had fallen. Who had fallen, Edith corrected herself as she stared at Effie's twisted body on the ground at their feet. The woman had landed exactly where they'd been standing before Cameron had half thrust and half dragged them out of the way. She couldn't have missed them by more than a hair, Edith thought with dismay, staring at her body.

"Oh, God's breath, m'lady!"

Edith glanced around at that voice, and just managed to brace herself before Jaimie threw his thin body at her and hugged her tightly. Unfortunately, short as she was, he was shorter, and his head landed between her breasts. Fortunately, however, she didn't have to say anything. As quickly as he did it the thin little man released her and jumped back, flushing brightly.

"I'm so sorry, m'lady. I was just so overset. Ye were nearly killed. Again! Ye should have waited fer me inside," he added, catching her arm and urging her around the body and back toward the door. "'Tis no' safe fer ye to be out o' the keep. Ye could have been killed. Again."

"Aye, 'tis almost as if God Himself were trying to strike ye down," Moibeal said under her breath.

Judging by the way Cameron's lips twitched, he heard the maid say that, but merely turned to Fearghas and said with resignation, "Ye'd best go fetch Tormod and the new laird. They'll need to hear about this."

Nodding, the soldier opened the door, held it for them to enter and then followed them inside and hurried quickly past them to rush out of the kitchens.

"Fearghas said ye were wanting a word with me," Jaimie was saying now. "Did ye want to break yer fast? Ye have no' done that yet. I can make ye a fine—"

"Nay," Edith interrupted. "Thank ye, but I wouldn't

want ye to take time out o' yer day to cook fer me. I just wanted to be sure that Duer and Iain delivered the cheese and capons I bought."

"Oh, aye, aye," he assured her, grinning. "'Tis all here. The cheese is in the larder and the capons look mighty fine and plump. I'm roasting 'em up for tonight's sup as soon as I finish gathering the herbs I need fer it."

"Oh, lovely, that will be nice," Edith murmured, patting his arm. "I should let ye get back to it then. That's all I wanted."

"Very well, m'lady. Now ye go sit down and try to settle yerself. Ye had a terrible scare there. I'll bring ye something light to settle yer stomach. Ye just go sit down. And *you*," Jaimie added sharply to Cameron, "keep an eye on her. We can no' lose our Lady Edith now we have her as lady fer good."

"I'm trying," Cameron assured him, catching Edith's arm and urging her along more swiftly. "But the lady can be stubborn."

"Nonsense. Lady Edith is an angel," Jaimie snapped as they reached the door. "And if ye let anything happen to her, it'll be naught but turnips and gruel fer ye til the day ye die, Cameron Drummond, so watch her well."

The soldier let the door close behind the three of them with a grimace, and pretty much marched Edith to the trestle tables.

"Sit," he ordered, and then grimaced and added, "Please."

Biting her lip to hold back her amusement, Edith sat, but she caught Moibeal's arm and dragged her down with her.

"Yer going to give Cameron fits," the maid said, glancing over her shoulder to eye the man as he began to pace back and forth behind them.

"Probably," Edith acknowledged.

"He is ever so manly though when he gets bossy, is he no'?" Moibeal said next, and then added, "He reminds me o' yer laird husband."

"Really?" Edith asked with surprise.

"Aye. He's so . . . commanding. I never really noticed how handsome he is before this," the girl said on a sigh.

Edith raised her eyebrows. "Does Kenny have some competition?"

"Oh, Kenny!" The maid waved her hand with irritation.

"What?" Edith asked curiously.

"Well, after seeing how good and kind and considerate the laird is with ye, and hearing how he pleases ye in bed . . ." She grimaced and shrugged. "I'm thinking Kenny is no' trying very hard. Mayhap he's no' the one fer me."

"Ah," Edith murmured, not wanting to say it, but glad the girl was thinking that way. She hadn't thought much of Kenny and the way he treated Moibeal from the start. Turning, she glanced at Cameron consideringly and then nodded and turned back to say, "Well, I like Cameron. So ye have me blessing if yer interested in him."

"I am," Moibeal assured her on a little sigh. "Now if only he'd notice me."

Edith shrugged. "Stay with me and he'll have to take notice."

"DEAD."

Niels grimaced at that announcement from Rory as he straightened from examining Effie where she'd fallen. He'd been able to tell that himself without even touching the woman. "Are all o' her injuries from the fall, do ye think?"

"Aye," Rory said. "I do no' see any bruising or scratches to suggest she was injured ere falling from the wall."

"Do ye think she heard us in the stairs, thought we were coming up, and jumped?" Geordie asked.

"That'd be my guess," Tormod said grimly. "She must have kenned we'd have found her poisons and bow in the bedchamber and were on to her."

"Her jumping was probably a last desperate effort to kill our lady and end herself as well."

Niels turned at that sour comment to see the cook approaching with a large basket full of freshly picked herbs.

Nodding at him, Jaimie informed them, "She nearly landed on Lady Edith's head, and surely would have killed her had Cameron no' pushed her and Moibeal out o' the way." Heaving out a sigh, he shook his head and peered down at Effie's broken body. "She must have been mad. All these killings . . . and fer what? No doubt she started out hoping to see her lady running Drummond as the lass wished, but instead she killed her too with her silly actions. She was probably just trying to kill Lady Edith out o' spite once she learned she'd unintentionally killed her Victoria."

"Aye," Geordie and Tormod said, nodding solemnly.

Niels noticed that Rory wasn't commenting, but was staring down at Effie, his expression troubled. "What are ye thinking, Rory?"

His brother hesitated, but then shook his head helplessly. "I do no' ken what to think. Certainly what Jaimie says makes sense. Everything seems to suggest Effie was our culprit and killed herself rather than be caught. 'Tis sad really."

Niels peered down at the woman again, and then up at the top of the wall. He frowned, but then simply turned and strode back into the kitchens and through. He needed to talk to Edith.

Pushing out into the great hall, Niels saw that his wife was still sitting whispering away with her maid at the table. Movement made him glance toward the fireplace where Ronson's grandmother was warming her hands by the fire, and looked to be lecturing her grandson. Probably about how filthy he was, Niels thought with a small smile. It looked as if the boy had been rolling in dirt. Laddie was not much better, he noted as his gaze fell to the dog. The two needed another visit to the loch. And that seemed as good a place as any to have that talk with Edith.

Niels headed for the table and his wife.

"M'LAIRD."

Edith turned at that low murmur from Cameron, and smiled uncertainly at her husband as she saw him approaching. She couldn't tell from his face whether he was angry with her for going out into the gardens or not. She couldn't read his expression at all. His eyes were troubled, his mouth smiling, but his jaw tight with tension. It was most confusing.

"I think I'll go clean up the bedchamber now that the men appear to be done up there," Moibeal said, hopping up from the bench to make her escape.

Edith nodded, but the word *coward* floated through her head as the maid slipped away and she had to force her smile to widen for her husband's benefit.

"Ronson and Laddie need another bath," Niels announced abruptly once he reached her.

Edith stared at him blankly. Those were the very last words she'd expected to hear come out of his mouth as she'd watched him approach.

"Ronson!" Niels called, and Edith followed his gaze to the boy who was following his grandmother to her chair. The lad cast a hopeful glance their way at the call.

"Aye, m'laird?" he asked, hurrying toward them with Laddie on his heels.

"You and Laddie need another bath. How the devil did ye get so dirty?" he added with exasperation. "Ye've mud from yer shins to yer withers."

"We were playing," Ronson said as if that should explain everything.

"Well, go tell yer grandmother we're going to the loch to clean the two o' ye up," Niels said, and then told Edith, "I'll ready me horse. Ye may want to gather some linens and fresh clothes while I do."

He was off heading for the keep doors before she could respond. Edith pursed her lips as she watched him go, and then stood and hurried above stairs, aware that Cameron and Fearghas were following.

Edith collected fresh clothes for herself and Niels, and linens for all three of them to dry off with, but she also grabbed soap and some furs as well. She rolled

the furs and tied them with string while Moibeal
stuffed everything else in a sack for her. She was hurrying back downstairs in no time.

Cameron and Fearghas both offered to carry the
items for her as they followed her from their position where they'd waited outside the bedchamber, but
Edith just shook her head and kept going. She was glad
she had when Tormod called the two men to him as
they hurried down the stairs. Cameron and Fearghas
slowed and looked to her, but she waved them on.

"Go ahead. I'll just go peek out the doors and see if
me husband is ready yet."

Nodding, the men rushed toward Tormod as they
hit the bottom of the steps, and Edith turned to hurry
to the keep doors. Hefting the sack over her shoulder,
she pushed one door open and peered out, her eyebrows rising when she saw Niels coming up the stairs,
a shield in hand. His horse was at the foot of the stairs
with Laddie lying beside it in the dirt, and Ronson
standing in front, holding the reins.

"Where are yer guards?" Niels asked when she
pushed out of the keep with her items.

"Tormod called them over to the table. I said I'd
just look and see if ye were ready."

Niels nodded, and then took the rolled furs from her,
tucked them under his arm and grabbed the sack as
well. Raising the shield over her head, he said, "Come
on. We'll go without them this time. I want to talk."

He ushered her quickly down the stairs, handed her
the shield to hold over her own head and then lifted her
up onto the saddle. Edith almost tried to sit sidesaddle,
but at the last moment thumbed her nose at propriety
and shifted her legs so that she landed astride. Niels

then quickly attached the sack and furs to his saddle before lifting Ronson up to sit in her lap. A moment after that he was in the saddle behind her and steering the horse out of the bailey.

"Ye can lower the shield now," Niels said once they were beyond the wall.

Edith lowered it with relief and let it hang beside them so it rested against her leg. It had been awkward holding it up like that. It had kept bumping into Niels's face. She'd tried to prevent it from happening, but bouncing around on the horse made it hard.

They didn't talk on the way out to the loch. Niels had the horse moving at a speed that made that difficult, but Edith didn't mind. She was enjoying the feeling of the cool wind in her hair and the heat of Niels's body behind her. So much so that she was almost sorry when they arrived at the loch and had to dismount.

"I'll set up the furs if ye want to get in the water," Niels suggested as he set her on the ground.

Edith smiled faintly, but shook her head. She planned to swim with him and Ronson this time, not by herself constantly anxious that she might be seen in her chemise. She'd still wear her chemise since Ronson was with them, but wasn't shy about her husband seeing her in it. She helped him unroll and lay out the furs, and then gathered the linens and fresh clothes and hung them from the branch she'd used last time.

Once done, Edith undid the ties of her gown and slid it off, surprised when Niels groaned behind her.

"Ah, lass," he sighed, moving toward her. "Ye make it hard to think when ye do stuff like that."

"Like what?" she asked on a breathless laugh as he slipped his arms around her from behind and pulled her back against his chest. Edith nestled against him briefly, enjoying the contact, but when his hands began to rise toward her breasts, she caught them and whispered, "Behave. Ronson is here."

"Aye," Niels sighed. Releasing her, he added dryly, "And I was fool enough to invite him too."

Edith chuckled at the comment and started into the water.

It was much more fun swimming with Ronson and Niels than without, she decided as they splashed and played in the water. This time she got to enjoy it with them rather than listen to them have fun. She even enjoyed washing Laddie, despite his jumping on her and dunking her under the water twice. But eventually they had to get out.

"There ye are," Edith said brightly as she followed Ronson out of the water. "Yer clean as a newborn babe now. That should please yer grandmother."

"Thank goodness," Ronson growled with childish annoyance. "I thought she'd fair have a fit when she came out o' the garderobe and saw me."

"The garderobe again?" Edith teased with amusement.

"Aye. I told ye, she's always in there," Ronson complained, accepting the linen Edith handed him and beginning to dry himself off. "She was heading in when she sent me out to play, and was just coming out when I came back in."

Edith paused with the linen half-wrapped around herself and peered at the boy as he dropped the linen and donned the clean, if worn, clothes his grandmother had sent with him. His words replayed in her head as she watched him. But when Niels caught up to them, she started moving again and finished wrapping the linen around herself. Holding it in place with one hand, she left Niels to dry off and dress in his shirt and tartan and followed the boy to the furs, saying lightly, "Tell me about your grandmother, Ronson."

He turned to look at her blankly, and then dropped onto the furs and asked, "Tell ye what about her?"

Edith hesitated, unsure herself what she was hoping to learn, but then suggested, "Tell me about yer life ere ye came to Drummond."

She'd meant for him to tell her about his home ere coming to Drummond, but he misunderstood and told her about his more immediate life before arriving here. Grimacing unhappily, he said, "Well, we walked fer a long time. I thought me feet'd fall off we walked so long."

"What about the other castles ye stopped at on the way?" Edith asked. Bessie had told her they'd stopped at every castle between here and their old home in northern England, but no one would take them in.

Ronson peered at her with bewilderment. "There were no other castles, m'lady. None I saw anyway. All there was on the way here were woods and more woods. We did no' even pass anyone else traveling."

"I see," Edith murmured. Bessie had obviously lied. Either the castle they'd come from hadn't been in the north of England as Bessie had said, or they'd stayed off the paths and trails to avoid running into others. That was possible and would have saved them getting robbed or attacked by bandits, but it would have been slower going and had its own dangers. They were lucky they'd avoided being attacked by wild wolves and bears on their way to Drummond.

"Do ye remember how many nights ye slept on the way here, Ronson?" she asked abruptly.

He paused and considered the question, and then shook his head. "Too many to count. Hundreds maybe."

Edith seriously doubted it had been hundreds, but she also didn't think the boy could count yet. Or if he could, he probably couldn't count too high. But his answer told her they must have traveled a good distance.

"Winter had just ended when we started," he added suddenly. "'Twas terrible cold still."

Edith nodded and relaxed a little. Ronson and his grandmother *had* been traveling quite a while to get to Drummond. Perhaps even as much as a couple of months. That seemed a bit much, but . . . It was late July, however they'd arrived at Drummond in late May. If they started their journey at the end of March . . . She frowned, but supposed they could have been walking that long. Ronson had little legs and was young, his stride would have been much smaller and they would have had to travel much slower than two adults . . . and apparently they'd done so without stopping once at any of the castles or villages along the way.

Mouth tight, she asked, "What did ye eat on the way to Drummond?"

"Gran always went out and hunted up a rabbit or a bird after we stopped fer the day," he said and then added proudly, "She's a fair hand with the bow. So was me ma. Ma used to take me hunting with her. She promised me she'd teach me to use the bow just like Gran taught her, but then she died." Ronson paused briefly, and then as Niels finished dressing and came to join them on the furs, the boy added sadly, "I miss me ma."

"I imagine ye do," Edith said, but asked, "What about the last castle ye lived at ere Drummond? Do ye remember that?"

"Aye." He reached out to pet Laddie when the dog dropped onto the grass beside the furs and was silent for a minute, but then said, "It was okay. We had the nicest cottage in the village, Gran and Ma and me. But Ma was always having to go up to the castle cause the laird wanted her to work. It made Gran curse something awful when he sent his men fer her. She said he was a rapping bastard, or something."

Edith's eyebrows rose. "Do ye mean raping?"

"Aye." Ronson's brow cleared. "That was it. He was a raping bastard."

Edith sat back briefly, and then asked, "What was yer mother's name?"

"Wife," Niels growled under his breath.

"Glynis," Ronson said with a smile. "She was ever so pretty, m'lady. And she was no' always off in the garderobe like Gran. She liked to play with me." He frowned. "At least she did when she was no' too sore."

"Too sore?" she asked, ignoring the scowl Niels was directing at her.

"Aye. Ma was always falling down and bumping into things while working fer the laird and coming back sore and bruised. She could no' play with me then," he said sadly.

"Is that how she died?" Edith asked. "Falling down or bumping into something?"

"Aye, she fell off the cliff," Ronson said unhappily. "'Twas terrible. She must no' have realized how close she was. She just walked right off o' it. I tried to warn her. I shouted and yelled and ran as fast as I could trying to catch up to warn her, but she did no' hear me and I could no' run fast enough."

"I'm sorry to hear that, Ronson," Niels said gently, "But I'm sure she kens ye tried to warn her."

The boy grunted, and began scratching Laddie behind the ear, making the dog's leg start kicking in the air.

Edith watched silently for a minute and then asked, "Is that when ye left?"

"Wife," Niels snapped now, obviously wanting her to stop asking these questions of the boy. Fortunately, Ronson answered anyway.

"Aye. The old laird came down and told Gran we had to leave," he muttered with a scowl, and then said, "But I think he must have meant someone else."

"Meant someone else to leave ye mean?" Edith asked uncertainly.

"Aye. I think he was mixing us up with someone else. He did no' even ken Gran's name. He kept calling her Ealasaid."

Edith stared at Ronson, a sound like rushing water in her ears as she tried to grasp what he'd said. When the sound began to recede, she finally said carefully, "Lad, did ye say he called her Ealasaid?"

"Aye." Ronson scowled. "She was so angry at him I do no' think she even noticed. But I did, and after he left I tried to tell her he was confused and she should go up to the castle and explain it to him, but Gran just told me to hush and go to bed and sleep, we were leaving at first light."

Ronson grimaced and admitted, "I think mayhap she was a bit overset by it all, because while she packed she kept muttering about going home, but we *were* home," he said earnestly and then heaved out another breath. "Anyway, then we left and walked all the way here, and it was hard, m'lady. The hardest thing I've done in me whole life. Sometimes I fell asleep on me feet and woke up to find Gran carrying me. I was ever so glad when we got here and ye let us stay."

Edith smiled crookedly, but had no idea what to say to that. She liked Ronson a great deal, but at that moment she couldn't honestly say she was glad that he and his grandmother had come to Drummond and that she'd let them stay. In that moment, she was quite sure it had been the biggest mistake of her life.

"Did ye—" she began.

"Ronson," Niels interrupted her grimly. "I need to have a word with me wife. We'll only be over there by the horse. Stay here until we return."

"Aye, m'laird," Ronson said through a yawn, and then flopped onto his back on the furs to stare up at the sky overhead.

Chapter 16

EDITH EYED NIELS WITH CURIOSITY AS HE LED her to his mount. He seemed terribly angry, and she got the feeling it was with her, though she couldn't imagine why. Until they reached his horse and he turned on her to demand in a growl, "What are ye doing making the lad talk about such upsetting matters?"

"Did ye hear what he said?" Edith asked with amazement, for while he'd missed the part about Bessie being so handy with a bow and arrow, he'd been there when the boy had said the names Ealasaid and Glynis.

"Aye. His poor mother was most like raped by their last laird and driven to take her own life. The old bastard then threw out Ronson and his poor old grandmother and they walked fer what must have been weeks to get here to Drummond."

"And the names?" she asked.

Her question brought him up short, and Niels frowned and asked, "What names?"

Edith gave a huff of impatience. "His mother for one."

Niels's mouth twisted and he glanced down briefly, obviously trying to recall. Finally, he shrugged and said, "Glenna?"

"Glynis," she corrected. "Me father's sisters' names were Glynis and Ealasaid," she reminded him.

"Oh . . . aye," he said finally, and glanced back to Ronson with a frown. "But Ronson's grandmother's name is Bessie."

"Bessie is what ye call a child or an old woman named Elizabeth," she pointed out patiently. "And Elizabeth is English fer—"

"Ealasaid," he finished for her with realization.

"Aye. Which is what the old laird called her," Edith reminded him and turned to peer at the boy. His eyes were closed now, though his foot was wagging, so she knew he was awake.

"And yer father's name was Ronald," Niels murmured, following her gaze to Ronson.

"And he said his grandmother kept muttering about going home," Edith added grimly.

"Aye." He stared at Ronson briefly and then shook his head. "But ye said yer father's sisters were dead."

"That is what I was told," Edith said solemnly.

"So . . . could this all be a strange coincidence?" he asked doubtfully.

Edith shook her head. "Ronson has complained to me a time or two about how much time his grandmother spends in the garderobes. He said she spends the better part o' the night in there," she told him quietly. "I just assumed it was a result o' age. But when we were coming out o' the loch today, I commented on how his gran would be pleased that he was so clean, and he mentioned that she'd told him to go out and play on her way into the garderobe and when he returned from playing, she near had a fit when she came out o' the garderobe and saw him."

Niels shook his head, obviously not sure what that had to do with anything.

"When I came below after leaving ye and the men to search the bedchambers and tunnels, the hall was nearly empty. There were the two guards at the kitchen door, and perhaps a handful o' servants at the tables including Moibeal, but Ronson and Laddie were nowhere to be seen. Neither was Bessie."

"Ronson was probably already out in the bailey playing with Laddie, and Bessie was in the garderobe," he said easily.

"Aye, that's what ye'd think, but the minute I got below I checked each o' the garderobes in search o' the hidden entrance Tormod mentioned and each one was empty."

Niels stilled. "She could no' have been in the kitchen."

"Nay. The guards would no' have allowed her past. And she could no' have gone above stairs, the men were guarding the landing and hallway to prevent it," she pointed out.

"Ye think she kens about the passages because Bessie is yer father's sister Ealasaid and that Ronson's mother was not her daughter, but her sister Glynis," he reasoned slowly.

"Nay. I suspect Bessie is Ealasaid, and that Ronson's mother really was Bessie's daughter, but she named her Glynis after her sister. They were quite close apparently."

Niels nodded, and then said, "And ye think the boy was named after yer father?"

Edith nodded.

"But ye think Bessie has been sneaking through the passages up to yer father's room and sleeping there?"

"I think she's been doing more than that," Edith said quietly. "I gather me father's mother was very skilled with healing and poisons and was teaching Ealasaid and Glynis everything she knew ere they all died. Or ere they supposedly died," she added dryly.

"So, she could have kenned enough about weeds to poison everyone," Niels murmured, and then his mouth tightened and he added, "And her being skilled with healing means she'd have kenned where the heart was and the best way to stab to stop it too."

Edith nodded. "I ken the men want to blame Effie fer all that has happened here, but as I told Rory, Effie—"

"Had palsy in her hands and arms and could no' aim straight. Aye, he told us when we found the bow and poisons under the bed," Niels admitted and explained, "We had already decided that Effie could no' be the culprit before we got word she was dead. But we still had no clue who it could be, so we decided to pretend we believed it in the hopes that the real culprit would relax enough to make a mistake as well as perhaps fall into the trap we planned."

"What trap?" she asked with interest.

"The one where we leave yer drink alone in the chamber where Alick is hiding and can witness yer would-be murderer dousing it," he said and then asked, "Did ye no' notice that Alick did no' come down with the rest o' us? No one kens he's here but the two guards in the hall and they've been sworn to secrecy."

"Oh." She nodded, recalling the plan he'd mentioned that morning. It seemed so far away now.

"How old would yer aunt be were she still alive?" Niels asked suddenly.

"Ealasaid and Glynis were seven and ten years younger than me father," she said and then explained, "Grandmother lost several bairns after Father before Ealasaid was born."

Niels shook his head with disappointment at this news. "Bessie is ancient, Edith. She could no' be yer father's sister. She's also deaf as can be, hunched with age and . . ." He shook his head again. "I'm no' sure she could manage a bow and arrow any better than Effie would have."

"Ronson said she is good with a bow and arrow and hunted up their food every night on the way to Drummond," Edith told him solemnly, and then frowned and said, "And she . . ."

"What?" he asked when she hesitated.

"Well, she does *seem* terribly old, but Ronson said she carried him on the walk here. And while she seems deaf as a wooden post, and blind too most o' the time, she's never had a problem threading her needles, and there are times she's heard me mutter things under me breath that she should no' have been able to were she as deaf as she often seems to be."

"Ye think she's feigning being that old," he said with realization.

Edith nodded. "I think we need to talk to her, husband."

"Wife, she's no' going to just admit to everything. 'Twould mean her hanging fer murder," Niels pointed out.

"Aye." Frowning, she glanced away, trying to figure

out how to prove what she suspected was true. Or prove it wasn't true.

"We could test her," Niels said suddenly.

"How?" Edith asked at once.

He thought briefly and then suggested, "Throw something at her and see if she is quick enough to prevent it hitting her. Or we ride back and you run inside and say Ronson has been hurt something terrible and see if she moves more swiftly to get outside to him than she should."

"That might work," she said with a slow smile. "That last one especially. Whatever else is true about her, she does seem to love Ronson."

"Aye. And if that does no' work, we'll chain her up in the oubliette and make her tell us the truth," Niels decided grimly, and then caught her by the waist and lifted her up in the saddle. The moment she was settled, he turned and shouted, "Ronson! Come! We're leaving."

Edith glanced around sharply at that, and quickly shouted, "Nay!"

Ronson paused, halfway to his feet and then straightened uncertainly and peered from her to Niels.

"Stay there," she said, and quickly dismounted again as Niels turned to her in question. He was quick enough to catch her by the waist and ease her to the ground, and Edith murmured a "thank ye," and then turned toward him.

"I thought ye wanted to talk to Bessie?" he said once she was facing him.

"Aye, but we can no' take Ronson back for it. She's his grandmother," she said anxiously. "'Twould be terribly upsetting to him, especially if we end up having her dragged away to the oubliette by the soldiers."

"Aye, I suppose ye're right," Niels murmured, and then frowned. "But I do no' like the idea o' his being left here on his own. Even with Laddie."

"Nay," Edith agreed. "So ye'll just have to stay here with him while I go question her."

"The hell I will," Niels said at once, his voice just this side of a roar. "If anyone is staying here with the boy, 'tis you."

Edith narrowed her eyes grimly and her chin came up. "'Tis me father, brothers and uncle that she killed. I want to be there when she is questioned."

Niels ran a hand around his neck and scowled briefly, but then stilled and lowered his hand. "All right. I'll no' talk to her until ye're there. I'll ride back to the castle, find Bessie and quietly escort her down to the oubliette. I'll lock her up in one o' the cells down there and then ride right back to get the two o' ye. That way Ronson'll no' see anything to alarm him, and ye'll get to question her with me."

Edith considered the suggestion slowly and then nodded her head. "But promise me ye'll take Tormod and yer brothers with ye when ye look fer Bessie and lock her up."

"I can handle one little old woman, wife," he said stiffly.

"She's killed a lot o' people, husband. I'd rather ye were no' counted among their number. So promise me," she insisted.

"Aye, fine," Niels said with exasperation. "I'll take me brothers and Tormod with me to look fer her."

"Thank ye," Edith whispered.

Nodding, he turned toward his horse and then paused and swung back, removing his sword as he did. "Take this."

Edith accepted the weapon, but frowned. "What if ye need it?"

"I'll be riding fast both ways, Edith. I'll no' need it. But I do no' like leaving ye out here alone and unarmed . . . even fer the short while I expect to be gone."

"I'm never unarmed, husband, I carry me *sgian-dubh* at all times," Edith reminded him solemnly, and then added, "Besides, I'm hardly alone. I'll have Laddie and Ronson with me, and we've often come here together without coming to harm."

"Just hold on to me sword," Niels ordered, and then bent to press a quick kiss to her lips before finally mounting his beast. Glancing down at her then, he shook his head. "I do no' like leaving ye here."

"I'll be fine," she insisted. "Just hurry."

"Aye," he sighed, and then nodded one last time and urged his horse away.

Edith watched him until he disappeared into the trees and then turned to walk back to the furs. Ronson was lying down again with his eyes closed, she saw, and Laddie had snuck onto the furs to curl up next to him. She considered prodding the dog and making him get off the furs, but it looked to her like Ronson had dozed off and she didn't want to risk waking the boy. Leaving the dog alone, she settled on the fur next to the pair, laid her husband's sword beside her and eyed the boy sadly.

Ronson was a good lad, and for his sake she almost hoped she was wrong about his grandmother being

behind the deaths at Drummond. But Edith suspected
she wasn't. Although, what she thought that she'd
learned brought up more questions than answers. If
Bessie was Ealasaid still alive, why had her father
been told she was dead? Had any of them died? Were
Glynis and their mother still alive? Probably not the
mother now, she acknowledged. And had her father
even really been told Ealasaid and the others were
dead? Edith wanted to believe he wouldn't have lied
about something like that, but after everything that
had happened, she didn't know what to think.

And then there was the other part of it . . . if Bessie
was Ealasaid, and her father had been as close to his
sisters as her mother had claimed, how had he not recognized her when she came to Drummond? More importantly, why would she kill him?

Edith was lost in such thoughts when Laddie suddenly lunged from the furs, barking and making
a beeline for the woods on the edge of the clearing
across from her.

"Laddie!" Ronson cried sleepily, on his feet before
he was even quite awake. "Come back."

"Ronson, no!" Edith shouted, and tried to catch
his arm, but the boy was almost as quick as the dog
and was off across the clearing before she could stop
him. Cursing, she stood to hurry after him, but paused
abruptly after only a couple of steps when she heard
Ronson cry, "Gran! What are ye doing here?"

"I just wanted to be sure ye washed behind yer ears."

Frozen to the spot, Edith heard that response and
then backed slowly to the furs and bent to pick up the
sword by its hilt. Gripping it tightly, she watched the
woods, simply waiting, and then tensed further when

Ronson led his grandmother out of the trees and toward her with Laddie nipping at their heels.

To say that Ronson's grandmother looked vexed was something of an understatement. She was eyeing Laddie like she'd like to kill and skin the poor beast, Edith noticed. More importantly, in her vexation, she was walking straight and at a normal pace, rather than in the slow, hunched-over manner she usually used. Even as Edith noted that, the woman began to slouch and lean forward, her pace slowing. She also changed her expression to a more servile attitude as she turned her attention to Edith.

"Oh, m'lady. 'Twas such a long walk to get out here," she said waving her hand before her face as if she felt quite faint from the exertion. As well she should. This spot was a good distance from the keep. Too far for her to have walked here in the time since Edith, Niels and Ronson had left the keep. She must have a horse somewhere nearby, Edith thought to herself.

"Laddie!" Ronson roared, releasing his grandmother's hand, and charging after the dog when he suddenly raced off into the woods.

While Bessie frowned after the boy, Edith never took her eyes from the woman. As long as Ronson stayed close to Laddie, he should be fine. She, on the other hand, was in a pretty tricky situation. The woman had come out here to kill her, she was sure. The question was whether she'd planned to do it in front of her grandson and hope he wouldn't tell anyone, or had planned something else. Since she should know that Niels had left with them, the most likely approach would have been for her to shoot arrows at them from the cover of the trees so that

Ronson had to witness the deaths, but not who caused it, she thought, and asked, "Where's yer bow and arrows, Ealasaid?"

"Where's me—?" the older woman began with feigned confusion, and then paused abruptly. Eyes narrowing, she asked softly, "What did ye call me, m'lady?"

"Ealasaid," Edith repeated quietly and then raised her eyebrows. "It's yer name, is it no'? Ealasaid Drummond. Sister o' one Glynis and mother to another. Sister to me father, as well as his murderer."

The woman eyed her for a moment, and then gave up her hunched stance and straightened, her mouth compressing.

"I presume ye came to kill Niels and me, and brought yer bow to do it," Edith said when the woman just stared at her. "Right in front o' yer grandson, too," she added grimly. "That would have been cruel."

"Aye." Bessie nodded solemnly. "It bothered me to have to do it in front o' him, but it needs doing. And I will no' let him see me do it. In fact, that's why I do no' have me bow now. The minute the dog came running and I heard Ronson chasing after him, I hid me bow and quiver under a bush."

Edith felt like she'd been punched in the stomach. She'd sorted it out and had thought she knew what was what, but finding out she was right was different than suspecting she was. And it appeared the woman still intended to kill her. "Why?"

The question slid out unbidden, and then just hung there in the air between them for a moment before Bessie snapped, "Why do ye think?"

"I really have no idea," Edith admitted. "Until today

I thought every last member o' me family was dead and ye were just some old woman trying to look after her grandson. Now I find out the aunt I thought died before I was even born is alive and behind the murder o' the rest o' me family."

"Is that what yer father told ye? That I was dead?" she asked with a hard laugh.

"Nay, me mother did," Edith said mildly. "The subject upset me father too much to talk about it."

"I bet it did," Bessie said with cold sarcasm and then held her arms out and said, "Well, ye can see that was a lie. I'm alive."

"Aye," Edith agreed. "So then are Glynis and yer mother alive still too?"

"What?" she asked with surprise. "Nay. O' course, no'. They died from the sweating sickness near to thirty years ago. Just before me father threw me out like I was rubbish and told me never to return."

"Me father was told ye died with Glynis and yer mother," Edith said solemnly.

"Aye. Well, I would no' doubt it. Our father was enough o' a bastard to do that. But I do no' believe fer a minute that someone else here did no' tell Ronald the truth in private afterward. He must have kenned."

"If that were true he would have come to find ye like he did Cawley after his father died," Edith said with certainty.

Bessie scowled at the suggestion and snapped, "Where's that husband o' yers?"

"By now he should have been back at the castle fer quite a while. Certainly long enough to have told everyone who ye really are and that ye're the one behind so many deaths. No doubt they're now all searching the bailey and keep fer ye and trying to decide if ye should be hanged, or just left to rot in the oubliette."

Bessie closed her eyes briefly in defeat, and then opened them again and glanced around as Ronson came running back into the clearing and hurried excitedly to them with Laddie on his heels.

"Look what Laddie found, m'lady. A bow and quiver. And look, they are no' broken or anything. Are they no' fine?"

"Aye, Ronson, very fine," Edith agreed, never taking her eyes off his grandmother.

"Do ye think I could have it fer me own?" he asked hopefully. "It might have been Lonnie's and his family may want it. Maybe I—"

"I'm quite sure 'tis no' Lonnie's," Edith assured him and then, arching an eyebrow at Bessie, said, "If yer grandmother says 'tis all right, then aye, ye can have them."

"Gran?" Ronson asked, hurrying to her. "Can I? I've always wanted a bow o' me own. It's all I've wanted me whole life. Can I have it?"

Bessie peered at him sadly and then nodded. Voice gruff, she said, "Aye. 'Tis yers, lad. Now go practice on that tree down by the water, and let us talk."

"Come on, Laddie," Ronson cried excitedly.

"Be careful ye do no' shoot yerself in the foot," Bessie called out. "And do no' shoot the dog either."

"Aye, Gran," he called back happily.

Sighing, Bessie peered back to Edith and then raised an eyebrow in question. "What now?"

"Now ye answer me questions," Edith said solemnly.

Bessie's eyes narrowed. "What questions?"

Edith hesitated, and then said, "Ye were thirteen when ye were supposed to have died and that was nearly thirty years ago."

"Aye."

"So, ye're forty-two or three?"

"Forty-two."

Edith nodded and then asked, "How did ye make yerself look so old?"

Bessie laughed grimly and said, "Me hair was always so fair it looked white. As fer the wrinkles on me face, some are strategically smudged dirt, but some are mine. Peasants do no' have the same luxury a lady does in avoiding the sun," she explained sourly.

"What happened to ye?" Edith asked with bewilderment. She couldn't imagine any circumstance that would lead to Ealasaid, the daughter of one of Scotland's most powerful and wealthiest lairds, becoming the servant, Bessie.

"What happened?" Bessie muttered harshly, and then shrugged and said, "As I learned too late, while a peasant can no' become a lady, a lady can certainly become a peasant does she dare to go against her father . . . I dared to go against me father."

"How?" Edith asked at once.

"He'd arranged a marriage fer me to a smelly old bastard I could no' even bear to look at. I decided I was no' marrying him, but I was no' stupid enough just to refuse. He simply would have put guards on me and forced me to go through with it. But me father could no' force me to marry if my maidenhead was gone I thought, so I got clever. I seduced a visiting English lord. Adeney." Her mouth tightened, "At least, that's what I like to say. The truth is I had no idea what I was doing. All I really did was slip into Lord Adeney's bedchamber through the secret passage in naught but me shift. The next thing I kenned I found meself lying on the bed with me shift thrown up over me face as this fine laird plowed into me, tearing me asunder. And he did it repeatedly through the night.

"Come the morning I could barely even walk the pain was so bad. But I dragged meself from that bed and made me way back to me own to lay there whimpering all day. All the while completely ignorant o' the fact that me sister and mother had fallen ill with the sweating sickness in the night.

"The morning next I felt a little better and sent fer me father to tell him triumphantly that I was ruined and he could no' force the marriage. He heard me out and then told me that Glynis and me mother were dead, and I was now dead to him too. I'd chosen Adeney and would be leaving with him. He could do with me as he wished."

"He did no' make him marry ye?" Edith asked with dismay. Despite everything this woman had done, Edith still managed to feel pity for the child Ealasaid had been and her foolish choices. A more honorable lord would have sent the girl back to her room. This Lord Adeney obviously hadn't been a very honorable man. He also obviously hadn't married the child he'd ruined. But Edith found it hard to believe that her grandfather, bastard though he might have been at times, hadn't made Adeney marry Ealasaid.

"Lord Adeney already had a wife. I knew that when I chose him," Bessie admitted, and then suddenly moved swiftly toward her.

"WELL?" NIELS ASKED AS HE LED HIS BROTHERS out of the passages and into the laird's bedchamber where Tormod stood waiting.

The old man shook his head solemnly. "The men have searched everywhere. She's no' in the gardens, the bailey or down in the village, and no one has seen her since Moibeal saw her slip into the garderobe."

"Well, she was no' in the passages or the bedchambers," Rory said with a frown. "Where else could she be?"

"We did no' check the tunnel," Geordie pointed out quietly. "We looked down it a ways, but did no' follow it to the end. Ye do no' think she went that way and is trying to escape?"

"Escape from what?" Alick asked dryly. "No one has seen her since shortly after Niels and Edith left fer the loch with Ronson. We did no' ken until Niels returned that she was really Edith's aunt and behind the killings, so there was nothing to escape from."

"The tunnels come out halfway between the keep and the loch," Niels muttered, worry beginning to gnaw at him.

"Aye, m'laird," Tormod said with a frown. "Ye're no' thinking Bessie used the tunnels to follow ye to the loch, are ye? If so, then Lady Edith is there alone and—"

The old man's words died abruptly as Niels turned on his heel and hurried from the room. He had a bad feeling that that was exactly what the old woman was doing. She'd probably hoped to kill two birds with one stone, or both him and Edith in one go . . . And he'd left his wife alone and defenseless in the woods with naught but a boy and a dog to protect her.

Chapter 17

EDITH WAS SO STARTLED BY BESSIE'S SUDDEN lunge toward her that she was slow bringing up the sword she held. Not too slow, thank goodness, and Bessie paused abruptly as the sharp tip pressed against her stomach.

They eyed each other briefly and then Bessie backed up a step, just enough to get the point away from her skin. She then shrugged as if to say she'd had to try.

Edith just stared at her. She'd thought sure once the woman knew that others would now be aware of her perfidy and all was lost, she'd stop trying to kill her. It seemed not, though . . . and that made Edith wonder if the woman was mad or just stupid.

Or perhaps Bessie had decided she could poison every last person at Drummond, blame it on someone else and yet claim the title fer herself, Edith thought suddenly. She had no idea. But whatever the woman was thinking, it was obvious Edith couldn't let her guard down again. Bessie was much closer than she'd been before that lunge. Another trick like that and Edith could wind up dead.

"Did ye have any more questions?" Bessie asked accommodatingly.

Edith narrowed her eyes, took a cautious step back, and then another. Once she was a safer distance away, she asked, "How did Lord Adeney and his wife feel about yer care now being his problem?"

"I have no idea how Lady Adeney felt, but he was fine with it," she assured her tersely. "As far as he was concerned, this was all grand. He had a wife, and now he had me, whom he could do whatever he wished with. It turned out what he wished was to dump me in a cottage in the village where his wife would no' have to look at me, and send fer me whenever he felt the need to do some plowing."

"O' course, I got with child," Bessie said conversationally. "But that actually turned out to be a good thing. Once I grew big, he was no' interested in me and I got some respite from his rough attentions."

"The babe was Glynis?" Edith asked.

"Nay. That first babe did no' take and was born too soon. It came early and dead. That happened several times ere Glynis was born. Adeney's seed was weak. Fer twelve years he plowed me, giving me nothing but weak seed and babes who were either born dead or died in me arms in their first moments."

"Until Glynis," Edith murmured.

Bessie smiled grimly. "Aye, but wee Glynis was no' Adeney's child. Her father, William, had strong seed."

Edith raised her eyebrows. "And who was William?"

"He was one o' Adeney's soldiers, and a good, kind man. He often had to escort me to the keep and back.

He kenned how miserable I was, and how Adeney made me suffer." Pausing, she explained coldly, "The lord was as weak as his seed. As the years passed it became more and more difficult for him to get hard, until he could no' perform unless I was in pain. He took pleasure in giving me pain."

Edith didn't know what to say to that. Offering sympathy to a woman who had killed so many people just seemed wrong, so she didn't say anything, and Bessie continued, "Fer years William carried me back to me cottage when Adeney was done with me and tried to tend me wounds. He was so kind and gentle . . . I fell in love with him, but when he told me he loved me, I spurned him. I kenned Adeney did no' like to share and our feelings would be trouble. But the day came when Adeney was called away to court for longer than his usual few weeks. The king wanted his consult and company and kept him for more than half a year."

Bessie smiled faintly. "'Twas like the heavens had opened up and sprinkled happiness from the clouds. The days were warm and sunny, the flowers were in bloom and William . . ." Sighing, she looked down. "After the first couple o' weeks when we tried to fight it, we spent every minute o' every day o' those months together. He taught me that the bedding needn't be terrible painful and horrid, and he taught me that all men were no' selfish, evil bastards like me father and Adeney. He wanted me to run away with him, but I was too afraid. I loved him so, but . . ." Bessie scowled. "But at least there I had the cottage and food. Had we fled . . ." Staring down at her hands, she shook her head. "Our love cost him his life."

"Adeney found out?" Edith asked.

"Oh, aye. I do no' ken who told him, and he did no' confront me at the time so we had no warning he kenned. But shortly after he got back, Adeney sent William to deliver a message with two o' his more loyal men and William did no' return. They claimed he fell from his horse and broke his neck and they'd buried him in the woods along the way."

Bessie gave a short hard laugh. "Fool that I was I believed it when Adeney told me. I thought mayhap God was punishing me." Shaking her head, she continued. "Glynis was born a mere six and a half months after Adeney returned. She was full-term, but wee, and I felt sure Adeney believed me when I said she was just early . . . because he pretended to. Right up until she was twelve."

Expression hardening, she said grimly, "I had gone out to collect some healing weeds fer one o' the women in the village who had the flux. I'd been using the skills me mother had taught me and added to them over the years. That day I returned to the cottage to find poor, wee, beautiful Glynis bloody and weeping on the bed in the cottage while Adeney enjoyed an ale at me table," she said bitterly. "The child had barely started her courses, but he'd raped her and tore her asunder just as he had me all those years earlier."

Her mouth tightened. "I flew into a rage. How could he do this to his own child? How could he? And he sneered and said, *'Ye mean William's child, do ye no'? She's no kin to me.'* And then he smiled real cruel like and said, *'Terrible his dying ere he could see his bastard. But he should no' have played with what was mine.'*"

Bessie let her breath out on a slow sigh and added, "He walked to the door then saying, *'In the end, William did me a favor though. She's a pretty little thing, even prettier than ye were in yer day. She'll be the one the soldiers come to collect from now on, Ealasaid. I tire o' yer ugly old body.'* And then he just walked out, leaving me there kenning me love had killed William and put our daughter in the same hell I'd endured."

Closing her eyes, she heaved out a long breath and then said, "True to his word, Glynis was now transported up to the keep each night. It broke me heart. She'd cry and beg me no' to let the soldiers take her, but there was naught I could do."

Ye could have packed her up and left, Edith thought, but held her tongue.

"After a handful o' months, Adeney's seed finally took in the girl and Ronson was born a year and a month after the first raping."

Bessie glanced to where the boy was trying and failing to pull the bowstring far enough to propel an arrow more than a foot or so before it flopped to the ground. "Despite his being Adeney's, Glynis loved that boy. We both did. He was the one bright spot in our lives. But even so, he was no' enough. She killed herself this past spring. Threw herself from the cliffs behind the castle." Mouth twisting bitterly, she added, "With no care at all as to how it would affect me."

Edith had to dig her nails into her hand to keep from commenting as the woman continued.

"The men had barely got her body back up from the rocks and laid her on our kitchen table when Adeney arrived to see if 'twas true she was dead. He took one look at her broken body and then shrugged and announced that Ronson and I had to leave Adeney. Come noon the next day the cottage would be set afire whether we were in it or no'."

"So ye packed up Ronson and headed here," Edith said.

"Aye. I had nowhere else I could think to go," she said resentfully. "I had no one to help me, no one to care, and then I got here and me own brother did no' even recognize me. He just looked over me and Ronson like we were a couple o' beggars, passed us off to ye and went about his merry way. He had you and his boys and this fine castle and I had nothing. No home, and naught but me grandson to feed and the clothes on me back. I had no one!" she shrieked.

"Ye had no one because o' yer own cowardice and selfishness," Edith snapped, tired of the 'poor me' tales.

"What?" Bessie gasped, taking a furious step forward, but pausing again when Edith moved the sword forward until it nearly touched her. Scowling, she said, "I've been sore done by me whole life and ye dare to judge me? None o' this was me fault. None o' it was—"

"I'm sorry, did I misunderstand?" Edith interrupted pleasantly. "I thought ye went to Adeney hoping he'd take yer maidenhead so ye could flout yer father's wishes and force him to break yer marriage contract."

"Aye, but—"

"And after that, did ye really expect yer father to just say, 'Aye, daughter, well that's fine then, let's have some wine and pastries'?"

"He threw me away like rubbish!" Bessie snapped.

"He gave ye to the man ye'd apparently chosen," Edith countered grimly. When Bessie just stood there glaring at her furiously, Edith added, "Through yer whole story I heard nothing but 'poor me' and ''twas someone else's fault.' Ye do no' see any o' yer own actions as even playing a part in yer downfall. 'Twas yer father's fault, and Adeney's fault and even *Glynis's* fault." She said that last with disbelief and then shook her head.

"Ye chose to go to Adeney's room and he did exactly as ye wished," she said firmly. "Mayhap more roughly than ye would have liked, but he did it. And then ye suffered the consequences, but ye blamed yer father and Adeney fer yer misery the whole while. And then after years o' apparent wretchedness as Adeney's mistress, ye met a man ye said was kind and good and gentle, who wanted to take ye away, but ye were too cowardly to do it. Or mayhap ye just did no' wish to leave yer fine cottage that Ronson says was bigger than all the others in the village. Why trade that fer an uncertain future, even if 'tis with the man ye claimed to love," she said harshly.

"Ye as good as killed him yerself. Ye must have kenned Adeney would find out. *And do no' try to tell me ye did no',*" Edith said heavily when Bessie opened her mouth on what she suspected would be a protest. "Ye ken as well as I that there is nothing that happens in a castle and village that the laird does no' find out about eventually. William was in yer bed fer *six months*. I'm sure he was seen coming and going by dozens or more people at Adeney, and at least half o' them would happily run carrying tales."

Mouth tightening, she added, "If ye did no' ken

Adeney would find out, 'twas only because ye did no' *want* to ken it. Ye were comfortable enough in yer miserable life that ye did no' wish to risk leaving it fer the unknown . . . and that was what got William killed. Yer own cowardice and selfishness and the fact that ye did no' love him enough to see past it."

Edith shook her head grimly. "The poor man must have loved ye a great deal to no' have abandoned ye and fled when ye refused to go with him. Because I guarantee he kenned he would die fer being with ye. As fer Glynis," she added with disgust. "Ye blame the child fer killing herself because o' how it affected *you*?" Edith shook her head. "Ye killed that poor child as surely as ye did me father and brothers."

"Me?" Bessie cried with disbelief. "'Twas no' me fault she killed herself."

"Aye, it was. Because ye did no' leave Adeney the day he raped her. Instead, ye let him continue to rape her and just stood idly by calling him a bastard as if ye had nothing to do with it, when ye were condoning it *every day ye remained there*."

"We had nowhere to go," Bessie snapped.

"Ye could have come here as ye did when she died and Adeney threw ye out," Edith pointed out coldly. "Had ye done so, ye'd still have yer daughter. Instead, ye let her be raped by that bastard fer five years or better. I bet she wanted to flee too like William, but ye argued against it."

A flicker of guilt on Bessie's face told Edith she'd hit the target on the nose with that guess.

"Yer a selfish coward, Bessie, much like me brother Brodie. Ye've spent yer life caring fer yerself and yer own wants above those who loved ye, and they paid the price. Including me own father and brothers and everyone else ye've killed here."

Bessie narrowed her eyes coldly.

"As fer me father no' recognizing ye—ye arrived here bent and hunched, yer white hair scraped tight back and yer face covered with dirt and lines. Ye looked ancient. I'm no' surprised he did no' recognize ye. And while ye blame him somehow fer that, *I* blame *you*. Ye did no' tell us who ye were," she pointed out coldly. "Instead ye gave a false name and then proceeded to lay ruin to me family more cruelly even than Adeney did to you," she said grimly.

"What?" Bessie glanced up quickly. "I—"

"I took ye in, despite no' even kenning ye were kin, and ye repaid me by killing every last member o' me family and even trying to kill me," she said harshly. "And why? What excuse do ye intend to give fer that? 'Twas no' yer fault I'm sure. If Father had recognized ye all would have been fine? Or is the truth that ye hated him fer having Drummond and kin who loved him so ye wanted to punish him fer it and, incidentally, claim Drummond fer yer own?"

Bessie's arm twitched and Edith noticed that she held a dirk in her hand that hadn't been there before. She watched the woman's hand clench and unclench around the hilt of the dagger like she was trying to decide where to stab her. Edith withdrew her *sgian-dubh*, but simply held it out in the open for the other woman to see that she didn't just have the sword and asked, "Will ye really make me kill ye with Ronson here to see?"

"Do ye think ye can?" Bessie asked grimly.

"I'm no' sure," she admitted. "But I'm younger and stronger and have a lot to live fer."

"Aye, that husband ye love so much," Bessie said dryly, and then something in Edith's expression made her eyebrows raise. "Ye did no' ken ye love him? Or did ye no' realize it was plain to see fer anyone who bothered to look?"

Edith remained silent, but her mind was working. Did she love him? It was a question she'd asked herself earlier, but never found the answer to.

"Niece, yer so eager to please him ye slapped preserves on his fiddle and tried to play it with yer mouth," she said dryly. "If that's no' love, I do no' ken what is."

Edith stiffened. Well, that answered the question she'd had earlier as to whether there were peep holes in the bedchambers, she thought grimly.

"Wanting to please another is a sign o' love," Bessie told her. "As is caring fer their well-being more than yer own."

Edith let her breath out slowly. If Bessie was right, then it seemed she loved Niels, because she wanted desperately to please him and make him as happy as he made her. And she was quite sure she'd throw herself in front of an oncoming bear or arrow to save him. She'd rather die in his stead than live without him. Aye, it seemed likely that was love. Edith just wished she'd realized it earlier and told him while she'd had the chance. She might not get another one.

"At least that's what me mother used to say," Bessie added now.

Edith peered at her silently, unwilling to let this woman sully what she felt for Niels by talking about it. Determined to get the answers to as many questions as she could, she said, "Ye've been at Drummond since May yet did no' start the poisonings until a month later. Why did ye wait so long to start killing people?"

Bessie shrugged and lowered her hand to her side so that her dirk was hidden in the folds of her skirts. Trying to lull her into a false sense of security, Edith supposed. The woman was like a snake waiting to strike and Edith was suddenly glad it was her here and not Niels. Her husband was very fond of Ronson, and if one of them had to kill the boy's grandmother, making him hate them, she'd rather it was her.

"At first I did no' plan to kill anyone," Bessie admitted. "I was just so stunned that me own brother did no' recognize me, I . . ." She shrugged. "I just tried to get by day by day and see what was what."

"And pretended to be half-deaf and near blind and much older than ye really are," Edith pointed out.

"The deaf do no' have to answer questions they do no' like," Bessie pointed out with a smile that suggested she thought she was clever. "Besides, thinking me deaf, no one worried about talking in front o' me. They did no' think I could hear them."

"And pretending to be half-blind and frail meant ye were allowed to sit and mend rather than being expected to actually work," Edith pointed out.

"Aye," Bessie agreed unapologetically.

Edith nodded solemnly. "Did ye poison the wine cask or pitcher the night me father died and me brothers fell ill?"

"The cask," Bessie said without an ounce of remorse.

"Ye poisoned the food brought to me when I fell ill," Edith added.

"Every night," she admitted and then added bitterly,

"Fer all the good it did me. Ye just would no' die." Her face and expression suddenly became furious.

"And ye poisoned the ale Brodie's men took with them," Edith guessed.

Bessie nodded.

"Lonnie?" she asked.

"I'd heard Brodie tell his wife they were going to the family lodge. I wanted to follow them to keep an eye on things. I worried that if one o' the men drank the ale ere the others, they may be warned off o' it. I'd put a lot o' poison in this time. Any death by it would no' have been mistaken fer illness. So, as I say, I wanted to follow and keep an eye on developments, but *servants* are no' allowed horses, which hampered me somewhat. So that evening, I took the tunnels out to watch fer anyone returning. They must have drunk the ale right away on arriving at the lodge. All but Lonnie, o' course. Because I barely got out o' the cave the tunnels open into when he came riding up. I ducked behind a bush, let him pass and then shot him in the back. Then I took his horse and weapons and rode out to the lodge." She shrugged. "The poison worked well. They were all dead."

"Nessa?" she asked, thinking of Victoria's missing maid. "Where is she?"

"In the well," Bessie told her with a smile. "I thought to blame it all on Victoria's maids, so I dragged the lass to the well and dumped her in so she would no' be found. I did no' consider that she'd float on the water's surface," she added with a grimace. "I was positive she'd be found as I rode back. When she was no' discovered, I felt sure the heavens were smiling on me."

Edith's mouth tightened. It was more like the heavens had been weeping, and that had saved the woman from being discovered, she thought as she recalled that Niels had gone to the well, but the bucket had been sitting there collecting rain in the storm they'd been seeking cover from. He hadn't had to draw any water. He'd simply used the rainwater in the bucket. If he'd had to draw water from the well, he would have noticed Nessa.

"What did ye do with Lonnie's horse?" Edith asked.

"He's back in the woods a ways. I've been keeping him in the cave the tunnel opens into. I thought I might need him a time or two yet. I could no' ride him all the way out here today, for fear yer Niels would hear the horse approaching."

"He probably would have," she acknowledged.

"No doubt," Bessie said dryly.

"Cawley? Why'd ye kill him? A half brother would hardly inherit Drummond if a full-blooded sister was discovered," Edith pointed out, finding she was growing weary at the thought of all the killing this woman had done. Or perhaps from Bessie's complete lack of compunction regarding those killings.

She shrugged. "He had it easy here while I suffered when he was only a bastard half brother."

"So ye killed him out o' spite," Edith said dryly, and then asked, "Effie? Ye threw her off the wall?"

"Aye."

"She was awake?"

Bessie nodded. "She woke up the day after ye moved her. The men did no' notice at first and she heard them talking on how they suspected her poor Victoria being behind the poisonings. So the old fool feigned that she was still unconscious to avoid possibly incriminating her girl." Bessie glanced toward Ronson briefly and then continued, "I saw her up and about from the tunnels later that day when the healer went below to fetch more broth for her. So I slipped in and—"

"How did ye ken about the passages?" Edith interrupted her to ask. Tormod had said that traditionally, only the Laird and Lady of Drummond knew about them.

"I discovered them as a child while playing," she said with a shrug. "It was me secret place when I wanted to get away. No one ever used them. I'd walk through, looking in the bedchambers and watching me father and mother abed, or me sister sleeping or look down on the hall."

Edith nodded, and then turned the conversation back to her original explanation. "So ye slipped into the room Effie was in and . . . ?"

Bessie shrugged. "I pretended to be sympathetic and promised to bring her real food and news until we sorted out how to keep her lady safe. O' course, I only brought her news that would be useful to me. Fer instance, I could hardly tell her Victoria was dead else she would have had no reason to feign being unconscious anymore. I could no' risk her telling anyone about the passage I used to get in and out o' her room, or that she'd even spoken to me. And I could no' kill her until I succeeded at killing ye. After all, how could she be blamed fer yer death if she was already dead?"

"Why'd ye throw her off the wall then?"

"That was yer fault," she accused at once. "Had ye

kept yer mouth shut about her having no feeling in her feet and legs, all would have been well, but the minute ye said that I kenned the men would go poke her somewhere else, realize she was awake and question her. Fortunately, yer husband was delayed just long enough for me to slip into the passage through the garderobe entrance and get above stairs to sneak Effie out through the tunnel to the laird's chamber. From there I took her through the second tunnel and up the stairs to the wall. I had her wait fer me at the top o' the stairs while I listened to as much as I could when ye all were in the laird's chamber. I had to duck into the stairs a couple times since ye all kept poking into the passage, but I heard enough that I kenned Effie had outgrown her usefulness."

"So ye took her up on the wall and threw her off."

"Aye." She gave a laugh. "I could hardly believe me luck when I glanced down and saw ye standing below. I thought the Fates were smiling on me again and pushed Effie over. But she missed ye," she added with disgust.

"And now there is no one to take the fall but you," Edith said quietly, and then cocked her head as she heard a faint, far-off drumming. "I believe I hear me husband and the others approaching. Several horses it sounds like." Watching Bessie's knife hand, she added, "Failing finding ye at the keep, they must have realized ye'd come out here."

Bessie turned the knife in her hand, her eyes flashing as she tried to decide what to do.

"Everyone at Drummond kens who ye truly are and what ye've been up to," she pointed out, and then couldn't resist adding, "It was all fer naught. Ye'll never be lady. And Ronson, like all the others who have ever loved ye ere him, will no doubt suffer as a result o' yer actions. He'll mourn the gran he loves, but hate and be ashamed o' what ye did."

Bessie stilled and protested, "Ye can no' hurt Ronson like that."

"I have no choice," Edith said without apology.

"Aye, ye do," Bessie countered. "The men all think Effie did it. Let them continue to think that."

"Ye want to blame yet another fer yer actions?" she asked with disbelief. "And expect me to agree?"

"Why not? Effie has no family to care or be hurt by it. No' like me Ronson," Bessie pointed out, and then added, "And I'm yer aunt."

"Who tried to kill me," Edith said dryly, and then shook her head. "Besides, ye're no' me aunt. Both me aunts Ealasaid and Glynis died ere I was born. Yer the servant Bessie who killed me father, Ronald, me uncle Cawley, me brothers Roderick, Hamish and Brodie, Brodie's wife, Victoria, both her maids and the six warriors who rode out with them. That's fourteen people," she pointed out in an empty voice. "The only future fer ye is to hang, or be locked up in the oubliette fer the rest o' yer days."

"Ye'd put Ronson through that?" Bessie asked with disbelief. "He'd hate ye fer it and I ken ye care fer the lad."

"Ye've given me no choice," Edith said firmly. She saw Bessie's arm start to move and then Ronson was suddenly in front of her.

"I hear horses, m'lady. Do ye think it's the laird? I'd really like to show him me new bow."

"I'm sure 'tis the laird," Edith said, watching Bessie

warily. She wasn't at all sure the woman might not try to throw her dirk at her despite Ronson's presence.

"Ronson, come here," Bessie said suddenly, and before she could stop him, the boy had slipped away and to his grandmother.

Edith tensed, half expecting Bessie to throw her dirk at her now that the boy was safely out of the way, but instead she handed the dirk to her grandson. "Take this. It's yers now too."

"Really?" he asked excitedly, taking the weapon. "Oh, wait til I show the laird this."

"Why do ye no' go wait fer him at the edge o' the clearing?" Bessie suggested.

"Aye." He ran off toward where Niels had stopped his horse the last two times they'd come here, clutching the knife to his chest, and Edith was briefly distracted watching him with concern. She was hard-pressed not to yell at him that he should not run with the knife, but then realized she'd allowed herself to be distracted and glanced warily back to Bessie in time to see her lower her hand from her face. Edith narrowed her eyes suspiciously as she caught a flash of blue in her fingers.

"What's in yer hand?"

Bessie hesitated and then sat down on the corner of the furs before holding her hand out and open to reveal the small blue vial she held. When Edith stared at it blankly, Bessie said, "Ye can tell the boy I had a heart attack or something."

"Poison," she realized.

"He'll never need ken what I did," Bessie said simply, and then as Niels rode into the clearing with his brothers and Tormod following, she smiled and added, "And ye can no' punish me fer what I've done. I win."

Edith stared at her blankly. As far as she was concerned, no one won here, and the words were so childish, so . . .

Turning her back on the woman, she walked toward her husband and her future.

Chapter 18

"WHERE THE DEVIL ARE THEY?" NIELS muttered, walking to the door and opening it to peer up the hall. There was still no sign of Edith and Ronson.

Sighing, he closed the door and crossed back to the bed, scowling when he saw Alick poking the needle again into Bessie—or Ealasaid. He was no' sure what to call her. Her true name was Ealasaid, but Edith refused to call her that and would refer to her only as Bessie. He suspected part of the reason was because she did not wish to slip up and confuse Ronson, but suspected too that she wished to deny the woman had any connection to her.

"Alick, fer the love o' St. Peter, stop poking the woman with that damned needle. Ye heard Rory. She's dead," Niels growled when the younger man stuck it into Bessie's still body again.

"How can we be sure?" Alick asked stubbornly. "Ye heard Edith. Even after kenning ye were back here telling us that she was the culprit, she lunged at her with the knife."

"Aye, but—"

"And she's fair knowledgeable about weeds," Alick continued grimly. "What if what she took was something just to make her *appear* to be dead and she's really alive and sleeping? Mayhap she's just waiting fer us to let down our guard and leave the room so she can rise up, use the passages to go below and poison the well so that all at Drummond die and she can claim it fer her own."

Niels hesitated, and then glanced at Geordie, not at all reassured when he saw the same sudden uncertainty in his brother's eyes that he knew was in his own.

Cursing under his breath, Geordie pulled his dirk, crossed quickly to the bed and plunged it firmly into Bessie's body where her heart would be. If she actually had one, Niels thought grimly. It was hard to tell from her actions.

"There," Geordie said with satisfaction. "If she was no' before, she's definitely dead now."

"Aye," Niels muttered, and then reached down quickly to tug the linens up to cover the knife in Bessie's body as the door opened behind them.

"Here we are, Ronson. Ye just come say yer goodbyes to yer grandmother now and then Geordie and Alick will sit with the body until burial."

Frowning, Niels turned at those comments in his brother Rory's voice and asked, "Where is Edith? I thought she was bringing Ronson."

"Aye, she was, but then she asked me to do it and to send ye to her," Rory explained, ushering Ronson to the bed. "I believe she's waiting fer ye in yer—What the devil is that?"

Frowning, Niels turned to see that the linen hadn't

hidden the knife very well at all and it was obvious
what was poking up out of Bessie's chest. Fortunately,
Rory had his hands over Ronson's eyes as he scowled
at Geordie and Alick and mouthed, "Get it out."

"Well, we had to be sure," Alick muttered as Geordie grimaced, pulled the linens aside and tugged his
knife out of the woman's chest.

"I told ye she was—" Rory frowned down at
Ronson, and then mouthed, "dead."

"Aye, but ye said Effie was unconscious too and she
was no'," Alick pointed out.

Rory's eyes narrowed and he opened his mouth
looking ready to blast their younger brother, but Niels
lost his patience at that point and snapped, "Where is
she waiting?"

"Who?" Rory asked, even as Geordie muttered,
"She's probably no' waiting at all, but went straight
to—" Pausing to glance worriedly at Ronson, he
merely pointed down at the floor.

Presumably to indicate that Bessie had gone straight
to hell, Niels supposed and scowled at him. "I meant
me wife."

"Oh, well ye'll have to ask Rory that then," Geordie
said, wiping his blade clean as he moved away from
the bed.

"I was," Niels snapped and then turned to see Rory
grinning at him. Eyes narrowing, he asked, "What?"

"'Tis just so nice to see ye so happy and in love," he
said with amusement.

Niels glowered at him and then turned and strode
to the door, muttering, "I'll find her meself."

"Try the bedchamber first," Rory suggested, and

before Niels closed the door, added, "The old laird's chamber."

Eyebrows rising at that last part, Niels strode down the hall to the last door and then thrust it open and stepped inside . . . and immediately froze. The room had been cleaned and completely transformed. All the old laird's personal items had been moved out and his and Edith's moved in. Aside from that, the old bed curtains had been removed and replaced with new ones and colorful tapestries hung on the wall. But the room was empty. At least he thought it was until his gaze reached the fire and he saw Edith curled up on a large fur in front of the hearth as naked as she'd come into the world.

Niels kicked the door closed with one foot and then strode quickly across the floor, shedding his tartan and tugging off his shirt as he went.

Edith watched him, her eyes growing wide. But the moment he stepped onto the furs and started to swoop down at her, she was off them and backing away.

"Where are ye going?" Niels asked with surprise, straightening to peer at her.

"I wanted to talk first, m'laird," Edith explained, backing away as he started forward.

"Wife, ye do no' need to be naked to talk," he informed her, stalking her like a wolf after prey. "In fact, 'tis more detrimental to talking than helpful."

"I ken, but I . . . I just want to tell ye . . . ." She paused and glanced around and down with a frown as she tripped over one of the rush mats.

"Tell me what?" Niels asked, swooping in to catch her while she was distracted and pull her into his arms.

Sighing, Edith braced her hands against his chest and said, "This is important."

"Talk," he suggested, bending his head to nibble at her ear.

"I . . . I want to please ye," Edith breathed as his lips ran down her neck.

"Ye do," Niels muttered against her skin.

"Aye but I—I'd throw meself between you and an arrow to save yer life," she said, the words ending on a moan as he cupped and clasped her breasts.

"I would no' let ye," he assured her.

"Aye, but I would, and I'd throw meself between ye and a bear too. I—Oh, I should have kept me clothes on until after," Edith muttered, sounding vexed. "This is hard."

"That's what ye do to me," he muttered, grinding his hardness against her.

"I'm trying to tell ye I love ye," Edith groaned and Niels froze.

Lifting his head, he peered at her solemnly. "What?"

Edith took a moment to clear her mind and then nodded solemnly. "I love ye, Niels. I realized it when I was in the woods with Bessie. She said love is wanting to please another, and caring fer their well-being more than yer own."

Niels grimaced. "'Tis rather disturbing that ye're taking advice on love from a woman who killed fourteen people and hurt so many others."

"Aye, I ken," she admitted wryly. "But if it makes ye feel better, she said her mother said it."

"Hmm," he murmured and decided that perhaps that made it more palatable, especially if it had led to Edith telling him she loved him. Cupping her face between his hands, he peered into her eyes and said, "I love ye too, Edith. I would no' have thought it possible to come to love someone so quickly, but ye . . ."

He paused, grasping for the words to express how he felt and then sighed and admitted, "I do no' ken how or when it happened, but ye've pushed yer way into me heart and made a place fer yerself there. And yer so firmly entrenched, I can no' recall life ere ye arrived in it, and can no' imagine life without ye at me side."

"Oh my," Edith breathed.

Smiling, Niels added, "But I'd no' let ye take an arrow fer me, and I'd definitely never let ye get between me and a bear, because I feel the exact same way about you."

Edith smiled and caressed his cheek gently. "Remind me to write Saidh and thank her."

"All right," Niels said slowly, a little confused by the abrupt change of subject, and then he tilted his head and asked with curiosity, "What do ye need to thank her for?"

"For you," she said solemnly. "Her sending ye to check on me was the greatest gift o' me life."

Swallowing a sudden lump in his throat, Niels scooped her up into his arms and carried her to the bed. But the whole way he was thinking that perhaps he'd write his sister a "thank ye" too. Because Edith was a gift to him as well, one he would enjoy unwrapping all the days of his life.

Keep reading for a
sneak peek of *New York Times*
bestselling author Lynsay Sands'
next Argeneau novel,

TWICE BITTEN

Available April 2018!

$\mathcal{E}$LSPETH BLINKED HER EYES RAPIDLY, TRYING to adjust to the much dimmer interior of the Night Club as she stumbled to the bar along the back. Her eyes weren't adjusting as quickly as they should, a result of her being low on blood, so she switched to rubbing her eyes in an effort to move the process along. She sensed, rather than saw, the bartender approach.

"A Virgin Mary without the Worcestershire, Tabasco, or lemon," she requested quietly.

"So . . . blood?" the bartender asked, his deep voice full of amusement.

Elspeth nodded with a sigh and breathed, "Yes, please," as she gave up on her eyes and sank onto the nearest barstool. She was staring wearily at the black stone countertop of the bar when a tall, blue tinted glass of red liquid was set in front of her. Elspeth pounced on it like a starving person on food and quickly gulped it down.

"Another?" the bartender asked as she lowered the now empty glass.

Nodding, Elspeth braced her hands on the bar top as the blood hit her system. She was struck with a brief light-headedness and a sense of being off kilter. It was like standing on a listing ship and trying to keep your balance, an effect of her system rushing to collect the blood in her stomach and redistribute it.

"Here you are, El," the bartender said, setting a fresh glass in front of her.

She glanced up with surprise on hearing her name and then stilled, her eyes widening incredulously as she gaped at the giant on the other side of the bar. Six foot seven with a twelve-inch, green Mohawk that took him to seven foot seven, the man was as wide as a linebacker with his padding on, and awash in tattoos and piercings. G.G. She'd encountered him many times at the Night Club back in London, an establishment that, like this one, was geared toward immortals and had a doorman who usually steered mortals away. It was a place for her kind to relax and enjoy blood-based mixed drinks in the company of other immortals. Her parents had taken her and her sisters to the Night Club in London to celebrate special occasions like birthdays, graduations, et cetera, but Elspeth had also been there many times on her own while at university. G.G. had always manned the door, and had always been very nice to her. He'd often even joined her inside and chatted with her about life and such on her visits.

"G.G.," she breathed with amazement. "What are you doing here?"

"I own the place now," he said with pride.

"Really? How? Why?" she asked with amazement. "Did you sell the Night Club in London?"

G.G. shook his head. "I still own it, and I've done well there. So, when Lucern called up saying he was interested in selling the Night Club here, I jumped at it."

"Wait a minute. Lucern owned this place?" she asked with confusion. "My cousin, Lucern Argeneau?"

G.G. chuckled at her expression, but nodded.

"I had no idea," Elspeth admitted, her eyes wide.

"I guess no one knew," G.G. said with a shrug. "I gather he was afraid certain relatives might take advantage if they knew he was the owner."

Amusement curved Elspeth's lips. "I can see that. Thomas probably would have before he met Inez. If for no other reason than that it would have annoyed Lucern."

"I suspect he was more concerned about Jean Claude than anyone else." G.G. said quietly.

"Oh, yes," Elspeth said, frowning as she thought of her now dead uncle. There was nothing more unpleasant than an immortal with a drinking problem, unless it was one with a drinking problem who was mean as a snake after consuming a drunk's blood. Although, to be fair, Jean Claude had been mean as a snake when sober too. Pushing thoughts of that unpleasant man away, she forced a smile and said, "So you bought it, but still own the Night Club in London too?"

G.G. nodded again. "I like London. But this is a good investment. Besides, my parents will soon have to move out of London again for that whole 'decade thing' you immortals got going on, to keep mortals from noticing you aren't aging, and they were talking about Canada as a possible destination for the next ten years, so this seemed fortuitous. I can travel back and forth between England and Canada, keep an eye on both places, and visit my parents while doing it whether they're there or here. It's all good."

"Yes," Elspeth agreed with a nod, and then shook her head and said, "I can't believe Lucern owned it. He isn't the Night Club type."

"It was one of his investments," G.G. said with a

shrug. "But now that he and Kate are going to start a family, he's decided to divest himself of some of his businesses. This is one he felt needed more time than he might have in the near future."

"He and Kate are pregnant?" she asked with amazement. Good Lord, the man knew more about her family than she did.

"Not yet," he said at once. "But Kate is retiring from Roundhouse Publishing later this year and they're going to start trying for a baby then."

"Oh." Elspeth nodded, not surprised to hear Kate was retiring. She'd worked at Roundhouse when she'd met Lucern and been turned, and it had been more than the usual ten years since then. It was time for her to move on. Otherwise she risked someone picking up on the fact that she wasn't aging.

"So, I'd heard you'd moved here to Canada," G.G. said with a grin. "Good for you. I think getting away from your mother will be good for you."

"You heard?" Elspeth asked with amazement. She hadn't told him. She hadn't been to the Night Club in London the last four years. Not since the family had moved out of London for the family home in York. But she supposed she shouldn't be surprised he knew about her move. The immortal grapevine was faster and more efficient than the mortal grape vine. Everyone seemed to know everyone's business.

"Yes, Lissianna and Jeanne Louise came in a few weeks ago for a girl's night and invited me to sit with them to catch up on things. They mentioned it, and were planning to drag you out with them on their next girl's night. They said you were busy getting settled in and they'd bring you next time."

"Oh," Elspeth smiled. Lissianna had invited her out about three weeks ago, but she'd been expecting her furniture to be delivered, and after three weeks living in a mostly empty apartment, she hadn't wanted to reschedule. Lissianna had offered to change the outing date but Elspeth hadn't wanted to disrupt her plans and had said no. She'd join them next time. And she would . . . if her mother didn't try to prevent it, she thought grimly, and then glanced to her purse with a frown as her phone began to ring. Sliding the leather bag off her shoulder, she set it on the bar and quickly dug out her phone. She wasn't surprised to see "Mother" listed as the caller. She'd been out of Martine's sight for half an hour. Of course, she'd call.

Hitting decline, Elspeth dropped her phone back in her purse and then glanced up to see G.G.'s raised eyebrows. He'd obviously noted who the caller was. Forcing a smile, she tried to steer his thoughts away from the call.

"So," she said brightly, "You work the bar here instead of the door?"

G.G. shook his head. "No, I work the door here too . . . when we're open."

Elspeth blinked at him with confusion, and then turned to peer around the club. She was the only person there. The Night Club had other rooms, of course, but she suddenly suspected they were probably empty too as she realized it was just a little after seven. The sun was still up and would be for at least another hour. The Night Club was only for immortals, and so was run differently than the average bar or nightclub. For one thing, it was only open from sunset to sunrise. Everyone knew that.

"Oh, crap," she muttered and turned back to G.G. with dismay. "I'm so sorry."

"It's fine," G.G. said with good humor. "My own fault. The phone was ringing when I came in and I rushed to answer it and forgot to go back and lock the door."

"Yes, but I know the club's hours, I can't believe I didn't think of that when I headed here." She began scrambling through her purse for her wallet. "You should have just sent me on my way. I just—Why on earth did you give me my drinks?"

"Because you were pale as death and looked like you needed the blood," he said quietly. "And you don't look much better after just the one glass, so stop fussing with your wallet and drink. You can pay me after."

"Thank you," she said with a sigh, and set her wallet down so that she could pick up the glass of blood and take a long swallow.

"Rough day?" G.G. asked, leaning his arms on the counter and offering her a sympathetic smile.

"The worst," Elspeth admitted with a grimace. "I got home this morning to find Mother and my sisters had decided on a surprise visit. They were already in bed. Mom in the guest room and the twins in my bed," she added with disgust.

"Pretty presumptuous of them," G.G. commented.

"I know, right?" she said, glad to have the support.

"Did you kick them out of your apartment?" he asked.

"No, but I kicked the twins out of my bed. Made them sleep on the air mattress in the living room. They weren't too happy about it though, and drank me out of blood before I got up."

"Punishing you," he said with a nod.

"Yeah, but hell, I don't know what they have to be angry about. They're the selfish twits who couldn't last two months alone with Mother and dragged her over here. Now they all might be moving here. Plus Dad," she added as an afterthought. "Although, I don't mind Dad. He's great, and Mother behaves a little better when he's around. Problem is he's always off running his 'empire.'"

"Hmm," G.G. murmured. "So you moved here to get away from your mother, and now she's moving here."

"Worse than that, Mother told Mortimer this morning that she was going to be a hunter and work with me. I'll have her hovering over me all damned night every night."

"Wait, wait, wait," G.G. said with confusion. "Lissianna said you got a position at the university, teaching criminology."

"I did," she said on a sigh. "But it doesn't start until the summer and, even then, it's a part-time gig. I've been volunteering at the Enforcer house, helping to sort through all the tips they get to see what might be real threats and what aren't. I wanted to see if I like it, and if I do, maybe I can work there officially in the future. At least part-time. And I do like it. At least I did, but now . . ."

"But now if you do work for the enforcers, you'll have your mother working with you," he said with understanding.

"Yeah," Elspeth sighed the word and then shook her head. "It's my own fault. I should have headed back to the Enforcer house when I got stabbed this morning rather than go home. She never would have known

I was working for them if I had," she said, and then frowned and argued her own point, "But it's not like I knew they were at the apartment, so why would I?"

"Wait, wait, wait," G.G. said with amazement. "You got stabbed this morning?"

Grimacing, Elspeth nodded. "I stopped to check out a soft call on my way home and a mortal stabbed me in the back and slashed my leg."

Much to her amazement that made him throw back his head and laugh loudly.

Elspeth stared at him wide-eyed, noting a little absently how the green strands of his Mohawk caught the bar lights as his head bobbed with laughter. Finally, she scowled and asked, "What's so funny about my getting stabbed?"

"Oh," he gasped, and shook his head. Making an obvious effort to control his amusement, he waved his hand and finally got out, "No, not your getting stabbed. That's not funny at all, but the fact that you got stabbed this morning and didn't include it as part of why today was your worst day ever is."

Elspeth blinked, and then sagged where she sat as she understood. He was right. She hadn't even considered the stabbing as part of her rough day. In comparison to the appearance of her mother in her new home, getting stabbed was like a pesky paper cut. Frankly, she'd rather be stabbed every day of her life than have her mother back ruling her.

"I knew that was blood on your car seat."

Elspeth swiveled sharply and gaped at the man standing beside her. Wyatt. How the heck had he snuck up on them like that? They should have heard the door open at the very least. Well, unless he entered while G.G. was laughing so uproariously at her misadventures. He must have, she realized and asked, "What are you doing here?"

"Forget that," he said, waving his hand impatiently. "You were stabbed this morning?"

Elspeth gaped at him briefly, and then sighed and narrowed her gaze as she concentrated on sending her thoughts out to search his mind, take control and—Whoa! What the hell? Her thoughts were crashing up against a black wall of nothing. Mouth tightening, she redoubled her efforts with the same results.

"Elspeth?" Wyatt said, frowning now as well. "Answer me. Were you stabbed this morning?"

"It was nothing," she muttered and slipped off her stool. Mortals weren't really welcome at the Night Club. She had to get him out of there. Casting a regretful glance at her drink, she picked up her wallet and quickly pulled out money, saying, "Thanks, G.G. We'll go now."

"Finish your drink," both men said at once, and Elspeth glanced from one to the other with surprise. G.G. was looking stern and insistent. He knew she needed the blood and felt she should drink it before she left. Wyatt just looked kind of annoyed. She had no idea why.

"Finish it," Wyatt repeated. "You had to rush off to have it, so finish it. In fact, I'll have a drink too. A beer," he decided, settling on the neighboring stool. "Because I want to hear about this getting stabbed business where Gran can't overhear and be upset."

Elspeth hesitated, but then said, "Fine. But we'll have to go somewhere else. The club isn't open yet. Besides, they don't serve alcohol here."

"What? A Night Club that doesn't serve alcohol?" he asked with open disbelief.

"Night Club is just the name," she said on a sigh. "It's not a real nightclub. At least, not like your normal nightclub. It's more like a coffee shop. A place where people can gather, relax, and drink . . ."

"Power drinks," G.G. said when she floundered.

"Power drinks," Wyatt echoed with disbelief and shook his head. "A night club that serves power drinks instead of alcohol."

"Yes," Elspeth said, casting G.G. a grateful look.

"Damn hipsters are ruining everything," Wyatt muttered, and then glanced at her glass. "What's that then? I thought it must be a bloody Mary, but the color isn't quite right and if they only serve power drinks, it—"

"It's beet juice, tomatoes, kale, spinach, kelp and a bunch of other disgusting things I wouldn't drink if you paid me," G.G. lied glibly, interrupting him.

"You just sling the drinks and don't consume them yourself, huh?" Wyatt asked with amusement, his mood suddenly lightening . . . although, she wasn't sure why. Had he worried his grandmother had rented to a lush?

"Pretty much," G.G. said solemnly. "Elspeth's right, we aren't open yet, but she needs a few more power drinks to help her heal, so I'll mix you up a power drink too if you like. Or I keep some soft drinks here for myself. Some Coke, Ginger ale, maybe some Root beer. What'll it be? A power drink or—?"

"A Coke," Wyatt said firmly. "Thanks."

Nodding, G.G. grabbed a glass, threw some ice in it and then retrieved a can of Coke from the refrigerator under the counter and poured it as he carried it back to them. He set it in front of Wyatt, and then nodded at Elspeth's drink.

"Knock it back and I'll get you another, Elspeth. You obviously lost a lot of blood this morning and need it," he said, his tone brooking no argument.

Grimacing, she did as he instructed. The moment she set the empty glass down, G.G. whisked it away and moved off to prepare another . . . at the other end of the bar. He was being careful that Wyatt not see what he was working with, she realized and glanced nervously toward the windows to see that the day was waning, but slowly. Still, other immortals would start arriving the moment the sun was gone and then Wyatt's presence would be a problem.

"Who stabbed you and where?"

Wyatt's question drew her attention back to him and she grimaced. "It was during work. I was checking out a tip and encountered a mentally ill man. He attacked his wife and then stabbed me when I rushed to help her."

"I meant where on your person were you stabbed?" he said grimly. "There was blood on your car seat."

"Oh." She grimaced, but admitted, "He stabbed me in the lower left side of my back, and slashed my left leg."

His gaze immediately slid to her side, but of course he couldn't see anything through her clothes and jacket. Even if she'd been sitting there naked there wouldn't have been much to see. When she'd got up that evening the wound had healed to the point that it was a large, dark, ugly scar. She'd needed more blood for the healing to continue. Elspeth could feel it happening again now that she'd had more blood. It was like someone was repeatedly jabbing her with a handful of needles in the spot. Most unpleasant, and she was holding herself very still to try to keep from flinching or otherwise give away that she was in pain.

"And you aren't in the hospital because . . . ?" he asked dryly.

"Because it was just a flesh wound, a scratch really," she lied. Actually, it had been pretty bad. Were she mortal she would have bled out within minutes. Fortunately, she wasn't mortal.

Elspeth glanced at Wyatt and saw that he was shaking his head. Scowling, she asked, "What?"

"I didn't realize your job was so dangerous," he admitted, his gaze on his glass as he turned it on the counter top. "Gran made it sound like your position was mostly analytical. A desk job."

"It is." Elspeth said, and glanced toward G.G. wishing he'd hurry. The sooner she finished this next drink, the sooner she could get Wyatt out of there. It would have been easier if she could have slipped into his thoughts, rearranged them, and sent him back to his grandmother's without recalling any of this, though. The thought made her turn to peer at him again to try to do just that. Nothing. She just kept coming up against a black wall of nothing. Either the man was brain dead, or—

Elspeth shied away from the "or" and smiled in gratitude at G.G. as he returned with her blood. Aware of the man beside her and the time crunch, Elspeth downed half of it at once, careful not to come away with a blood mustache afterward.

"But you got stabbed," Wyatt pointed out. "How did you get stabbed working a desk job?"

"There are some days when stuff happens and I end up going out on calls. This morning was one of those days," Elspeth said vaguely, and cast a pleading glance G.G.'s way, hoping he'd change the subject. He did. Just not to a subject she liked any better.

"So what are you going to do about your mother?" he asked abruptly.

"Her mother?" Wyatt asked G.G. with interest and then turned to Elspeth. "What about your mother?"

"Nothing. She's just a little overprotective," she said firmly, and scowled at G.G. as she picked up her drink.

"Martine is more than a little overprotective," G.G. told Wyatt as Elspeth drank. Apparently, he hadn't got the silent message behind the scowl, she decided as he went on, "She's a control freak and almost obsessive-compulsive about keeping her daughters near her. They've all led very sheltered lives."

"She's not that bad," Elspeth countered, which was an absolute lie. Martine Argeneau Pimms wasn't almost obsessive-compulsive about keeping her daughters near her, she was full on, certifiably obsessive-compulsive about it.

"Really?" Wyatt asked G.G., apparently believing him over her, which was kind of ironic when she thought about it. He trusted the big tattooed bartender with a Mohawk over a clean-cut woman he believed worked for the police. Go figure.

Maybe he had trust issues with women, Elspeth thought.

"Oh, yeah," G.G. told him. "Martine wouldn't let them out of her sight for a minute as kids. All three girls were home schooled until university. Never let out of the house. Never allowed friends."

"We had our cousins," Elspeth argued stiffly.

"Whom you saw once every couple of years or so," G.G. said dryly.

"How do you know that?" Elspeth asked with surprise.

"Julianna," G.G. said at once and then grinned and added, "Did you think you were the only member of your family to skip uni classes at least once a week and slip away to the Night Club to hang out with other im—club members," he finished, catching his own slip with a grimace.

"Damn," Elspeth breathed. It had never even occurred to her that her sisters might skip classes. It should have, she supposed. Elspeth had made a practice of signing up for an extra class every term. She'd show her mother her schedule once she got it, and then cancel the extra class. Her mother would think she was in university during that time, while she was actually at the Night Club chatting with G.G., or at a movie, or just shopping, taking time for herself. However, when G.G. had asked how she'd managed to slip away from her mother the first time they'd chatted, she'd simply said she was supposed to be in class.

She didn't explain it now, either, but simply set her empty glass on the bar top and glanced to Wyatt as she slid off her stool. "We should go. You have to pick up flowers for Meredith."

"He can go, but you're not going anywhere, Elspeth," G.G. said firmly, and then picking up her empty glass, he added, "You're looking better, but you need at least two more of these before you go anywhere."

"Fine," she snapped a bit irritated at all this boss-

ing about. It was like being with her mother. That
thought made her scowl at Wyatt as she said, "I'll
have two more. But you should go before Meredith
worries."

"I called and explained things before I came in
here." He smiled like the cat that caught the canary
and said, "I can keep you company while you have
your power drinks."

That brought a soft chuckle from G.G. as he moved
to the other end of the bar to fetch her another "drink."

Elspeth hesitated, wanting to just walk out and
leave, but in the end, she sank back onto her stool.
G.G. was right. She was feeling better, but still cramp-
ing and achy. Two more of the twenty-ounce glasses
should see her right.

"Those power drinks really seem to be working,"
Wyatt commented now, peering at her face. "You are
looking a little better. You have more color in your
cheeks. Maybe I should try one of those drinks myself."

Elspeth's eyes widened with alarm, and then she
asked abruptly, "What are you doing here? Did you
follow me?"

"Yes," he admitted without hesitation and when
she gaped at him, Wyatt shrugged and said, "Look,
Gran's already been burned once by a tenant who was
supposed to be a friend, and she nearly fell for that
iTunes scam too. Now there's you who already has
a key to her apartment." Scowling, he added, "And
then . . ." He paused briefly, several expressions flashing across his face and simply said, "Once I saw the
blood on your car seat I was suspicious, and followed
you to make sure you weren't up to no good."

Elspeth stared at him. Between the expressions that

had crossed his face and the way he'd hesitated, she suspected he was leaving out something. Had he overheard the argument she'd had with her mother in front of the house?

"Elspeth up to no good?" G.G. asked with amusement as he returned to place two tall blue glasses in front of her this time.

"He thinks I'm after his grandmother's money," Elspeth explained quietly as she picked up one of the drinks.

G.G. snorted at the suggestion. "Elspeth's family has money. Loads of it. Besides, like I said, she's led a pretty sheltered life. I think your grandmother's money is safe."

Wyatt considered G.G. briefly and said, "So, a beautiful young creature like Elspeth is really just friends with my very sweet, but very old grandmother because . . . ?"

Elspeth blinked and blushed. Did he really think she was beautiful? Aware that G.G. was grinning at her reaction with amusement, she raised her glass and hid her red face by chugging down the blood he'd just brought her. Chugging was better. Elspeth wasn't especially keen on the taste of blood. She preferred consuming it from the bag where you didn't have to taste it at all.

"I'd imagine she's more comfortable around older people," G.G. said as she drank. "She's spent very little time around young people. Instead, most of her life has been spent around the very old."

Elspeth almost snorted at G.G.'s words. He wasn't kidding. Most everyone in her life was well over two or three hundred years old. Heck, she herself was twice as old as Wyatt's grandmother. In comparison, Merry was a youngster. Setting down the now empty glass, Elspeth slid it toward G.G. and wrapped her hand around the other glass he'd brought her.

"Hmm," Wyatt murmured, and then before she could lift the second glass, asked, "Is that why you rented from her? Because she was older and you were comfortable around her? No other reason?"

Elspeth rolled her eyes at the question. "I didn't know your grandmother was the landlady when I rented the apartment. I didn't know who owned it at all. I found and applied for it while still in England. I've always loved old Victorian houses, and there were pictures of the front of your grandmother's house with the listing on the internet. It . . ." Elspeth grimaced. Not sure why, but unwilling to tell him that it had looked familiar to her, like home for some reason. Instead, she said, "It looked charming and homey."

"She advertised on the internet?" Wyatt asked with surprise. "Gran doesn't have a computer."

"Meredith uses a Management company to rent the apartments," she explained. "They posted the pictures and a description on a rental website. They're whom I dealt with."

"So you didn't pick my grandmother?" he asked slowly. "That was just a coincidence?"

Elspeth had no idea what he meant by coincidence, but assured him, "I didn't know about Merry owning or living there until the day I arrived when she introduced herself and offered me a plate of cookies as a welcome gift." Glancing to G.G., she added, "Merry makes some killer cookies."

"Yeah, she does," Wyatt said with a faint grin.

"You're making me jealous," G.G. said with a sigh. "Mom used to make great cookies too, but she and Alfred travel so much now . . ." He shrugged, and then commented, "I was wondering why you hadn't bought instead of rented, but if you had to arrange it all from England . . ."

Elspeth nodded. "I would never buy a house or condo without seeing it first. So, I planned to rent for a year or so while I checked out the city and where I might want to live, and then buy later," she said, which was true. But she also hadn't bought because she hadn't been at all sure her escape plan might work. There had always been the chance that her mother might have caught a stray thought of hers, realized what she was doing, and put an end to it.

Fortunately, she hadn't. But now Martine was here, in her apartment, and planning to move to Toronto as well. There was a good possibility that Victoria was right and her mother would try to make her move into whatever house she and father bought here.

Elspeth lowered her glass and bit her lip at the thought, but then recalled how she'd been able to resist her mother's mind control efforts today. Martine had managed to make her stop, briefly, in her apartment, but hadn't been able to make her stay until she'd got close enough to touch her on the stairs, and then she hadn't been able to stop her at all during her second attempt to leave. The pain she'd been suffering had helped her to push past her mother's efforts to take control. At least, Elspeth thought that must be how she'd managed to escape. If it was, she might have to stab herself once a day to make sure she could have a life not controlled by her mother.

Elspeth considered that as she downed the last of the blood. She'd have to keep a knife on her at all times, and maybe stab herself each morning before she left her room. That way, her mother couldn't sink her hooks into her mind and control her life. It didn't sound pleasant, but hopefully she wouldn't have to do it long before her mother gave up and stopped trying to control her.

"Right. I'll just hit the bathroom and then I'll walk you to your car," Wyatt said when she finished and set down her glass. Glancing to G.G., he asked, "Where are the washrooms?"

G.G. pointed toward the back, and Wyatt nodded and murmured, "Thank you," before following the silent instructions.

"Well?" G.G. said the minute Wyatt was out of hearing. "What are you going to do?"

"I don't know. I understand why Mother acts the way she does, and I've tried to be patient, but . . ." Elspeth closed her eyes with frustration. "She doesn't realize what she's doing to us. And tonight I think she was actually trying to get me to break council law so that I'd be banished and sent back to England."

"That sounds whacked," G.G. said, his eyebrows climbing his forehead, and then he grimaced and added, "But I meant what are you going to do about your friend."

"Wyatt?" she asked with surprise.

"Is that his name?" G.G. asked innocently, and then pointed out, "You never introduced us."

"Oh! I'm sorry, you're right," she said with amazement. She'd been so befuddled by her inability to read and control him that she'd—

"You couldn't control him," G.G. said as if reading her mind.

"How do you know that?" Elspeth asked with surprise.

"Because you didn't control him and make him leave," G.G. said dryly. "Besides, I saw you look at him like you were trying to fry him with your eyes. I assume you were trying then to read or control him?"

"Yes," she admitted solemnly.

"And couldn't," he said with certainty and when she nodded, added, "So . . . life mates?"

Elspeth grimaced, but shook her head. "If we were life mates, we would have had shared dreams today while I slept. He's staying with his grandmother on the floor below my apartment," she pointed out. "We should have had shared dreams and didn't. Ergo, we are not life mates."

"Or maybe he wasn't sleeping. He is mortal after all and was probably awake all day while you slept," G.G. pointed out. When Elspeth sighed, her shoulders sagging in defeat, he smiled and said, "So, Wyatt is your life mate."

Elspeth closed her eyes unhappily. This was not something she wanted to have to deal with just now. She had enough on her plate. Taking a deep breath to calm herself, she opened her eyes and shrugged. "A possible life mate."

G.G. tilted his head. "You don't want him for a life mate?"

Elspeth avoided his gaze, her mind returning to that incredible kiss on Meredith's back porch. Finally, she said, "It's not that I don't want him, I just . . ." Closing her eyes briefly, she sighed and then admitted, "I want to have a life, G.G. You were right when you said I've led a sheltered life. I haven't been able to do anything. I've never dated, never been kissed properly until today, never had a girl's night—unless you count the pajama party we had for Lissianna's birthday when she met Greg. And even then our parents were all there," she added with a grimace. "I want to experience at least some stuff before I settle down to a life mate. I want to go on dates, go dancing, eat popcorn in movie theaters, have fun girl's nights, and . . ." She shook her head unhappily and then noticed the crooked smile on G.G.'s face and raised her eyebrows. "What?"

"I was just thinking God must have an ironic sense of humor," he admitted with mild amusement.

"How's that?" she asked with curiosity.

"Well, most immortals are pining for their life mate, and probably on their knees praying every night to find them, but they don't," he said solemnly. "While you, who isn't at all interested in finding her life mate, and who just wants some freedom to experience life for a change, has your life mate thrown at you right out of the gates." He shook his head. "I sometimes think God, or the fates, or whoever it is he puts in charge of this stuff, really needs a good slap up the side of the head."

Elspeth smiled wryly, thinking he might be right. After all, she wasn't the only example of God's sense of humor. There was G.G. himself, a mortal whose mother had been widowed while he was still a boy, and then found herself a life mate to an immortal. She'd allowed the immortal to turn her, and then when G.G. was eighteen, had offered to use her one turn to turn her son. But where most mortals would give a lot for such an opportunity, G.G. wasn't interested. Of course, that had crushed his mother. She didn't want to have to watch her son grow old and die. So his step-father had bought the Night Club and given it to G.G. on his eighteenth birthday with the hope that one day, an immortal would walk in that G.G. might be a life mate for, and he might yet agree to be turned.

"Wow, this place is something special."

Elspeth turned at that comment as Wyatt returned from the washroom.

"The bathrooms are first class, and I spotted a room through a glass door on my way there that looks like a high-class New York dance club."

"If this place is anything like the Night Club in London, there will be other rooms too, all with different themes," Elspeth said with a faint smile and then glanced to G.G. "Are there?"

He nodded. "Lucern had it set up pretty good, but I did redecorate a couple of rooms to my own taste when I bought it."

"You own this place?" Wyatt asked with amazement. G.G. nodded.

"Wow," he breathed, and then said solemnly, "Well, you have a real classy place here. Nice job."

"Thank you," G.G. said with dignity.

"We should get going," Elspeth said, standing up. "My mother and sisters are probably still with Merry, and I wouldn't want to inflict them on your grandmother for any longer than necessary. Besides, I do have to get to work eventually."

"Yeah." Wyatt got up and pulled out his wallet. "I've got our drinks."

Elspeth exchanged a glance with G.G. and then

quickly rolled up the money she'd taken out earlier and passed it to G.G. in a handshake as she murmured, "Thank you."

"My pleasure," G.G. said solemnly, but held on to her hand. "You're going to have to confront her, Elspeth. I know there's a reason for her behavior, but this isn't healthy for any of you. Not only is she making you and your sister's lives miserable, she's hampering your development. The twins are like a couple of sixteen-year-olds, and you . . ." He shook his head. "This has to end. You have to find a way to end it."

"Yes," she said on a sigh, and withdrew her hand when he released it. Noting the curiosity on Wyatt's face, she forced a smile. "Shall we go?"

Nodding, Wyatt held a fifty out toward G.G. for what he thought were a Coke and four power drinks, "Will this cover it?"

"It's all good," G.G said, waving the money away and walking around the bar. "I'll see you guys out and lock the door."

Wyatt tried to protest, but fell silent, his eyes widening incredulously when the man reached them. Wyatt was probably an inch over six feet tall and well built, but G.G. was a giant in comparison, and twice as wide.

Grinning, Elspeth took Wyatt's arm and urged him toward the door. "Come on. Let's get moving and let G.G. finish getting ready for the rush."

Lynsay Sands

The Highlander Takes a Bride

978-0-06-227359-8

Raised among seven boisterous brothers, comely Saidh
Buchanan has a warrior's temper and little interest in
saddling herself with a husband . . . until she glimpses
the new Laird MacDonnell bathing naked in the loch.
Though she's far from a proper lady, the brawny
Highlander makes Saidh feel every inch a woman.

Always

978-0-06-201956-1

Bastard daughter to the king, Rosamunde was raised
in a convent and wholly prepared to take the veil . . .
until King Henry declared she would wed Aric, one of
his most valiant knights. While Rosamunde's spirited
nature often put her at odds with her new husband,
his mastery in seduction was quickly melting her
resolve—and capturing her heart.

Lady Pirate

978-0-06-201973-8

Valoree has been named heir to Ainsley Castle. But
no executor would ever hand over the estate to an
unmarried pirate wench and her infamous crew.
Upon learning that the will states that in order to
inherit, Valoree must be married to a nobleman—and
pregnant—she's ready to return to the seas. But
her crew has other ideas . . .

LYS8 1016